The Look in Her Eyes

Frank Toich

巫

The bagua 八卦
Qian 乾 (Heaven)
Kun 坤 (Earth)
Xun 巽 (Wind)
Zhen 震 (Thunder)
Li 離 (Fire)
Kan 坎 (Water)
Gen 艮 (Mountain)
Dui 兌 (Valley)

ISBN: 978-0-578-79315-3

Acknowledgments

My voice in the night, my guiding light, Charlie November Hotel, who brought me home.

For every battle, the silent warriors, the quiet professionals, you helped make me a man with how you endured.

Shamans everywhere and everywhen, showing me, me.

Dedication

My wife, Signe, a healer, wait for me.

Frankie and Abby, I hope to leave a world worth living in.

My sister Pat, happiness, at least.

Anya, I will always love you for the light of a moment, for eternity.

Tommy X, Brother, we'll sink some links together soon.

Jackie, to have a daughter such as you.

All those cats who passed through my life, now Mr. Playfair has my six.

Dizzy, you beautiful bastard, through all iterations, at my side.

Always, Anders, you showed me the true meaning of the word Courage.

Exordium

Mad Frankie, present time, in the woods:

It is difficult to even speak of what I know. So here I am writing it down, trying to piece together the path that was shown to me. A path several others have joined me on. Together we walk, always aware of each other even if darkness precludes sight. Six of us move silently through this jungle. Bound together by some force I cannot define and, I believe, none of us can.

All of this started in a small office on East 10th Street. The Doctor and the group he has gathered around. I was working closely with the Doctor on several missions, forays into increasingly perilous terrain. Little cover, no help, no rescue. We were out there operating without any regard for the rules of engagement. The Doc had more to lose in terms of rank, status, respect, and a shot at any future peer acceptance. I could give a fuck. I owed the Doc plenty and was willing to grease any stuffed shirt in our way.

As it turns out, even I was unprepared for the total collapse of time and space. How does it feel to be cast adrift in places undreamed and unimagined? To be unexpectedly sat down among the dead, the yet to be born, the lost…how do you equip yourself for a journey like that?

What follows is one such journey. One in which I appear on stage playing a part I was born to play with the group filling out other parts of this reality. I cannot explain how this world was conjured up, or how the moment in time was selected. Maybe just a coalescence of chance, one big Fan Tan game. So, join me with the triad of wandering souls, Nigel Larsson, Giuseppe Finnegan, and me. Go careful; everyone should go careful in a place like this.

Explanations not forthcoming,

Mad Frankie

P.S. Dizzy, I did my best…

Part One

"The future ain't what it used to be."

~Yogi Berra

Chapter 1

I shake out two Gabapentin 300 mg into my hand and carry them into the kitchen, washing them down with a pull of milk. I close the refrigerator door, I look at my reflection in the stainless steel. Maybe this whole string has been played out. Maybe the words will not clear a path. Have I been fooling myself? As usual I need to occupy myself until the pills shut my mind up. If only the memories would fade, would end. The good ones, the bad ones, just an avalanche of despair. Dizzy, can you hear me? Dizzy, maybe you are in your study typing away or are you drawing? Can you make it stop? I close my eyes. Back I go, back I go, back I go.

Giuseppe Finnegan: Chinatown, New York, 1906:

I sit on the edge of the bed. The light in the room is fading, as the sun bids us farewell. The darkness wins. Two days in an opium joint on Pell Street, wearing my stained collarless shirt and rumpled suit, sack coat of dark grey with matching pants patterned with dumpling dipping sauce. Bearded and unwashed. Stopped at a joss house on the way home where I saw an angel standing in the sun; I saw the beast lurking in the shadows. Where will I stand? Time is running down. I am losing the ability to distinguish between my opium dreams and reality.

Reality: that's a real comic word. Because, my friends, the opium dreams seem so much more real. My past, my present, my future have all been revealed.

The light level continues to drop but still enough to see my way out, my choice. The well-oiled Webley lies on my nightstand. A gift from my uncle when I joined the Hong Kong police force, just slightly used killing a few Boers.

There are no yesterdays, only tomorrows, and all the tomorrows fill me with despair. I pick up the Webley. I love the heft of it, the grounded feel of the hard rubber grip. I pull the hammer back and raise the gun. The barrel feels cool on my throat in the summer heat of my room.

Simmering Chinese delicacies spread into the room from the open window, along with the sounds of pots, pans, and woks, always accompanied by the constant music of the Canton dialect.

Pull the trigger, come on you cunt, just squeeze it and end this misery. Come on, do it now! I put pressure on the trigger and it begins to slip back. One more pull, you bastard.

There is a knock of authority at my apartment door. I lovingly lay the Webley Mark IV back on my nightstand.

I get up and move to the kitchen, which is how you enter the apartment through the hallway door. I pull open the door and there is an unexpected sight. Well, really, any sight is unexpected because I almost left my brains on the bedroom ceiling. Why did I stop to answer the door?

The man standing before me is certainly a toff, wearing a dark suit with a white waistcoat and dotted necktie. He is carrying a fashionable Homburg and gloves. He asks in a slight accent, vaguely Germanic, "I'm looking for a man named Gilhooley. Are you that gentleman?"

I say, "No, but you certainly don't look like a bill collector and most definitely not a copper."

I open the door wider and bid him enter. He slowly walks into my kitchen. He looks dead serious but decides on a little lesson. "Etymology is rarely an exact science. When you mentioned copper, I believe I am correct in assuming its derivation is from 'cop,' in the sense of 'capture' or 'catch,' first recorded in 1704. It may be derived from the now obsolete verb 'cap,' to arrest, from a related Old French word."

While he is speaking, he reaches into his spotless waistcoat, pulls out a card, and hands it to me. It reads:

Dr. Daniel Distanziert, Alienist
Köstlergasse 3
Vien, Austria
By Appointment Only

I turn the card over. On the back it reads:

Dr. Daniel Distanziert, Alienist
In Residence

Hotel Royalton
44 West 44th Street
By Appointment Only

I look up from the card. "This man, Gilhooley, he need help? I mean, is he crazy?"

The doctor seems slightly perplexed and says, "So I see you are familiar with my profession. Well, Mr. ...?" He pauses tilting his head to the right.

I answer, "Finnegan. Giuseppe Finnegan."

The doctor says, "Mr. Finnegan, I cannot really discuss the nature of my visit, but am I correct in my assumption that Mr. Gilhooley is a fellow countryman?"

"Sorry, Doctor, I was born in England. My father is Irish."

"Giuseppe?" The doctor almost begins to smile.

I try to fill in with more information. "It is my grandfather's first name. Mother is from Venice."

"Ah," the doctor says, "Venezia, the capital of the Veneto region. I have visited many times. I can still taste the *rixoto de gò*, the *fegato alla veneziana*—what a magnificent cuisine."

"Well, Doctor, I cannot help you, so..." I turn to open the door.

"Mr. Finnegan, please contact me if you hear anything of this man. It is essential that I speak with him."

The doctor moves toward the door but turns slightly at the threshold. "Go careful, Mr. Finnegan. Everyone should go careful in a place like this."

With that he walks past the threshold and out of my space.

A door opposite my flat opens and I see Barbara making her way out. As she is closing her door, she looks at me. Barbara Goldstein owns the building. She is always well dressed with a fit figure and a serious attitude. Once you get to know her, she is warm and welcoming. Her husband died about two years ago, and at first I thought he left her this building but I was wrong. He turned his back on his Hebrew faith to chase prostitutes and pile up gambling debts. He was knifed and bled out on Doyers Street; no one was ever charged. One witness claimed the killer was a woman, but he changed his story a few days later. Mrs. Goldstein, Barbara, never mentions him.

6

She says, "Good evening to you, Mr. Finnegan, I trust you are well?"

"I am, thank you, Mrs. Goldstein."

She gives me a slight nod and an ever slighter smile. A very capable woman is Mrs. Goldstein.

I wander back down the hallway to my bedroom and sit on my bed. I look over at my Webley. I lay my hand on it and I'm calmed by the slight feel of gun grease. This has become an almost, daily ritual, the room, me, the gun. How many times? The room is dim, very dim. I imagine my parents receiving the telegram: "Sorry to inform you that your son painted the walls of his bedroom with most of his brains." Well maybe worded with a little more tact. Once again I subverted their expectations. Dad would curse me but it would tie up his guts. Mum would never understand because no matter what I did, her love was unconditional.

Well, Mr. Finnegan, you came all this way so better get to it. I glance to my right and the folded newspaper on the bed. I pick it up and look at the circled advertisement. It reads:

Wanted: Able-Bodied Man to work with
Enquiry Agent. Must have Military or
Police background. Own Firearm.
Please apply: Raymond Clark Enquiry Agency
8 Warren Street, 3rd Floor

The doctor has left me with a strange feeling. Is Gilhooley real? I seem to recall a fella named Gilhooley, but it might have been in an opium dream. Preliminary plan, go to Wu's Bath Emporium. Bathe, shave, let Wu roll the Zhou yi and see if this enquiry job holds good fortune. After all, Wu handed me the paper with the circled posting. I head out to Wu's Bath Emporium on Baxter Street.

It is August 10, 1906, almost to the day eight months ago I set foot on American soil. I was born in Manchester, England, on December 27, 1881, on the edge of a small area called Medlock. I'm blessed with the combination of the temperament of an Irish father and an Italian mother. An unlikely pair but they are perfect for each other. Dad,

Michael Finnegan, quick tempered and sharp tongued; mother impervious to both.

Dad and his boyos hail from working-class Dublin and are all hawkers of one sort or another. Mum, she is Venetian, has the blood of merchants, bankers, and statesman. Nicoletta Tonetti was her maiden name. She came from wealth but her father disowned her for marrying well beneath her standing. That changed when I was born. Grandpa Tonetti could not resist a grandson, even one with a mick name. Baptized Giuseppe Finnegan, I am straddling both worlds. I became a diplomat early in life.

We were not rich but more comfortable than most. It was not until Manchester's Unhealthy Dwellings Committee came about that the city's slum dwellings began to be refurbished. At first hundreds of homes a year and then thousands, changing Manchester from the shit hole it was to the city it has become.

We resided in one of the first refurbished homes containing a shop on the ground floor consisting of a takeaway food counter and an odd assortment of tables. Nicoletta had brought with her a recipe from the old country, a baked flat bread topped with whatever was fresh at the market that day.

Dad was popular among his crowd; always good for a touch if your pockets were empty. So the place was always packed with his cronies. Mum loved her food and it showed in what she produced from her ovens. Ovens that Grandpa Tonetti had imported from Naples, Italy. Grandpa has many business concerns and some are in Naples. He owns a factory producing surgical sutures and violin strings. He had already started to import to America and his tales of New York City ignited in me dreams of adventure at an early age. So, before my 21st birthday, I convinced my parents that I was ready to see some of the world.

I always had an interest in China so I set sail, saw many sights on the mainland, and finally landed in Hong Kong, where I got a job as a constable at the Old Stanley Police Station, constructed in 1859, in Stanley on Hong Kong Island. Hong was a rough-and-tumble place in those days, and I had my share of clashes with the Chinese criminal element. Spending time there could really colour one's opinion of the

Chinese people. Somehow I was drawn to the culture, the language, the food, the people.

One night, I remember…

We are busy breaking up a gambling house with an unconnected small structure across the road. My sergeant tells me and Jenkins to check it out, sharpish. Jenkins kicks the door in and we both barge into the one-room hut. Empty. Wait—a few candles are burning in the corner in front of a small reed mat. The mat is occupied by a very frail-looking old man. Jenkins laughs, turns, and walks out the now shattered front door. Once Jenkins is gone, the old man's eyes open and he beckons me closer. I stop in front of his mat. He pushes both hands down. Sit.

I sit. He speaks. "Many years ago I learned your language at a young age, as my father was involved with negotiations between English trading companies. I was called to help maintain some face during and at the end of the second opium war; but after, because of the disastrous defeat of the Qing army, the death of the Emperor, and the burning of the summer palace, we had nothing with which to bargain. Now all that is left is rebellion. From the East it will come but it will not restore the Ming."

I look at him, perplexed. "So, you can tell me the future, old man?"

He answers, "When the world began, there was heaven and earth. You will seek your fortune elsewhere. You have done terrible things, been the tool of great injustice, drunk, gambled, smoked the poison, and given in to the pleasures of the flesh. You have mashed your boot on the innocent and guilty alike. While you have used women of my race as things for your satisfaction, there is one who will come out of the East. She will be of the Dao, and the look in her eyes will show you your true path."

I laughed, more nervous reaction than humour. I stood up and left the old man to his delusions. Crossing the road I saw the boys were already cracking heads and throwing limp bodies into the Mother's Heart. We had a black-painted covered wagon that we liked to refer to as Mother's Heart, because there was always room for one more.

After two years cracking skulls and being knifed three times breaking up gambling, opium dens, and alleged secret societies, I had enough and set sail for the west coast of America. Made my way over-land to a new place in my heart, New York City, where I slowly and gently eased myself into the local milieu.

Chapter 2

Night has fallen, the air is filled with the exotic smells of Chinese cooking and the sounds of one of its many dialects. I leave my rooming house on Mott Street to have a bowl of congee with dried mushrooms at Big Wong. While there a woman I know comes in, name of Jeannie Culbard, and walks over to my table.

Jeannie has been around, originally born in south Chicago, of Scottish parents. She started working at the Lone Star Saloon in '98. The Lone Star Saloon was in the city's South Loop neighbourhood on South State Street. She was employed as a house girl by none other than the manager of the place, a one Michael "Mickey" Finn.

You may be familiar with the name and that would come from his practice of using knockout drops and then robbing some of his patrons. Jeannie would befriend a patron and then slip a little chloral hydrate into the unsuspecting nob's drink, just enough to look and act very drunk so Mr. Finn would have an excuse to remove him from the joint, leaving him a lot lighter in the wallet that when he entered.

She lost her job when, in 1903, the police shut down Mr. Finn's saloon. They hardly stopped the practice, since I believe Jeannie brought it with her from the south side. I have seen her rubbing elbows with some Hip Sings. She's always been nice to be around and I enjoy her company, but always watched my drink.

"Well, you're looking quite scrubbed and polished, Mr. Finnegan. Mind if I join you?"

"Not at all, Miss Culbard, please have a seat."

I motion to Big Wong and he quickly brings over a bowl of congee. This dish has some dried shrimp in it. Wong knows it is Jeannie's favourite.

"Why thank you, Mr. Wong," she says. "It looks quite delicious."

Wong gives her a small nod and returns to stand behind his big pots of congee. Always next to Wong is a big grey male tomcat named Yinglong, who, Wong is always telling me, is the most famous dragon in Chinese mythology, he is the god of rain. Wong tells stories of people in different places praying to Yinglong in order to receive rain. He also has told me he, Wong, is *Descendant of the Dragon*. I have heard this many times, and it is very important to the Chinese as a sign of their ethnic identity.

Both Yinglong and Wong have the same satisfied look on their faces. Once a drunk patron kicked the cat across the room. Wong cut off one of the patron's ears. The one and only warning to never let Big Wong lay eyes on you again.

I sit and watch Jeannie eating, her blond hair still with a sparkle to it, her eyes still full of life. I am overcome with sadness for some reason. I guess it is Jeannie. She has had a rough life so far, but there is always that tipping point. The point where the streets extract that last ounce. Maybe it is just life. Maybe in the end we are just overwhelmed, knocked down one last time and never get up. She looks up at me and smiles and gives me a wink. Almost like she knows and is all in, anyway.

I stand and say, "Enjoy your congee, Jeannie. It's time for me to head out and see what the night brings."

"Mind your temper now, Mr. Finnegan." Her smile tells me this is her way of saying stay out of trouble.

It is early but I am anticipating a long night of gambling. I have on my red silk underwear, brought with me from Hong Kong, ready for business as I make my way over to Pell Street. Walking along I check out various shops selling kitchen pots, pans, bowls, religious statues, clothes, and all descriptions of food, some cooked, some uncooked, attracting many of the local flying insects.

I finally stop in front of 8 Pell Street and gaze at its faded red door before knocking on it three times, slowly. The door opens and I am allowed to enter the dimly lit hallway. Two men are stationed further down the hall. I know one from my frequent trips to this establishment. As I pass him he smiles and tries to slap me on the shoulder, a sign of bad luck; he is hoping to profit from my loss. I spin and he misses me and hits only air. I meet his gaze. The air in the cramped space holds some tension. He nods and I turn and walk toward a plain door with a single sheet of white paper proclaiming in pinyin *yat ye' hoi p'i*, simply stating the game runs day and night. The game is Fan Tan.

I am here to make money. I like this place because they make it simple, strictly cash, no *s'in tsz* or Chinese cash. With the Chinese cash, you have to deposit a bank note and you are given a Chinese playing card. At the table there are different counters that represent denominations of bets. Like I said, I like to just lay down my dollars and have at it.

I descend a steep flight of stairs to a sparsely furnished room. The walls have a few white paper tablets; directly to my left is a board upon which hangs a white tablet explaining the rules of the game. They are simple. In the middle of the room is a table about four feet high covered with Canton matting. There is a table on either side. On each table is a piece of tin upon which the numbers one to four are marked from right to left. Along one side is a railed space containing a high chair for the cashier. Besides the cashier, on his left, is the tan kun, ruler of the spreading out. The cashier is called the ho kun.

The tan kun takes a handful of bright-white buttons from a pile before him and covers them with a shallow brass cup about three inches in diameter. The betting is now open. The winning number is called open and is derived by the tan kun using a curved bamboo stick and removing white buttons four at a time. If there is one button left, one is said to be open and so forth. If there are no buttons left, then four is open.

I chose the table that draws me to it. Tonight it is the table to my left. A man approaches me and nods. He is a young Chinese, well dressed, a Hip Sing. I am in a Hip Sing house. Floor above a small restaurant, above that opium joint. There is very little conversation in this room, none at the tables. The young man is abreast of me. I know him only as Liu and whisper in his ear, "No Tommy?" a friend I gamble with.

Liu looks at me. "A cart blocked his way on Pell." He knows I will understand.

I move to an open spot at the table, wait as the tan kun takes a handful of bright-white buttons from the pile before him and covers them with a shallow brass cup, then place a five on one; betting closed.

The tan kun begins removing the buttons four at a time. The tan kun is finished. There are no buttons left; a loss. I place the same bet, with the exact same result. I place a bet beside three; betting closed. The removing begins; two left, a loss. I repeat the bet and win. Temporary relief, because on this night for every time I win, there will be threefold losses.

The hours pass unnoticed. The joss house visit to Guan Gong was not accepted, the red brings me no luck. It is a new day of the same old things. I leave the den, hungry, heading for my favourite restaurant, a few doors up the block.

The sun is up and the day is already hot. It is very hot in the packed, rather small, restaurant, not aided by the steam spewing forth from the open kitchen. This summer has been warm, not overly so, it is only early August, so plenty of time left to sweat. My three char siu bau buns and bowl of dan dan mian noodles are set noiselessly on the table before me by the same diminutive woman who has served me almost every day for the past three months. She never makes eye contact. I often observe her as she moves effortlessly around the small, overly crowded space. Her movements consist of ever widening and contracting circles. Each time I am sure a collision is imminent, she is not at the point of contact.

It is difficult to discern her age, but she is not young. I let go of my interest and focus on the plates before me. I did not experience the same immigration problems as the Chinese, being English born. Having eaten as much I care to, I head for the front door, meeting Liu on the threshold entering from the opposite side. We pause for the briefest of moments and he whispers in my ear, "Lay low tonight."

I pass into the street without acknowledging. A warning from a Tong member is not to be ignored. I decide on some refreshment before any other ideas on what to make of the day. Any decision will have to leave plenty of time to be tucked in before whatever acts of violence will be perpetrated.

I swing uptown on Canal, toward Broadway. As I turn the corner, I almost run into Margo Gutmann.

"Yissl"—it's what she calls me—"where are you going in such a hurry?"

Margo is one of my first friends in New York. She's a tall woman of indeterminate age, with a shock of white hair. She's told me stories of her days playing in Yiddish theatre with Jacob Adler, including his performance as Shylock in a 1903 production of *The Merchant of Venice.*

In those days Margo Gutmann moved back and forth between the city's leading Yiddish-language and English-language stages. She worked all the big Yiddish places like the Bowery Garden, the National, and the Thalia.

Lately, however, she has been hired to oversee the Chinese Opera House on Doyers. After the violence in August, 1905, Mock Duck ordered several of his *boo how doy* to take care of business, once and for all. He chose his favourite gunman, Sing "The Scientific Killer" Dock. They entered the Chinese theatre and opened fire using exploding firecrackers to cover their gunshot. Four On Leongs were killed. Now an element of dread crept into Chinatown's popular imagery, and the Chinese Opera House, attended by a few whites until that awful night, felt the immediate effects. The uptown crowd has kept away, and the owners are looking for a way to bring them back. Margo is well known in certain circles and I think their faith in her will be rewarded.

"Sorry, Mrs. Gutmann, I was not paying any attention."

"Yissl, I'm glad I ran into you or rather you ran into me. In a few days we are putting on a production of The Peony Pavilion. I will leave a ticket at the office for you. It is a Ming classic about a young girl, Du Lijiang, who takes a walk in the garden, where she falls asleep. In her dream Du Lijiang encounters a young scholar, identified later in the play as Liu Mengmei, whom in real life she has never met. Du Lijiang becomes so preoccupied with her dream affair she wastes away and dies. Later Liu Mengmei, in the same garden, falls asleep and dreams of a woman, whom he recognizes as the deceased daughter of a Ming official, Du Lijiang's. The story evolves but it is a terribly romantic opera."

"Thank you, Mrs. Gutmann. Let me know the date and I will attend."

With that Margo turns and walks away humming a strong tune.

A short walk later, I arrive at McGinnity's Saloon and shove open the doors. I stroll over to the bar and slide a coin under Old Tom's paw. McGinnity loves this old-school practice that dates back to the old gin palace days in London.

The barkeep slaps a glass down and fills it with gin. I throw it back, savouring the slightly sweet warmth sliding down my throat.

I then realize there is soft, syncopated music being played on the saloon's old piano. I never pay much attention to music but I recognize the style as being currently popular. I turn and get my first surprise, for the man at the piano is obviously of African descent. He is fashionably dressed in an older style. He continues to play his slow, offbeat music that sounds oddly like a march.

I turn to where McGinnity is standing and give him my wide-eyed, what-the-hell-is-this look.

He heads in my direction and says, "Interestin' a lad."

I ask, "You might say. There is a story here—let's have it."

McGinnity shakes his head and lets out a laugh and begins. "Well, I wanted someone to play that old piano and liven things up a bit. I got word there was an Ernest Hogan who would play days, as he had other engagements during the night. Far be it from me to turn down a lad with the name Hogan, so I said sure, and this guy turned up. Name of Ernest Hogan, although I found it very hard to believe, and was going to throw him out the door when he sat down and started playing. He told me the old thing was severely out of tune but it would only add to the atmosphere. Atmosphere? Damn, I didn't know this place had an atmosphere. So I thought what the hell, might be good for business."

I turn back to watch Mr. Ernest Hogan play, and a mixture of the gin and the music's odd syncopation relaxes me, almost brings a smile to my face. I nod at the barkeep and he refills my glass. I down it and lean against the bar. I gesture to the barkeep to pour a shot and bring it over to the man at the piano.

When the glass hits the piano edge, Hogan briefly looks up, continuing on until he finishes the tune. He reaches over and drinks the shot in one gulp and turns to face the bar. When I raise my hand, he gets up from the stool and walks over to me.

"Thank you for the drink, sir." He reaches out his hand with a slight smile. I take his hand and we shake.

I say, "Finnegan, that is a very popular type of music today." He turns and leans on the bar. "Name's Hogan, my stage name so to speak. That piece of music sold over a million copies. One million! And now I am going to be the first African man to star in a Broadway show."

"Impressed, Mr. Hogan. What is the name of the show?"

"Called *The Oyster Man*. Right now we are putting together the production."

I shake my head. "A million copies. You must be a very famous man."

16

Now it is Hogan's turn to shake his head. "That song I just played brought me a lot of grief in and out of show business. You see, it's called 'All Coons Look Alike to Me.' It created a whole type of music called coon songs. I get the blame for that from many of my kind, but you see, Mr. Finnegan, a new musical rhythm was given to the people. All because I wrote down the music I heard in different places. Coon songs will fade but the rhythm, that will last a mighty long time."

I down my last gin and bid Mr. Hogan good luck with his show. I am sure I will run into him again. As I walk out of McGinnity's, the piano is already playing music that Mr. Ernest Hogan named ragtime, but now a man I know only as David is playing a cornet in accompaniment to Mr. Hogan's music. David's playing is always lyrically tinged with a sense of melancholy.

Occasionally I have been in McGinnity's and David has been playing some parlour music that McGinnity loves so much, accompanied by a singer named Lindsay LeFleur. She tends horses for the Hip Sing laundry wagons. Liu told me that they believe she can communicate with the horses. She always knows when one is ailing. Liu claims she is some kind of—what's the word—shaman. I do not fully understand, but I saw many mystics and seers in China and know that the Chinese hold powerful beliefs about the afterlife and all things spiritual.

A few steps down Broadway and I feel it: that presence, the darkness, the demon. My legs feel like lead, my mind burns with rage. It is happening again. There is only one place to run to, so I do—and find myself at Wu's Bath Emporium.

I lie on a pallet, resting my upper body on pillows musty with incense. I hold a plain wooden pipe in my hands watching the old man gently rotating the thin metal needle above the opium lamp; the small ball of tar at the end is ready. He places it over the small hole at the end of the pipe and I take a long pull, feeling my lungs fill with smoke from the hop. I hold it and as I exhale, my eyelids slowly descend. I see the words of Milton before me, floating in the air, written in red.

"...though this by some supposed True Paradise..."

The barge drifts down the Yi River, propelled by twin oarsmen at the rear. Each stands on a slightly raised platform, allowing them greater visibility upstream, downstream, port, and starboard.

I lie on a canopied bed covered in pillows and silk. A sing-song girl on either side. One with food and drink, for those who want; the other keeps the porcelain pipe handy and the opium lamp lit. An elderly man plays an erhu, above which a tune floats away on the gentle, fragrant breeze.

Mad Frankie, in the woods, present time:

I shake out two Gabapentin 300 mg into my hand and carry them into the kitchen, washing them down with a pull of milk. I close the refrigerator door, I look at my reflection in the stainless steel. Maybe this whole string has been played out. Maybe the words will not clear a path. Have I been fooling myself? As usual I need to occupy myself until the pills shut my mind up. If only the memories would fade, would end. The good ones, the bad ones, just an avalanche of despair. Dizzy, can you hear me? Dizzy, maybe you are in your study typing away or are you drawing? Can you make it stop? I close my eyes.

Giuseppe, Chinatown, New York, 1906:

The room is hazy with smoke from a large brazier, bathing me in lavender, and it brings me back, back to Shandong province. I step through a door into the courtyard, facing east. The sun striking my face is pleasant. The large square, while not overly crowded, contains many young women all dressed in red. They wear red coats, red trousers, red hats, red shoes, and each carries a red lantern in one hand and a red fan in the other. Their hair is not worn in the traditional way, their feet are not bound. All together they sing. The Chinese is understood:

> *Wearing all red,*
> *Carrying a small red lantern,*
> *Whoosh, with a wave of the fan,*
> *Up they fly to heaven,*
> *Learn to be a Boxer, study the Red Lantern,*

Kill all the foreign devils and make the churches burn.

Again and again they sing. I know them: they are all members of the Hóng dēng jì shǎn líng, 紅燈記閃靈, The Red Lantern Shining. They are all young woman convinced that they can leap up to heaven when they wave their red fans. I just know they will kill many yang guizi, 鬼子. They will all stand very still and their spirits will join the battle.

They all turn toward me. But even though they take no notice of me, I see Her. The woman from the restaurant, much younger but the same one. Her movements are masterful, holding a terrible beauty to them. With a wave of her fan, she locks gazes with me. The look in her eyes holds me as she raises her red lantern.

With that, I am back in my Hong Kong flat, lying on hot sweaty sheets. A young woman lies beside me. Sleep envelops her. Long black hair covering one side of her face. I roll my head and see a man sitting in the chair I had placed in one corner of the room, at the moment, placing it on the opposite side of a shaft of light illuminating my side of the room but placing all but a highly polished pair of Balmorals, one under the other of his crossed legs, in the shadows. I know him. It is Gilhooley. I reach a hand out to him, palm up, fingers ready to grasp, as he speaks. "I'm afraid that's all the time we have."

My eyes roll open, with difficulty, as the opium still weights my eyelids.

I am on the cheap wooden pallet in Wu's Bath Emporium. The sound of rain striking the covered windows and the momentary flash of lightning play like an after-vision of my opium dream.

Mad Frankie, in the woods, present time:

I shake out two Gabapentin 300 mg into my hand and carry them into the kitchen, washing them down with a pull of milk. I close the refrigerator door, I look at my reflection in the stainless steel. Maybe this whole string has been played out. Maybe the words will not clear a path. Have I been fooling myself? As usual I need to occupy myself until the pills shut my mind up. If only the memories would fade, would end. The good ones, the bad ones, just an avalanche of despair. Dizzy, can you hear me? Dizzy, maybe you are in your study typing away or are you drawing? Can you make it stop? I close my eyes.

I am back in Hong Kong. Back in my room. Back with Gilhooley. Back with the man who calls himself Dizzy.

His voice, like a gentle soporific, speaks. "I want you to go back, back to the dream of the bamboo hut and the old man on the mat. The old man who spoke of the future, my future, but it was no dream. It happened just as I described it. I will meet a woman, the look in her eyes will show me my true path." I am having trouble staying awake; in my dream I am falling asleep talking to Gilhooley. My eyes close. I step through a door into the courtyard, facing east. The sun striking my face is pleasant. The large square, while not overly crowded, contains many young women all dressed in red. They wear red coats, red trousers, red hats, red shoes, and each carries a red lantern in one hand and a red fan in the other. Their hair is not worn in the traditional way, their feet are not bound. All together they sing. The Chinese is understood...

...I see Her. The woman from the restaurant, much younger but the same one. Her movements are masterful, holding a terrible beauty to them. With a wave of her fan, she locks gazes with me. The look in her eyes holds me as raises her red lantern.

My eyes roll open, with difficulty, as the opium still weights my eyelids.

I am on the cheap wooden pallet in Wu's Bath Emporium. The sound of rain striking the covered windows and the momentary flash of lightning play like an after-vision of my opium dream.

Mad Frankie, in the woods, present time:

I shake out two Gabapentin 300 mg into my hand and carry them into the kitchen, washing them down with a pull of milk. I close the refrigerator door, I look at my reflection in the stainless steel. Maybe this whole string has been played out. Maybe the words will not clear a path. Have I been fooling myself? As usual I need to occupy myself until the pills shut my mind up. If only the memories would fade, would end. The good ones, the bad ones, just an avalanche of despair. Dizzy, can you hear me? Dizzy, maybe you are in your study typing away or are you drawing? Can you make it stop? I close my eyes.

I am back in Hong Kong. Back in my room. Back with Dizzy.

His voice, like a gentle soporific, speaks. "I want you to go back, back to the dream of the bamboo hut and the old man on the mat. The old man who spoke of the future, my future, but it was no dream. It happened just as I described it. I will meet a woman, she will be of the Dao, and the look in her eyes will show me my true path." I am having trouble staying awake; in my dream I am falling asleep talking to Gilhooley.

Jenkins kicks the door in and we both barge into the one-room hut. Empty. Wait—a few candles are burning in the corner in front of a small reed mat. The mat is occupied by a very frail-looking old man. Jenkins laughs, turns, and walks out the now shattered front door. Once Jenkins is gone, the old man's eyes open and he beckons me closer. I stop in front of his mat. He pushes both hands down. Sit.

I sit. He speaks. "Many years ago I learned your language at a young age, as my father was involved with negotiations between English trading companies. I was called to help maintain some face during and at the end of the second opium war; but after, because of the disastrous defeat of the Qing army, the death of the Emperor, and the burning of the summer palace, we had nothing with which to bargain. Now all that is left is rebellion. From the East it will come but it will not restore the Ming."

I look at him, perplexed. "So, you can tell me the future, old man?"

He answers, "When the world began, there was heaven and earth. You will seek your fortune elsewhere. You have done terrible things, been the tool of great injustice, drunk, gambled, smoked the poison, and given in to the pleasures of the flesh. You have mashed your boot on the innocent and guilty alike. While you have used women of my race as things for your satisfaction, there is one who will come out of the East. She will be of the Dao, and the look in her eyes will show you your true path."

My eyes roll open, with difficulty, as the opium still weights my eyelids.

I am on the cheap wooden pallet in Wu's Bath Emporium. The sound of rain striking the covered windows and the momentary flash of lighting play like an after-vision of my opium dream.

Wu is standing over me. "You go upstairs now, take bath, go to restaurant, have bowl of dan dan mian noodles. You beginning to look like ghost."

I raise my hands and look at them. I do not recognize either.

Wu is still looking down at me. "Go, your gui ren, 贵人 is waiting."

I know what Wu is talking about but I have grave doubts that a person exists who can come and be a great help in my life.

My eyes close. I step through a door into the courtyard, facing east. The sun striking my face is pleasant. The large square, while not overly crowded, contains many young woman all dressed in red. They wear red coats, red trousers, red hats, red shoes, and each carries a red lantern in one hand and a red fan in the other. Their hair is not worn in the traditional way, their feet are not bound. All together they sing...

...I see Her. The woman from the restaurant, much younger but the same one. Her movements are masterful, holding a terrible beauty to them. With a wave of her fan, she locks gazes with me. The look in her eyes holds me as raises her red lantern.

I slip into the bath, images from the opium dream fading into the night of my mind.

Chapter 3

I must have fallen asleep. I do not remember falling asleep; if I did, I have no idea how long I was asleep. The bath water is still warm, but Wu always makes sure that those not fully in this world are at least afforded the luxury of a bath kept warm.

I look over at the bench where I dropped my clothes, still where I left them but now cleaned and pressed. The service at Wu's Bath Emporium is always tip-top. I climb out of the bath, dry, and dress. Time to go see a man about a job.

I arrive at 8 Warren Street wearing my newly cleaned and pressed suit, washed and starched shirt, dark tie. Checking the lobby directory, I find the Clark Enquiry Agency is located on the third floor, office 317. Why not try the Otis elevator in the lobby? It lifts me effortlessly to the fifth floor. I follow the sign to office number 317, knock, and enter. The office air holds faint traces of cigars and joss sticks, an interesting combination.

I am in an outer office looking at a young man behind a small desk containing a new-looking Underwood No. 5 typewriter, telephone, pad, inkwell, pen. He looks up from a paper he is reading and places it down on the desk, while removing his hand from below the desk.

I say, "I've come about the ad. Name's Finnegan. I sent my information ahead."

He rises and sticks out his hand. "Marcus. Let me tell Mr. Clark our candidate has arrived."

Marcus partially opens the rear solid wood door and says something I do not catch. He listens, opens the door further, and waves me to enter the inner office.

Raymond Clark is sitting behind a Ming rosewood desk, spare, except for the Tiffany Counter-Balance Desk Lamp. Blown-glass damascene gold Favrile 12-inch shade with wave pattern, on a counter-balance base. Next to an open notebook, a Parker 30, black hard-rubber eyedropper filler, 13.7 centimetres long, gold-filled overlay with scrollwork and diamond pattern, pen catalogued at $10. The one with the Lucky Curve feed with side cut-outs, responsive Lucky Curve nib. Immediately to his right on a red cloth lies a well-oiled Colt .45-calibre

Rimless automatic pistol. In its 1906 catalogue, Colt boldly proclaims this: "The Most Powerful Small Arm Ever Invented."

I raise my eyes and see Mr. Clark is motioning me into the chair in front of his desk, while holding a folder in his left hand. Without a word of greeting, he turns his notebook and slides it across to me. I can feel his eyes on me as I read:

<u>New Notes</u>

A person's heart and mind are in chaos.

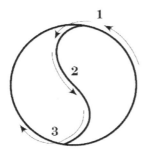

Concentration on one thing makes the mind pure.

If one aspires to reach the Dao, one should practice walking in a circle.

I know I have one shot at this, so I better make it my best. I turn the notebook around and pass it back to Clark. He leans back in his chair.

I speak with as much confidence as I can muster. "It's Daoist philosophy, their method of meditation. They believe the universe is in constant motion, therefore in order to meditate one should be in motion, and the proper motion is called circle walking."

With a slight nod and a wisp of a smile, he asks, "Finnegan, you ever fire a weapon at another man?"

"Yes, sir."

He asks, "The outcome?"

"Well, he was killed, sir."

Clark nods again. "How'd that make you feel, son?"

I tell him what happened. "He had knifed a woman, a prostitute, and was approaching me with the knife. I ordered him the drop it but he just kept coming."

"No, I mean, I want to know how you felt afterwards, not why."

"Sorry, sir. To be honest...I lost my lunch."

Clark smiles. "Good. What weapon do you own?"

"A Webley Mk IV."

He smiles. "Excellent weapon. Among the most powerful top-break revolvers ever produced. Fires the large .455 Webley cartridge. Might have more stopping power than my .45 rimless."

Clark pages through the folder, stopping to read a bit, then closes the folder.

"Finnegan, I have in my folder a telegram from the Hong Kong police, an answer to my enquiry. On the whole they endorse you but with similar reservations as my own. I know you are friendly with some Hip Sings, that you frequent Hip Sing gambling and opium dens. As long as things are kept at a level to my satisfaction, you will be useful. On the other hand, if you compromise this organization, if you give information to those with whom we are at odds, you will be terminated. Am I clear in my meaning?"

"Yes, Mr. Clark, I understand the consequences of disloyalty."

"I am counting on it, Finnegan. The river is no place for a young man to end up." He lets that sink in then adds, "You will carry, in concealment, your weapon at all times hence. You are now a member of the Clark Enquiry Agency."

He pulls a picture from the notebook and slides it across the desk. "Your first assignment. I want you to keep tabs on this gentleman. Nothing overt, I just to want to know his comings and goings. Particularly if he frequents a loft on 23rd Street, which I believe provides storage for a fencing outfit."

The photo shows a tall, thin, middle-aged man, greying with a slight beard. Damn familiar face. I stand to leave but Clark asks me to be seated. He looks at me for a few seconds and leans back in his chair. "Now go and bring back something useful, and we'll see about your pay level."

With that Clark presses something under his desk. A moment later Marcus opens the door and walks up to the desk. Clark hands him my file. "Show Mr. Finnegan out. He has an assignment."

Marcus, file in hand, says, "Yes, sir, Mr. Clark. Will do."

Marcus looks at me and inclines his head toward the door. I make haste for the exit. Once we are back in the outer office, I let out a breath, turn, and ask, "Do you have any advice, Marcus?"

"Yeah. Whatever Mr. Clark told you to do, I suggest you do it. I do not want a repeat of Dan Dinwitty."

"Dinwitty?" I say.

Marcus smiles slightly. "Let's leave that story for some another time, Mr. Finnegan."

On that note I shake Marcus's hand and leave the office. Riding on the quiet Otis elevator to the lobby, I wonder if the Zhou yi was right about this one. Only time will tell.

I slowly make my way back to Chinatown, thinking about my interview, with the intention of having a bite at Big Wong's. I enter the place and move up to the counter. Big Wong is there, because Big Wong is always there. He ladles a bowl of my favourite and I take it to the nearest table. I notice Jeannie at a back table, talking with a well-dressed gentleman. Best not to interrupt. I quickly finish my bowl and am about to leave when in walks the neighbourhood pest.

About five foot four inches tall, wearing a dirty pea coat. and watch cap pulled down over sparse grey hair to go along with a grey unshaven face, surrounding an almost toothless mouth. Added to all this, a nasty piece of work. He is always demanding handouts from shopkeepers and pedestrians alike. I have no idea why the Chinatown shopkeepers put up with him.

Now he's in Big Wong's place, cursing and complaining with a hand out. Some say he's an old sailor, but I've known my share of salts and drunk or sober they never acted like this old bastard. More to my liking is the story he's a former member of the Whyos, whose specialty was "jacking 'em out," price to you $15 for the service. The story goes that he was politely asked to fuck off after the cheap gin rattled his brains. He's never been known for "doing the big job, prices starting at $100."

There he is, standing in front of Big Wong with his grubby hand out. Wong half fills a bowl, and as he is handing it over, Yinglong comes around the counter to give the deadbeat a sniff.

The Old Bastard sees Yinglong and shouts, "The devil! I used to skin cats, I hate them. Sign of bad luck."

He spits on Yinglong, and the cat quickly retreats behind the counter. Big Wong stares at the old man and speaks, a rare thing for Wong. "Last bowl, no more congee. You come into Big Wong no more."

The old man takes it like you would expect. "Fuck you, you fat chink. You'll feed me anytime I please or the next time I'll burn this shit hole to the ground."

He then proceeds to slop most of the congee around his mouth and beard and throws the empty bowl over his shoulder and staggers out, cursing.

As I'm bending over to pick up the broken bowl, I glance over at Big Wong, who is gently wiping Yinglong's coat with a clean towel. Picking up the pieces, I notice all the Chinese in the room are looking down at their meals, nobody talking. Jeannie appears beside me to help clean up the broken crockery.

She whispers in my ear, "I'd like to add a little something to his next bowl." She's dead serious.

We finish and dump the mess into the garbage. I want to say something to Big Wong, but he is standing there with his head bowed. Why? Why did he allow this to happen? Losing face in his own place of business. Is the Old Bastard protected? Is he untouchable? Why would the *boo how doy* allow this to happen to Big Wong?

Not the time to ask. I nod to Jeannie and walk out.

Two days later I'm tucked into a doorway across from a loft space on 23rd Street. I've been here for about four hours, and I'm beginning to wonder if this assignment is to test my stamina when I see my mark leaving the building with none other than the Old Bastard from Big Wong.

The mark says a few words and walks off west on 23rd, while the Old Bastard walks east, crossing over Fifth making a right onto Broadway. I've connected the mark with the loft; maybe I can get some information out of the Old Bastard.

The mark disappears into a carriage and continues west.

I move out of the doorway and begin to trail the old man. Not too difficult, as he is slowly sauntering with a little weaving thrown in. After few blocks a vacant lot comes up on our right. Time to brace the old man. I quicken my pace and catch up to him. He realizes too late he's prey, and before he can fully turn around, I pull him into the vacant lot.

"I ain't got nothing," he snarls, reaching into his jacket pocket with his right hand while waving his left hand about.

I lift a finger and shake my head. "It's a few words I'm looking for, worth a fiver." He relaxes slightly.

I ask, glaring into his eyes, "Who is the man you were talking to?"

He spits out, "What? No one to me, just hitting him up for some change."

I press, "You came out of the building together." I pull out the fiver and hold it up.

He eyes it, moistening his lips. A little drool as he speaks. "I know a chink, he pays me to pass on some gibberish to that cheap mick. I don't owe them nothin'."

"What sort of gibberish?"

He says, "Some chink saying, they're always saying shit that don't mean nothin'. They made me memorize it, and when I'm told by some big shot chink, I come here and tell the mick."

I press a little harder. "What? You tell him what?"

He says, "Eight immortals cross the sea. The chink always gives me a nice touch but the cheap mick never gives me an Indian. Just tells me to keep my mouth shut. Fuck him."

He grabs the fiver. I let him. He begins to turn as he says, "Fuck you, too."

Now I know why Big Wong did nothing. It's Tong business.

I'm about to turn away when the Old Bastard says, "And fuck you mother, too."

Sudden roaring in my head, pounding in my ears, screen of red before my eyes. I smell his cheap gin breath, his cabbage stink. He makes no sound, drool running down his chin. His legs begin to buckle. I give the knife one more twist; he jerks. I pull out the blade and step back. He falls to his knees and onto his side, kicks once and is still. I clean my knife off on his pea jacket. Then pick up his watch cap and stuff it into my pocket.

As I walk away, I realize I have just severed a Tong tie, interfered with Tong business, let my rage control me. Yes, I got information for Clark, but I have crossed a line no man wants to cross, putting myself in opposition to a Tong. I am going to need help on this one.

I find myself in front of Big Wong's. I open the door and walk in. Wong sees me and smiles. He begins to fill a bowl with congee. I glance down at Yinglong, who raises his head in recognition. I hand Wong the watch cap. He looks at it a moment, and I see realization in his eyes. He lifts his head. His face holds both the most loving and saddest expression I have ever seen. He drops the cap in front of Yinglong, who gives it a sniff, which raises the fur along his spine. Wong picks up the cap and throws it into the burner. He turns to me and bows his head. He knows I may have forfeited my life to restore his face.

I sit on the edge of the bed, still vibrating from the encounter of this evening. I have put myself in a bad spot. I see Big Wong's face. I owed him that much, especially Yinglong.

Have to dwell on making it right. How? I have no idea.

I finally lie down as dawn approaches. I have a few hours before I have to report back to Clark. I am willing myself to relax but can't. I am furious at myself for killing the old man. Wait, no I'm not. The way the blade slid in, it was real tasty.

What have I become? As to be so immune to violent death, from murder. Suddenly I feel a presence in the room. I want to reach for my revolver but I cannot move, my body is immobilized. Now I feel it: a malevolent being washing over me, pushing me into the mattress. I am terrified. I try to open my mouth to shout. Did I shout for help? The terror is overwhelming. My right big toe twitches. Just like the presence came, it is gone.

I sit up, soaked in sweat. Hands shaking. I throw some clothes on and run out of the apartment, all the way to Wu's Bath Emporium. I shove open the doors so violently that several people whirl around and stare at me, one being Wu himself. He says something to his assistant and motions me over. In no time I am soaking in a hot bath.

A young Chinese man comes in and shows me a pipe. I quickly nod yes. He leaves to gather some hop and I begin to calm down.

Wu comes into the bath and looks down at me. I tell him the story.

He nods. "A ghost followed you home, a *bei gui ya*. A ghost that presses down, in your case a *gǔdú-guǐ*, a venomous ghost. Someone who was hateful in life. You finish bath, no hop. Come downstairs, I take you to see wu, 覡."

I look at him. "You're Wu. Who's the other one?"

Wu thinks for a few seconds, then says, "Not this Wu, someone who talks to spirits. His name Ching Ling Foo."

I slip out of the bath, dry myself off add a little herbal powder and dress. Wu is waiting downstairs. I follow him out and two doors down to a small Chinese herbal shop with a sign above depicting a beautiful crane at the edge of a pond.

We go into the shop. It is dimly lit. Wu beckons me to follow him to the back, where a few candles are burning in the corner in front of a small reed mat. The mat is occupied by a very frail-looking old man. The old man's eyes open and he beckons me closer. I stop in front of his mat. He pushes both hands down. Sit.

I sit. He speaks. "Many years ago I learned your language at a young age, as my father was involved with negotiations between English trading companies. I was called to help maintain some face during and at the end of the second opium war; but after, because of the disastrous defeat of the Qing army, the death of the Emperor, and the burning of the summer palace, we had nothing with which to bargain. Now all that is left is rebellion. From the East it will come but it will not restore the Ming."

I look at him, perplexed...

Chapter 4

Mad Frankie, in the woods, present time:

I shake out two Gabapentin 300 mg into my hand and carry them into the kitchen, washing them down with a pull of milk. I close the refrigerator door, I look at my reflection in the stainless steel. Maybe this whole string has been played out. Maybe the words will not clear a path. Have I been fooling myself? As usual I needed to occupy myself until the pills shut my mind up. If only the memories would fade, would end. The good ones, the bad ones, just an avalanche of despair. Dizzy, can you hear me? Dizzy, maybe you are in your study typing away or are you drawing? Can you make it stop? I close my eyes. I feel my mind unclench, as I let out a long breath. I feel my qi move down in my body. I am elsewhere as the moment slips away.

Mad Frankie, in the woods, alternate time:

David and I stare straight ahead as the last chord of The Little Fugue in G slowly dissipates. There are a few moments of silence then a knock. I slide off the wooden stool and head for the front door. David only gives a slight tilt of his head in recognition of the event.

I open the door; it's Dizzy. He slips through the opening and into the house.

"Any word?" I softly ask.

At first I think he did not hear me, but he does a slight turn, spinning on his wingtips. "Yes, this morning; they are trying to obtain enough fuel to get here."

"What are the chances?"

He says, "Good. They have some favors they can call in."

I nod. "So, we wait." Not a question; I already know the answer.

We move into the kitchen area. David has already made a musical selection. Brian Eno's "Final Sunset" fills the space. How ridiculously fitting. Dizzy pulls out a stool and sits. Without looking at David, he asks, "Did you bring it?"

David just nods. In mid-nod Dizzy turns his head and catches the last movement, saying, "Good."

I begin to mix a batch of martinis. I decide to stir rather than shake. A nod to the old-school bartenders at the original Waldorf Hotel.

Where did it all go wrong? Where can we take it from here?

The project started with good intentions all around. It seemed to get away from us at a rapid pace—really, not long after my meeting with agent Ancient Soul in the old part of Jerusalem. Did she ever trust my intel? I guess it is the old "Trust but Verify" policy.

She has tried to kill me at least three times. Let's see, the first was after the job we completed in the Brazilian/Venezuelan jungle by Angel Falls. She creased my head after she claimed her gun got caught on a branch. Then there was the time at that restaurant in some backwater town on Long Island, but that was a surrogate assassination by waiter. The last was in my hotel room at The Temple Mount. Her gun misfired, if you can believe that. Anyway, we both had an uncomfortable laugh and then went out and enjoyed a kosher Thai dinner.

I finish up a batch of three martinis, in each, two dashes orange bitters, one-third Dolin Vermouth de Chambéry Blanc, two-thirds Hayman's Old Tom Gin, twist of lemon. David accepts his with a slight smile and an open hand. Dizzy eyes his as if it's the last martini on the planet. Maybe he's right. He takes the cocktail, raising his glass and glancing at David, who also raises his glass.

Both look at me and know what's next. I raise my glass. "Here's to us and fuck everyone else"—the old Green Beret toast from a conflict relegated to the memories of a few.

I hear a car pull into the driveway. They're here.

Dizzy pushes out his wooden stool and heads to the front door to greet them. I begin to mix a new batch of cocktails. Jeannie and Margo enter, followed by Dizzy. There's a moment of anxiety, but agent Ancient Soul enters a heartbeat behind. I feel under the cooktop for my well-greased Webley. Not enough stools to go around, so I direct them to the couch area and let them know cocktails are on the way.

Margo states that the only other person who would be mixing cocktails at a time like this would have been Noel Coward. I take it as a compliment. It takes a few minutes to put together another batch, put them all on a tray, and bring them into the sitting area. Dizzy is standing looking out the large slider that has a view of the gardens. While everyone is sipping their cocktails, I move around with a tray of appetizers because what's a drink without a nosh? As we are nibbling and sipping, Nigel walks into the area and lies down on the gold-tone Nepalese rug, knotted in Nepal and dye washed in Switzerland.

Everyone is staring at a cat who is a character in a novel, but here he is. Nigel, unaware of the group's confusion, quietly cleans his right paw.

Jeannie is the first to ask, "I know the answer to this, but is this Nigel?"

"Yes," I say in an unsure voice. "I have another surprise for you. Someone is here to give one explanation as to the root cause of the phenomenon that has been affecting our lives. I'll be right back."

I leave the sitting area and enter one of the guest bedrooms. I gesture to the man lying on the bed to follow me. He does just that and we return to the group in the sitting area. The man follows me and stands in the middle of the rug. I sit down in an armchair, crossing the legs of my Charles Tyrwhitt Grey Glen Check suit. Dizzy knows the man, and he looks quite pleased with himself.

You see, despite all the philosophical, scientific, and religious data, he believes I have conjured up this reality in an effort to avoid a reality I cannot control. Does everyone in the room exist outside this moment? Does anyone?

Well, let me get this over with. "Members of the group, let me introduce our guest speaker, noted mathematician and crippled soul, Dr. Watson Page."

Everyone is looking at each other, most with worried expressions. Meanwhile, Dizzy is rubbing his hands together as if to say, *Now the fun is going to start.*

Watson waits for no further introductions, although he seems a little peeved at my crippled soul remark. But before he can speak, there is a tentative knock at the door, which was preceded by Nigel lifting his head, flipping his ears forward, and raising his nose. Dizzy nods, so I get up and open the door. There is a woman standing on the front deck. It's Lindsay.

"I wanted to be here," she states.

I look at her a moment; it seems simple. "Of course. You're involved now, please come in." She bends down and to pet Nigel. He turns his back and lifts his tail, allowing her to touch his coat. Satisfied, he walks slowly toward the sitting area, where the rest of the group is assembled.

Watson waits patiently as Lindsay takes a seat. I offer her a martini; she is about to say no thanks, but Barbara gives her a best-not-refuse-him look, so she takes it from me.

Watson finally begins. "In a universe that is defined thermodynamically, time can only run in one direction. But who here believes One Universe was created at the beginning of time? Was there a beginning? We are experiencing local events that have reshaped our belief in the arrow of time, that systems always move from lower to higher entropy."

He pauses to assure himself of our attention then continues. "Rip it all up. Time compression is occurring, and it is due to a very simple and terrifying fact. Two supermassive black holes have coalesced, emitting a linear momentum with amplitude as large as 4,000 kilometers per second, perhaps larger. This has caused the ejection of the coalesced black hole completely from the center of our galaxy. It is now less than 1,000 light-years from us. Too far away to disrupt orbital integrity, but massive gravity waves are causing time phenomena that are affecting our world. You are all tied to some quantum state that is pushing you into the near past, while maintaining a group energy state. In other words, you are all experiencing the same past events. You are all being pulled together, coalescing around a unifying quantum state. I believe at some point your future memories will catch up with your past actions."

The only one laughing is Dizzy. Well, here's to us and fuck everyone else. I lean into the comfort of two martinis and my favorite chair. My eyes roll close and I imagine I'm involved in some other plan. I see us all moving back, back to another state, another stage.

Giuseppe, McGinnity's Saloon, Broadway, New York, 1906:

I push open the saloon door and cross the threshold into the unexpectedly sedate atmosphere of McGinnity's place. Hogan is at the rickety upright playing his syncopated style. He is smiling; he always smiles when he plays. It's evening. I am unsure if Hogan's Broadway show has started, but here he is.

I slide a coin under Old Tom's paw, the bartender slaps a glass down, and fills it with gin. I throw it back and nod for another; he obliges. It follows the last one. I turn and lean back against the bar. Strange, because the gentleman beside me does exactly the same thing, at the same moment. Now here we are both facing outward and turning our heads to give each other the once-over.

He is well dressed, maybe too well dressed. He casually sticks out his hand and says, "Gilhooley."

I grab his outstretched hand and shake it. "Giuseppe."

I glance back and notice his glass is empty. I turn and look at him. "Gilhooley, an Irishman with an empty glass spells trouble. Let me fill it for you."

He gives me a slow smile and an even slower nod. "Whiskey."

I'm watching Hogan at the keys, and when I turn back, I notice Gilhooley glance at three men sitting at a back table. Not a real stare, mind you, just a slow sweep of the room. I feel the tension when his gaze rolls across the three men but know enough not to mention any-thing.

Instead I lean in and say, "Another?"

His head moves but his eyes are back on the men as he says, "Why, no thanks, but allow me to return the favour, as I was just leav-ing." He nods at the barkeep, who promptly fills my glass. As I'm emptying the glass, Gilhooley pushes off the bar. "Good night, Giuseppe, I hope you enjoy your evening."

With that he slowly walks out of the saloon, without a glance at the men of interest. I lay my glass down and drop a bill on the counter. The barkeep smiles and sticks it in his vest pocket. As I turn I notice the three men leaving McGinnity's, and they are not dawdling. Two leave quickly through the door while the third is looking back at me. I turn back around and raise my glass as I glance in the mirror at the third man pushing open the door and leaving.

None of this is my business, but I can never keep my nose out of a fight and this promises to be a short ugly match. I make my way through the place to a back table and Jones. Jones is sober, but Jones is always sober. He works for McGinnity. I sit down next to him. His eyes never leave the crowd as I ask, "Jones, a quick favour—go out the door and have a smoke and see if there is anyone hanging around, someone you've been eyeing."

He gives me a quick nod and exits. Back in no time. A shake of his head no. I'm about to press a bill into his hand but his stare tells me I'm paid up.

Back out on Broadway, I'm looking both ways, trying to decide on a direction, when I spy the last of the three gentleman to leave make a left by Great Jones Street onto West Third, taking him past the Broadway Central Hotel. As he makes the turn, I pick up my pace. When I'm about 10 feet from the corner, I cross the street, head down, not looking back. I hear footsteps quickly heading away. Going to ambush me, you little shit.

I move back around the corner and lean against the wall, pulling my Webley out of my shoulder holster. I break it open and spin the cylinder, then close it. I peer around the corner and see my man about a block and half ahead. There's some traffic on West Third, even at this hour. I slide into the crowd, not letting him get too far ahead.

These three are local thugs, paid by someone to put my bar companion down, maybe forever. Each step tells me to go back, leave it be. You know how it is…well, maybe you don't. There is a moment of recognition. My mind is telling me I need this man alive and well. Why? It may have nothing to do with this world.

I keep eyes just off my target, something I learned in Hong Kong: never stare at the back of someone you are following. They can sense your presence.

After a left onto Sullivan Street, I stop. Gilhooley is staying at the Broadway Central Hotel so he is doubling back to Broadway. Damn. The El casts a shadow over Bleecker Street. I hurry and make a left onto Bleecker, heading toward the elevated station at Bleecker and West Broadway. As I pass Thompson Street, I hear a gunshot. I pull my Webley, carrying it low, and run toward the sound.

There, under the El, the three have joined up and have cut off Gilhooley. One man is lying on the ground looking quite dead, the product of the derringer in Gilhooley's hand. Gilhooley is holding his side;

it looks black, blood. All of his attackers have knives. Not so stupid to bring a knife to a gun fight when there are three of you and the other guy has a one-shot derringer.

Gilhooley looks like running is not an option. The final two begin to advance on him, so I raise the Webley and pull back the hammer. In a very calm voice I say, "Stop right there, boyos, fun's over for tonight."

They both turn. One snarls, "Why are you so interested? We's got orders, so fuck off."

I shoot the little fuck and he drops like a sack of shit. The lone thug runs like hell, obviously the smart one of the bunch. I hear a police whistle, and quickly holster the Webley and take Gilhooley by the arm. "Can you walk?" I ask. He nods.

I say, "Let's see if we can avoid the coppers and get you back to McGinnity's. He knows a good sawbones name of Larsson."

Gilhooley puts his arm around my shoulder and says, quite clearly, into my good ear, "Haven't we done this before?"

I half drag, half carry Gilhooley along Bleecker. As we pass Wooster Street, I look up the street, where two thugs appear out of the shadows. The low light from the streetlamp casts them as in a shadow play. They clearly intend to do us harm.

I ease Gilhooley to the ground. He grunts, as he is barely conscious. I reach into my jacket and feel an empty holster. Dummy—that is why the damn thing has a deadeye on the end, a fitting for a lanyard. Prevents losing your weapon in a fight. This one is not going to be pretty. I reach behind me for my Nepalese Gurkha Kukri Bhojpure Fighting Knife, pulling it out of its soft leather scabbard.

The two thugs start to move my way as one draws a pistol, the other a nasty-looking knife. I know I can take the clown with the knife, but the pistol is going to be a problem. Although I know he has to get fairly close because his weapon of choice looks like an Apache revolver, which incorporates a fold-over knuckle duster forming the grip with a rudimentary fold-out, dual-edged knife. French designed, manufactured and a piece of shit unless you're close enough to be able to use the blade.

Something changes; I feel it in my belly. Time slows down, everyone appears to be underwater. Out of the deep shadows a figure emerges. All in black, including mid-back-length hair. It is a woman, a diminutive woman. She seems to glide and pivot to face the approaching thugs. Her arms and legs move as one as she comes to a halt, adopting a stance I recognize as a Chinese martial art fighting posture. Her left leg out, straight, foot inward, right leg bent and carrying the weight. Both arms up, left arm extended palm up, right arm back palm up, flowing into left leg pulled back, both arms down and crossing her chest, fists closed, shifting her legs, right leg forward, body into a crouch, arms extended, palms open, thumbs facing down, flowing back to her original posture. All with an incredible grace that holds a sense of power. It seems like a long time between movements, but she is controlling time and space: it may have been a second or forever.

The boyos stop their forward progress and at the same time both laugh.

One speaks. "Go home, little girl, we have business with these two."

As they begin to move past her, she is suddenly behind the gunman and grasping his gun arm, pulling it down and striking his back. He is propelled forward, releasing his gun as he hits the pavement. In one kick the gun is out of sight. All this happens just out of the peripheral vision of the knifeman. As he realizes what is happening, he turns and thrusts his knife at the empty air. She grasps his knife arm, pulling it down as she moves beside him. He falls to his knees but still has the knife in his hand. She whirls in a circle and delivers a devastating kick to the side of the assailant's head. He is out before he bounces off the pavement. She is everywhere and nowhere, passing like an empty cloud. Gone, without even waiting for a thank-you.

Chapter 5
Guanlin Temple

Guanlin Town, Luolong District, Luoyang, China, sometime before 1906:

Kong Biàn passes the Opera Tower on her right as she moves toward the main gate of the Guanlin Temple. Crossing the threshold by extending her right leg over the barrier, the purpose of which is to prevent ghosts from entering. She moves to the small wooden table and begins to write out a prayer for we know not what or whom, to hang on the tree of intentions. Upon finishing she takes a small piece of red twine and attaches the prayer to a branch of the tree. She brings her hands to her forehead in a sweeping gesture, three times.

It is time to enter the main temple area. She carries with her a red sash, long joss sticks, and devotion. She places her right foot over the threshold of the Courtesy Gate, passing the Bell Tower on her left and the Drum Tower on her right. Pausing at the rows of *qilin* statues on her right and left, no two alike, she picks one and hangs her red sash over its head, joining other sashes in prayer unique to each sash.

Walking up the three steps takes her to the large brazier that sits in front of the Enlightened Sage Hall. She places three burning joss sticks in the brazier, then brings her hands to her forehead in a sweeping gesture, three times. Moving past the brazier, she bows and enters the hall, kneeling at the altar, before a 20-foot statue of Guan Yu, Guan Gong, Lord Gong, General Gong—so respected that when he was defeated in battle and his head brought to Cao Cao, he ordered a body of wood be made so Guan Yu would be intact for the battles of the next world. There are 12 wooden carvings on the walls in the Enlightened Sage Hall, telling the story of what happened in the Romance of the Three Kingdoms.

Biàn moves to her right around the Enlightened Sage Hall. She passes between it and the Hall of the God of Wealth containing the statues of Guan Yu reading the book *Chunqiu* and one of him sleeping. These express people's respect and love for him.

She now stands before the Five Tigers Hall. During the Three Kingdoms period, the "Five Tiger Generals" referred to five generals from the state of Shu Han: Guan Yu, Zhang Fei, Zhao Yun, Ma Chao, and Huang Zhong. All are represented as large statues, ten feet tall.

She places three burning joss sticks in the brazier, then brings her hands to her forehead in a sweeping gesture, three times, in reverence to those towering figures. The term "Five Tiger Generals" moved into the culture so that any outstanding group of five can have the title bestowed upon them.

Biàn moves to pay her respects before the last hall. Because Guan Yu often stayed up nights reading *Chunqiu*, Cao Cao asked construction workers to build Chunqiu Hall for him. In this hall, a statue of Guan Yu on the left is reading the book.

Finally she comes to the Stone Lane with a stone tablet, 6 meters high and 3 meters wide. The characters on the lane are written to commemorate Guan Yu. At the altar Biàn places two oranges and an apple and bows her intentions. She turns and is at the tomb. Facing the front of the tomb, to her right, there is a stone tablet, which was built in the Qing Dynasty, carved with the highest of inscriptions of Guan Yu by many emperors. She brings her hands to her forehead in a sweeping gesture, three times. Following her beliefs she makes offerings to create positive energy and develop good qualities such as giving with a respectful attitude and gratitude.

Giuseppe, somewhere in China, somewhen:

I lift myself off the bamboo matting that has been placed upon the rosewood bed frame. Her fragrance still lingers there. I quietly wander out into the rear garden. The early-morning sunlight reflects off the pines. I am facing east, the direction the rear garden is to be enjoyed, bathed in a most gentle light.

The centre of the garden is occupied by her. She has been here since dawn. Walking the circle, she concentrates on its centre. Her body is in constant motion, duplicating the movements of the cosmos. She is always becoming, always changing, beautiful, poetic, divine.

The whirling circles of BaGua Zhang. The BaGua, signifying its roots in the Zhou yi. She is the Lion 乾, the Monkey 兌, the Rooster 離,

the Dragon 震, the Phoenix 巽, the Snake 坎, the Bear 艮, the Qilin 坤. She is standing, turning, striking, ever changing. Watching her I am as empty as I have ever been.

Giuseppe, Chinatown, New York, 1906:

I sit on the edge of the bed. The light in the room is fading, as the sun bids us farewell. The darkness wins. Two days in an opium joint on Pell Street, wearing my stained collarless shirt and rumpled suit, sack coat of dark grey with matching pants patterned with dumpling dipping sauce. Bearded and unwashed. Stopped at a joss house on the way home where I saw an angel standing in the sun; I saw the beast lurking in the shadows. Where will I stand? Time is running down. I am losing the ability to distinguish between my opium dreams and reality.

Reality: that's a real comic word. Because, my friends, the opium dreams seem so much more real. My past, my present, my future have all been revealed.

Mad Frankie, in the woods, present time:

I shake out two Gabapentin 300 mg into my hand and carry them into the kitchen, washing them down with a pull of milk. I close the refrigerator door, I look at my reflection in the stainless steel. Maybe this whole string has been played out. Maybe the words will not clear a path. Have I been fooling myself? As usual I needed to occupy myself until the pills shut my mind up. If only the memories would fade, would end. The good ones, the bad ones, just an avalanche of despair. Dizzy, can you hear me? Dizzy, maybe you are in your study typing away or are you drawing? Can you make it stop? I close my eyes.

Chapter 6

Giuseppe, McGinnity's Saloon, Broadway, New York, 1906:

We place Gilhooley on a table in one of McGinnity's back rooms after we clear away a few dinner dishes and glasses and throw a fresh table-cloth over the stained surface. We are as gentle as possible, but he emits a soft groan and then is quiet. I had given him a long pull off a bottle of Wampole's Tonic; it seemed to ease his suffering after the journey from the El on Bleecker Street.

The visions of the fight keep running through my mind. It seemed so fantastic, so much so that I could easily believe it never happened. In my mind's eye all I can see are those whirling circles, that vortex of movement. Thoughts for later. Right now I have to focus on Gilhooley.

The door opens and in wobbles the Doc, Butcher Larsson, former head of surgery at Bellevue Hospital and noted hophead, which accounts for the "former" preceding member of the surgical staff. Butcher, not a moniker usually associated with a surgeon but let me tell you about Doc Larsson.

All I needed to know about Doc Larsson I heard from McGinnity. Doc Larsson and what happened at the battle of Gettysburg. Anyway, on July 1, 1863, things were pretty much touch and go between the two sides at that point in the American Civil War. The two armies came together to engage in the pivotal battle of the war, outside a small town called Gettysburg. Back in 1761 Samuel Gettys settled at a crossroads and opened a tavern as a resting place for travellers. The town grew from there.

General Robert E. Lee marched his Army of Northern Virginia into Pennsylvania in late June 1863, after he won a major victory over the Union at Chancellorsville, Virginia. Too bold a move? He decided to strike and destroy the Army of the Potomac and then roll north, maybe as far north as Philadelphia, with the hopes that the North would sue for peace. It did not work out for him or the Army of Northern Virginia. July 1, 1863, the first day of the battle of Gettysburg, involved some light engagements with the hastily formed Union lines to the northwest of town failing to hold but no real advantage was gained.

Doc's story starts on July 2, 1863, which would make him about 17 years old, maybe 16, at the time, a member of II Corps, Second Division, 1st Brigade, 1st Minnesota. This was the second day of battle. By afternoon Major General Sickles' III Corps units had been repulsed and were crossing the open space toward Cemetery Ridge, pursued by two Confederate brigades. Major General Winfield Scott Hancock, sensing he was about to lose this vital position, ordered the 1st Minnesota to charge into the gap to buy time for him to regroup his position. There were 262 men in the 1st Minnesota. They were about to be out numbered five to one. Colonel William Colvill repeated the order, and all 262 men double-timed down the slope and broke the Confederate front line with bayonets. Nearly surrounded, they held out for some time, and when they retired, upon the approach of Confederate reserves, 215 had been killed or wounded, an 82% casualty rate. Two men were awarded the Medal of Honor. Their colours fell and were raised five times. They captured the battle flag of the 28th Virginia. Forty-seven men retired from the field of battle toward Cemetery Ridge, still in line. Doc Larsson was one of these 47. They bought time with their lives, saving the day and perhaps the battle.

That night Doc found his true calling. What must have his young eyes seen? What must have his young ears heard? He performed many amputations, true testament to what kind of carnage a .577-calibre ball could do. He worked through the night and in the morning, covered in his brothers' blood. His comrades, lovingly, gave him the moniker "Butcher."

Doc stops himself by extending his hands and making contact with the table. He looks down at Gilhooley, muttering, "Cut away his shirt. He's still bleeding but nothing major was hit or he would have bled out by now. Also, get a bowl of hot water and some soap."

This process takes about five minutes. All the while Doc stands by the table gazing down at Gilhooley's face. I wonder, did the hop blur all those faces he looked at on the ridge? Did it quiet the last cries of the dying?

July 3, 1863, was the final day of battle, the day of great miscalculation. The charge across an open terrain to engage an enemy who occupied the high ground. It was doomed before the first Confederate foot moved forward. In hand-to-hand combat, Doc took a bayonet through the shoulder.

While at the field hospital, the wound festered for a time but he re-covered, as much a testament to his youth than to the prowess of the medical staff. The wound left him with a lifelong scar and an on-again, off-again addiction to the painkiller liberally given. The invention of the hypodermic needle in the late 1850s, and the isolation of morphine sulphate in the early 19th century, combined to have left almost half a million soldiers addicted and Doc was one.

With the delivered water, Doc rolls up his shirt sleeve and scrubs his hands and forearms. It is a strange sight, but Doc has his own ways and I am not about to question a man of his experience. Anyway the last joker who offered the doc some advice needed his attention. Doc wobbles over to the table and asks me to remove the pressure he asked me to apply. Good thing since my arms are going numb. Doc looks at the wound, cleans it with a sponge, and with a grunt, orders, "You are going to assist me, so stay sharp and when I ask for an instrument be quick. I will point to what I need and you will hand it to me. Now go take off that jacket and go wash your hands and forearms."

Doc quickly unwraps a collection of surgical instruments and starts to work on Gilhooley. His first movement is to pull a loaded syringe out of a green alligator case and, after tying off one Gilhooley's arms, injects the fluid directly into a main vein. This done he steps back, laying the syringe down and closing his eyes, almost like he had taken the shot himself. Gilhooley's body visibly relaxes, and Doc's eyes open with a ghost of a smile.

Chapter 7
The End of the World

Mad Frankie, Earth, distant future:

I'm standing on a small outcrop of red granite, which juts out of the side of a hill. The view looks out over a calm ocean. I have no idea which one. Low grass pops up here and there, kept down by the constant wind blowing in from the water. The air has a slight chill with a light ozone quality.

I look up at an awe-inspiring sight, a sight no humans should ever see. The Sun, bloated and red, fills much of the heavens, its luminosity reflected in the narrow dust belt circling the horizon. Long ago the Moon reached the Roche limit and began to fall toward the Earth, breaking up and forming our own Saturn ring. The object of so much literature and thousands of years of the Moon festival, long gone. Where has Chang'e, the Moon Goddess, gone now?

There is a small disturbance behind me, as someone has kicked a few loose rocks on the way toward me. I turn to see Gilhooley.

He nods and walks up to stand beside me. "Is this it?" he asks.

No one has ever been more stranded.

"Possibly," I answer, "but it could be an anomaly that will rectify itself and slingshot us back to some past point in time."

Gilhooley looks dubious. "It's the end of the world," he says without a trace of fear. I smile, closing my eyes, feeling the chill wind on my face.

Chapter 8
Wàn Suì Yé

Nigel Larsson, Forbidden City, Hyde Park, New York, alternate time:

Consciousness returns by olfactory stimuli. A divine citrus scent, mixed with a delicate hint of white tea and jasmine, gently prods me awake, while lightly coming to rest on my face. Awake, I am lying on a sea of silks. Silks dyed in shades of red and yellow. A feather-light comforter covers me to my waist, red, bordered in yellow, decorated with a large five-clawed yellow dragon with red eyes. The immense bed sits on a round dais within a perfectly square room. The ceiling is set with blue ceramic tiles. A set of large windows to my right are open, allowing a gentle breeze carrying a light whiff of working braziers.

Two men approach the bed, dressed in servant attire. At a certain distance, they drop to their knees and bow their heads to the floor.

They address me, "Wàn Suì Yé, 萬歲爺/万岁爷, many dishes have been prepared, tasted, and are ready for consumption."

Servants often addressed the emperor as Wàn Suì Yé. Was I really the Lord of Ten Thousand Years? The servants rise and bow their way back out the door.

I continue to bask in the coolness of the room and the softness of the silk. Funny thing, though, being addressed as Wàn Suì Yé yet spoken to in English.

I roll my head to the left. There, sitting on a high-backed Ming, rosewood chair, is Gilhooley. "Enjoying yourself?" he asks.

Bastard! My mind explodes with incomprehensible images: a swirling black hole, ingesting its fill. A strange group of people sitting in wait, a small hot, stuffy room with a wooden pallet, me standing over a body, knife in my hand, me sitting in a chair petting a grey cat. I sit up, answering Gilhooley's question. "Yes, as a matter of fact, I am."

He crosses his long legs, after a slight tug of his dark-grey American-cut suit pants. He gives me a slight smile. "I can tell on the carriage ride up the main entrance, I saw the heads. It appears as if beheading is the order of the day."

I throw the comforter aside, feeling the anger rise, and quote Hong Xiuquan: "'In my hand I wield the killing power in Heaven and Earth. I slay the evil, preserve the righteous, and relieve the people's suffering. My eyes see through beyond the West, the North, the rivers, and the mountains, my voice shakes the East, the South, the Sun, and the Moon. The glorious sword of authority was given by the Lord.'"

Gilhooley takes it all in stride and has his say. "Really, 20 million Chinese were left dead because of the Taiping Rebellion. Listen to me, this is all an illusion. You are not the Lord of Ten Thousand Years. You're Nigel or Giuseppe but not Hong Xiuquan or Qin Shi Huang or whatever that outfit is about. In case you haven't noticed, we are not even in China. We are currently in Hyde Park, New York, specifically on what was known as the Springwood Estate. The estate, which comprises one square mile of land, was bought in 1866 by James Roosevelt, father of the 32nd President of the United States, Franklin Delano Roosevelt. All this appears to be gone. History that I learned, places I visited in the past. All replaced by a one-square-mile Forbidden City. Look at the Chinese characters above your bed."

I turn and see these characters in red lacquer, above the bed: 奈杰尔.

Gilhooley continues, "You know that's a literal translation of your name, a non-Chinese name, Nigel. Have you heard the servants say your name, thinking you were out of earshot? *Nài jié ěr*. A rough pinyin of Nigel?"

I look at him. "You're jealous. Now who's in the position of power? With one clap of my hands, I could have you removed."

Gilhooley turns his head but not before I see the look of sadness wash over his face.

He whispers, "I'm angry too. I'm furious. Mad as a hornet. This reality we are sharing. It's the first shift where I have retained memory of another persona, other places. Why is it occurring on this timeline? I know one thing: this must be an aborted loop, the whole gestalt is all wrong. It has been constructed based on your fantasy. It all concerns your preoccupation with China and all things Chinese. Your dreams of righting all the wrongs, of putting those that you despise on pikes. It is anger that drove you here. That has forged every detail of this set. That is the energy that has pitched you down this timeline. We both know we need to find a way back; back to the main trunk of our timeline.

Away from this impossible—no, correction—improbable world." With that he slumps into his Ming chair.

I am taken aback and for the briefest of moments we are connected on a conscious and subconscious level. I have to ask, "What brought you down this timeline? I didn't create this reality alone. No, it was our combined energies multiplied by the force of anger, the power of anger, our anger. The heads are just a demonstration of the depth of it."

He looks confused for a moment, then just nods. "I know, he speaks without any regret in his voice. I have known for a while. Our brain quantum states on occasion act as a single entity. I think that the energy of anger pushes us to some tipping point, where in moments of time dilation we are one. The question before the house is, how do we abort this loop?"

I rise off the bed and in a flash two servants begin to slip on a large royal-blue robe embroidered with the Twelve Symbols of Sovereignty representing a symbolic interpretation of the universe. These symbols of imperial authority assume a cosmic significance and represent the emperor as the Son of Heaven.

Sun (日 rì)
Moon(月 yuè)
Constellation of Three Stars (星辰 xīngchén)
Mountain (山 shān)
Dragon (龍 lóng) Five-clawed
Pheasant (華蟲)
Two Goblets (宗彝 zōng yí)
Seaweed (藻 zǎo)
Grain (粉米 fěn mǐ) [rice grain; literal: rice powder]
Fire (火 huǒ) [flame]
Axe head (黼 fǔ)
Fu symbol (黻 fú) To distinguish between Good and Evil

As I am being outfitted, two other servants are opening a pair of beautifully glazed doors situated at the far end of the room, allowing a blond-haired woman to enter. She's wearing on her feet, slippers with peony pattern embroidery. Above them she is wearing a long white silk pleated skirt under a silk peach waistcoat with porcelain buttons. Her arms are filled with peonies, red peonies. She bows slightly, turns, and begins placing the flowers in a Ming dynasty, Xuande mark and period (1426–35), imperial blue-and-white vase, which sits upon a deeply lacquered, green Ming-style stand.

The moment is perfect. The flowers, her robe, the sun striking her hair as she pauses, five flowers in the vase, one she is holding in her left hand—the perfect tableau, a Caravaggio vision. Only a breath, a second, revealing a minuscule island of beauty surrounded by darkness and coming doom.

Gilhooley is staring at the woman. His lips move, his face trance-like: "Jeannie."

I have had enough. I wave my right arm and everyone rushes out of the room, leaving one red peony on the green slate floor. Gilhooley stays. As I look at him, the solution comes to me, the way to break the loop, even one that can last 10,000 years. All I have to do is have Gilhooley beheaded.

Darkness descends on the room like a final curtain. Then, a bright flash, then another. I walk to the window and see swirling clouds of a deep amber, so beautiful, like nothing I have ever seen before. I turn and clap my hands, bid the servant to bring the Wu. I turn back toward Gilhooley, still sitting in the Ming chair, a brief glimmer of hope in his eyes. The Wu enters, carrying a tablet. Gilhooley gets to his feet, shaking his head, suddenly looking quite pale.

The Wu stops at the appropriate distance and bows. She reads from the tablet. The divination was performed at the proper moment and has revealed itself to be Wu Wang, 無妄, Heaven flowing over Thunder. An incredibly bright flash, followed by a rolling bass line. I speak to the Wu. "We must ascend and receive these messages from Heaven." I motion for the Wu to follow. Turning to invite Gilhooley, I see him approaching me. Two imperial guards step from the shadows. In a moment Gilhooley will be dead.

I raise my hand. "I am permitting him to enter my circle."

Gilhooley speaks with a certain desperation in his voice, pointing to the Wu. "Don't you recognize her?"

"Of course. She is the court Wu. She divines from the Zhou yi, the way of change."

Gilhooley is shaking his head. "No, no, it's Barbara, Barbara from The Project, Barbara from Chinatown, Barbara from our past, our present, our future, who the hell knows at this point."

I turn toward the stone stairs that lead to the roof. One of the guards rushes pat and heads up the stairs. The other, gripping his sword tightly, eyes Gilhooley as we mount the stairs. Once on the roof, the cycling clouds shift from amber to dark red with fringes of red-violet. The lighting strikes end in a bright, fiery red-orange. Is Heaven so close? My robes billow in the wind. Gilhooley is looking around at the assembled members of the court.

He has to shout above the deep rolling bass line. "They're all here. Look"—he points at an Imperial guard—"that's David." His right arm moves west. "There"—he singles out two women, both wearing red quju, 曲裾, standing before a large bronze brazier emitting the smoke of dragon's blood and copal—"It's Margo and Lindsay." His arm continues its arc and lands on the blond woman wearing the peony slippers and peach waistcoat over white silk pleated skirt. "It's Jeannie. Everyone is here. Why?" he shouts the last question.

I glance at the guard standing behind Gilhooley, the one he calls David, sword at the ready. All he needs is a slight nod and this journey ends. The Wu, whom Gilhooley calls Barbara, steps forward. A purple flash and thunder physically striking my chest causes my right foot to slide backward.

She speaks. "The Oracle has spoken, Wu Wang, Heaven flowing over Thunder. Below Heaven thunder moves. Fate belongs to Heaven."

I understand. Sadness envelops me. It is all going away. The energy that brought me here drains away, for the moment, I am empty now. I pivot, raising my arms to Heaven. The central tenet, Wu Wei, 無爲, I laugh as loud as I have ever laughed. A massive bolt of lightning strikes. The wave comes.

I jerk forward, the wooden pallet creaks, my eyes take in the dim surroundings of Wu's Bath Emporium. I draw the pipe close, like it is the only lover I'll ever know. My eyes close.

Chapter 9
Mano Nera

Giuseppe, Chinatown, New York, 1906:

I am at the bar in McGinnity's. As if from a fog I emerge, with sounds, sights, and the ambience of the room slowly coming into focus. Looking at myself in the mirror, which runs the full length of the bar, I take stock. I'm wearing a light-blue check suit, sack cut, with matching waistcoat buttoned high exposing a white wing-collared shirt and a dark-grey, diamond-pattered tie done up in the four-in-hand style. No crease, dark-blue contrasting pants with roll-ups. All ending in a pair of over-the-ankle, toe-cap dark-brown boots. On my head, slightly pushed back, is a dark-blue derby.

Armando is standing just off to my left in his—out of place here—starched white shirt, turned-down collar, black waistcoat, and pants with a red-striped bow tie, having poured out two of his martini cocktails.

As I bring mine up for a taste, the man on my right is doing just that and both of our glasses hit the bar at the same time. He's dressed in a slightly older style with frock coat, straight bagged trousers, over-the-ankle square-toed boots, all in black. Black double-breasted waistcoat with white turned-down-collar shirt, adding a blue paisley ascot tied under the collar.

I've known Tony DiRusso for about two months. Business brought us together. Both of us have Italian roots. Tony is damn handy with a stiletto.

Do not let his mild manner fool you. Tony is a dangerous man.

At the moment, he is flush and paying our way tonight.

He insisted, I complied. He is well paid for his sideline talent of letter writing. It's what is known as *Mano Nera*—Black Hand—letter writing. I have seen his work; it is quite impressive. He's well schooled and in good with a few of his Neapolitan cousins. His latest note was sent to a mick swell named Gilhooley. I do not know what connection Raymond Clark has with the cousins, but they approved the mark and the amount was paid in full.

I turn my head slightly toward Tony and ask, "*E 'andata bene, penso?*"

"*Ha pagato senza lamentarsi.*" He gives a slight laugh.

Tony switches to the Neapolitan. "*L ièvace 'e dièbbet.*"

I give him a nod. "Indeed, Tony, indeed."

I pull out my B. W. Raymond pocket watch. About the middle of the 1860s, a group of watchmakers and mechanical engineers produced their first pocket watch movement, named for the then investor and Chicago mayor B. W. Raymond. The watch is exquisite. The Elgin National Watch Company was born.

I think it is time to visit Wu's. Tony wanted to give the hop a whirl, so what better place than Wu's. Wu will be gentle. I nod toward the door, we both pick up our cocktails and finish them off. Tony drops a bill on the bar, I tip my hat to Armando, and off we go.

As we walk through the doors of McGinnity's, we hear cursing. Jones has just tossed someone into the street. "Stay away, old man, I warn you. You've worn out your welcome."

Jones turns around, nods to us, and proceeds back inside. While I am looking down at the man, I recognize him as the Old Bastard who made the scene at Big Wong's restaurant. I realize Tony has quietly slipped into the shadows. The Old Bastard picks himself up, looks at me, and says his usual, "Fuck you, who you lookin' at?" He then staggers off down Broadway.

I move over to where Tony is standing. He looks at me and says, "He insulted my cousin Roberto and his wife on the street one night in full view of many countrymen."

"*Bene,*" I answer.

Tony says, "*Devo vendicare l'onore di mio cugino. Si tratta di vendetta.*"

I look at him and say, "I owe the Old Bastard, too."

We begin to tail the Old Bastard, not too difficult as he is slowly sauntering with a little weaving thrown in. After a few blocks a vacant lot comes up on our right. Time to brace the old man. We quicken our pace and catch up to him. He realizes too late he's prey, and before he can fully turn around, we pull him into the vacant lot.

"I ain't got nothing," he snarls, reaching into his jacket pocket with his right hand while waving his left hand about. Tony steps forward and grabs the Old Bastard's right hand as he slides his stiletto between the man's ribs in one fluid motion.

He says in a grim voice, "*Questo è il bacio di Tosca!*"

The Old Bastard makes no sound, drool running down his chin. His legs begin to buckle. Tony gives the knife one more twist; he jerks. Tony pulls out the blade and steps back. The Old Bastard falls to his knees and onto his side, kicks once and is still. Tony cleans his knife off on the Old Bastard's pea jacket. Then I pick up his watch cap and stuff it into my pocket. Tony looks down at him and says,

"*È finito.*"

In no time at all, we are pushing open the doors of Wu's Bath Emporium. I see Wu standing off to one side. He gives me a disapproving look but motions for a young girl to serve us. Tony and I move up the rickety wooden staircase to the den. The girl leads us into a room with four pallets, none of which are occupied. She makes a stylized gesture inviting Tony to recline on one of the pallets.

"Tony," I say, "jacket off, loosen the ascot, and make yourself comfortable, going to be a long night."

I see him eyeing the ball of dope the young girl is placing on the needle as I say, "*Riposare, il tempo per sognare.*" He gives me a weak smile and lies down.

I lie down on my own wooden pallet in the gloom of Wu's Bath Emporium's opium den. Everything a hophead would want, meaning a nice ball of dope. I've never noticed how beautiful the young Chinese woman is as she twirls the ball of dope over the opium lamp. Maybe it's because she has the thing I want. The thing that so fleetingly quenches the fire.

All set, she hands me the plain pipe. Her eyes are averted as I notice she is missing the ring finger of the hand offering me the pipe. I take it from her, bringing the stem to my mouth with more anticipation than with any lover. I take a long pull, allowing my head to fall back among the cheap pillows. As I exhale time slows and the cosmos opens to its terribly beautiful, infinite possibilities, but it is one I am falling toward. I dream of a ship that sails away, far, far away.

Consciousness returns by the olfactory sense of Chanel No. 5 perfume. Coco Chanel, from her earliest days, found mystical meaning in

the number five, seeing in it a thing's embodiment and spirit. I stare down at a cocktail on the inlaid demilune bar. The dream fades as I am fully on set.

I am at Sherry's bar in the Metropolitan Opera House on 39th Street and Broadway.

Someone beside me says, "I really enjoyed that first act. Renata is in fine form as always."

I turn to my right to see Tony holding a coupe cocktail glass to his lips.

"Yes, yes, in fine form." As I say it, I feel a hand on my shoulder and turn. It is Armando with a woman, white hair in a French twist, beside him. I give him a hug.

His eyes twinkling, he says, "She is remarkable. The divine beauty of her floated pianissimo high notes just carry me away. Oh, sorry, you both know Margo Gutmann?" He gestures to the woman beside him. "Margo, this is Giuseppe and Tony."

She takes my hand with her light-blue-gloved right hand. "Pleasure." She is wearing an off-the-shoulder dress with a sweetheart neckline, princess seams, and below-the-knee slightly flared skirt, all in light-blue satin, with a dark-blue satin wrap.

Armando looks at me and smiles. "Here it is March already, and the last time I saw you was New Year's Eve at Birdland. Wow, what a night that was."

I just laugh.

Armando asks, "How is 1955 treating you?" I wish I could re-member but just nod OK.

Tony taps me on the shoulder. "Time for act two."

I turn toward him and notice how well his thin, satin-lapelled tux-edo with white carnation and red bow tie looks on him. Then I smile and say, "Yes, it is time to hear Renata sing 'Vissi d'arte.'" We link arms and head to our seats, bidding Armando and Margo farewell.

We are in our seats when the second act of Tosca begins.

Scarpia summons Tosca in the hope of using her lover, Cavaradossi, as leverage in finding Angelotti. Tosca arrives, and upon hearing Cavaradossi's cries of pain, she betrays the whereabouts of Angelotti. Having the information he wants, Scarpia proposes a bargain: if Tosca gives herself to him, he will free Cavaradossi. She refuses but realizes

Cavaradossi is about to be executed. Tosca turns centerstage and begins her plea to the Divine: "Vissi d'arte, vissi d'amore."

After the aria is finished, Tosca will submit to Scarpia, if he provides safe conduct out of Rome for herself and her lover. Scarpia, knowing that it is all a sham and intends to kill Cavaradossi and have Tosca for himself, agrees. As he is signing the document, Tosca slides a knife off the table and as Scarpia turns to embrace her, she sticks the blade in him and announces, "Questo è il bacio di Tosca!"

I jerk forward, the wooden pallet creaks, my eyes take in the dim surroundings of Wu's Bath Emporium. I draw the pipe close, like it is the only lover I'll ever know. My eyes close.

Chapter 10
El Dorado

Nigel, The El Dorado Club, Berlin, 1932:

Consciousness returns by overwhelming stimuli. Music, voices, laughter, smoke, perfume. I am sitting on a hardback wooden chair, looking at myself in an enormous mirror. My hair is slicked back. I have on a set of evening wear in midnight blue, a deep blackish blue, which even in this bright light appears muted in hue, yet still appearing to be darker and richer than black.

The jacket sitting long on my hips, with moderately wide peaked lapels, cuffed at the wrists with satin trim. Single breasted, of course. Two flap pockets on the front, and a slit breast pocket containing a lavender scarf.

The trousers, a matching midnight blue, very high waisted, held up by a pair of lavender suspenders, with a satin stripe down each leg. The pants are cut narrow and cuffed.

The shirt, starched white, crisp with a wingtip collar and French cuffs, buttoning up the front with mother-of-pearl buttons. Keeping with the popular style, the cuff links are initialed "AB," in midnight-blue enamel.

The waistcoat is a stylish white brocade with a straight waist lined "tub" fashion, high-waisted cut with no points.

The bow tie is a silk lavender matching the scarf tucked into the breast pocket. On the left jacket lapel, a boutonniere containing a lavender rose.

The shoes are simple black patent-leather slip-on pumps with small stacked heels, the toes slightly pointed.

I am sitting at a table with four other people. Now I am fully in this moment. Sitting on my immediate left is a stunning woman. Not just measured by her looks but by the fact she is wearing a full-length mink coat, gold chain around one ankle, and is completely naked beneath the coat. Her only other adornment is a small monkey clinging to her shoulder. The monkey is sleeping. I look into her eyes and feel my soul sliding down a chute. She gives me a smile of utter contentment. Her eyes are pinned. Mainly because of the cocaine injection, dangerous even for her trained hand, which is the main reason she followed it up with an injection of morphine, maybe later a bowl of opium. I realize I have deep feelings for this woman, Anita Berber. I am overwhelmed with sense of loss because somehow I know that this will end in utter sadness.

On my right sits a middle-aged woman wearing an evening dress with a matching jacket adorned with silk-covered buttons of carrots and cauliflowers. The dress and jacket are lilac, each a slightly differ-ent shade. The outfit is unmistakably an Elsa Schiaparelli design, so the woman must have money. She ties it all together with a violet shade of lipstick. She looks vaguely familiar but I cannot place her.

To her right, two gentlemen in English tweeds, if you could be-lieve it!—then I recognize Christopher and his pal, a man I know as Hugh. Hugh is a fairly well-known poet but I have not read any of his works.

Anita lays a hand on my arm. I am about to say something when the woman to my right speaks in a fairly deep voice, "It's Margo and Lindsay."

I turn to where she is pointing and see two woman dressed in men's dinner jackets dancing together. Not an uncommon occurrence in this club.

I turn back to the woman at our table and say, "Excuse me, mad-am, but I feel I know you. Have we ever met before?"

"Of course you have damn it," she says. "It's me, Gilhooley."

Yes, it's coming back to me, I am beginning to remember, but it is hard to get past the violet lipstick. Gilhooley looks cross and a little nervous. "What the hell are we doing here, and how the hell are we going to get out?"

I look at Gilhooley—or Glenda, as Hugh keeps addressing him/her—and say, "I have no intention of leaving. This is my moment. I have money, interesting friends, I work in the film industry. By the way, did you see *Number 17*? I did it in 1928; it was a silent feature, a crime story. Sound made no difference to me, I was the cinematogra-pher. At that time I was going under the name of Eduard Hoesch. Hitchcock remade it last year as a talkie." All the while Gilhooley is staring at me with his wide-open, massacred eyes.

Anita applies a little more pressure on my left arm. I turn to her, she leans into me. "Let's go back to my place. Invite your friends, if you like. Do you want to fuck the guy in the Schiaparelli?" Before I can answer, she gives me a languid smile. It's her sense of humor that I love so much.

As I signal for the waiter, a young man in an SA uniform asks me if I would like to dance. "Sorry, some other time, we were just leaving. Good night, soldier." He beams and strides away. The waiter appears with the check on a silver tray. I glance at it and drop a stack of marks that could paper a wall. Looking at the waiter, I slip him a $5 bill. For that I get a sweet kiss on the cheek and a gentle caress of my genitals. I love the El Dorado.

Outside it is a crisp early morning. Anita's car is at the curb, quietly humming, and what a magnificent vehicle it is, a 1930 Duesenberg J. Walker LaGrande Torpedo Phaeton, reported to have cost her over $30,000. With its unsynchronized gearbox, it is a difficult machine to drive. Just look at it, though: interior coachwork by LeBaron in red leather. The exterior is finished in a high-polished black with enough chrome trim and chrome wire wheels to blind you. All this with a powerful straight-eight motor, it can produce 265 horsepower from dual overhead camshafts and four valves per cylinder. It is capable of a top speed of 94 miles per hour in second gear. Driving with Anita you quickly learn the vehicle's capabilities.

Two people climb into the rear seats, Gilhooley and a man introduced as Dr. Distanziert. The rest scramble into cabs waiting at the entrance. I give them Anita's address, because there is no way they will be able to keep up with Anita's Duesenberg. She tears away from the curb and flies through the streets with utter abandon. Whatever is chasing her, she is giving it a run for its money.

We arrive at Gedendktafel 10707 Berlin-Wilmerdorf, Zahringerstrasse 13, Anita's house in Berlin. She informs the doorman to allow the stragglers to come right up to her apartment. He nods, familiar with the routine. We take a silent lift up to her top-floor apartment and enter the flat. As Anita disappears into her bedroom, Dr. Distanziert strolls into the parlor.

Every time I look at the decor of this room, it always draws me in, longs to hold me in an embrace like a gentle soporific. As if Le Corbusier has made an offhand remark, there is no sofa in the room. Your eyes first land on the chaise lounge. It has perfect dimensions, with stylized vines, leaf and fruit carved in a three-dimensional style which exemplifies the unique style that could only be Dufrêne. The fabric, a stylized floral motif, complements the bleached white wood. Occupying the perfect location, a Tomaso Buzzi floor lamp with a Murano glass, Alga glass, shade sitting on copper piping. The doctor seats himself in one of a pair of armchairs, in beech and fabric, by Jindrich Halabala. The chairs have a very dynamic appearance, due to the curved base that ends fluently in the armrests. The dark-brown-stained wood contrasts beautifully with the green and off-white fabric upholstery in a scribble pattern.

The doctor pulls out a package of cigarettes and reaches for the Karl Wieden (KW) lighter sitting on a side table, model H259 by Jindrich Halabala, in oak ebonized legs and oak varnished top with exquisite wood-grain details. The floor is covered by an area rug of white wool mixed with grey designed by the Finnish artist Greta Skogster. Pulling you in further and finishing the look and feel of the room, occupying the far wall, is a French Art Deco rosewood cheval mirror by Maurice Dufrêne.

I am about to join the doctor when Gilhooley grabs my arm and motions me to fall behind. He looks around and, for whatever reason, seems to be satisfied he can talk. He turns to face me, looking quite lovely under the entranceway light, a simple chrome pendant with central frosted glass disc by Josef Hurka. He asks, "What year do you think it is?"

Seems an odd question but it has been an odd evening. "Why, it is fall 1932," I say.

"Really," he says, "if that is the case, then once again we are on an aborted timeline."

I'm puzzled. "Why do you say that? Everything is as it should be, I see no anomalies."

He says, "I am going to let you in on a little secret. Do you remember the last iteration? Don't answer—I do, and for similar reasons I know this is an unrealized reality. There is an anomaly here."

"What anomaly?"

He lets go of my arm and shakes his head. "The past I know, or is it the present? Never mind, it contains the fact that Anita Berber died in November of 1928 from complications brought on by her alcohol and drug consumption. Yet, in this world, she is still very much alive in what you call the fall of 1932."

I am spared the need to respond when the doorbell rings out the "Ode to Joy." I turn and let the rest of the partygoers into the flat. It appears the crowd has grown but Anita will not care. They all spread out into the parlor. The biggest question facing them is what drug to choose.

I slide over to the rosewood bar, tucked into an alcove. I mix myself an Old Tom style martini; and as I add the twist, I decline a gilt mirror piled high with cocaine. Anita emerges from her bedroom wearing a dressing gown in a sheer blue silk fabric. Its soft flowing lines accent her lithe body. Her feet are encased in red Moroccan slippers, matching the shock of short-cropped hair on her head. She is perfection. I feel it all the way to my toes. She moves next to me, sliding an arm around my waist, while her scent envelops me entirely. The laughter, the room, the warmth of Anita's body—the moment is perfect. It will not last, but then again what does?

I notice a beautiful amulet around her neck.

"What does this represent?" I ask.

She answers and her words come for another time and place. "It is Nuba, she is the Chinese goddess of drought, the daughter of the Yellow Emperor. I use her as a character in one of my plays. She'll suck the life right out of you. She is also known as Ba." Anita slides closer and presses her lips to my ear, whispering. "Call me Ba." With that she begins to pull me into the bedroom, while over her shoulder she says to the crowd, "Anyone for the white rose follow us." I notice Gilhooley and the doctor heading our way, along with the two women in dinner jackets from the El Dorado.

When we enter the spacious bedroom, decorated in what can only be described as Alice in Wonderland, there are two women lounging on the bed, both dressed in men's tailored pinstripe double-breasted suits. The toenails of their bare feet are painted black. There is also a young man passed out on a matched Machine Age lounge chair and ottoman by Thonet Frankenberg that Anita had reupholstered in white covered with red hearts.

Anita Laughs and says, "I don't think we'll all fit on the bed. The blonde is Jeannie, the brunette is my favorite pharmacist, Barbara."

At that Barbara gets off the bed and leaves the room. Jeannie opens her arms and Anita falls into them. It is a moving sight.

I look over at the young man passed out in impeccable evening wear, a highly polished cornet in his lap.

Gilhooley notices where my eyes are focused and whispers to me, "That's David." Do I know that?

Barbara returns carrying an onyx bowl containing a liquid with white rose petals floating on its surface. As she passes us, the odor from the bowl hits me like a Max Schmeling right. Anita's favorite, white rose petals soaked in ether and chloroform.

Barbara offers the bowl to Anita and Jeannie first. Each put a petal in the other's mouth. The bowl makes the rounds. It doesn't take long. I am swaying on my feet, like Max landed that punch, feeling stupid and completely happy at the same time. The doctor is circumscribing small circles and muttering, "I feel so dizzy." I laugh to myself. Dizzy, Dizzy and Gilhooley.

I turn toward Gilhooley. His mascara is beginning to run. He slides into my arms, my lips grazing the sapphire earring of his left ear. I whisper into that ear, "Please leave me here."

He turns his head, a tear running down his cheek. "I'm afraid that's all the time we have," he says as the next wave comes.

I jerk forward, the wooden pallet creaks, my eyes take in the dim surroundings of Wu's Bath Emporium. I draw the pipe close, like it is the only lover I'll ever know.

Chapter 11
That Feeling

Night draws close like my knife and the Old Bastard. I lie on a wooden pallet in the gloom of Wu's Bath Emporium's opium den. Everything a hophead would want, meaning a nice ball of dope. I've never noticed how beautiful the young Chinese woman is as she twirls the ball of dope over the opium lamp. Maybe it's because she has the thing I want. The thing that so fleetingly quenches the fire.

All set, she hands me the plain pipe. Her eyes are averted as I notice she is missing the ring finger of the hand offering me the pipe. I take it from her, bringing the stem to my mouth with more anticipation than with any lover. I take a long pull, allowing my head to fall back among the cheap pillows. As I exhale time slows and the cosmos opens to its terribly beautiful, infinite possibilities, but it is one I am falling toward. I dream of a ship that sails away, far, far away.

I am on set in the middle of a conversation. I'm seated at a large round table. I recognize the place as the Port Arthur Restaurant on Mott Street. I can't quite put my finger on what I'm doing here, but the more urgent question is: why are Jeannie, Barbara Goldstein, Margo Gutmann, David, Lindsay, and Gilhooley sitting around the table with me?

Gilhooley says, "This is a great idea, the group getting together at a Chinatown restaurant." They all nod. I have something to say, but before I can speak, Jeannie is pulling my arm. I turn toward her.

She says, "This is my dream, let me finish the story." She continues to pull my arm, as I realize my eyes are closed. When I open them, I'm back on the wooden pallet at Wu's. The young Chinese woman is pulling my arm and speaking to me in Chinese. Wu enters and says a few harsh words to the woman and she runs out. He turns and looks down at me.

He places a hand on my forehead, lets out a sigh, and says, "She say you dead, you left this world, on your journey."

I didn't even flinch, knowing somehow she is partially correct. There is a soft rustling outside my field of vision. I see Wu bow once and walk away. The figure slowly glides into a position opposite my pallet. He is old, very old, but emanates an overpowering energy.

He looks down at me, bows slightly, and speaks. "I am Ching Ling Foo. I recognize you for what you are. You exist in this moment, only in an unearthly realm. Sit up and look back at yourself."

I sit up yet my body is still lying on the pallet. I say, "Another world, another life, I know there is a sphere just beyond my senses. Somehow I am tied to another time. I cannot grasp it, I want to hold on but I cannot."

Ching Ling Foo lays a hand on my arm and speaks in an exquisite voice of the Divine. "It is time for the truth of the Dao. The world belongs to those who let go."

The pilgrims were weary, some sick, some just worn out, yet onward they drove, onward to the Western Lands. Onward to the book of the way of all things, change. It is a holy quest, a Divine quest. They have sacrificed all for a glimpse of the way of all things. Soon, soon the book will be theirs and they will be famous even in heaven.

That night they were set upon by bandits and slaughtered for what little they had, the way of change.

Chapter 12
Farmville

Nigel, Virginia, alternate time:

I-95 to I-64 to Powhite Parkway to Va-2887S to US 60 to Midlothian Turnpike toward Powhatan, quick bear left, then right, US 60 toward Powhatan, about 35 miles, turn left onto Cumberland Road, 18 miles arrive at Farmville and an abandoned tobacco farm.

John Rolfe is widely given credit for importing *Nicotiana tabacum* seeds to Virginian to grow a species of tobacco that is less harsh when smoked. Farms like this one, built in 1906 by Marshal Whittle, grandson of Bolling Whittle, late of the 38th Virginia Infantry, Confederate States Army, where acres and acres of tobacco were grown until the extinction of the 1950s cheap labor.

I sit at a worn-out kitchen table in a not uncomfortable wooden chair. The oil lamp casts lonesome shadows across the room, where the whiff of pecan pie has faded like the yellow wallpaper with posies.

I glance at my Rolex Triple-Date Moonphase Padellone with manual winding movement, steel case, and crocodile-skin bracelet, circa 1950. It is early fall, sun down, moon up, but I'm feeling quite comfortable in my purple-label modal/pima athletic pants with matching textured cashmere sweater, all under a black, water-resistant jacket.

I sit patiently. I have plenty of time. I stifle a yawn just as headlights splash across the chipped kitchen cabinets. Did I just smile? The front door scrapes the entrance floor upon opening and then again upon closing. The floor, no longer used to traffic, complains about the footsteps. She stops at the doorway, her upper half still in shadow. I use my foot to slide the chair opposite me out as an invitation. At the same time I lay my Glock G30S on the table.

She emerges from the shadows. She is wearing a jet-black Chanel 03C trench coat, two-on-four button, double breasted with a notch lapel, two silk detachable black camellia pins on the right one, self-belt with a square black enamel buckle with "CHANEL" embossed on it; cuff has a detachable belt with two buttons on each, buttons are black with enamel "CC" on each. The coat is slightly open showing a pair of Chanel black wool gabardine trousers with pleated front.

She sits in the chair, placing a box on the table, and leans back into the chair. I glance at the box; it is a Cailler Signature Assortment Dark Chocolate collection, an assortment of dark cocoa tempered with hazelnuts, caramel, almonds, coffee, and citrus, the large assortment. You all heard of the anecdote of bringing a knife to a gun fight, but what about bringing a box of chocolates?

It's Ancient Soul, with that same look on her face, not smug but supremely confident. I speak first since it's protocol. "We have some wet work. Contract consisting of a 30% increase over your last payment, also including a passport to your named destination. We have to come to terms on the currency."

She just sits there.

I continue. "Dollars? European euro? Japanese yen? Swiss franc?" I smile and nod, I think I got it. "Israeli new shekel?"

I still get no response. I continue. "Russian ruble? Saudi Arabian riyal? Swedish krona? Norwegian krone? Pound sterling? Netherlands Antillean guilder? Australian dollar?"

Where the hell is she planning on going.? "Hong Kong dollar? Chinese yuan renminbi? New Zealand dollar? Belize dollar? Philippine peso? Cape Verdean escudo? Cambodian riel? Costa Rican colón? Nepalese rupee? Nigerian naira? Peruvian sol? Gold? Silver? Stocks, bonds, futures?"

She has not moved a muscle.

"OK, what?" I look at her, slightly annoyed.

"Nothing," she says.

"Nothing," I echo.

"Nothing," she says.

"So you'll do it for free?"

"No," she says.

"Then what do you want?" Frustration is a little on the rise.

"Nothing. Nothing, because I am not accepting. I'm out." She leans forward slightly, the light reflecting off her dark eyes like fire.

I give her my best hurt look. "So you drove all the way out here to, let me put this as non-sexist as I can, have the balls to tell me you're out? As we both are fully aware, nobody gets out alive."

I lift my right hand off my lap and lay it on the table. She catches the movement without having shifted her gaze. I reach over and slide the box of chocolates over to me and open it. Inside is a Beretta BU9 Nano. Small, powerful, the perfect concealed-carry weapon. I give her my second-best hurt look.

"Oh, stop," she says. "I wasn't going to shoot you, at least I don't think I was going to shoot you." She shrugs.

Am I going to have to shoot her? I'm looking down at my Glock.

I look up at her. "I have an idea: why don't we shoot ourselves? Then we're both out."

She laughs and says, "I might miss and then you'd be dead."

"I bet you'd miss me," I say.

I hold up my hands. "Wait, before this goes any further, look at this." I slide a picture across the table.

She picks up the faded black-and-white photo, her eyes lift, she looks at me in disbelief. "Him?" she asks.

I grimly nod to her and say, "We have no choice. We have to go back and eliminate him, he is the key to it all."

Now it's her turn to look grim. "Why didn't you say so in the first place? This changes everything." A slight shiver passes through her body. Whether from the chill of a fall night or what this news signifies, I am not sure.

Chapter 13
The Long Night
(All of about 10 minutes)

Nigel, Farmville, Virginia, sometime, apologies to Mr. Eugene O'Neill:

I wake up to the chill of a small disheveled bedroom, lying on an iron-hard bed. Directly across from me, sitting, facing the small, dirty window, is a woman. She appears to be of medium height, her figure full but graceful. She turns toward me, revealing herself to be middle-aged and beautiful. She wears no makeup; her hair is thick, white, and pushed back from her forehead. Her eyes are deeply dark, reflecting the bottom of the Liffey Head Bog.

She smiles at me. "So you're awake, fella." Her voice has a soft Irish lilt.

Maybe, I think to myself, if I can only remember who the hell she is and where I am. Slowly, very slowly, the fog begins to fade. I'm still at the old tobacco farm in Virginia. I met with Ancient Soul last night…was it last night?

The woman ties off her arm, takes a shot, and melts back onto the bed. She drapes a languid arm over me. I look into her coal-black eyes and feel myself sliding down a chute on a long journey. She has a warm smile and a still-striking face. The years have not been good to her, but there is still something there. She moves into me and I embrace her.

"Mary," I whisper into her ear. What? Who is Mary?

She pulls me closer and says, "I am so happy you changed everything, well, almost everything. I still love the morphine. I can feel the warmth of its embrace. I am finally free of a husband who ceased to love me and two sons who are boors."

I am getting a vague feeling but I am not up to interrupting her monologue. Mary gets off the bed and opens a small free-standing closet. As she reaches into the closet, she says, "I was so very tired of all the Irish angst, the drinking, the bad family ties, the wasted lives."

She turns to me holding a white dress against her body, a wedding dress. "I never have to pray again," she says as I watch her in silence. The play forever changed.

Chapter 14
Dizzy's Place
(Part 1)

Nigel, unknown location, alternate time:

A cool breeze gently brings me back. I'm sitting on a greying teak bench, dressed in a simple set of pajamas of a soft cotton in a robin's-egg blue, with matching cotton robe. My feet are encased in a pair of dark-blue leather Moroccan-style slippers. In my field of vision is a grove of fruit trees covered in small white flowers. There is some expectation of a pleasant scent but none reaches me.

I am trying to decide what kind of fruit trees they are when a voice to my left asks me a question. It is the first inkling I have that I am not alone on the bench. I slowly turn my head, a bit annoyed at being interrupted contemplating my tree conundrum.

The middle-aged man sitting at the far end of the bench is dressed in a Brooks Brothers Regent Fit Plaid 1818 Suit, white starched shirt, Tonal Sidewheeler Stripe Tie in shades of blue, legs crossed showing a pair of light-grey socks and cordovan, unlined penny loafers. He sits, a sense of calm surrounding him, as he awaits an answer to the question that hangs before us.

A woman, dressed as I am, walks behind the bench, passing a circular bed of pastel tulips. It's Sarah. I voice this observation to the gentleman on the bench, adding that she is a friend's, David's, fiancée. I attended their kiddushin but I cannot remember where or when. She smiles at me as she walks by. As I look at her back, I am a little embarrassed as I recall a dream where Sarah is transformed into Bouguereau's model in *The Wave*. Mr. 1818 just sits, a slight smile on his face, not pressing for an answer, as if he had all the time in the world.

The question—I have thought about little else, but that does not mean I am close to an answer. The question—I cannot run, I cannot hide. A plastic face, the huge bribe, the hot car, a million miles, nailed every step of the way. I know what he wants to hear, do I? I can give an answer, can I? Contemplating it is just so painful. So painful and I am so tired. Fuck him. I pull more of myself inside my robe, thinking like a turtle. The breeze flows over my shaved head and he just sits there, his left foot moving to a heartbeat rhythm. A drug-induced slow rhythm.

I look up at the warming spring sun that is at the exact same spot it was whenever I sat down on this bench. When was that? More of the surroundings begin to fall into place. It clearly was a working farm at one time. The main house has been remodeled and upgraded with a large attachment. A funny observation strikes me that all the buildings are painted the same robin's-egg blue as my attire. I want to close my eyes and sleep, what dreams may come?

Sorry, Hamlet, you dumb fuck, with all your elaborate schemes. You did ask the right questions, it's just that you had no answers. Oh, and he's the dummy, not the one sitting here in a robe? Well, what answers are there? Plenty of questions, small set of reliable answers. I cast a million seeds and pray to the god of probability. I glance over at Mr. 1818. He just sits there, his left foot moving to a heartbeat rhythm.

It's just too damn frightening. How can all those times and places exist inside one mind? I've discussed all the permutations. Nigel on his quest to find the Western Lands; Raymond battling with, oh yes, they can call themselves "The Militia United in Righteousness" but they were Magic Boxers; Giuseppe, the opium-addicted detective tasked with protecting/observing Gilhooley. The same group of people in iteration after iteration, and the question stands.

My eyes open as cool breeze gently brings me back. A woman dressed in a mirror image of my sartorial splendor stands before me, a benign smile on her face. As she leans forward to speak, a small hamsa hand, the Hand of Miriam, attached to a silver chain, falls from between her pajama opening.

She says, "Would you care for a chocolate?" as she offers me a section from an ornate Belgian box.

I know her. "No thanks, Barbara." Why has she broken my train of thought? Where was the train going?

She nods and says, "Maybe later, when we're with the group."

She covers the box before Mr. 1818 can select a piece. He withdraws his hand. Barbara turns and walks away up the bluestone path lined with a dozen varieties of daffodils, thinking there are 25 different species of daffodils. I watch her until she disappears.

70

I glance over at Mr. 1818. He just sits there, his left foot moving to a heartbeat rhythm. Finally he speaks. "Time to rejoin the group for today's session."

I do not really react, a little confused because Barbara had mentioned the same thing. Mr. 1818 stands and walks over to me, slipping his right arm in my left and gently pulling me to my feet. I am a little unsteady.

Mr. 1818 whispers in my ear, "Not to worry, I'm holding you, these people have decided that you meet the criteria for disorganized schizophrenia and have embarked on a treatment of 50 mg chlorpromazine combined with group therapy."

I feel light, as if I'm gliding across the bluestone, feeling safe, covered in warmth, Mr. 1818 holding me. We pass through a set of oak-stained, double doors into a large open room, with bleached oak flooring. Along both side walls is a collection of Eames Molded Plywood Lounge Chairs, six to a side. At the far end sits a Distil Desk in bleached wood, designed by Todd Bracher. It is bare except for the Teco Rocket Vase in red used by Frank Lloyd Wright, holding three Unicum tulips of red-orange with brightly variegated foliage. Behind the desk is an Eames Soft Pad Management Chair, in tobacco-colored leather. Sitting in the Eames chair is a perfectly coiffed handsome young man in an Anderson & Sheppard (Savile Row tailors) single-breasted three-button jacket with matching single-breasted waistcoat with light-grey bone buttons, cut from light-grey Prince of Wales flannel with a light-blue overcheck. White French-cuff shirt with a bird's-eye cashmere tie in navy.

I have no idea what they are paying this kid but it's a little hard to take, with me dressed in my pajamas and robe. The light is provided by a large trapezoidal window and nine dropped lights with Murano glass shades.

In one corner, behind the desk area, sits a BeoPlay A9 sound system featuring an elegant domed case in white, seamless white fabric disc cover, three removable maplewood legs, individual USB, line-in, Ethernet ports, wireless 2.4GHz and 5GHz WLAN, AirPlay, DLNA and Bluetooth 4.0 connectivity, designed by Øivind Alexander Slaatto, playing one of my favorite duets from *La Bohème*, "O soave fanciulla." More impressive, it's the 1912 recording featuring Enrico Caruso and Geraldine Farrar.

Mr. 1818 waits until the aria is over before he speaks. "We're heading for the sunroom and our group session. You'll be fine," he says in a melodious voice. I do not object; I'm floating high above, my heart open and soaring with each note of "Si, mi chiamano Mimi," Renata Tebaldi with the Orchestra of the Accademia di Santa Cecilia.

Suddenly I stop. I have to hear the climax of the aria. Life seems a little sweeter when Renata is singing. I touch the heavens. Mr. 1818 looks a little startled at first but soon realizes what is transpiring. A small smile creases his lips and we wait. After the ending we proceed toward the sunroom, closed off by oak French doors with stained-glass geometric prairie-style design. These doors come from the sunroom of a prairie-style house in Glencoe, Illinois. The Midwest has a large number of houses designed by Frank Lloyd Wright in the prairie architectural design.

We are ushered through the doors by "Santa Lucia Luntana," sung by Luciano Pavarotti. The group sits in a semi-circle on the same Eames Molded Plywood Lounge Chairs; by the way, they are not really that comfortable. Mr. 1818 leads me to the single unoccupied chair. He turns and, of course, sits in an Eames Soft Pad Management Chair, a duplicate of the one in the entrance hall.

I look around at my fellow travelers, all dressed in the same pajamas of a soft cotton in a robin's-egg blue, with matching cotton robe. No one else is wearing Moroccan slippers. I glance back at Mr. 1818, the haze is lifting. Anxiety begins to rise. Wait. If I could only remember the question he asked. It must mean something. I try and try but cannot recall our bench conversation. Sweat beads my forehead. I know Mr. 1818—it's Gilhooley, it's Dizzy. This is his group session.

Yes, yes, I've been committed. I am suffering from disorganized schizophrenia. I look around the room and there's Barbara, still holding her box of chocolates; Jeannie, wrapped in her own arms; Margo, waiting for her entrance cue; David, holding the hand of someone not in this moment; Tony, holding a single daffodil, anguished. Tony, I want to tell him to let it go, but I hold on more than anyone else.

Dizzy swivels his head toward me. "I would like to know whom I am addressing this question, can you tell me?"

I am on the spot: he wants an answer before he will continue. Why, why is he doing this to me?

72

I relax and say, "I was trying to…" I cannot seem to get the words out, I need to know what kind of trees are in the grove. What happened to the bench? It was so nice there.

"What kind of trees are outside?" I finally get it out but not quite the way I intended. I continue, "I'm from England." Was that the question?

Today, let's see. I glance over at Barbara. Her grip on the box of chocolates seems to tighten. I remember now, she's afraid I'll blow her cover. Got to think of something to get Dizzy off the scent. Everyone is looking my way. Why? Was I supposed to start the session?

Jeannie, is she really Jennifer? I just saw her, where was that. Yes, placing red peonies in a Ming dynasty vase, Xuande mark and period (1426–35), imperial blue and white. It was sitting upon a deeply lacquered, green Ming-style stand. That was yesterday, right?

David, we shared the warmth of a fire on a cold evening. David, he was playing the cornet, someone was playing the piano, an oddly syncopated music. I was having a drink. What was the place?

Margo, we were watching a Chinese opera, 戲曲 together, *The Woman Prisoner*, 女起解, when was that? Last week, right?

I look over at Armando . His smile reminds me of someone, just cannot remember. We were talking yesterday, I'm sure, about his sister. I recall thinking she is a shaman, a Wu. Armando , you have the same powers. You can see into the spirit world. Enjoy the ride.

Tony, his right cheek has a small scar, not his cheek, his heart. Did I put it there? Tony, there is something that binds us, why do I fight it? *La grazie è dicesa dal cielo*, Grace descends from heaven.

I look back at Dizzy, who's satisfied he's gotten what he wanted.

Chapter 15
Dizzy in G Major
(Dizzy's Place, Part 2)

Nigel, unknown location, alternate time:

A cool breeze gently brings me back. I'm sitting on a greying teak bench, dressed in a simple set of pajamas of a soft cotton in a robin's-egg blue, with matching cotton robe. My feet are encased in a pair of dark-blue leather Moroccan-style slippers. In my field of vision is a grove of fruit trees covered in small pink flowers. A sweet scent reaches me.

I am trying to decide if I'm in China, why, when a voice to my left asks me a question. It is the first inkling I have that I am not alone on the bench. I slowly turn my head, a bit annoyed at being interrupted contemplating my placement conundrum.

The middle-aged man sitting at the far end of the bench is dressed in a simple set of pajamas of a soft cotton in a robin's-egg blue, with matching cotton robe. His feet are encased in a pair of dark-blue leather Moroccan-style slippers. He sits, a sense of calm surrounding him, as he awaits an answer to the question that hangs before us.

A woman, dressed as I am, walks behind the bench, passing a circular bed of pastel tulips. It's Sarah. I voice this observation to the gentleman on the bench, adding that she is a friend's, David's, fiancée. I attended their kiddushin but I cannot remember where or when. She smiles at me as she walks by. As I look at her back, I am a little embarrassed as I recall a dream where Sarah is transformed into Bouguereau's model in *The Wave*. Mr. Pajamas just sits, a slight smile on his face, not pressing for an answer, as if he had all the time in the world.

The question—I have thought about little else, but that does not mean I am close to an answer. The question—I cannot run, I cannot hide. A plastic face, the huge bribe, the hot car, a million miles, nailed every step of the way. I know what he wants to hear, do I? I can give an answer, can I? Contemplating it is just so painful. So painful and I am so tired. Fuck him. I pull more of myself inside my robe, thinking like a turtle. The breeze flows over my shaved head and he just sits there, his left foot moving to a heartbeat rhythm. A drug-induced slow rhythm.

I look up at the warming spring sun that is at the exact same spot it was whenever I sat down on this bench. When was that? More of the surroundings begin to fall into place. It clearly was a working farm at one time. The main house has been remodeled and upgraded with a large attachment. A funny observation strikes me that all the buildings are painted the same robin's-egg blue as my attire. I want to close my eyes and sleep, what dreams may come?

Sorry, Hamlet, you dumb fuck, with all your elaborate schemes. You did ask the right questions, it's just that you had no answers. Oh, and he's the dummy, not the one sitting here in a robe? Well, what answers are there? Plenty of questions, small set of reliable answers. I cast a million seeds and pray to the god of probability. I glance over at Mr. Pajamas. He just sits there, his left foot moving to a heartbeat rhythm.

I realize he's holding a sketch pad, on it, a partial pastel drawing of the cherry grove. It's just too damn frightening. How can all those times and places exist inside one mind? I've discussed all the permutations. Nigel on his quest to find the Western Lands; Raymond battling with, oh yes, they can call themselves "The Militia United in Righteousness" but they were Magic Boxers; Giuseppe, the opium-addicted detective tasked with protecting/observing Gilhooley. The same group of people in iteration after iteration, and the question stands.

My eyes open as cool breeze gently brings me back. A woman dressed in a mirror image of my sartorial splendor stands before me, a benign smile on her face. As she leans forward to speak, a small hamsa hand, the Hand of Miriam, attached to a silver chain, falls from between her pajama opening.

She says, "Would you care for a chocolate?" as she offers me a selection from an ornate Belgian box.

I know her. "No thanks, Barbara," I reply. Why has she broken my train of thought? Where was the train going?

She nods and says, "Maybe later, when we're with the group."

She covers the box before Mr. Pajamas can select a piece. He withdraws his hand. Barbara turns and walks away up the bluestone path lined with a dozen varieties of daffodils, thinking there are 25 different species of daffodils. I watch her until she disappears.

"Would you care for a chocolate?" as she offers me a selection from an ornate Belgian box.

I know her. "No thanks, Barbara," I reply. Why has she broken my train of thought? Where was the train going?

She nods and says, "Maybe later, when we're with the group."

She covers the box before Mr. Pajamas can select a piece. He withdraws his hand. Barbara turns and walks away up the bluestone path lined with dozens of brightly colored zinnias, thinking there must be 25 different shades of zinnias. I watch her until she disappears.

"Would you care for a chocolate?" as she offers me a selection from an ornate Belgian box.

I know her. "No thanks, Barbara," I reply. Why has she broken my train of thought? Where was the train going?

She nods and says, "Maybe later, when we're with the group."

She covers the box before Mr. Pajamas can select a piece. He withdraws his hand. Barbara turns and walks away up the bluestone path lined with a dozen varieties of tea roses, thinking that they are the most popular species of garden roses. I watch her until she disappears.

Each iteration, an attempt to hold her here, yet she always disappears. I realize I should have taken a chocolate. I glance over at Mr. Pajamas. He just sits there, his left foot moving to a heartbeat rhythm. Finally he speaks. "Time to rejoin the group for today's session."

I do not really react, a little confused because Barbara had mentioned the same thing. Mr. Pajamas stands and walks over to me, slipping his right arm in my left and gently pulling me to my feet. I am a little unsteady.

Mr. Pajamas whispers in my ear, "Not to worry, I'm holding you, these people have decided that you meet the criteria for disorganized schizophrenia and have embarked on a treatment of 50 mg chlorpromazine, combined with group therapy."

I feel light, as if I'm gliding across the bluestone, feeling safe, covered in warmth, Mr. Pajamas holding me. We pass through a set of oak-stained double doors into a large open room, with bleached oak flooring. Along both side walls is a collection of Eames Molded Plywood Lounge Chairs, six to a side. At the far end sits a Distil Desk in bleached wood, designed by Todd Bracher. It is bare except for the Teco Rocket Vase in red used by Frank Lloyd Wright, holding three Unicum tulips of red-orange with brightly variegated foliage. Behind the desk is an Eames Soft Pad Management Chair, in tobacco-colored leather. Sitting in the Eames chair is a perfectly coiffed handsome young man in an Anderson & Sheppard (Savile Row tailors) single-breasted three-button jacket with matching single-breasted waistcoat with light-grey bone buttons, cut from light-grey Prince of Wales flannel with a light-blue overcheck. White French-cuff shirt with a bird's-eye cashmere tie in navy.

I have no idea what they are paying this kid but it's a little hard to take, with me dressed in my pajamas and robe. The light is provided by a large trapezoidal window and nine dropped lights with Murano glass shades.

In one corner, behind the desk area, sits a BeoPlay A9 sound system featuring an elegant domed case in white, seamless white fabric disc cover, three removable maplewood legs, individual USB, line-in, Ethernet ports, wireless 2.4GHz and 5GHz WLAN, AirPlay, DLNA and Bluetooth 4.0 connectivity, designed by Øivind Alexander Slaatto, playing one of my favorite duets from *La Bohème*, "O soave fanciulla." More impressive, it's the 1912 recording featuring Enrico Caruso and Geraldine Farrar.

Mr. Pajamas waits until the aria is over before he speaks. "We're heading for the sunroom and our group session. You'll be fine," he says in a melodious voice. I do not object; I'm floating high above, my heart open and soaring with each note of "Si, mi chiamano Mimi," Renata Tebaldi with the Orchestra of the Accademia di Santa Cecilia.

Suddenly I stop. I have to hear the climax of the aria. Life seems a little sweeter when Renata is singing. I touch the heavens. Mr. Pajamas looks a little startled at first but soon realizes what is transpiring. A small smile creases his lips and we wait. After the ending we proceed toward the sunroom closed off by oak French doors with stained-glass geometric prairie-style design. These doors come from the sunroom of a prairie-style house in Glencoe, Illinois. The Midwest has a large number of houses designed by Frank Lloyd Wright in the prairie architectural design.

We are ushered through the doors by "Santa Lucia Luntana" sung by Luciano Pavarotti. The group sits in a semi-circle on the same Eames Molded Plywood Lounge Chairs; by the way, they are not really that comfortable. Mr. Pajamas leads me to an unoccupied chair. He turns and sits in an identical Eames Molded Plywood Lounge Chair. I take a hard look at Mr. Pajamas, his eyes are pinned, doped to the hairline, just sits there holding his sketch of the cherry grove. Sitting on the Eames Soft Pad Management Chair, in tobacco-colored leather, is an elderly Asian man I do not recognize. Bach's Fantasia for organ in G major begins to play. Maybe a little too loud but I love Bach.

The Asian gentleman looks directly at Mr. Pajamas and says, "Dr. Gilhooley, we all would like to hear about your sketch, tell us about your inspiration."

Mad Frankie, in the woods, present time:

I shake out two Gabapentin 300 mg into my hand and carry them into the kitchen, washing them down with a pull of milk. I close the refrigerator door, I look at my reflection in the stainless steel. Maybe this whole string has been played out. Maybe the words will not clear a path. Have I been fooling myself? As usual I need to occupy myself until the pills shut my mind up. If only the memories would fade, would end. The good ones, the bad ones, just an avalanche of despair. Dizzy, can you hear me? Dizzy, maybe you are in your study typing away or are you drawing? Can you make it stop? I close my eyes.

Chapter 16
David in G

The Beach at Waikiki 17.0

Nigel, alternate time:

A warm, salt-scented breeze gently brings me back. The azure ocean waves rhythmically roll toward me and whoosh, tumble to shore. I am slowly rocking back and forth in a brown-striped linen hammock. A soft-as-can-be pillow cradles my head. Behind me someone is playing a ukulele, dolce to my ears. Just to my left, a man stands gazing out at mother ocean, a couple of billion years old, and not quite in her prime.

The air is pleasantly warm. He is dressed in an Italian Nile-blue linen suit. The jacket has natural shoulders, two buttons of a corozo beige, peaked lapels, single vent in the rear. He has pulled back the jacket by thrusting both hands into the slant pockets of his pants, showing a pair of dark-brown suspenders attached to suspender buttons. The pants are cuffed, just touching a pair of dark-brown wingtips.

I recognize the music as "I Wonder Where My Hula Girl Has Gone." Knowing that the song is fairly new, must mean it is before the war. What war is that? I cannot remember.

I feel the warmth of a south-sea sun. I am bare except for a wrap-around Javanese batik of an orange geometric pattern. The right side of my body is tattooed, mostly with devotional phrases. All in traditional Chinese script. I lift my left arm, languidly.

The man in Nile blue turns toward me and says, "I am going back to the cottage, she probably has arrived by now."

I give him no answer as he walks out of my field of vision, the sun reflecting off his steel-rimmed glasses. All business, I think to myself and laugh, but it's stifled by the realization I have no idea what that business might be. I sit up for a few seconds and watch the long boards pounding through the waves carrying beautifully cut men before pushing myself off the striped hammock. My feet feel the soft texture of the warm sand.

I turn toward my path to the cottage and see the young musician strumming his ukulele. The woman beside him is singing in an exquisite contralto. David, his cornet lost to another time, now so attached to the young contralto and his ukulele. Journey well, kids. I have a very bad feeling about this moment.

The chords from the song push me past the tall palms onto a bamboo path lined with Jasmine Sambac "Belle of India" surrounding me with wonderfully fragrant, elongated white flowers. I reach the crest of a small hill.

I look down at a small cottage tucked into a black bamboo grove that ends after 50 yards or so with a view of a jagged peak running down to the water. I walk down stone steps to the doorway surrounded by purple bougainvillea. The bamboo grove, the bougainvillea; the smell, the sight, all trigger memory of another place, another time, and I think of Guangdong Province. I knock on the front door, the door swings open, and there is Armando, beckoning me toward the parlor. He raises his head, smiles, and gestures toward a small gold brocade davenport. He is dressed in a guayabera shirt. I think guayabera is said to have originated from the word *yayabero*, the nickname for those who lived near the Yayabo River in Cuba.

The person I am looking for is sitting on a rosewood Ming long-arm chair wearing a diaphanous gown of pale blue. Her rouged nipples are showing, unashamedly, matching the shock of her chopped red hair. Time has passed; a good deal of time. Her face is old but no less beautiful. It is Anita. I place my hands on my hips and give her my best tough-guy stare. She reaches out to the table beside her and picks up a Limoges porcelain coffee cup by Legrand from a Dutch tile-top small size drinks table with Delft ceramic. She pours me a cup from a beautiful Tiffany sterling tea and coffee service in the rare bird's-nest pattern.

I take the cup and settle back onto the gold brocade. Before I hit the back, a large silk pillow embroidered with red dragons is slipped behind me and I sink into comfort as I take a sip of coffee. Armando lightly brushes a lock of my hair off my forehead. The ambient light filtered by the bamboo is warm and inviting. A slight scent of sandalwood reaches my nose and a soft melodic tune drifts on the coffee aroma. Armando sits on a bench playing a Cuban tres guitar. It is the

80

perfect setting. Only a moment and it will be gone. Yet I have a feeling I am missing something. There is something I should do. Something I should remember. I just do not know what.

The Shadow of the Sphinx

Operation Omega: Precognition Experiment #17.0
Subject: Mr. N
Interrogator: Ralph Henry Van Deman - Maj. Gen. (Ret.) - RHVD
Time: 15:36, October 23, 1941

RHVD: Mr. N, at this time can you relate to us your perceptions as to where, when, and what you saw. Please take your time.

Mr. N: I was on a beach, there were people with me. A well-dressed middle-aged gentleman, a young man playing a ukulele, a woman singing. I am comfortable but somewhere in the corner of my mind there is a nagging feeling I forgot something.

RHVD: Something you forgot, a fact or a task? Tell me more of your impression of the people.
Mr. N: They seem to be American but I am not sure. The sea, the sand, men out on the waves with surfboards, the music, I just got the impression that it was Hawaii.

RHVD: OK. Did you see anything that was, let's say, out of the ordinary?

Mr. N: Yes. After I left the beach, I walked to a cottage and there I was met by a man who seemed to know me and I him, but how I just cannot say. Plus, there was a woman there. She spoke to me and offered a cup of coffee, which I took. After I took a sip, a sense of dread took over, a sense I should have done something, something terribly important.

RHVD: That was well done, Mr. N. Please rest now. We will try for another viewing later.

The Beach at Waikiki 17.1

A warm, salt-scented breeze gently brings me back. The azure ocean waves rhythmically roll toward me and whoosh, tumble to shore. I am slowly rocking back and forth in a green-striped linen hammock. A soft-as-can-be pillow cradles my head. Behind me someone is playing a ukulele, dolce to my ears. Just to my left, a man stands gazing out at mother ocean, a couple of billion years old, and not quite in her prime.

The air is pleasantly warm. He is dressed in an Italian Nile-blue linen suit. The jacket has natural shoulders, two buttons of a corozo beige, peaked lapels, single vent in the rear. He has pulled back the jacket by thrusting both hands into the slant pockets of his pants, showing a pair of dark-brown suspenders attached to suspender buttons. The pants are cuffed, just touching a pair of dark-brown wingtips. I know him, it's Dr. G. There is something I want to ask him but music breaks my train of thought.

I recognize the music as "I Wonder Where My Hula Girl Has Gone." Knowing that the song is fairly new, must mean it is before the war. What war is that? I cannot remember.

I feel the warmth of a south-sea sun. I am bare except for a wraparound Javanese batik of an orange geometric pattern. The right side of my body is tattooed, mostly with devotional phrases. All in traditional Chinese script. I lift my left arm, languidly.

The man in Nile blue turns toward me and says, "I am going back to the cottage, I would like to fix a nice breakfast. I am pretty sure our guest has arrived."

I give him no answer as he walks out of my field of vision, the sun reflecting off his steel-rimmed glasses. All business, I think to myself and laugh, but it's stifled by the realization I have no idea what that business might be. I sit up for a few seconds and watch the long boards pounding through the waves carrying beautifully cut men before pushing myself off the striped hammock. My feet feel the soft texture of the warm sand.

I turn toward my path to the cottage and see the young musician strumming his ukulele. The woman beside him is singing in an exquisite contralto. David, his cornet lost to another time, now so attached to

82

the young contralto and his ukulele. Journey well, kids. I have a very bad feeling about this moment.

The chords from the song push me past the tall palms onto a bamboo path lined with Jasmine Sambac "Belle of India" surrounding me with wonderfully fragrant, elongated white flowers. I reach the crest of a small hill.

I look down at a small cottage tucked into a black bamboo grove that ends after 50 yards or so with a view of a jagged peak running down to the water. I walk down stone steps to the doorway surrounded by purple bougainvillea. The bamboo grove, the bougainvillea; the smell, the sight, all trigger memory of another place, another time, and I think of Guangdong Province. I knock on the front door, the door swings open, and there is Armando, beckoning me toward the parlor. He raises his head, smiles, and gestures toward a small gold brocade davenport. He is dressed in a guayabera shirt. I think guayabera is said to have originated from the word *yayabero*, the nickname for those who lived near the Yayabo River in Cuba.

The person I am looking for is sitting on a rosewood Ming long-arm chair wearing a diaphanous gown of pale blue. Her rouged nipples are showing, unashamedly, matching the shock of her chopped red hair. Time has passed; a good deal of time. Her face is old but no less beautiful. It is Anita. I place my hands on my hips and give her my best tough-guy stare. She reaches out to the table beside her and picks up a Limoges porcelain coffee cup by Legrand from a Dutch tile-top small size drinks table with Delft ceramic. She pours me a cup from a beautiful Tiffany sterling tea and coffee service in the rare bird's-nest pattern.

I take the cup and settle back onto the gold brocade. Before I hit the back, a large silk pillow embroidered with red dragons is slipped behind me and I sink into comfort as I take a sip of coffee. Armando lightly brushes a lock of my hair off my forehead. The ambient light filtered by the bamboo is warm and inviting. A slight scent of sandalwood reaches my nose and a soft melodic tune drifts on the coffee aroma. Armando sits on a bench playing a Cuban tres guitar. It is the perfect setting. Only a moment and it will be gone. Yet I have a feeling I am missing something.

I look down at my Rolex, 18-karat yellow gold rectangular with stepped case, leather band. It is 7:01. There is something I should do. Something I should remember. I just do not know what.

The Shadow of the Sphinx

Operation Omega: Precognition Experiment #17.1
Subject: Mr. N
Interrogator: Ralph Henry Van Deman - Maj. Gen. (Ret.) - RHVD
Time: 20:13, October 23, 1941

RHVD: Mr. N, I am told that while you were resting you had another vision. If you would like to, please tell me what you experienced.

Mr. N: I was on the same beach, there were people with me. A well-dressed middle-aged gentleman, I believe he is a doctor I know. Again, a young man playing a ukulele, a woman singing. I am comfortable but somewhere in the corner of my mind there is still that nagging feeling I forgot something.

RHVD: Something you forgot, a fact or a task? Do you have any thoughts as to what you forgot? Any impressions?

Mr. N: Yes. There was the same cottage, the same Spanish man greeting me at the door, the smell of coffee.

RHVD: The man at the door was Spanish? How do you know?

Mr. N: Did I say he was Spanish? Yes, that I know but not from Spain. Just an impression of his manner and dress.

RHVD: The smell of coffee, is that a new?

Mr. N: No, just a stronger impression, and the fact I glanced down at my watch. I distinctly remember it was 7:01.

The Beach at Waikiki 17.2

A warm, salt-scented breeze gently brings me back. The azure ocean waves rhythmically roll toward me and whoosh, tumble to shore. I am slowly rocking back and forth in a blue-striped linen hammock. A soft-as-can-be pillow cradles my head. Behind me someone is playing a ukulele, dolce to my ears. Just to my left, a man stands gazing out at mother ocean, a couple of billion years old, and not quite in her prime.

The air is pleasantly warm. He is dressed in an Italian Nile-blue linen suit. The jacket has natural shoulders, two buttons of a corozo beige, peaked lapels, single vent in the rear. He has pulled back the jacket by thrusting both hands into the slant pockets of his pants, showing a pair of dark-brown suspenders attached to suspender buttons. The pants are cuffed, just touching a pair of dark-brown wingtips. I know him, it's Dr. G. There is something I want to ask him but music breaks my train of thought.

I recognize the music as "I Wonder Where My Hula Girl Has Gone." Knowing that the song is fairly new, must mean it is before the war. What war is that? I cannot remember.

I feel the warmth of a south-sea sun. I am bare except for a wrap-around Javanese batik of an orange geometric pattern. The right side of my body is tattooed, mostly with devotional phrases. All in traditional Chinese script. I lift my left arm, languidly.

The man in Nile blue turns toward me and says, "I am going back to the cottage, I would like to fix a nice breakfast. I am pretty sure our guest has arrived."

I give him no answer as he walks out of my field of vision, the sun reflecting off his steel-rimmed glasses. All business, I think to myself and laugh, but it's stifled by the realization I have no idea what that business might be. I sit up for a few seconds and watch the long boards pounding through the waves carrying beautifully cut men before pushing myself off the striped hammock. My feet feel the soft texture of the warm sand, the majority of which has been imported from Manhattan Beach, a city in southwestern Los Angeles County, California.

I turn toward my path to the cottage and see the young musician strumming his ukulele. It's David. He says, "Beautiful Sunday morning, isn't?"

"Yes, David, it is. Morning, Sarah, you're in fine voice this morning."

I still cannot shake a very bad feeling about this moment.

The chords from the song push me past the tall palms onto a bamboo path lined with Jasmine Sambac "Belle of India" surrounding me with wonderfully fragrant, elongated white flowers. I reach the crest of a small hill.

I look down at a small cottage tucked into a black bamboo grove that ends after 50 yards or so with a view of a jagged peak running down to the water. I walk down stone steps to the doorway surrounded by purple bougainvillea. The bamboo grove, the bougainvillea; the smell, the sight, all trigger memory of another place, another time, and I think of Guangdong Province. I knock on the front door, the door swings open, and there is Armando, beckoning me toward the parlor. He raises his head, smiles, and gestures toward a small gold brocade davenport. He is dressed in a guayabera shirt. I think guayabera is said to have originated from the word *yayabero*, the nickname for those who lived near the Yayabo River in Cuba.

The person I am looking for is sitting on a rosewood Ming long-arm chair wearing a diaphanous gown of pale blue. Her rouged nipples are showing, unashamedly, matching the shock of her chopped red hair. Time has passed; a good deal of time. Her face is old but no less beautiful. It is Anita. I place my hands on my hips and give her my best tough-guy stare. She reaches out to the table beside her and picks up a Limoges porcelain coffee cup by Legrand from a Dutch tile-top small size drinks table with Delft ceramic. She pours me a cup from a beautiful Tiffany sterling tea and coffee service in the rare bird's-nest pattern.

I take the cup and settle back onto the gold brocade. Before I hit the back, a large silk pillow embroidered with red dragons is slipped behind me and I sink into comfort as I take a sip of coffee. Armando lightly brushes a lock of my hair off my forehead. The ambient light filtered by the bamboo is warm and inviting. A slight scent of sandalwood reaches my nose and a soft melodic tune drifts on the coffee aroma. Armando sits on a bench playing a Cuban tres guitar. It is the perfect setting. Only a moment and it will be gone. Yet I have a feeling I am missing something.

I look down at my Rolex, 18-karat yellow gold rectangular with stepped case, leather band. It is 7:12. There is something I should do. Something I should remember. I just do not know what.

The Shadow of the Sphinx

Operation Omega: Precognition Experiment #17.2
Subject: Mr. N
Interrogator: Ralph Henry Van Deman - Maj. Gen. (Ret.) - RHVD
Time: 09:53, October 24, 1941

RHVD: Mr. N, if you would like to, please tell me what you experienced during your last vision. Take as much time as you like.

Mr. N: I was on the same beach, there were people with me. A middle-aged gentleman, well dressed, I believe he is a doctor I know. Again, a young man playing a ukulele, a woman singing. I remember the young man remarked what a lovely Sunday morning it was. I am comfortable but there is still somewhere in the corner of my mind that nagging feeling I forgot something.
RHVD: You are sure the young man said it was Sunday morning? Do you have any more insight as to what you may have forgotten?

Mr. N: I am sure he said it was Sunday morning. After that there was the same cottage, the same Spanish man greeting me at the door, the smell of coffee.

RHVD: You still feel the man at the door is Spanish.

Mr. N: Spanish? Yes, that I know but not from Spain. Just an impression of his manner and dress.

RHVD: The smell of coffee again?

Mr. N: Yes, that and the fact I glanced down at my watch. I distinctly remember it was 7:12.

The Beach at Waikiki 17.3

A warm, salt-scented breeze gently brings me back. The azure ocean waves rhythmically roll toward me and whoosh, tumble to shore. I am slowly rocking back and forth in a yellow-striped linen hammock. A soft-as-can-be pillow cradles my head. Behind me someone is playing a ukulele, dolce to my ears. Just to my left, a man stands gazing out at mother ocean, a couple of billion years old, and not quite in her prime.

The air is pleasantly warm. He is dressed in an Italian Nile-blue linen suit. The jacket has natural shoulders, two buttons of a corozo beige, peaked lapels, single vent in the rear. He has pulled back the jacket by thrusting both hands into the slant pockets of his pants, showing a pair of dark-brown suspenders attached to suspender buttons. The pants are cuffed, just touching a pair of dark-brown wingtips. I know him, it's Dr. G. There is something I want to ask him but music breaks my train of thought.

I recognize the music as "I Wonder Where My Hula Girl Has Gone." Knowing that the song is fairly new, must mean it is before the war. What war is that? I cannot remember.

I feel the warmth of a south-sea sun. I am bare except for a wrap-around Javanese batik of an orange geometric pattern. The right side of my body is tattooed, mostly with devotional phrases. All in traditional Chinese script. I lift my left arm, languidly.

The man in Nile blue turns toward me and says, "I am going back to the cottage, I would like to fix a nice Sunday breakfast. I am pretty sure our guest has arrived."

I give him no answer as he walks out of my field of vision, the sun reflecting off his steel-rimmed glasses. All business, I think to myself and laugh, but it's stifled by the realization I have no idea what that business might be. I sit up for a few seconds and watch the long boards pounding through the waves carrying beautifully cut men before pushing myself off the striped hammock. My feet feel the soft texture of the warm sand, the majority of which has been imported from Manhattan Beach, a city in southwestern Los Angeles County, California.

I turn toward my path to the cottage and see the young musician strumming his ukulele. It's David. He says, "Beautiful Sunday morning, isn't?"

"Yes, David, it is. Morning, Sarah, you're in fine voice this morning."

I stop for a moment to admire David's playing. He just looks so smart in his dress whites and his head adorned with his Dixie Cup at a jaunty angle. I still cannot shake a very bad feeling about this moment.

The chords from the song push me past the tall palms onto a bamboo path lined with Jasmine Sambac "Belle of India" surrounding me with wonderfully fragrant, elongated white flowers. I reach the crest of a small hill.

I look down at a small cottage tucked into a black bamboo grove that ends after 50 yards or so with a view of a jagged peak running down to the water. I walk down stone steps to the doorway surrounded by purple bougainvillea. The bamboo grove, the bougainvillea; the smell, the sight, all trigger memory of another place, another time, and I think of Guangdong Province. I knock on the front door, the door swings open, and there is Armando, beckoning me toward the parlor. He raises his head, smiles, and gestures toward a small gold brocade davenport. He is dressed in a guayabera shirt. I think guayabera is said to have originated from the word *yayabero*, the nickname for those who lived near the Yayabo River in Cuba.

The person I am looking for is sitting on a rosewood Ming long-arm chair wearing a diaphanous gown of pale blue. Her rouged nipples are showing, unashamedly, matching the shock of her chopped red hair. Time has passed; a good deal of time. Her face is old but no less beautiful. It is Anita. I place my hands on my hips and give her my best tough-guy stare. She reaches out to the table beside her and picks up a Limoges porcelain coffee cup by Legrand from a Dutch tile-top small size drinks table with Delft ceramic. She pours me a cup from a beautiful Tiffany sterling tea and coffee service in the rare bird's-nest pattern.

I take the cup and settle back onto the gold brocade. Before I hit the back, a large silk pillow embroidered with red dragons is slipped behind me and I sink into comfort as I take a sip of coffee. Armando lightly brushes a lock of my hair off my forehead. The ambient light filtered by the bamboo is warm and inviting. A slight scent of sandalwood reaches my nose and a soft melodic tune drifts on the coffee aroma. Armando sits on a bench playing a Cuban tres guitar. It is the perfect setting. Only a moment and it will be gone. Yet I have a feeling I am missing something.

I look down at my Rolex, 18-karat yellow gold rectangular with stepped case, leather band. It is 7:20. I lay my head back, focusing on a picture on the wall. It is a picture of the Forbidden City; below it hangs a calendar. There is something I should do. Something I should remember. I just do not know what.

The Shadow of the Sphinx

Operation Omega: Precognition Experiment #17.3
Subject: Mr. N
Interrogator: Ralph Henry Van Deman - Maj. Gen. (Ret.) - RHVD
Time: 14:27, October 24, 1941

RHVD: Mr. N, if you would like to, please tell me what you experienced during your last vision. Take as much time as you like.

Mr. N: I was on the same beach, there were people with me. A middle-aged gentleman, well dressed, I believe he is a doctor I know. Again, a young man playing a ukulele, a woman singing. Two things struck me. The well-dressed man said he was going to make a Sunday breakfast, and I remember the young man remarked what a lovely Sunday morning it was. I knew his name, David. He was dressed in tropical whites and a cap; on his upper left sleeve, he wore a Signalman 2nd Class insignia and rating.

I am comfortable but there is still somewhere in the corner of my mind that nagging feeling I forgot something.

RHVD: You are sure the young man said it was Sunday morning? You are sure he was a seaman? Do you have any more insight as to what you may have forgotten?

Mr. N: I am sure he said it was Sunday morning. After that there was the same cottage, the same Spanish man greeting me at the door, the smell of coffee.

90

RHVD: You still feel the man at the door is Spanish.

Mr. N: Spanish? Yes, that I know but not from Spain. Just an impression of his manner and dress.

RHVD: The smell of coffee again?

Mr. N: Yes, that and the fact I glanced down at my watch. I distinctly remember it was 7:20. After that I glanced at the far wall and saw a picture of the Forbidden City above a calendar.

Follow-up notes on information and subject:

RHVD: The subject Mr. N has taken a minor sidetrack. We realize we have no power over what he sees, hears, and experiences while he is in his trance-like state. We also believe that he does not have any power over his projection. He represents one of many channels currently being developed. Mr. N is a strange man and his talents may just represent an auditory hallucination, someone hearing something that is not there. It is the most common type of hallucination. A visual hallucination is when one has seen something that is not there. Can Mr. N be having both? *Ecco homo*, Mr. N, here is the man.
We have given him some time to himself. The sessions will resume on the 26th. Somehow that sailor boy is the key. I just feel it.
Interesting note: each time he mentions looking at his watch, the time has advanced. This gives me some hope he is not caught in a replicating loop.

The Beach at Waikiki 17.4

A warm, salt-scented breeze gently brings me back. The azure ocean waves rhythmically roll toward me and whoosh, tumble to shore. I am slowly rocking back and forth in an orange-striped linen hammock. A soft-as-can-be pillow cradles my head. Behind me someone is playing a ukulele, dolce to my ears. Just to my left, a man stands gazing out at mother ocean, a couple of billion years old, and not quite in her prime.

The air is pleasantly warm. He is dressed in an Italian Nile-blue linen suit. The jacket has natural shoulders, two buttons of a corozo beige, peaked lapels, single vent in the rear. He has pulled back the jacket by thrusting both hands into the slant pockets of his pants, showing a pair of dark-brown suspenders attached to suspender buttons. The pants are cuffed, just touching a pair of dark-brown wingtips. I know him, it's Dr. G. There is something I want to ask him but music breaks my train of thought.

I recognize the music as "I Wonder Where My Hula Girl Has Gone." Knowing that the song is fairly new, must mean it is before the war. What war is that? I cannot remember.

I feel the warmth of a south-sea sun. I am bare except for a wrap-around Javanese batik of an orange geometric pattern. The right side of my body is tattooed, mostly with devotional phrases. All in traditional Chinese script. I lift my left arm, languidly.

The man in Nile blue turns toward me and says, "I am going back to the cottage, I would like to fix a nice Sunday breakfast. David is due back to his ship. I am pretty sure our guest has arrived."

I give him no answer as he walks out of my field of vision, the sun reflecting off his steel-rimmed glasses. All business, I think to myself and laugh, but it's stifled by the realization I have no idea what that business might be. I sit up for a few seconds and watch the long boards pounding through the waves carrying beautifully cut men before pushing myself off the striped hammock. My feet feel the soft texture of the warm sand, the majority of which has been imported from Manhattan Beach, a city in southwestern Los Angeles County, California.

I turn toward my path to the cottage and see the young musician strumming his ukulele. It's David. He says, "Beautiful Sunday morning, isn't?"

"Yes, David, it is. Morning, Sarah, you're in fine voice this morning."

I stop for a moment to admire David's playing. He just looks so smart in his dress whites and his head adorned with his Dixie Cup at a jaunty angle. On his upper left sleeve he wears an E-2 insignia, Seaman Apprentice second class.

I still cannot shake a very bad feeling about this moment.

The chords from the song push me past the tall palms onto a bamboo path lined with Jasmine Sambac "Belle of India" surrounding me with wonderfully fragrant, elongated white flowers. I reach the crest of a small hill.

I look down at a small cottage tucked into a black bamboo grove that ends after 50 yards or so with a view of a jagged peak running down to the water. I walk down stone steps to the doorway surrounded by purple bougainvillea. The bamboo grove, the bougainvillea; the smell, the sight, all trigger memory of another place, another time, and I think of Guangdong Province. I knock on the front door, the door swings open, and there is Armando, beckoning me toward the parlor. He raises his head, smiles, and gestures toward a small gold brocade davenport. He is dressed in a guayabera shirt. I think guayabera is said to have originated from the word *yayabero*, the nickname for those who lived near the Yayabo River in Cuba.

The person I am looking for is sitting on a rosewood Ming long-arm chair wearing a diaphanous gown of pale blue. Her rouged nipples are showing, unashamedly, matching the shock of her chopped red hair. Time has passed; a good deal of time. Her face is old but no less beautiful. It is Anita. I place my hands on my hips and give her my best tough-guy stare. She reaches out to the table beside her and picks up a Limoges porcelain coffee cup by Legrand from a Dutch tile-top small size drinks table with Delft ceramic. She pours me a cup from a beautiful Tiffany sterling tea and coffee service in the rare bird's-nest pattern.

I take the cup and settle back onto the gold brocade. Before I hit the back, a large silk pillow embroidered with red dragons is slipped behind me and I sink into comfort as I take a sip of coffee. Armando lightly brushes a lock of my hair off my forehead. The ambient light filtered by the bamboo is warm and inviting. A slight scent of sandal-wood reaches my nose and a soft melodic tune drifts on the coffee aroma. Armando sits on a bench playing a Cuban tres guitar. It is the perfect setting. Only a moment and it will be gone. Yet I have a feeling I am missing something.

I look down at my Rolex, 18-karat yellow gold rectangular with stepped case, leather band. It is 7:23. I lay my head back, focusing on a picture on the far wall. It is a picture of the Forbidden City; below it hangs a calendar. The month is boldly proclaimed in faux Chinese script: "December." There is something I should do. Something I should remember. I just do not know what.

The Shadow of the Sphinx

Operation Omega: Precognition Experiment #17.4
Subject: Mr. N
Interrogator: Ralph Henry Van Deman - Maj. Gen. (Ret.) - RHVD
Time: 09:36, October 26, 1941

RHVD: Mr. N, I hope you feel rested. If you would like to, please tell me what you experienced during your last vision. Take as much time as you like.

Mr. N: I was on the same beach, there were people with me. A well-dressed middle-aged gentleman, I believe he is a doctor I know as Dr. G. Again, a young man playing a ukulele, a woman singing. Two things struck me. The well-dressed man said he was going to make a Sunday breakfast, and I remember the young man remarked what a lovely Sunday morning it was. I knew his name, David. He was dressed in tropical whites and cap; on his upper left sleeve, he wore an E-2 insignia, Seaman Apprentice second class. Someone mentioned he needed to get back to his ship.
I am comfortable but there is still somewhere in the corner of my mind that nagging feeling I forgot something.

RHVD: You are sure the young man said it was Sunday morning? You are sure he was a seaman? Did he or anyone else mention the name of his ship?

Mr. N: I am sure he said it was Sunday morning. No, I do not recall hearing the name of his ship. After that there was the same cottage, the same Spanish man greeting me at the door, the smell of coffee.

RHVD: Does the Spanish man ever say anything?

Mr. N: No, he just greets me warmly and ushers me into the cottage.

RHVD: What about the woman, is she American? Each time does she offer you a cup of coffee and you take it?

Mr. N: Yes, yes, I take the coffee cup but this time it dawned on me that she spoke to me in perfect German.

RHVD: German? She is a German national? This is the first time you got that impression.

Mr. N: Yes and no. Please let me explain. In the context of these visions, she is what I have come to call a phantom. She appears in many of my visions. She is almost never in context of the vision. I believe she and I have a strong connection. So it usually is a non sequitur. She is just there. It could be the same with the others. They are filling out reality, giving me verbal or visual clues. It's up to me to crack the paranormal code. Are you familiar with the term 'paranormal'?

RHVD: Yes, coined around 1920 as an attempt to explain the unexplainable. I assure you, Mr. N, we are here to gather information. Let others categorize what we do here. Please feel no bounds. Did you happen to glance at your watch?

Mr. N: Yes, it was 7:23 and I read the calendar month. It said December.

Follow-up notes on information and subject:

RHVD: Note, the time on his watch is advancing albeit by minutes. I agree with his assessment of the German woman. I strongly reject the opinions that she represents a German spy and is the true key to the vision.
Now we have a month, December, a time, 7:23, and a day, Sunday. Are we close to a threshold event or could this just be an infinitely sequenced series of pictures? Maybe, given the woman, it's just a personal event, confined to Mr. N's life. I noticed he is increasingly fatigued. We have to push forward no matter the cost to Mr. N.

The Beach at Waikiki 17.5

A warm, salt-scented breeze gently brings me back. The azure ocean waves rhythmically roll toward me and whoosh, tumble to shore. I am slowly rocking back and forth in a red-striped linen hammock. A soft-as-can-be pillow cradles my head. Behind me someone is playing a ukulele, dolce to my ears. Just to my left, a man stands gazing out at mother ocean, a couple of billion years old, and not quite in her prime.

The air is pleasantly warm. He is dressed in an Italian Nile-blue linen suit. The jacket has natural shoulders, two buttons of a corozo beige, peaked lapels, single vent in the rear. He has pulled back the jacket by thrusting both hands into the slant pockets of his pants, showing a pair of dark-brown suspenders attached to suspender buttons. The pants are cuffed, just touching a pair of dark-brown wingtips. I know him, it's Dr. G. He works with me. We are working on a project together. An important project. I must collect as much information as I can. There is something I want to ask him but music breaks my train of thought.

I recognize the music as "I Wonder Where My Hula Girl Has Gone." Knowing that the song is fairly new, must mean it is before the war. What war is that? I cannot remember.

I feel the warmth of a south-sea sun. I am bare except for a wrap-around Javanese batik of an orange geometric pattern. The right side of my body is tattooed, mostly with devotional phrases. All in traditional Chinese script. I lift my left arm, languidly.

Dr. G in his Nile blue turns toward me and says, "I am going back to the cottage, I would like to fix a nice Sunday breakfast. David is due back to his ship. Can you remember what ship it is? I am pretty sure our guest has arrived."

I give him no answer as he walks out of my field of vision, the sun reflecting off his steel-rimmed glasses. All business, I think to myself and laugh, but it's stifled by the realization I have no idea what that business might be. I sit up for a few seconds and watch the long boards pounding through the waves carrying beautifully cut men before pushing myself off the striped hammock. My feet feel the soft texture of the warm sand, the majority of which has been imported from Manhattan Beach, a city in southwestern Los Angeles County, California.

I turn toward my path to the cottage and see the young musician strumming his ukulele. It's David. He says, "Beautiful Sunday morning, isn't?"

"Yes, David, it is. Morning, Sarah, you're in fine voice this morning."

I stop for a moment to admire David's playing. He just looks so smart in his dress whites and his head adorned with his Dixie Cup at a jaunty angle. On his upper left sleeve he wears an E-2 insignia, Seaman Apprentice second class.

"By the way, David, will you be going back to your ship today?" I ask.

"Yes, I am due back for the afternoon watch."

"Do I know what ship you are on?"

"I never mentioned it. USS *Vestal*, it's a repair ship," he says.

I remember now. "Oh, thanks."

David adds, "She's at Pearl now, moored next to the *Arizona*."

Somehow I know. "If it's the afternoon watch, then you have some time."

The chords from the song push me past the tall palms onto a bamboo path lined with Jasmine Sambac "Belle of India" surrounding me with wonderfully fragrant, elongated white flowers. I reach the crest of a small hill.

I look down at a small cottage tucked into a black bamboo grove that ends after 50 yards or so with a view of a jagged peak running down to the water. I walk down stone steps to the doorway surrounded by purple bougainvillea. The bamboo grove, the bougainvillea; the smell, the sight, all trigger memory of another place, another time, and I think of Guangdong Province. I knock on the front door, the door swings open, and there is Armando, beckoning me toward the parlor. He raises his head, smiles, and gestures toward a small gold brocade davenport. He is dressed in a guayabera shirt. I think guayabera is said to have originated from the word *yayabero*, the nickname for those who lived near the Yayabo River in Cuba.

The person I am looking for is sitting on a rosewood Ming long-arm chair wearing a diaphanous gown of pale blue. Her rouged nipples are showing, unashamedly, matching the shock of her chopped red hair. Time has passed; a good deal of time. Her face is old but no less beautiful. It is Anita. I place my hands on my hips and give her my best tough-guy stare. She reaches out to the table beside her and picks up a Limoges porcelain coffee cup by Legrand from a Dutch tile-top small size drinks table with Delft ceramic. She pours me a cup from a beautiful Tiffany sterling tea and coffee service in the rare bird's-nest pattern.

I take the cup and settle back onto the gold brocade. Before I hit the back, a large silk pillow embroidered with red dragons is slipped behind me and I sink into comfort as I take a sip of coffee. Armando lightly brushes a lock of my hair off my forehead. As he does he speaks to me. "This is the final iteration. Remember all you see and hear."

I don't know exactly what he means, but I feel in my bones he is right.

The ambient light filtered by the bamboo is warm and inviting. A slight scent of sandalwood reaches my nose and a soft melodic tune drifts on the coffee aroma. Armando sits on a bench playing a Cuban tres guitar. It is the perfect setting. Only a moment and it will be gone. Yet I have a feeling I am missing something.

I look down at my Rolex, 18-karat yellow gold rectangular with stepped case, leather band. It is 7:55. I lay my head back, focusing on a picture on the far wall. It is a picture of the Forbidden City; below it hangs a calendar. The month is boldly proclaimed in faux Chinese script: "Sunday, December 7." I rise off the couch as the ground under the cottage is stuck by a bassline wave, then a booming reaches my ears. Several minutes pass as the booming continues.

Anita is gone, Armando is gone, someone is banging on the front door. My adrenaline is flowing. It is hard to even get to the front door. I pull it open to find my blond neighbor, Jeannie, and her roommate, Margo. They are wide-eyed and seem to be shouting something. I try to focus, surrounded by distant thunder.

They both exclaim, "Something is happening at Pearl, some kind of accident!"

I push out of the door and run up the stone walk to the beach, just in time to see David cutting through the palms toward the road.

I fall back on my seat with the realization that this is what I was struggling to recall, this event. What is really happening? The air is swirling around me, there's a faint ozone smell in the air. Focus. I must collect as much information as I can gather. It seems important. I glance down at my watch, 8:53—almost an hour has gone by. The thunder is non-stop.

I look up: a man is standing before me. He is dressed in an Italian Nile-blue linen suit. The jacket has natural shoulders, two buttons of a corozo beige, peaked lapels, single vent in the rear. It is the Doctor. He reaches out a hand. I take it, firmly. He pulls me up and shouts over the thunder, "David was the key, the clue we kept missing."

We hear planes over the water. We both look: dark-green military aircraft, on their sides is a large red sun. It is Sunday, December 7, but what year?

The scene vanishes, like a film running out of its sprockets.

The Shadow of the Sphinx

Operation Omega: Precognition Experiment #17.5
Subject: Mr. N
Interrogator: Ralph Henry Van Deman - Maj. Gen. (Ret.) - RHVD
Time: 19:00, October 30, 1941

RHVD: Mr. N is in no condition to be questioned further. He is near collapse, a complete mental and physical breakdown. I have read and reread his description of his last vision. I am awestruck. He related a story of Japanese aircraft attacking Pearl Harbor. He related the date: Sunday, December 7. We have a complete list of years December 7 falls on a Sunday—1941, 1947, 1952, 1958, 1969, and so forth. Which one is it? If it is 1941, we must act quickly.
Who was the doctor who seemed to know the nature of this experiment? We checked the USS *Vestal*'s rolls and found 12 Davids, one was an E-2. Clean record. Under interrogation, he denies any knowledge of such a place. The only facts that correspond are he is dating a Sarah and does play the ukulele. I am afraid that this project is over. I will submit my findings.

Follow-up notes on subject:

I have great admiration for Mr. N. He currently resides at a private sanitarium in Virginia, under the care of a Dr. Gilhooley. The doctor claims to know what is ailing Mr. N and thinks he can be cured. I do not share his optimism.

Final Deposition Project Omega:

RHVD's report read by Naval and Army High Command is restricted. Classified: Top Secret.

Chapter 17
Adios Is Not So Long

Nigel, Texas Panhandle, alternate time:

All summer it has been hot and dry, cotton-growing weather. The two of us are sitting on the front porch of a rundown farmhouse, Dizzy in his favorite rocker, me in a floral-print parlor chair. Mid-day, sun high, heat shine off the highway, sweat forging a small river between my shoulder blades. I glance at Dizzy. He's staring out toward the horizon. Seeing nothing but the occasional jackrabbit listlessly wandering among the sagebrush. The sweat gathering in his beard and finally dropping onto his chest. His blue work shirt trying to absorb the liquid and failing.

"We've lost them haven't we?" I say.

Dizzy slowly turns his head and says, "Yes, we have. Did you really think they would follow us to this garden spot?"

With a fair amount of frustration, I say, "It was what the predictors said. We had no choice."

A ghost of a smile from Dizzy. "We had no choice, the predictors never said anything about the rest of them."

I shake my head, which encourages another stream of sweat to roll off my bald dome and run into my eyes. "This is a special kind of hell but we've been in tougher spots."

Dizzy chuckles. He reaches between us and turns on the tabletop Catalin radio by Addison Industries. It takes a moment to warm up and then we hear the voice of Hank Snow.

Suddenly I notice a dust cloud rising, moving toward us. A car, running fast, the driver unconcerned about the advance warning. As it gets closer, I recognize the car and by connection, the driver. It is a 1955 Mercury Montclair two-door hardtop in black and grey with a 429 engine and a C6 auto trans. The driver pulls hard right while stomping on the brake, causing the car to perform a beautiful drift as it slides to a stop 50 feet from the porch. Coating us in fine grit. The driver opens the door, moving clear, and then slams it shut and casually leans against the front panel.

The predictors never said a damn thing about this but they didn't need to. I knew she'd show up. The situation demanded it. I smile at her while she is looking us over in her crisp field tan and not a bead of sweat.

She says, "Did you really think I would leave you two assholes to rot in this iteration?"

Dizzy says, "You rode off into the sunset, content to dwell in a non-replicating closed loop. Said good-bye, adios."

I am trying to hide my emotions but I say, "We need you on this one, we need the old magic."

She smiles at us. A slight wind begins to pick up, carrying a promise of rain. Adios is not so long.

Chapter 18
He Puts His Hand in Mine

Giuseppe, McGinnity's Saloon, New York, 1906:

The last note sounds, holds a shimmering beauty, then slowly drifts off into nothingness. Yet I still vibrate with its frequency. I pick up the cocktail glass and drain off the last of my Martinez. I drop some crumpled notes onto the bar, too many but who's counting. Armando, tending bar, is talking quietly with his Polish friend Michal. He's some kind of Count or Prince, I never did get it straight. Anyway, Armando gives me a nod and a wink. He makes a great Martinez.

I turn slowly to rejoin the room. Hogan sitting at his piano both hands in his lap. David clutching his cornet, leaning against the wall, loaded. Jeannie holding a swell upright, helping his wallet out of his jacket. Him with a choral hydrate smile. Margo sitting at a table with a woman whose face is partly in shadow but I recognize as Bertha Kalich, the actress currently playing Miriam Friedlander in *The Kreutzer Sonata*, a play based on a story by Leo Tolstoy, adapted from a Yiddish play, performing on Broadway.

Then my eyes fall on her, upright, proper, stylishly dressed. Half smile on her face. She turns and her dark eyes hold mine with a million questions and not one answer. She leaves me, her eyes, that is, but I still hold the promise. Behold her, sitting, with her friend—friend?—Max Zweifach, born Maximillian Zweifach, known as Kid Twist. I turn around and stare into the bar mirror. I look back at her, the mirror our only connection as she makes one last point with Max. He stands, nods, and leaves. She had a suitor at one time, an older man. I heard Zweifach came between them. She was told the man left for somewhere in the southern part of America but my Mano Nera friends claim Zweifach put him in the river.

The smoke in the room gives the mirrored reflection a dream-like quality. She, Barbara Goldstein, still sitting at her table. Her reflection is all I have. I move off the bar as Hogan and David resume their ragtime moment. I give McGinnity a thumbs-up; he points his little finger down, meaning I can pass through the red door.

Inside an old Chinese man plays an ancient tune on an upright string instrument. There's hop in the air but that's not what I want. I make my way into the dim interior. Candles flickering light over a few pallets occupied with the dead, dying, loaded, does it matter which.

Butcher Larsson is sitting in one of two parlour chairs separated by a small table. His eyes are closed but I know he can still see Cemetery Ridge. I sit down next to him. His eyes slowly, very slowly, open while his head turns to see his visitor. He frowns at me. I have to ask, "Please, Doc. She's out there."

The Doc could never refuse a man in pain, physical or psychic. He nods. I stand and remove my blue-check jacket, sit and undo my cuff link and roll up my shirt sleeve. The Doc is standing over me tying off my arm, waits, then slides the needle in with a loving touch, depressing the plunger releasing the tie. My legs feel it first, my heart flutters, my body melts into the chair.

The Doc looks so sad as he puts his hand in mine.

Chapter 19
Dizzy Walks Away

Nigel, Vienna, Austria, alternate time:

So there I was sipping a Slivovitz at the Empress Club. The Empress Club was quite the hotspot before the war, before the darkness, before the facade that is culture got ground into dust. Now the place is filled with shady little scum and women looking to pick up a few bills of Army scrip. I had spent two months in this bombed-out vestige of the Hapsburgs, working on a disinformation campaign with decidedly mixed results.

I threw back the Slivovitz and ground out my Lucky in the crystal ashtray, tossing the rest of my Army scrip onto the bar. Tomas, the bartender, made a sideways glance at me with a ghost of a smile. The guy had been helpful on many fronts. Anyway, his father had been a bartender at the Old Waldorf and taught the kid how to make a proper martini. Even though he had to use that terrible German gin.

The operation was over but I had two threads to tie up. One was next to me, Jeannie. Jeannie who had no business being in this sector plying her trade. She would undoubtedly be caught in the next round-up. Repatriated behind the steel wall if she was lucky and shot if she was not. I owed her this one last act of kindness. She had been eyeing me in the faded bar mirror, afraid to ask the question to which she already knew the answer.

I reached into my pinstripe and pulled out the dark-blue passport and laid it on the bar on top of which I laid the pack of Luckies. During the 1870s gold rush, about four in a thousand hit a strike called a lucky strike. That's how the chewing tobacco, later to evolve into a cigarette, got its name.

I slid them both across to her. "Cigarette? Please keep the pack."

She tucked them both into her purse, still looking at me in the mirror.

I moved off the stool, bringing my mouth close to her ear. "*So Lange, meine liebe.*"

One last time enveloped in her delicate lily-of-the-valley scent. She never moved as I walked out of the Empress Club for the last time.

Outside, there was the Major sitting in the idling jeep, staring straight ahead. The Major…what have we become in this city of rubble? Old "L" Detachment buddies; there are three of us. Now the last thread. A ride which would take us through the cemetery and then a flight back to I know not what.

As we drove along, passing the devastation of what's left of this city, we do not speak. It's as if there's no longer any need for words. I pull my overcoat around me as I foolishly think the chill of the air blowing past the open jeep is making me shiver. We turn right onto the long boulevard with the cemetery rolling out on either side of us. I spot him ahead, walking alone, most assuredly after visiting that grave. We pull past him as I reach out and touch the Major's arm. He slows and finally brakes to a stop. I begin to climb out of the jeep. For the first time the Major looks at me. "There's not much time."

I glance at the lone figure and say, "I can't leave it like this."

The jeep drives off. The figure is maybe 20 meters away as I lean against an old cart, pulling out another pack of Luckies. I light one and inhale the smoke.

The trees are almost bare, the sky slate grey, the wind picking up and cold, as a few, not knowing they are dead, leaves flutter to the ground. Captain Gilhooley, we call him Dizzy, walks past me without a glance. I blow out the smoke but it doesn't feel like a Lucky Strike.

Chapter 20
De-light

Armando had just poured my second gimlet when the tangy sweet smell of Rose's Lime juice, which seemed to kill the German gin, is carried away by the scent of lily of the valley. The joint is near empty but she slides onto the stool next to me, an unlit cigarette between Max Factor red lips.

I let her have a light from my Automatic Ronson Standard Delight. Her hair is a lovely shade of dark red and she has a distant smile on her lips.

Turning back to my gimlet, glancing at her image in the bar mirror, I am impressed by her sleek suit in navy-blue velvet, bureau-drawer pockets with black plastic knobs, a Schiaparelli. I take a sip from the still ice-cold gimlet then turn my head to ask, "Cocktail?"

Smoke slides out from between her lips as she speaks, "Seventh Heaven, *bitte.*"

I look over at Armando; he is already pouring the gin into the bar glass. She says, "Have you been here long?"

The smoke is making swirling circles above our heads. I keep silent. A new game is being played out all across a ravaged landscape and a deadly form has followed me here.

"Not so long," I say.

Her smile widens about a millimeter. "A desolate landscape filled with the desperate, living out their ruined lives."

"Who lives?" I reply.

She takes another drag from her cigarette and blows the smoke out through her nose, picks up her drink and drains the glass, gesturing for another. As Armando is stirring, she leans in a little closer. Once again her scent brings me back, back to the Empress Club, now closed by the Commission. Her are lips so close to my ear I can feel her warm breath. "Barbara sent me. I have a message."

I am looking at her in the mirror. I turn slightly toward her and recite in a whisper, "'April is the cruellest month, breeding / Lilacs out of the dead land, mixing / Memory and desire, stirring / Dull roots with spring rain.'"

Armando already has his hand on the High Standard HD. He never misses but she recites from T. S. Eliot's *The Waste Land* in answer, "'Winter kept us warm, covering / Earth in forgetful snow, feeding / A little life with dried tubers.'" She adds, "Fitting for this place, in a surreal sort of way. The meeting is at 2:00 p.m. in the Prater. A blind man plays music just opposite the Riesenrad. Ask him this: 'Who has the Torah?' He will answer: 'Heschel Messias.'"

With that she drains her second drink and delicately slides off the barstool and out the door. I look over the shabby decor and I think it wasn't just the war, this place was always shabby. I look over at Armando, who just nods as if he read my thoughts. I drop a handful of the local stage money on the bar and leave.

As I ease out the front door, a chill wind hits me, so I raise the collar of my charcoal-grey wool overcoat and pull down on my grey trilby hat. Since it's about two hours until the meet, I decide to take a stroll past the rubble to the Prater. I wander for a while, finding myself in the area of the city known as Leopoldstadt. Fitting tribute to Leopold I by the locals, so named because Leopold drove the Jews from the area, making the inhabitants so grateful they named it Leopold's City. Did it end there? Even after nearly 10 years, I can still smell the smoke and hear the cries. *Kristallnacht* 1938, none of the synagogues survived, the Schiff Shul, the Leopoldstädter Tempel, the Türkischer Tempel, on and on, all gone. Just one fragment of one Torah was saved from the flames by Heschel Messias. Music blunted some of the sorrow. Verdi, *Nabucco*, "Chorus of the Hebrew Slaves." I heard it at Teatro alla Scala, before the world lost its mind.

Oh my country so beautiful and lost!
Or so dear yet unhappy!
Oh harp of the prophetic seers,
Why do you hang silent from the willows?

I arrive at the Prater 20 minutes before the meet. I stand off to one side and survey the area around the Wiener Riesenrad, the 212-foot-tall Ferris wheel. Newly repaired but not completely refurbished. I see the blind musician playing a zither. With him, on a long chain, a black bear is dancing a grotesque Viennese waltz.

I saunter over to the blind man and wait for him to finish his piece. The music ends, the bear sits, I drop a few coins in his metal cup, and say, "Who has the Torah?"

The blind man plucks a string and answers, "Heschel Messias." He takes my hand in both of his, slipping me a note. "*Danke*," he says. I thrust my hands into my overcoat and move off. As I turn I spot Harry walking toward the Riesenrad. He has other business and so have I. I also notice two young girls staring up at the Riesenrad.

I walk over to them and ask, "*Begleite mich Mit?*" They both looked down, unsure. I start toward the giant wheel, look back, and say, "*Kommen sie.*" They begin to follow, their excitement overcoming their trepidation. I see Harry and another man, whom I do not recognize, in a car alone moving upward. I pay the fare with a generous tip. The wooden door slides shut and we start to rise. The girls have their noses pressed to the window in awe of the view.

I reach into my overcoat pocket and bring out the note, unfold it and read the contents, written in English: "Now, the Universe is rotating."

I must have a quizzical expression on my face, but not really. Somehow I am familiar with the expression.

The sun is shining through the gondola's windows as we draw near the apex. The young girls are silent, that much closer to heaven. My eyelids are so heavy and I feel so very weary. They slide down, the fall of the curtain.

The sun on my face gently brings me back. I feel so rested as I open my eyes.

I am in an elegant bedroom. On the wall opposite the bed hangs a painting I recognize. It is the Young Sick Bacchus *by Michelangelo Merisi da Caravaggio. It must be a copy. I cannot remember where the original hangs but certainly not in a bedroom. I raise a hand to shield my eyes from the sunlight. The hand is old, wrinkled, and wears a small silver ring with inscriptions on each side: "Yesh me-Ayin, Ayin me-Yesh." I glimpse the infinite as my eyes close.*

Giuseppe, New York, 1906:

The manure and garbage smell pulls me back. I am at the foot of an alley off Broadway, wearing my favourite blue-check suit. The light from the electric streetlights grows dimmer the further into the alley I look. There are sounds of a struggle in the darkness.

I hear a man's voice. "Try to rob me, you little whore."

I move into the alley; I never could mind my own business. My eyes adjust—I see them now. A man with his hands around a woman's throat. I can only make out their outlines. He is choking her and banging her head against the wall. I am reaching for my Webley when I hear a muffled gunshot. There is a short guttural sound and the man slides down the woman's body and curls up on the ground.

Before I can move, another man from further down the alley yells, "Bitch!"

He is pointing something at the woman. The Webley in my hand fires, 218 grains of lead hollow-point design in a .455 cartridge, propelled by cordite. Fired at a relatively low velocity resulting in a milder recoil, the bullet taking on a tumbling action. The man cries out and slowly crumples down in the darkness, as if he just wanted to lie down for a minute.

I approach the woman. She is pointing a small firearm at me. I point the Webley at her, commanding, "Lower your weapon."

She says, "Mr. Finnegan, is that you?"

I recognize her voice. By God, it's Jeannie.

Giuseppe, a moment in time:

The whole scene fades as if I am engulfed in a dense fog. I am sitting at a table across from a woman dressed in a simple suit in a dark-blue fabric, her hair a lovely shade of dark red, and wearing has a distant smile. She has an unlit cigarette between Max Factor red lips. I let her have a light from my Automatic Ronson Standard De-light. Smoke slides out from between her lips as she says, "Barbara sent me. I have a message."

I turn toward her and whisper more from *The Waste Land*: "'Who is the third who walks always beside you? / When I count, there are only you and I together.'"

She recites in answer, "'But when I look ahead up the white road / There is always another one walking beside you.'"

She sighs. "I am Olivia De León. Thirty-two generations removed from my ancestor, Moses de León, Moshe ben Shem-Tov. All the iterations, all the lives, all the terrible deeds, all the beautiful sacrifice, all the devotion comes down to this: 'All the worlds below and above are all mysteriously one. Divine existence is indivisible.'" So wrote Moshe ben Shem-Tov in the Zohar."

Then she says, "The process has begun. Go back to the alley, help Jeannie and find Gilhooley."

The curtain falls.

Chapter 21
Beautiful Dreamer

Giuseppe, alley off Broadway, New York, 1906:

As if I'd step through a fine mist, I am back in the alley. I have both hands on Jeannie's shoulders. Her eyes are glazed.

I shake her gently. "Jeannie, you have to get out of here." Her eyes begin to focus.

"Go through the back alleys to McGinnity's. Knock on the back door. They will ask for a password. Tell them Beautiful Dreamer sent you. Now go."

She turns and begins to run down the darkened alley. I look down at the man at my feet, quite dead. I turn him onto his back and proceed to look for some identification. I pull out a billfold and extract a card.

Edison Laboratory
West Orange, New Jersey
Andrew McCabe

I drop the card, move on to the next victim. Damn if it isn't the same card with the name Michael Millbury. I slowly move down the alley and climb over two fences, disturbing a tomcat who stares me out of the yard. I reach the back of McGinnity's and knock.

"Who's pounding on my door?" a voice asks.

"Beautiful Dreamer is who I am."

The door opens. It's Jones. He jerks his head for me to enter. I move in quickly and hand him my Webley, saying, "She's been upset tonight. Calm her down, would you?"

Jones nods and smiles and after a pointed glance at my pistol says, "I'll take good care of your 'Lady of Bristol'" and winks.

I move through the back room and enter the main bar. I scan the crowd and spot Jeannie, holding a drink, at a table with David, his head held low, probably loaded. I feel my stomach tighten. I want a shot or a pipe but I push it off for now. I walk over to the bar, and without a word a glass hits the bar and a drink is poured, a stirred martini.

I look up and Armando is cleaning a glass, eyeing me, his waxed moustache moving ever so slightly up and down.

I know he wants to say something. All I have to do is tilt my head up and he says, "*No tenías elección.*"

"Armando?"

"You had no choice," he translates.

"How do you know these things?" I ask.

"My great-aunt is a spirit, an *orixá*. She speaks to me. You are a *despachar humanos al mundo de los espíritus.*"

I have no idea what he's talking about but somehow I know it is the truth. I throw my drink back, leave a nice tip for the tip. I move off the bar as David and Hogan resume their ragtime moment. I give McGinnity a thumbs-up; he points his little finger down, meaning I can pass through the red door.

Inside an old Chinese man plays an ancient tune on an upright string instrument. There's hop in the air and it's what I want. I make my way into the dim interior. Candles flickering light over a few pallets occupied with the dead, dying, loaded, does it matter which. I pick a wooden pallet and lie down among the musty pillows. There is a small table next to me, an opium lamp, a slender needle, a pipe. A hand reaches out and picks up the needle.

I've never noticed how beautiful the young Chinese woman is as she twirls the ball of dope over the opium lamp. Maybe it's because she has the thing I want. The thing that so fleetingly quenches the fire.

All set, she hands me the plain pipe. Her eyes are averted as I notice she is missing the ring finger of the hand offering me the pipe. I take it from her, bringing the stem to my mouth with more anticipation than with any lover. I take a long pull, allowing my head to fall back among the cheap pillows. As I exhale time slows and the cosmos opens to its terribly beautiful, infinite possibilities, but it is one I am falling toward.

A cool breeze gently brings me back. I'm sitting on a greying teak bench, dressed in a simple set of pyjamas of a soft cotton in a robin's-egg blue, with matching cotton robe. My feet are encased in a pair of dark-blue leather Moroccan-style slippers. In my field of vision there are hundreds of white tulips.

The sun breaks through the clouds, illuminating the white heads of each tulip like stars in an alternate universe. In the middle of the field stands a young man, a beautiful young man. The tears in my eyes catch the light like diamonds rolling down my cheeks. Somewhere, somewhen I know this young man. He gently places his hand over his heart. It all fades away.

Beautiful dreamer, wake unto me,
Starlight and dewdrops are waiting for thee;
Sounds of the rude world, heard in the day,
Lull'd by the moonlight have all passed away!

~Stephen Collins Foster, "Beautiful Dreamer"

Chapter 22
The Inferno

Giuseppe, Nigel, Mad Frankie, who's who, time again:

The smell of hop brings me back to the dimly lit room of McGinnity's opium den. I slowly sit up to the creaking of the wooden platform and swing my legs over onto the floor. My mind begins to clear enough to remember there was something I needed to do. Some message I needed to deliver, someone I needed to see. I just couldn't quite grasp what it was. It was like trying to hold on to a wet rope tossed to pull you out of the floodwaters. I'm drowning, not a life preserver in sight. Was Gilhooley still in the back room? When was that? I recall saving him from those thugs but when? I fall back onto the musty pillows; never mind, I just want to close my eyes for a few more minutes.

I-95 to I-64 to Powhite Parkway to Va-2887S to US 60 to Midlothian Turnpike toward Powhatan, quick bear left, then right, US 60 toward Powhatan, about 35 miles, turn left onto Cumberland Road, 18 miles arrive at Farmville and an abandoned tobacco farm.

John Rolfe is widely given credit for importing *Nicotiana tabacum* seeds to Virginian to grow a species of tobacco that is less harsh when smoked. Farms like this one, built in 1906 by Marshal Whittle, grandson of Bolling Whittle, late of the 38th Virginia Infantry, Confederate States Army, where acres and acres of tobacco were grown until the extinction of the 1950s cheap labour.

I lie on a stained feather mattress, which had been placed on steel-frame rail bed. There is a chipped white end table next to me covered in empty liquid morphine sulphate bottles. The room stinks of sweat and piss. My arms straight out, my feet crossed. Small rivulets of blood, some congealed, some still oozing, dot my arms.

Headlights splash across the dirty lace curtains. I hear footsteps creaking on the stairs. The hallway is dark. She emerges from the shadows. She is wearing a jet-black Chanel 03C trench coat, two-on-four button, double breasted with a notch lapel, two silk detachable black camellia pins on the right one, self-belt with a square black enamel buckle with "CHANEL" embossed on it; cuff has a detachable belt with two buttons on each, buttons are black with enamel "CC" on each. The coat is slightly open showing a pair of Chanel black wool gabardine trousers with pleated front.

She crosses the bedroom without blinking an eye at the terrible conditions. She sits on the edge of the bed. Her coat falls open on one side revealing a Glock G30S. I raise my head slightly and whisper, "Please, just do it."

She bends over and puts her arms around me, holding me in a loving embrace.

My head falls back onto the musty pillows. I just want to close my eyes for a few more minutes.

I am lying on the bottom bunk of a steel-frame bed. The cheap wool blanket stinks, crawling with lice. Each day the guards come and drag me to the windowless room and beat me, not for any purpose that I can understand. I am at the end of the line. Today I will die in that room.

The bedding above me shifts as my cellmate continues to pray. I can hear the Spanish words: "*Dios te salve, María, llena eres de gracia, el Señor es contigo.*"

I can see his rosary dangling over the side of his mattress. A pair of dirty feet appear and he jumps off the upper bunk. He sits quietly on my bed. It's the bartender from the La Bodeguita del Medio, Armando.

I raise my head slightly and whisper, "*Terminarlo.*"

He bends over and places a kiss on my battered cheek, while holding me, lovingly.

My head falls back onto the musty pillows. I just want to close my eyes for a few more minutes.

Smoke, fire, explosions, screaming. I am lying on my back upon a wooden deck. There is a burning ship next to the ship I am on. I try to rise up but it is almost impossible. I realize my right leg is gone below the knee, blood staining the deck. Suddenly there is a sailor kneeling beside me, furiously tying off my leg above the knee. I recognize him, a young man I met on last shore leave, David. I strangely feel nothing, maybe the end is near. I notice David's right side is burnt, he must be in pain. Why stop to help me? I raise my head slightly and whisper, "Save yourself," but he does not hear me above the noise. He places his right hand on my forehead, while holding me with his left.

My head falls back onto the musty pillows. I just want to close my eyes for a few more minutes.

I am sitting at my dressing table with my head lying on my arms. Three of the six lights are out on my backlit mirror. Makeup scattered over the top. An Old Tom Gin bottle almost empty sits next to a co-balt-blue shaker and glasses. I'm so very tired, and the stage manager keeps yelling. He is in a rage, while my agent sits quietly in the corner.

"I've had it, you drunken sod. William Fucking Shakespeare, Hamlet—how many times have you performed the role? What the fuck did you have in mind tonight? The whole play is an internal dialogue. That Hamlet may or may not have killed both his father and drowned Ophelia. Murdering Polonius because he pushed the marriage, and of course my favourite: that Hamlet loved Horatio all along. Let's not forget that you rewrote the most famous soliloquy in all of literature. That the *to be* part was thrown out of the play. You reduced the entire play to mass murder and suicidal rumination."

With that he exits stage right, slamming the door. My agent rises, sighs, and walks out.

I never hear her enter until a cool hand is on my neck, moving down to hold me. It's my Ophelia, Margo.

My head falls back onto the musty pillows. I just want to close my eyes for a few more minutes.

I am crouched against the wall of a shell hole, the bottom of which contains a headless Frenchman and muddy, bloody water. Crouched across from me is my comrade, who calls himself a psychologist and worked in some clinic in Leipzig. No matter; we are now members of the 12th Division, 23rd Regiment of the Prussian/German Army. We were sent out to reconnoitre the French positions and now have become trapped in no-man's-land during a barrage. During light flashes, I look into his eyes and he mine, both seeing the same hope: Let it be quick.

We have been here for three hours. Soon it will be light and the French will attack. Our choice: death by French bullets or German Maxim guns. We both know we must try it. I make hand signals that I will crawl out first. He nods. I make it 15 meters and a shell lands to my right, throwing me, dirt, wire, and assorted debris into the air. I come down on my back. I try to lift my right arm but it is not there. I am heading for shock and death. Suddenly I am picked up and carried the final meters to our trenches. My comrade is screaming the pass-word and for a medic at the same time. We make it over the wall and onto the floor of the trench. I am fading as the medic is working as fast as he can. The psychologist with the steel-rimmed glasses is holding me. The sun comes up.

My head falls back onto the musty pillows. I just want to close my eyes for a few more minutes.

Doc quickly unwraps a collection of surgical instruments and starts to work on Gilhooley. His first movement is to pull a loaded syringe out of a green alligator case and, after tying off one Gilhooley's arms, injects the fluid directly into a main vein. This done he steps back, laying the syringe down and closing his eyes, almost like he had taken the shot himself. Gilhooley's body visibly relaxes, and Doc's eyes open with a ghost of a smile.

Two hours later, Doc is washing his hands in the sink, Gilhooley is resting quietly, and I need a shot. Doc must sense what I'm thinking as he turns around and frowns. I plead with my eyes. He jerks his head toward the back rooms. I slip through the red door.

Inside an old Chinese man plays an ancient tune on an upright string instrument. There's hop in the air but that's not what I want. I make my way into the dim interior. Candles flickering light over a few pallets occupied with the dead, dying, loaded, does it matter which.

I move to the back and sit in one of two parlour chairs separated by a small table. The Doc sits in the other. The Doc could never refuse a man in pain, physical or psychic. He nods. I stand and remove my blue-check jacket, sit undo my cuff link and roll up my shirt sleeve.

The Doc is standing over me tying off my arm, waits, then slides the needle in with a loving touch, depressing the plunger and releasing the tie. My legs feel it first, my heart flutters, my body melts into the chair.

After a brief time, I realize I want to hear some music, some ragtime music that I can faintly hear through the walls. I make my way to the main room and it's crowded. Hogan and David are playing as one. I spot a table with one patron, Jeannie. I wobble, side to side, over to her table, slurring the words, "May I sit?"

Jeannie looks sadly at me, but her face changes to a smile. I sit down next to her. A cocktail is out on the table in front of me and I drain the glass. Jeannie leans in and speaks in a low voice, "You're loaded." I answer, "Yes, miss, I believe I am." Nearly incoherent but understood.

She puts and arm around me and says, "Thank you, Finnegan, I am in your debt."

I laugh as two more cocktails are placed on the table. I drink half and spill the other half. Jeannie lovingly holds me closer. Looking at the barkeep, she says, "I believe Mr. Finnegan has had enough."

The barkeep replies, "Yes, I believe he has."

Chapter 23
It's Always Winter Here

"But I don't want to go among mad people," Alice remarked.
"Oh, you can't help that," said the Cat: "we're all mad here. I'm mad.
You're mad."
"How do you know I'm mad?" said Alice.
"You must be," said the Cat, "or you couldn't have come here."

~From *Alice's Adventures in Wonderland*, Lewis Carroll

Nigel, Siberia, alternate time:

The paths leading to the Divine or to Madness are sometimes indistinguishable. I've lost so much. Unable to intervene, bring forth the Divine; save the ones I love, have loved through so many iterations. My head is bloodied and bowed. I want to paint the sky red. My rage knows no bounds but neither does my love.

After a month of chasing the dragon in my rural retreat, I received a personal note of such a touching level of sympathy that it brought me back. The details which led me here are hazy at best. I received a message using Advanced Encryption Standard, AES, which is a symmetric encryption algorithm and one of the most secure. It was a simple message from a known Mossad agent. A very well-known agent to me.

I step off the Trans-Siberian Railway with a single bag at the Krasnoyarsk-Passazhirsky station, the main station of Krasnoyarsk. Krasnoyarsk, on the Yenisei River, is the third largest city in Siberia with a population of a little over 1 million. The station was originally built in 1895 and since then has undergone a bit of restoration.

There are the usual rip-off cabs circling the station entrance but I spot my contact right away. He is sitting in a two-tone black and brown 1975 Mercedes Benz 300D. I slide into the cold rear seat. The driver is looking at me in the rearview mirror, smiling. He speaks in perfect English, "It is too cold in car, maybe, for soft westerner?"

I worked with the driver, Vasily, before. I had to reply, "The Soviets still had an empire the last time this car had a heater that worked. I'm booked at the Novotel, 123 Karla Marksa Ulitsa."

Vasily laughs. Vasily Ivanovich Surikov is the great-grandson of a Russian realist painter from Krasnoyarsk. "I know the address. I met a young Swedish woman at that hotel this summer. The Swedes still think it exotic to sleep with Siberian."

After crossing the Communal Bridge over the Yenisei River, Vasily drops me off in front of the Novotel Krasnoyarsk Center Hotel, right in the heart of the business center of the city, very convenient for the traveling businessperson but not for my kind of business. I hand some rubles to Vasily just to make it look good. He booked me into a suite at 3,500 rubles a night. Vasily knows a good thing when he sees it.

I carry my own bag up to the room but still tip the bellhop. No use pissing off the staff. Here I will sit and wait, in Russian luxury, waiting for the word to start the trip to Yakutsk, part of the Sakha (Yakutia) Republic, situated entirely on the west bank of Lena River. With the A360 (Lena Highway or The Amur-Yakutsk Highway) running on the east bank, the highway terminates in Nizhny Bestyakh, a settlement of 4,000 people opposite Yakutsk on the east bank of the Lena. The word will be that the river is frozen enough to permit our truck to drive over it into Yakutsk. There is no bridge over the Lena River into Yakutsk. Twenty days into November, the wait should not be long. Anyway the Novotel hotel bar is open seven days a week, 24 hours a day.

After two days of meals in my suite and a few cocktails at the bar, I get word from the bellhop, a Vasily plant, that I should prepare for a little drive in the country. My room is open-ended booked. Good thing I didn't stiff the kid. Oh, and dress warm. Thanks, kid.

The next morning I take the knapsack the kid hands me and walk two blocks south and wait for Vasily. The temperature in Krasnoyarsk is a balmy 22 this morning. I do not have long to wait as a TGL series, flatbed body, 10-ton, 250-horsepower, steel air suspension, German-made MAN truck, flashing its lights, pulls over. Vasily nods for me to get in. As I slam the door, Vasily says, "I got this special, comfortable cab, warm, plenty of food and drink, just right for western who is, is this the expression, a cream puff. Sit back, relax, Yakutsk is Siberian close, just 4,142 kilometers away. A short 57 hours and we meet your contact. By the way, the temperature will not be above -30 degrees Celsius."

I say nothing. While I may be a cream puff, I know Vasily is not. Vasily Ivanovich Surikov was at the Dubrovka Theatre on October 23, 2002. He was there as a Spetsnaz operator from the Federal Security Service (FSB), Alpha team. Forty to 50 Chechens took 850 hostages, heading them into the main hall. The hall was only reachable by a 30-meter corridor and up a long staircase. The Chechens had planted explosives along the path and rigged a powerful explosive in the middle of the hall where all the hostages were held. Their demand was simple: withdraw all Russian forces from Chechnya.

After more than two days and two hostages executed, the word came down to assault the terrorist position. First the Spetsnaz operators pumped an undisclosed chemical agent into the hall's ventilation system and then they assaulted. One hundred and thirty hostages died due to inhalation of the agent but over 700 were saved. The Spetsnaz operators killed every Chechen terrorist they found.

The Russians received plenty of criticism for their tactics, but one noted Security analyst listed Russia as one of the most dangerous places to be a terrorist.

I settle back into the not uncomfortable seat and fall into a slight doze. Less than one hour out, we are pulling off the road and into a café, gas, small settlement area. I ask, "Vasily, we need gas already?"

"No, my friend, this is where an *algus* lives."

Not surrendering but I ask, "An *algus*, someone who performs blessing rituals?"

"Yes, we must strengthen our minds, spirits, and bodies for the long trip ahead, for the journey. It is called an *aitchelaan*, a Sakha word, meaning to bless a journey."

Leaving the truck into the already frigid air, Vasily lifts a box out of the back of the truck then we move around the café to a small house behind. A young woman answers our knock and bids us enter.

The interior is small in dimension with a low ceiling but there is a vastness here. A welcoming energy immediately lifts my spirit. Vasily places the box on a small painted table. The woman smiles, then leads us out the back door to a small hut. Inside is the *algus*, the cultural leader of his community.

When an *algus* performs an *aitchelaan*, it consists of ritual song or chanting and burning of a tree bark made special by "spirits." The ritual is a connecting with, and follows the concept that it is a journey within, the natural land in all its cycles. Centuries old, it is an acknowledgment of the nature of Siberia and the absolute need to understand an environment that is extreme. Emphasizing that on any journey through Siberia's vastness, it is essential to know and respect its landscape.

We sit in one corner of the hut, directed there by the *algus*. I'm sure our placement is of significance. The drumbeat, the chanting, the burning of the tree bark are all marks of the ceremony. The bark has been collected from dense conifer forests of northern Siberia and is selected from trees that form a distinct physical form, which is believed to have been created by spirits. The drum beats, beats, beats, the *algus* chanting, chanting, chanting. The room grows dimmer with each beat until...

I'm sitting on a greying teak bench, dressed in a simple set of pajamas of a soft cotton in a robin's-egg blue, with matching cotton robe. My feet are encased in a pair of dark-blue leather Moroccan-style slippers. In my field of vision there are hundreds of yellow daffodils.

The sun breaks through the clouds, illuminating the yellow heads of each daffodil like stars in an alternate universe. In the middle of the field stands a young woman, a beautiful young woman. The tears in my eyes catch the light like diamonds rolling down my cheeks. Somewhere, somewhen I know this young woman. She gently places her hand over her heart. It all fades away. I'm back with the *algus*. The drum beats, beats, beats, the *algus* chanting, chanting, chanting. The room grows dimmer with each beat until...

I'm in a room with the beat of other music, spiritual, holding music. The smell of incense and death is here. Lying on a bed is the young woman but years have passed. She is much older, and I realize I am also. No, no, this is not my vision. I had this vision many years ago—I was lying in a bed and she was sitting in a sun-filled room, her grey head low, watching me die. It was always the way I saw it. No, once again I'm fucked. Life has taken this beautiful person and left this shell of a man. I realize my rage is pointless because I'm holding the short straw. No, the joke is on me because it's not chance, you see, they're all short straws. The drum beats, beats, beats, the *algus* chanting, chanting, chanting. The room grows dimmer with each beat until…

I am standing in a dense coniferous forest, sounds of the forest all around me. I make my way in a direction I can only follow, follow the path. I reach a small clearing, where a woman stands in the center. She is wearing a ritualistic costume. The costume is filled with metal pendants, each representing different ideas and having its own qualities. In the Yakut language she is an *ojun*, a shaman. The air around her vibrates, the vibrations of a female *ojun*. Hostile spirits are scared away by her presence. Her drum beats, beats, beats and in her song can be heard sounds imitating the howling of the wolf, and the voices of other animals, her guardian spirits. The sounds are from in front of me, next to me, behind me, they are everywhere. I deny her healing powers; looking up to heaven, I rage. I deny her healing powers; looking up to heaven, I rage.

I deny her healing powers; looking up to heaven, I rage—three times I deny her. The clearing grows dimmer with each beat until…

I jerk awake. I'm sitting in the Man truck cab, the only illumination from its headlights, the rest is total blackness.

Vasily looks over at me. "You're finally awake. We have been driving for five hours. Did you have a good sleep?"

I just nod. The terror of that one vision is fading, and that's when real hopelessness sets in because she really is gone.

We drive, hour after hour, nothing but our headlights and blackness. After a while Vasily pulls into a cutout. He looks at me and says, "Time to feed the beast. Engine running auxiliary gas tank on flatbed. You pump, I watch." With that he reaches behind his seat and pulls out an Auto Assault-12 automatic shotgun with a 32-round drum.

He just smiles at me. "No one, how you say, fucks with us. For you." Vasily hands me a Vityaz-SN, a 9×19mm Parabellum submachine gun developed in 2004 by Izhmash.

"Selector lever is on lowest setting. You pull trigger, it fires one bullet." Vasily can be very condescending. Then again, he has a right to be. Time for me to pump the gas.

It is a long and brutal journey, subfreezing temperatures and no Holiday Inn in sight. One positive is that the road is easily passable in winter. Spring and summer it is a mud pit, when even our Man truck would find it near impossible to negotiate. The road of bones, it is called, in homage to all the Gulag inmates from the Sevvostlag Labor camp who died and were buried along the road. Continuous construction occurred from 1932 until 1953.

It is dusk, and it feels like it has been dusk for hours, the sun painting the harsh whiteout landscape a delicate shade of red. The road goes on, goes on, goes on. We are quiet for hours, each surrounded by his own thoughts, visions, the truck hum, trance inducing. Sleep eludes me as the vision of the female shaman returns again and again and again. One of the metal pendants stands out. The one called the mother spirit, the mother animal. Twice in the life of a shaman the vision of this spirit comes: when he/she becomes a shaman and when he/she dies. Vasily pulls the truck into a large area carved out of a small hillside. He has been driving for hours. He needs to sleep. After a while I doze off. I am in front of the female shaman again, this time we are in a hut of some kind, kneeling on what at first I think is a mattress but is just a mat made from a woven fiber. We are both naked. The left side of her body is covered in numerous tattoos. At first I think they are sayings written in Chinese characters but realize they are in another language. The initial erotic feel of the moment soon fades as she drops a bunch of dried herbs on a brazier. Soon we are embraced by the strong scent of sage mixed with other herbs I cannot identify. She places her hand over her heart and says, "*Sayiina*," and points to me, if only I knew.

I am awakened by Vasily pulling his GSh-18 from a holster next to his seat.

I ask, "What's up?"

He answers in a tense voice, "Car pulled in behind us about 20 meters. Do not move, we are being watched."

A few minutes pass as I realize my weapon is stored behind my seat. "Vasily, I have no weapon handy."

He tells me, "Two men getting out of car. Roll down your window, reach into door compartment. Another GSh-18, round chambered."

I look in the side mirror and see a man approaching on my side. "Vasily, they split, one on my side." They are both carrying handguns, which they begin to raise as they draw near the truck cab. Vasily reaches to his right, keeping an eye on the side mirrors. Two beats and he flips a switch. Floodlights illuminate all around the truck. Our two would-be thieves both bring arms up to block the glare.

I wait for Vasily to shoot but instead he shouts, "Opustite oruzhiye i Otpravlyaysya!" I let you live. "Я позволяю вам жить.вы хотите кого-то убить, убейте некоторых чеченцев. YA pozvolyayu vam zhit.vy khotite kogo-to ubit, ubeyte nekotorykh chechentsev."

At the first words they began to back off toward their car. By the time Vasily is finished they are already past our truck.

I look over at Vasily. "I thought you would shoot, I almost did."

Vasily gives a short laugh. "Seen many of their kind get straightened out in the Army. They're just kids with not much and nothing else to do. I told them to go kill a few Chechens."

With that he starts the truck, looks at me, and smiles. "Shall we?"

Endless white, ice-packed road, I drive, Vasily drives, I drive, I sleep. Hoping each kilometer carries me further and further from tragedy, but each rotation of the wheels sings out the truth. There is no escaping, only one thing can change it, not writing, not religion, not mediating, not shooting, not whiskey, not sex, not drugs, not time, only death. Who knows, maybe even then our consciousness remains tormenting us forever.

Vasily continues driving while I slip in and out of the world. The forest shaman appears frequently in my dreams. She pierces her breast, she removes her head and holds it, she makes bird sounds, wolf sounds, bear sounds, reindeer sounds, sounds of swollen rivers, sounds of the wind through the conifers, sounds of ice cracking on the Lena, sounds of the dawn of the first day, sounds of the twilight of the last night. She shouts at me, she embraces me, she guards me, she will fight to the death for me.

We leave, take A360 onto the Ulitsa Lenina, or its designation the P504. The truck braking brings me back to this world of sorrow. I look out my window and see groupings of low buildings, smoke coming from almost all of them. I realize we have arrived at Nizhny Bestyakh. I turn to Vasily and ask, "Tired? Maybe we can rest here."

He answers, "Not just a rest stop, we are here to see the old man. The one who will tell us if it is safe to cross the Lena into Yakutsk."

I look dubious about this and say so. "Vasily, why do we need to ask an old man living in a shack if the Lena is frozen enough to cross?"

Vasily shakes his head and explains it to me. "Nothing to do with weather, my friend. In case you haven't noticed, there are demons on our ass. You brought them with you and somehow they have been kept at bay. Now we ask if he will lead us across the Lena to our operative."

I do not answer, knowing full well who has kept the demons away.

We exit the truck and walk to the first building. Vasily asks a young man a few questions in Russian. The door closes.

Vasily moves to his left while saying to me, "The old man is in the furthest building on the next block, we are expected."

We knock at the door, it opens, we are ushered into a sparsely furnished room. It is warm enough to take the chill off your bones.

A few candles are burning in the corner in front of a small reed mat. The mat is occupied by a very frail-looking old man. The old man's eyes open and he beckons me closer. I stop in front of his mat. He pushes both hands down. Sit.

I sit. He speaks in his native Yakutia. I look over at Vasily. He translates, "He is called Kuday. It means universe in Yakut. Also, he wants to know if you have caught the dragon you have been chasing?"

I do not know how to answer, not sure what he means. In the back of my mind I know I have been chasing the dragon, but is that what the old man is referring to?

I look at Vasily. "Tell him the dragon cannot be caught."

Vasily translates for him. A sadness passes over that weathered face and he nods. He takes both of my hands in his and speaks. Vasily translates, "Trust her. She was many things in many lives, in many worlds. You loved her, that love has brought her true self to you. Follow her. She can slay the demons. You will see it in the look in her eyes."

His eyes close. It is time to leave. He utters one more thing. I look at Vasily, who shrugs. "He said, 'Journey well, Sayiina.'"

Back in the truck, we head down the P504. Vasily says we are to make a right at the shopping mall. Shopping mall? We follow this road—and yes, there really is a shopping mall—until we reach the banks of the Lena. Now quite frozen with no ice flow. We begin crossing the Lena River. There are other vehicles, so it seems like a regular highway. You might not know it was just ice between your truck wheels and water.

My sleep patterns have been erratic. My thoughts are on the old man. How could he know about my dreams? How could he know about my nightmares? My eyes close, and the forest shaman appears. She is shrouded in a swirling mist of frigid air, she is in costume beating her drum, beating her drum, beating her drum. When I open my eyes, there is no frigid water separated by a meter or so of ice below us.

Vasily says, "Not long now, your contact is staying at the Gostinichnyy Kompleks Renabo. It sits right on a lake, quite beautiful spot even in winter."

After a drive on incomprehensibly named roads, we pull into the lot of the hotel. Vasily is right it: is a spectacular spot. I feel a sense of apprehension about this meeting, though. The operative was insistent that I come. Said she was onto something big. I've never known Ancient Soul to exaggerate.

We check into the hotel, go to our rooms. We are to meet Ancient Soul at the bar in two hours. It's hard for me to really care. I know what an endeavor we just undertook to get here. I realize it was all Vasily. I must face this question. Why is the shaman inhabiting my dreams? What does she think I can accomplish? I gaze at the calendar on the desk in my room. I have no memory of the year it displays. Somehow years have passed. Where have I been?

It is time for the meet. I wander down to the bar overlooking the frozen lake, piled with snow. Vasily protested long and loud as I tried to persuade him to wait in his room. Not a chance; he'll be at the bar. I spot her, Ancient Soul, at a far table with an ice-cold martini in front of her. I walk over to her table in a straightforward manner and sit down. She gives me a hint of a smile.

I look down at her drink. "Not vodka, I hope."

She gives a slight laugh. "Knowing I was meeting you, would I take that chance?"

She's right—I do not care where I am, anyone asking for a vodka martini is immediately shown the door. She signals the waiter, he's there in a flash. She orders for me in flawless Russian.

I look at her and have to ask, "What brought you back?"

She takes a long pull of her drink and her gaze drifts out the window for a moment. She takes in the expanse of white landscape and deep-blue sky. She turns back to me and begins, "How many times have we crossed paths, do you remember? Do you remember when? Do you have any details after I met you and Gilhooley at that rundown farmhouse?"

Now it is my turn. "I remember you arriving at the farm; after that, I'm not sure. Also, have you seen today's date?"

"Yes, yes, the boys back at the lab have done all the math. They're scared shitless. Something is controlling local time. At least they think it is a local phenomenon. Who knows, the disturbance may have far, very far, reaching effects, maybe outside our galaxy and beyond."

The waiter silently puts my ice-cold martini in front of me. I nod and he backs away.

I look at Ancient Soul. "Is this the plan to lure me to desolation? Are you going to finally kill me? Let me tell you something, there will always be a world where I survive with a family, grandchildren. My wife will grow old with me and close our eyes to this world. Is that so improbable?" I throw back my drink, stand, and look out over the lake.

The shaman is standing in the middle of the lake. In the mist she raises a knife in her right hand and brings it down, piercing her breast. I remember, I am kneeling in a small hut, sage fills the air along with pine bark. I am stripped to the waist, devotional tattoos covering the right side of my body. Ancient Soul approaches me, puts a gun to my head, and pulls the trigger. I am so very grateful.

I look at Ancient Soul. "Is this the plan to lure me to desolation? Are you going to finally kill me? Let me tell you something, there will always be a world where I survive with a family, grandchildren. My wife will grow old with me and close our eyes to this world. Is that so improbable?" I throw back my drink, stand, and look out over the lake.

The shaman is standing in the middle of the lake. In the mist she raises a knife in her right hand and brings it down, piercing her breast. I remember, I am kneeling in a small hut, sage fills the air along with pine bark. I am stripped to the waist, devotional tattoos covering the right side of my body.

There is an old man on a straw mat. He speaks in English:

"When the world began, there was heaven and earth. You will seek your fortune elsewhere. You have done terrible things, been the tool of great injustice, drunk, gambled, smoked the poison, and given in to the pleasures of the flesh. You have mashed your boot on the innocent and guilty alike. While you have used women of my race as things for your satisfaction, there is one who will come out of the East. She will be of the Dao, and the look in her eyes will show you your true path."

I look at Ancient Soul. "Is this the plan to lure me to desolation? Are you going to finally kill me? Let me tell you something, there will always be a world where I survive with a family, grandchildren. My wife will grow old with me and close our eyes to this world. Is that so improbable?" I throw back my drink, stand, and look out over the lake.

The shaman is standing in the middle of the lake. In the mist she raises a knife in her right hand and brings it down, piercing her breast. I remember, I am kneeling in a small hut, sage fills the air along with pine bark. I am stripped to the waist, devotional tattoos covering the right side of my body. Ancient Soul approaches, kneeling next to me. We wait for the Sakha *ojun* in costume. I am scared. I look at Ancient Soul, into her eyes; she returns my look, placing a hand on my shoulder. "I'm here now, I will face the demons with you."

The *ojun*, the Sakha shaman, enters with Vasily, who is dressed in local garb. She commences to beat the drum softly and to sing in a plaintive voice. Then the beating of the drum grows stronger and stronger; and in her song you can hear sounds imitating the howling of the wolf, the groaning of the reindeer, and the voices of other animals, her guardian spirits. The sounds seem to come sometimes from the corner nearest to where I am kneeling, then from the opposite end, then again from the middle of the house, and then to proceed from the ceiling. Her drum also seems to sound, now over my head, now at my feet, now behind, now in front of me. I can see nothing. Yet it goes on and on.

The fear dissipates into absolute calmness, just the frequency of the creation/destruction cycle of all things. The *ojun* says one word:

"Kini'je."

I know this is the name of the Yukaghir deity responsible for the flow of time. We are no longer in the middle realm in this world. The *ojun* is speaking directly into my conscious mind, telling me that Kini'je controls not only the flow of time but the passages from one to another of the uncountably infinite worlds.

I slump onto the pillows. Ancient Soul eases me onto my back, the room obscured by the smoke from the braziers. I want that bullet, but I know there is a world where the gun is empty.

Mad Frankie, in the woods, present time:

I shake out two Gabapentin 300 mg into my hand and carry them into the kitchen, washing them down with a pull of milk. I close the refrigerator door, I look at my reflection in the stainless steel. Maybe this whole string has been played out. Maybe the words will not clear a path. Have I been fooling myself? As usual I need to occupy myself until the pills shut my mind up. If only the memories would fade, would end. The good ones, the bad ones, just an avalanche of despair. Dizzy, can you hear me? Dizzy, maybe you are in your study typing away or are you drawing? Can you make it stop? I close my eyes. I am standing in another world.

Giuseppe, Chinatown, New York, 1906:

I look up and Armando is cleaning a glass, eyeing me, his waxed moustache moving ever so slightly up and down.

I know he wants to say something. All I have to do is tilt my head up and he says, "*No tenías elección.*"

"Armando?"

"You had no choice," he translates.

"How do you know these things?" I ask.

"My great-aunt is a spirit, an *orixá*. She speaks to me. You are a *despachar humanos al mundo de los espíritus.*"

I have no idea what he's talking about but somehow I know it is the truth. I throw my drink back, leave a nice tip for the tip. I move off the bar as David and Hogan resume their ragtime moment. I give McGinnity a thumbs-up; he points his little finger down, meaning I can pass through the red door. I feel at home, maybe this is where I belong.

Inside an old Chinese man plays an ancient tune on an upright string instrument. There's hop in the air but that's not what I want. I make my way into the dim interior. Candles flickering light over a few pallets occupied with the dead, dying, loaded, does it matter which.

I get a surprise as I spot Jeannie curled up on one of the pallets, her right hand lying on a pipe. I had no idea Jeannie chased the dragon.

I walk over to her and crouch down and place my hand on hers. Her eyes open slightly, a thin smile on her lips. I give her hand a light squeeze, and say, "'And flights of angels sing thee to thy rest.'"

It must have something to do with the alley gunfight. I wonder if Jeannie has ever killed someone. She's led a rough-and-tumble life so who knows. I believe there is bound to be trouble about two dead Edison men. We could seriously get the shovel and pick for this.

I spy an empty pallet and give the boss a tilt of my head. I loosen my tie and shoes, take off my jacket, and fall back on the musty pillows. This time I notice how beautiful the young Chinese woman is as she twirls the ball of dope over the opium lamp. All set, she hands me the plain pipe. Her eyes are averted as I notice she is not missing the ring finger of the hand offering me the pipe. I take it from her, bringing the stem to my mouth with more anticipation than with any lover. I take a long pull, allowing my head to fall back among the cheap pillows.

As I exhale time slows and the cosmos opens to its terribly beautiful, infinite possibilities, but is it one I am falling toward?

Moments pass like eons, I catch movement out of the corner of my eye. As I turn my head, there is someone standing at the front of the pallet. I realize I am lying on the pallet in a dense coniferous forest, sounds of the forest all around me. The woman standing before me is wearing a ritualistic costume. The costume is filled with metal pendants. The air around her vibrates, she begins to drum, drum, drum and in her song can be heard sounds imitating the howling of the wolf, and the voices of other animals. The sounds are from in front of me, next to me, behind me, they are everywhere. I am frightened.

Chapter 24
The Man in the Overcoat

Mad Frankie, unknown place, alternate time, chatting with Kurt Gödel:

So here I am, sitting outdoors around a beautified patina cold-rolled steel table in a red Adirondack chair, adorning a circular bluestone patio sitting atop a square mesa, surrounded on three sides by a luxurious growth of black bamboo. All this reached by a set of bluestone steps shaped into isosceles triangles. The work had to be by Rothe & Company, as the top step is embellished with an eagle and the initials E. J. R. Jr., son of the owner, lost in an accident.

I'm contently sipping tea from an 18th-century Chinese export coral and puce porcelain tea service. My cup just filled by a lovely Asian woman, missing the ring finger of her right hand. The flaw that makes perfection. Two other men at the table are both looking at me, waiting for an answer to a question asked 40 years from now.

I recognize Gilhooley, who is trying to look like he is following the drift but is clueless. I can't blame him, I guess, but I'm just as clueless. I'm dressed in a Gieves & Hawkes RAF-blue lightweight textured wool suit with a seersucker tailored-fit shirt and an embroidered paisley silk Jacquard tie. Gilhooley is dressed like he just returned from a camping trip.

The sun is quite low but the temperature is still late-summer warm. What's interesting is the third gentleman is dressed in an out-of-date dark suit, white French-cuff shirt, dark-maroon tie, silver tie clasp, matching cuff links, all topped off with a heavyweight wool top coat and scarf.

"No," I say, "I don't believe it is."

Gilhooley nods, the man in the overcoat smiles, picks up his teacup, smells the tea, and sets the cup back on its saucer. He adjusts his tortoiseshell glasses and says, "Then there is no way to explain the afternoon tea."

"Why do you say that?" I ask.

"Because you two gentlemen are from your present, sitting at a table in my present and your past. Have you come here to kill me?"

133

Somehow, I don't know how, I know he is right but I have no rec-
ollection of any such events. I believe I have known the professor for
years and I have to state that fact.

"No, I say, this is our usual afternoon tea, I have known you for
years."

He smiles. "Finnegan and Gilhooley sitting at a table with me dis-
cussing time and causation in a universe you both believe has no observ-
able justification. There is a fundamental contradiction in your belief
system: I have never seen either of you until I sat down at this table."

Gilhooley lets out a short laugh and says, "Professor, is it possible
that all this is just a figment of Finnegan's, if that is who he really is,
imagination? Travel into our own past contains violations of causality,
therefore is it not true that this is just a dream?"

"Quite possible, sir, that all this is an illusion, but another possibility is that your time travel involves not a single branch but multiple
branches, perhaps an uncountably infinite number of branches. This tea
is just one possibility, our conversation may be just an unrealized moment. Have you come here to kill me?"

My turn to laugh. "Why do you keep asking that question?"

"Because," he says, "you have murder's eyes."

With that Gilhooley stands up. "Gentlemen, let's explore that more
in our next session. That's all the time we have for today."

I look up at the two men dressed in white, taking each of us gently
by an arm, guiding us to our rooms. I lie down on my bed after the aide
removes my slippers. I'm dressed in robin's-egg-blue pajamas. I close
my eyes.

Giuseppe, Chinatown, New York, 1906:

I jerk forward, the wooden pallet creaks, my eyes take in the dim surroundings of Wu's Bath Emporium. I draw the pipe close, like it is the
only lover I'll ever know.

Chapter 25
Make the World Go Away

Mad Frankie, Safe House, Tunis, Tunisia, no date:

We are both kneeling on a bed of soft bamboo sheets in a pale green, the tears are running down my cheeks, my eyes beginning to bulge, sweat dotting my forehead. My tattooed right arm hanging limp at my side. My left arm is holding the rope. I can smell her Jo Malone Velvet Rose & Oud Cologne, feel her warm breath on my right ear, the sharp points of the nipples topping her breasts, slippery from the heat, pressed into my back. I am a gasper.

She tightens the rope around my neck with another twist. This strangulation game played by my partner is purely erotic. Nothing else matters to her but bringing me to the edge of death then orgasm. Who am I to argue with her premise. She, being a very smart mathematician of Syrian descent, coal-black, short-cropped hair with green eyes.

I am almost there, that point between this life and death, the moment when I enter a lucid, semi-hallucinogenic state, becoming hypoxic. Tighter, my love, almost, I'm thinking. Suddenly it's here, the moment I can see the door open, the moment I can step through and make this world go away.

Chapter 26
A Love Letter

Giuseppe, Chinatown, New York, 1906:

Dimly aware of my surroundings, I soon realize I am back on a pallet in Wu's Bath Emporium. I gaze across the candles and recognize the woman on the next pallet. It's Jeannie, the hop smoke framing her golden hair, a look of fleeting contentment on her face. Someone is tugging at my arm, it's the young Chinese woman who prepares my pipe. She is raising her hands as if she wants me to get up. Get up? My body is nailed to this pallet.

Finally I hear Wu's voice. "Sorry, you have visitor, please come. She is waiting, very important."

I manage to sit up and immediately regret the movement. My head is throbbing, being a common condition after indulging. I shake it off and stand. Christ, I feel slightly nauseous, my mind is blank, my suit rumpled, never felt better, tip-fucking-top. I stumble out into the low light of the entrance room of the bath. The light seems like a lighting strike, so I shield my eyes and finally recognize the woman sitting on the rosewood bench. It's my neighbour, a fellow Mancunian, Mrs. McShane. She is wringing her hands.

I feel a sense of shame that, whatever brought her here, she has to sit in this place and wait for someone to crawl out of an opium den.

I offer an apology. "Mrs. McShane, I am sorry you have to wait for me in this place."

"No, Mr. Finnegan, I am so sorry that I have to come to you with my problems. Ian, in the grave a little over a year, forgive me, but I needed someone I can trust."

"Anything I can do, Mrs. McShane, I will, just ask." I sit down next to her on the bench.

"It is truly terrible but I can hold it in no longer. I know our neighbour Mr. Rosen has been touching Margret and her being only 10." She begins to tear up, pulling out a lace handkerchief and wiping her eyes, which are already red. I sit back dumfounded. Rosen seemed a decent sort.

"Are you sure, Mrs. McShane? Please, I am not doubting you, but are you sure?"

She nods. "There was blood and she cried most of the night; she told me what happened in his place." She starts to weep.

"Go home, Mrs. McShane, avoid Rosen. I will deal with it."

"Thank you, Mr. Finnegan, I just didn't know where to turn."

She gets up and leaves Wu's. Damn, I need a drink. I nod to Wu, who is looking concerned, and make my way over to McGinnity's.

It is a little early for the usual crowd, but I spot Tony at the bar and move over to stand next to him.

He turns his head and smiles. *"Ciao amico, stai bene?"* Without asking, Armando places a Martinez in front of me. I nod thanks. He senses some business so he moves away.

"Pura malvagità. You know my next-door neighbour, Mrs. McShane? She just let me know that she believes the neighbour across the hall has molested her 10-year-old daughter. A Jewish tailor, name of Simon Rosen. What the hell can I do?"

"Niente. Devi dirlo alla signora Goldstein."

"English, Tony. I cannot think in another language right now."

Tony gives me a sad smile. *"Amico mio, l'italiano è il linguaggio più adatto alla vendetta.* English for now. Nothing. You must tell Mrs. Goldstein. I do not know this man, he may have connections. Mrs. Goldstein will know."

"Thanks, Tony, you're right. I have to talk with her." I motion to Armando, who looks up at me,

"Armando, un amaro per il mio amico, per favore."

I down my Martinez and turn, and guess who is seated at a table not 20 feet away, the stately Mrs. Goldstein. Slight problem, though: Max is with her and the Kid looks none too happy. I slowly walk over, keeping my hands in plain view.

As I reach the table, Mrs. Goldstein looks up and smiles at me. "Why, it's Mr. Finnegan, how are you tonight?"

"Fine, and I hope you are well. I was wondering if I might have a word?" All the while the Kid is eyeing me like I just took his last kreplach.

Still smiling she says, "Of course, please have a seat. I see your friend Anthony is here tonight." I notice Max sits up a little straighter.

I sit. Now…how to let her know? Dive right in, Finnegan. "Mrs. Goldstein, you know a tenant of yours name of Mrs. McShane?"

"Yes, her husband was killed in a terrible accident at the docks. I know you have helped her, and let me tell you I have done the same. Her with the adorable little girl."

"Well, Mrs. Goldstein, this concerns her and the neighbour across the hall, Mr. Rosen."

Mrs. Goldstein moves back in her chair. "I hope he has not been bothering Mrs. McShane, him being a bachelor and all."

Here it comes, Giuseppe, hold on to your hat. "The problem is not with Mrs. McShane and Mr. Rosen, it is between Mr. Rosen and her child, Margret."

Silence, then the Kid speaks. "What kind of trouble, Finnegan?"

I look at the Kid because I cannot bear to see Mrs. Goldstein's face when I say it. "He has molested the child."

The Kid's face grows hard. He turns toward Mrs. Goldstein and says, "*Rosen, er iz a toyt mentsh.*"

Mrs. Goldstein is pale, very pale. The Kid speaks again, this time one word. I understand the Yiddish and I know it's not good. "*Toyt.*"

Mrs. Goldstein holds up a hand. "Is this possible, Mr. Finnegan? A 10-year-old girl in my building?"

"I am asking you for a favour, Mrs. Goldstein, please let me handle it. Nothing will touch you or the building, my word."

Mrs. Goldstein looks over at the Kid. He slowly nods but has a few words to say to Mrs. Goldstein. "*Er beser nisht fak es aroyf.*" In other words, he'd better not fuck this up…

"Maximillian, your language, it is not necessary." Mrs. Goldstein looks at me, her eyes suddenly very hard. "Very well, Mr. Finnegan, perhaps someday you will do me a favour."

"Thank you and good night, Mrs. Goldstein, good night to you, Maximillian."

The Kid actually smiles. I head back to the bar and stand next to Tony. Armando comes over for my order but instead puts his hand over mine and speaks to me in Italian. "*È sulla tua anima. Chiedi perdono, più tardi.*" It's on your soul. Ask for forgiveness later.

Indeed Armando, indeed.

I turn to Tony. "Tony, I can do this myself."

Tony answers, *"Sono in debito con te, amico mio."*

I am touched; we will do this thing together.

I voice the plan. "Tomorrow night when three stars appear in the sky, we will act. His fate will be sealed at the end of Shabbat." Tony just shrugs.

Tony and I have been walking around Allen Street for 20 minutes, when people start to exit Ajutarul Bukarester Handwerker Congregation located at 192 Allen Street. I spot Rosen. He's not an imposing figure.

The plan is to grab Rosen and take him to an empty apartment Tony's family rents on Allen Street. We wait for a dark spot then step up on either side of Rosen. He looks frightened and says, "I have no money, please."

Tony responds, *"Sta zitto, Sei fica."* Shut up, you cunt.

Rosen slumps slightly and if it is possible looks more frightened.

I let him in on the score. "If you want to live, be quiet and walk with us."

He complies. We reach the building, Tony lets us in the front door, we climb the three flights of stairs to apartment 32, Tony opens the door, and we enter the almost bare apartment. Tony puts a gun to Rosen's head, forcing him onto a straight-backed kitchen chair. Rosen is scared stiff mainly because he cannot figure out what we want with a Hungarian tailor, so I let him in on the secret. "Rosen, tell us about Margret."

He looks at me blankly at first but then I see recognition but he makes a first attempt at deception. "I don't know any Margret."

I slap him so hard he tumbles off the chair. Tony yanks him back up by his jacket onto the chair.

"Tell us about Margret."

"Do you mean the girl from across the hall?"

I slap him off the chair again. He begins to silently weep. Tony yanks him back up by his jacket onto the chair.

"That's for the first lie. Lie again and we are going to be very upset and I do things I regret when I'm upset."

Rosen pulls himself together. "What has that little bitch been saying about me?"

I slap him off the chair again. He balls up on the floor; I kick him hard in the ribs. He yelps and holds up his hands.

"This is wrong, he says, I've been kind to that mick family."

I kick him again. I nod to Tony who, once again, drags him back onto the chair.

"Listen, you cunt, they're English and the next words out of your mouth better be what we already know or I promise you will die right now."

Rosen starts to weep. I could give a fuck. The atmosphere in the room changes to a deep vibration of dread. There is murder in my eyes. Rosen is sobbing, "Lies, it's all lies, I've been nothing but kind to them."

I lean down and speak in a very low, emotionless voice, "Who, Rosen. Say it, say her name."

He looks at me, eyes of hate, and spits out her name. "Margret," he snarls. "Margret, the ungrateful little bitch."

Rage—my knife is out, rage—he's a dead man. The moment is frozen, the room grows dim.

I am in a forest, a woman appears. The same woman frequently in my dreams. She pierces her breast, she removes her head and holds it, she makes bird sounds, wolf sounds, bear sounds, reindeer sounds, sounds of swollen rivers, sounds of the wind through the conifers, sounds of ice cracking on a river, sounds of the dawn of the first day, sounds of the twilight of the last night. She shouts at me, she embraces me, she guards me, she will fight to the death for me.

She lifts her arm and points to a path at the opposite side of the clearing. Suddenly the light is blinding. The light is warmth. The light is love. The light is devotion. The light is surrender. I feel the pull away from the light. The demons are locked in a battle with my female protector. She wills me forward to the light.

I am holding the knife to Rosen's throat. I stand, the rage is quenched. I turn and walk out of the apartment without a word. Two stairs down, I hear a single gunshot.

I love the Supreme because I came from Her. I devote myself to the Supreme because I wish to go back to Her. I surrender myself to the Supreme because she lives in me and I in Her.

Chapter 27
Holding You

Giuseppe, Chinatown, New York, 1906:

Cold, cold, cold forest, the conifer branches bent low by the weight of the pure white snow. I know I'm on a pallet in Wu's Bath Emporium, so this is a dream; is this a vision? Is this the past? Is this the future?

A low frequency begins in the forest floor, I can feel it through my boots. Getting stronger, penetrating my shins, thighs, hips. Spirit-awakening vibrations.

Suddenly I hear her voice from behind me, right to the centre of my skull. Sounds of all there is, was, will be. The primordial drone of all the uncountably infinite worlds. My body is several feet above the pine-needled floor.

It is too beautiful to bear, too painful to hear. We are not the author of our lives. It is the 32 paths of Kabbalah, the 72 names of G_D, the Alpha and Omega.

She appears angry, protective, loving. The sounds intensify, becoming deafening; it is the music of eternity, the sounds of existence. It contains all things. I am her, she is me. The Divine in us all and yet I turn to the darkness.

She sends me a paradox. A single mother who deeply loves her only daughter. She embraces me, holds me, and for a moment I see the path illuminated. Then she takes it away and I am lost. Yet my dream woman beckons, lovingly, she envelops me as I lay my head on her breast.

I jerk awake, the wooden pallet creaks, I hug the pipe to me but the feel of her embrace remains.

Chapter 28
The Beauty of Darkness

Mad Frankie, artist's loft, present time:

I am vulnerable. Heightened receptors of feminine energy lead me down paths of light and darkness. If I am totally honest with myself, I'd admit that I crave the allure of those standing in the shadows. Is it possible that those in Sanskrit called Shuddha, pure, appear in twilight? That's how this all started.

The shaman embodied herself in an earthly woman of the light. Her touch healing, the path illuminated. So, not to be outdone, the demons delivered a soul in torment, knowing full well I could not resist. Among the small crowd, she stood off to the side, standing in semi-darkness looking so lost.

What better connection—two people, one empty and battered from battle, one loss after another, the other just hurt.

As I approach her, I get a weak smile and glassy eyes. There is justice in that. She reaches out her hand with a wrist adorned with a thin scarlet string, her totem, a way to ward off misfortune brought about by the evil eye. She says, "I was watching you looking at her paintings. Now that you are close, I see you have tears in your eyes. It is a painful fucking world, is it not?"

I engage her hand with mine and reply, "It has just about taken all I can give."

She smiles at me, a beautiful transformation to the tender, the loving.

She pulls my hand closer and speaks into my good ear. "I have a studio one floor down, come and see how my visions affect you."

There is not a moment of hesitation; I am compelled to follow. We walk down one flight encased in a dimly lit staircase, painted a dull grey. After a short walk halfway down the hallway, she opens her studio door. Inside two rows of track lighting illuminate a number of large canvases.

The work is abstract, not my favorite, but I am surprised by the vibrant, warm colors, drawing me into a pleasant mandala. The angle of the tracks leaves a portion of the center of the studio in shadow. She leads me to a steel table lit by a small LED light. Then she turns and looks me in the eyes, and I know she has no doubts. She says, "You use, don't you? Nice pinned pupils, do you see me?"

I just fucking nod. This is dangerous. I know full well where this is going. Before I know it, she is holding a small bag with an off-white substance. That smile again. "Cut pretty heavy but it will do. Please join me. I hate to get loaded alone."

I almost take the bag, but at the last second my arm drops down. I explain the reality of the situation. "I'll stay but I'm already loaded and this mix is not what the Doctor would advise."

She gives a small laugh and takes two hits. Drops the bag on the steel table, sits down on the floor beneath a canvas of swirling colors, which draw you into her world. I sit down on the floor opposite her, her upper body in light with me cast in shadow and this only because she didn't want to get loaded alone.

Chapter 29
This Is Your Life

Mad Frankie, alternate time, both sides of the flipped coin:

Gentle, gentle lilting breeze caresses my face, those blue jays chatting again. Far-off rumble of sky-blue waves rolling toward shore. I open my eyes and watch the batik shades flap in the same breeze. Someone in the yard is strumming a ukulele. The smell of a grilling breakfast fish reaches my nose. She must be up already. I decide to soak in more of the early morning before I get up. Have I known more happiness? My writing has suffered but how can I complain, it might still come.

The bed moves and I turn my head as her hair envelops me in her citrus scent. I feel her warm breath on my ear. "You could lie in bed or get up and have coffee, eggs, and spicy grilled fish."

I bring my lips close to her cheek. "I should get some work done today, breakfast, and then tackle that problematic chapter. My characters are not cooperating."

She laughs. "That's because you are too nice to them."

I put my hands on her bare back, lithe but yet so strong. "I have no control over them, they keep making the right choices."

She looks me in the eyes. "Really, they are independent, free-willed individuals who are going about living their lives."

I nod. "Yes, the bastards defy me at every turn. I cannot write any tears or misery. Their lives are just too wonderful."

She caresses my face. "Darling, your analyst needs to be more involved in this whole thing. Does he know that your characters are so unruly?"

"If he does he won't say anything because he thinks all this writing is good for my soul. He should know."

"Let's eat." She begins to get up but I pull her back down just to inhale a little more of her scent. So happy to wake up with her in my arms, my life.

Hot, hot lilting breeze rolls the sweat off my face, those blue jays chatting again. Far-off rumble of black boxcars rolling toward market.

I open my eyes and watch the ripped shades flap in the same breeze. Someone in the yard is coughing up phlegm. The smell of leftover, fried fish reaches my nose. She must be up already. I am having trouble getting my legs to move this morning, so how can I get up? Have I known less happiness? My writing has flourished, so how can I complain.

The bed moves and I turn my head as her hair envelops me in her chemical scent. I feel her warm breath on my ear. "You could lie in bed and I'll fix us a pickup."

I bring my lips close to her cheek. "I can get some work done today, pickup, and then tackle that next chapter, my characters have will but fear me."

She laughs. "That's because you are a harsh task master."

I put my hands on her bare arms, so thin, so damaged. "I have no control over them, they are the ones who are fucking up."

She looks me in the eyes, reflecting her own pinned pupils. "Really, they are independent, free-willed individuals who are going about living their lives."

I nod. "Yes, the bastards defy me at every turn. I cannot write any happiness. Their lives are just too miserable."

She caresses my face. "Darling, your analyst needs to be more involved in this whole thing. Does he know that your characters are so unruly?"

"If he does he won't say anything because he thinks all this writing is good for my soul. He should know."

"Let's get loaded." She begins to get up but I pull her back down just to inhale a little more of her chemical scent. So scared to wake up with her in my arms, my life.

Chapter 30
Quantum Immortality

Mad Frankie, many bars, many realities, chatting with Hugh:

So there I am sitting in a pretentious bar with a studious-looking guy next to me waiting for a reply to his question. In front of us stands a rather tall bartender looking quite pleased, having just placed two small glasses of clear liquid in front of us. Off to my left someone knocks over a glass and it shatters, mixing shards of glass with liquid, over a small area of the bar. Behind me is a loud guffaw. To our right, a man and a rather attractive redhead are conversing in a language I do not understand.

I look at the studious guy with a questioning look on my face. He asks another question. "Do you speak English?"

"Yes, yes of course," I answer.

Evidently he repeats his first question. "Do you like aquavit?"

I am not sure I ever heard of it and do not know what he is talking about.

He plows on, "The drink in front of you, do you like it?"

I look down at the glass, raise it to my lips, and take a small sip. God, caraway seeds. I hate caraway seeds. I put the glass down, forcing myself to swallow the vile stuff. I give him my answer as he is throwing his back. "No, not really, I hate caraway seeds."

He meets my eyes and says, "Well, let me postulate that there is a world in which you love aquavit, but according to Bohr and his buddies, the reaction you had to aquavit is the only possible one. That the wave function has already collapsed. Of course, their theory has nothing to do with two guys entering a bar but only concerns itself with the microscopic universe and nothing else. I believe there is no collapse, only paths of uncountably infinite possibilities."

So there I am sitting in a pretentious bar with a studious-looking guy next to me waiting for a reply to his question. In front of us stands a rather chubby bartender looking quite pleased, having just placed two small glasses of clear liquid in front of us. Off to my left someone knocks over a glass, spilling the liquid over a small area of the bar. Behind me someone sneezes. To our right, two men are conversing in a language I do not understand.

I look at the studious guy with a questioning look on my face. He asks another question. "Do you speak English?"

"Yes, yes of course," I answer.

Evidently he repeats his first question. "Do you like aquavit?"

I am not sure I ever heard of it and do not know what he is talking about.

He plows on, "The drink in front of you, do you like it?"

I look down at the glass, raise it to my lips, and take a small sip. God, caraway seeds. I hate caraway seeds. I put the glass down, forcing myself to swallow the vile stuff. I give him my answer as he is throwing his back. "No, not really, I hate caraway seeds."

He meets my eyes and says, "Well, let me postulate that there is a world in which you love aquavit, but according to Bohr and his buddies, the reaction you had to aquavit is the only possible one. That the wave function has already collapsed. Of course, their theory has nothing to do with two guys entering a bar but only concerns itself with the microscopic universe and nothing else. I believe there is no collapse, only paths of uncountably infinite possibilities."

So there I am sitting in a pleasant bar with a studious-looking guy next to me waiting for a reply to his question. In front of us stands a rather young bartender looking quite pleased, having just placed two small glasses of clear liquid in front of us. Off to my left someone knocks over an empty glass, behind me someone coughs. To our right, a man is reading a newspaper in a language I do not recognize.

I look at the studious guy with a questioning look on my face. He asks another question. "Do you speak English?"

"Yes, yes of course," I answer.

Evidently he repeats his first question. "Do you like aquavit?"

I am not sure I ever heard of it and do not know what he is talking about.

He plows on, "The drink in front of you, do you like it?"

I look down at the glass, raise it to my lips, and take a small sip. God, caraway seeds. I hate caraway seeds. I put the glass down, forcing myself to swallow the vile stuff. I give him my answer as he is throwing his back. "No, not really, I hate caraway seeds."

He meets my eyes and says, "Well, let me postulate that there is a world in which you love aquavit, but according to Bohr and his buddies, the reaction you had to aquavit is the only possible one. That the wave function has already collapsed. Of course, their theory has nothing to do with two guys entering a bar but only concerns itself with the microscopic universe and nothing else. I believe there is no collapse, only paths of uncountably infinite possibilities."

So there I am sitting in a dimly lit bar with a studious-looking guy next to me waiting for a reply to his question. In front of us stands a rather decrepit bartender looking quite pleased, having just placed two small glasses of clear liquid in front of us. Off to my left someone raises an empty glass, there is no one behind us. To our right, a man is sitting alone, staring at his drink.

I look at the studious guy with a questioning look on my face. He asks another question. "Do you speak English?"

"Yes, yes of course," I answer.

Evidently he repeats his first question. "Do you like aquavit?"

He plows on, "The drink in front of you, do you like it?"

I look down at the glass, raise it to my lips, and throw it back. First time, caraway seeds. Not my favorite but it's OK. I put the glass down, swallowing the warming liquid. I give him my answer as he is throwing his back. "It's OK."

He meets my eyes and says, "Well, let me postulate that there is a world in which you love aquavit, but according to Bohr and his buddies, the reaction you had to aquavit is the only possible one. That the wave function has already collapsed. Of course, their theory has nothing to do with two guys entering a bar but only concerns itself with the microscopic universe and nothing else. I believe there is no collapse, only paths of uncountably infinite possibilities."

So there I am sitting in a Danish Modern design bar with a studious-looking guy next to me waiting for a reply to his question. In front of us stand rows and rows of bottles, behind which is a large mirror. The bar is empty.

I look at the studious guy with a questioning look on my face. He asks another question. "Do you speak English?"

"Yes, yes of course," I answer.

Evidently he repeats his first question. "Do you like aquavit?"

He plows on, "The drink in front of you, do you like it?"

I look down at the glass, raise it to my lips, and throw it back. A caraway seed aquavit. "I love it."

He meets my eyes and says, "Well, let me postulate that there is a world in which you hate aquavit, but according to Bohr and his buddies, the reaction you had to aquavit is the only possible one. That the wave function has already collapsed. Of course, their theory has nothing to do with two guys entering a bar but only concerns itself with the microscopic universe and nothing else. I believe there is no collapse, only paths of uncountably infinite possibilities."

Occam's razor rules against a plethora of unobservable universes, but what the fuck did Occam know.

Chapter 31
Boo How Doy

"Judgment Day is inevitable."

~From *Terminator 3: Rise of the Machines*

Giuseppe, Chinatown, 1906:

My eyes open of their own will. I am back on the wooden pallet in Wu's Bath Emporium. Someone is standing next to the pallet; it is Wu, and he is sweating. Wu never sweats. He is wringing his hands. Wu doesn't worry about anything. And Wu hardly ever speaks but this time he says, "Man in front, he wants to speak with you. A dangerous man, Mr. Finnegan, a very dangerous man. No highbinder, he's *boo how doy*. Maybe he is here to wash your body, understand? Finnegan, I translate to you what this man has to say. We go to my office. I cannot help you. I am sorry but I cannot, it is Tong business."

We enter Wu's windowless, small office. The Tong member is already sitting in Wu's chair. I don't recognize him. He is well dressed in wide-brimmed black hat, black jacket cut in mandarin style, black trousers. He has a long scar running from his left ear to his jawline and the coal-black eyes of generations of *boo how doy*.

He nods to Wu and begins to speak slowly in the local dialect. The phrase I recognize is *Shāshǒu jí yìngyòng*, 杀手级用. Basically he is saying I am a killer. I realize he must be talking about the Old Bastard. A chill runs through my body. My life hangs in the balance. At first Wu looks relieved, but as each phase is spoken he looks less satisfied. Finally he turns to me. "He say you murdered a Tong courier. Why?"

I say, "Yes, yes I did. He made my friend lose face in his place of business and he cursed my mother, so I stabbed him in a lot off 23rd Street."

My best shot, I'm sure this is common knowledge. I'm getting the cold-eye stare. A slight smile, very slight, then he speaks. Wu listens, his face blank. When the man finishes, Wu turns to me. "He say, justified but no matter. Tong business, you must pay debt but you are lucky, not with your life."

I visibly relax but Wu holds up his arm. "Wait, Mr. Finnegan. The Tong world is harsh, here is the payment he requests, you must kill a *ji*, a woman who works the bars and pays no tribute. You know her, Mr. Finnegan—Jeannie, she has blond hair. You must do it before next night."

I look at the man's stone face. They know full well she is a friend of mine. My guts turn to water. If I refuse, I am dead man. If I do it, I might as well be a dead man. This is true Chinese justice. Spare my life and let me live in agony and all over a little back and front. My time is running out so I better speak if I want to keep my Brighton Rock.

I look at Wu. "Agreed."

With that the *boo how doy* stands and lays a gun on the table. The gun I'm to use and then toss.

He begins to leave but has one last order. "Shoot *yīndao*."

He turns and walks out. Wu is looking pale. I know, I know why. More punishment, because I trespassed on Tong business. I am ordered to shoot her in her genitals. Wu and I stare at the gun. I slowly lay my head on Wu's desk but not before I see a tear in Wu's eye. After a few moments of silence, I get up, leave Wu's office without a word because there are no words.

I am back in the den on my pallet. The young Chinese woman hands me a readied pipe. How long can I chase the dragon? Well, tonight for sure. I hope in my dreams there will be an answer to this hell. Long pull, long pull, numbness in my legs but I still feel the gun in my waistband. I turn my head.

It's Jeannie on the next pallet, her legs pulled up and her arms pulled in, just like a little girl in her bed at home. I turn back. Here it is Finnegan, you fuckin' cunt. I have an idea: pull the gun and put one in your watch and chain. The whole scene fades.

I am walking down a dimly lit staircase, painted a dull grey. After a short walk halfway down the hallway, a woman opens a door. Inside two rows of electric lighting illuminate a number of large canvases.

The work is abstract, not recognizable, but I am surprised by the vibrant, warm colours, drawing me into a pleasant mandala. The angle of the lights leaves a portion of the centre of the studio in shadow. She leads me to a steel table lit by a small red light. Then she turns and looks me in the eyes, and I know she has no doubts. She says, "You use, don't you? Nice pinned pupils, do you see me?"

I just fucking nod. This is dangerous. I know full well where this is going, what the fuck is Jeannie talking about. Before I know it, she is holding a small packet with a pure white substance. That smile again. "Cut pretty heavy but it will do. Please join me. I hate to get loaded alone."

I almost take the packet, but at the last second my arm drops down. I explain the reality of the situation. "I'll stay but I'm already loaded and this mix is not what the Doctor would advise."

She gives a small laugh and takes two hits. Drops the bag on the steel table, sits down on the floor beneath a canvas of swirling colours, which draw you into her world. I sit down on the floor opposite her, her upper body in light with me cast in shadow and this only because I didn't want to leave Jeannie alone.

The Divine is in us all and yet I turn to the darkness. I am standing on a street. Looking at local produce, when I hear her voice say, "You made it."

I turn and see Jeannie, breaking sunlight in her hair, she slides into my arms, holding me against all there is. I say, "I'm so happy to see you." My words break the embrace. The scene fades.

I am back on the pallet in Wu's. I turn my head and see Jeannie is gone. I have about 10 hours before one of us is dead. Who I am I to ask the Divine to show me a path? Do I have any means to make that connection? My eyes close with the unbearable heaviness of it, of the soul-crushing effects of it. I beg for the path illuminated. The dragon is so powerful, so beautiful. I lurk around the edges of darkness, the edges of oblivion. Years of devotion and she is gone. A hug that lasted a moment, gone. Sometimes all you get is a moment, or so it seems.

Mad Frankie, present time, in the woods:

I shake out two Gabapentin 300 mg into my hand and carry them into the kitchen, washing them down with a pull of milk. I close the refrigerator door, I look at my reflection in the stainless steel. Maybe this whole string has been played out. Maybe the words will not clear a path. Have I been fooling myself? As usual I need to occupy myself until the pills shut my mind up. If only the memories would fade, would end. The good ones, the bad ones, just an avalanche of despair. Dizzy, can you hear me? Dizzy, maybe you are in your study typing away or are you drawing? Can you make it stop? I close my eyes.

Giuseppe, dreaming, Hong Kong, before 1906:

I am back in Hong Kong. Back in my room. Back with Dizzy. "I want you to go back, back to the dream of the bamboo hut and the old man on the mat, he can help you out of this," he says.

I'm not so sure and answer, "The old man who spoke of the future, my future, but it was no dream. It happened just as I described it. I will meet a woman, the look in her eyes will show me my true path."

Giuseppe, Chinatown, New York, 1906:

Listen, there is no way I am going to kill that young lady, no way. All she's been through, all those paths that lead her here. Finnegan, you are not going to write the ending. So what are my chances? Slim to none. No one can help. No one in their right mind would even consider helping. I can think of one very off-the-board bet, and I think I can find him at McGinnity's. I drag myself out the door. See the *boo how doy* watching. Always watching, right up until the time they bury a hatchet with a red ribbon in your back.

I push open the doors of McGinnity's Tavern, which is what he calls it now. I scan the crowd. A hand grips my heart: I see Jeannie at a table with a swell. How many times, Jeannie? How many times have I warned you about the Tong. How many times have you told me you are too small a fish to bother with. God, nothing is overlooked by the Tong. This is their world, they allow us to breathe for free. Maybe that will change.

The room feels like home. McGinnity in his usual spot, Armando behind the bar, Kid Twist having a seltzer, David playing a mournful tune on his cornet, the red door and behind it Butcher Larsson, the best fuckin' sawbones I ever met. I walk further into the large barroom, me and my Lady Bristol. Looking for the one person, the only one, who can help me. There he is, standing sideways to the room so he can keep one eye out. The glass of Old Bushmills in front of him, that cunt, Gilhooley.

I walk causally over to the bar and stand next to Kid Twist. McGinnity nods, Armando gives a slight smile and wink, the Kid looks sideways at me and says, *"Fayn arbet mit az baren. Er iz in di taykh, neyn balebatisheh yiden. Tony iz a mentsh ver halt zeyn vort."*

I guess the message: The job is done, he is in the river, Tony is a man who keeps his word.

The Kid smiles and translates, "The fuck went for a swim." I nod. Why the Kid insists on speaking to me in Yiddish I have no idea, but I take it as a compliment. The Kid nods and pushes off the bar and out the door. I gesture to Armando to refill Gilhooley's glass, which he does while jerking his head toward me. Gilhooley raises his glass to me and empties it and sets it down like it's his grandmother's crystal. He walks over to me and leans on the bar. I lean in and speak in a church voice, "It's a favour I be asking of you, Gilhooley."

He replies without looking up, "I'm in your debt, Finnegan, you fuckin' know that. Name it."

I begin, "It looks like I may be out of print. I crossed the Hip Sings. I done in someone you know, the Old Bastard. I may be off the hook, but I have to do their bidding and it ain't pretty."

Gilhooley gives no indication he gives a fuck one way or the other, but he thinks about it for a few seconds then says, "I heard about the Old Bastard, didn't know it was you. Whatever it is they want you to do, I take it you are not keen?"

I shake my head. "I am not keen."

Gilhooley raises a finger to Armando. He looks over at us and I nod. Seconds later an Old Bushmills and a Martinez hit the bar in front of us. Armando looks me in the eye and says, *"Che Dio ti aiuti."* He knows, and it's all anyone can ask for.

Just then David starts to play the "The Rose of Mooncoin." Gilhooley and I look at each other, turn back to our drinks, both thinking about our youth and things never to be again.

After a while Gilhooley looks up and says, "Let's go see if we can satisfy the Hip Sings."

He turns and heads for the door. I follow him out two doors down to a small Chinese herbal shop with a sign above depicting a beautiful crane at the edge of a pond. We go into the shop. It is dimly lit. Gilhooley beckons me to follow him to the back of the shop, where a few candles are burning in the corner in front of a small reed mat. The mat is occupied by a very frail-looking old man. The old man's eyes open and he beckons me closer. I stop in front of his mat. He pushes both hands down. Sit. I sit.

He speaks. "Many years ago I learned your language at a young age, as my father was involved with negotiations between English trading companies. I was called to help maintain some face during and at the end of the second opium war; but after, because of the disastrous defeat of the Qing army, the death of the Emperor, and the burning of the summer palace, we had nothing with which to bargain. Now all that is left is rebellion. From the East it will come but it will not restore the Ming."

I look at him. How many times am I going to hear this story? An old man, how is an old man going to appease the Tong?

He continues, "You seek the help of the departed. The spirits who aid those in trouble. What have you to offer? Do you come out of love, out of devotion, to surrender who you are?"

"I have nothing to offer. I cheated myself like I knew, all along, I would. I come for the girl, she doesn't deserve to die." The old shaman —that what he is, I realize now—says, "Come follow me, this is but one moment, one life, look." With that we leave the small shop.

I am alone on a windswept hillside. There is a man standing before me, dressed in a severely cut dark-grey suit. The jacket has a high clerical-looking collar and is buttoned all the way to his pale, thin neck. His chest has an emblem of a light red rose, in the centre of which is a red heart displaying a yellow cross. The rosy cross, what does this mean and what is this place?

The man speaks. "We are in total preparedness. Your word is all we await."

I realize I am in the same outfit. I know what I'm going to say, even if it makes no sense. "It is the final event, mankind is finished on this planet." I point to the man standing in from of me. "It is up to you machines to continue the brotherhood." The scene fades, one future.

The horizon is brightly lit in orange-red flaring gas jets. I am huddled in a half-destroyed house. There is a young girl in my arms, maybe 11 years old. She is not frightened, I am. In a few moments, the shock waves will reach us and all that is here will be no more. It is the end of the world. I gently place a small kiss on her head. Judgment Day, one future.

I am standing in a dense coniferous forest, sounds of the forest all around me. I make my way in a direction I can only follow, follow the path. I reach a small clearing, where a woman stands in the centre. She is wearing a ritualistic costume. The costume is filled with metal pendants, each representing different ideas and having its own qualities. In the Yakut language she is an ojun, a shaman. The air around her vibrates, the vibrations of a female ojun. Hostile spirits are scared away by her presence. Her drum beats, beats, beats and in her song can be heard sounds imitating the howling of the wolf, and the voices of other animals, her guardian spirits. The sounds are from in front of me, next to me, behind me, they are everywhere. The ojun spreads her arms; as she does, a shaft of light breaks through the dense canopy, illuminating her, and I am filled with love, I am filled with devotion, I surrender who I am.

Giuseppe, 1906, alternate take:

Walking along Broadway, with the sun shining and feeling quite good, I run into a conservatively dressed Jeannie.
I open my arms and say, "Jeannie, where have you been, I haven't seen you in two months."
She hugs me warmly and looks up at me. "I'm working with Alice Paul—you remember, the woman I met who is at the School of Social Work. We're suffragettes. She persuaded me to work with her to get the vote for women."

I smile and say, "Well, things couldn't get worse, so why not. Don't make yourself a stranger. And Jeannie, I couldn't be happier for you."

I open my eyes. I am sitting front of the shaman. How long have I been under his power? His spirit has taken me to places that exist, do not exist, might exist. The shaman lifts his arms and I stand. Looking around I see Gilhooley, eyes wide.

The shaman speaks. "She is protected, she will not be harmed. You have dreamed it, you have created the past, the present from the future. Go, the one is still waiting."

Chapter 32

Temple Mount
Part 1

HOLY LAND HOTEL
6 Rashid St., Jerusalem, Israel

Nigel, alternate time:

My eyes rest on the Al-Aqsa Mosque, which sits on the far south of the Temple platform and is a magnificent piece of architecture. Its southern exterior walls consist of the upper southern walls of The Temple Mount retaining walls. The Dome of the Rock sits on the western half of the middle of The Temple Mount, probably in the exact location of the Jewish inner Temples.

I never mention Al-Aqsa to her; we never speak of it. It is The Temple Mount, the first temple built almost 1,000 years before the birth of Christ. The place of the Ark, the place where Abraham bound Isaac for sacrifice, and is referred to as Mount Moriah but I do not want to start that argument again.

A voice behind me speaks: "אלוהים של עבודתו."

I turn and look at her, seated on the edge of my bed. She smiles, tilting her head. "You never would learn Hebrew, Nigel. It means God's work."

I shrug and say, "Old Testament God."

The Mossad agent gives me a slight smile and a nod. She is, perhaps, Mossad's deepest-cover agent. There are only hushed whispers in Jerusalem and everywhere else where decisions are made to destroy Israel. Whispers of fear. Whispers of awe. It is my third assignment with her and she still scares me.

I turn back to catch the last light reflecting off Al-Aqsa. We're in the Holy Land Hotel, home to some of the most deadly assassins hiding behind the cover of normalcy. Just like the woman behind me, Healer, Mother, instrument of God's wrath. I know because I revel in it. I am of the Old Testament.

I look back at her on my bed, and she is pointing a gun right at my mid-section, a suppressed HD Standard, the only choice. I look back at the pink-painted sky and speak in her language, "?האל רצון זה האם"

She raises an eyebrow and the barrel of the gun. She decides, in the end, to let me in on it, her voice as soft as the light off The Temple Mount. "I finally created an assignment that I knew you could not refuse. That you would undertake without all your background information. Printout after printout was bypassed because I pointed you to the perfect target. All your wrath of God talk, I knew this was too tasty for you to pass up. To answer your question, is it God's will?"

She tosses the gun on the bed. "They asked me too many times to kill you. Too many times I have obliged. The night has just begun and אין אלוהים של רצונו דוע, I know a great Thai restaurant."

I cannot argue with her logic and I am hungry.

I give her a slight smile and say, "You're right, God's will is unknown but the bastard deserved to die, so it was not a complete loss. If you have decided to be Barbara again, I have one question: Does your restaurant serve Shrimp Pik Pao?"

She looks at me with a grin. "You're a real bastard, Nigel."

Temple Mount
Part 2

I am looking at her across a sea of Thai food dishes. Yes, Thai food can be kosher. No shrimp paste so I have no idea how authentic the food we're eating is, but it tastes good. Extra plus, the waitress is Thai and seems to be enjoying her life in Jerusalem. I am formulating the question in my head. It is one I have been itching to have answered, since I read a stray memo about events occurring in the early-morning hours of November 5, 1991. The memo was simply a list of passengers and crew of the luxury yacht *Lady Ghislaine*. The yacht was owned by Ján Ludvík Hyman Binyamin Hoch, known to most as Robert Maxwell. They were cruising off the Canary Islands on that date, and he was last in contact with the *Lady Ghislaine*'s crew at 4:25 a.m. Later in the morning he was discovered missing, presumed to have fallen overboard.

No further documentation or sources sited.

Exit Strategy

Nigel, alternate time:

The plan was in the works for years. Attend one last meeting and then slip away into the cotton fields of Virginia where old times are soon forgotten. Are there still cotton fields in Virginia? Anyway, she had it all worked out to the last decimal place.

Sell the house using a third party who owed her a favor. Something to do with an extraction from Budapest after a mission went south. Her current persona as a psychiatrist in private practice, she could do in her sleep, simply because how many people in therapy have any real expectation of "getting better."

She informed her patients her office was being redecorated. No one seemed to mind it was on their dollar. She gave them all a new number to call, so as not to disturb the decorators, to make an appointment. These new appointments she would handle in 50-minute—how the hell did that come about?—phone sessions.

The phone number was actually a scrambled land line located in the basement of a Chinese laundry. All calls taken by a Tong member. Another favor connected to the control of the Hong Kong laundry trade. Why Mossad wanted in on the laundry trade in Hong Kong, I could never ascertain.

It took me months to discover the identity of the buyer of her house. In the end I had to work over a part-time art instructor at a local community college. That's not how I normally operate, but this one had a short shelf life. Regardless, I bought the poor sod a new Volvo, which seemed to buy his silence. That and the HD Standard I had pressed against his skull while I showed him those pictures. I may have misplaced the negatives, but he seems happy with the car and the bruises are just a little yellow now.

Listen, before you start to whine about how we got here, try to remember why we went down this path. I mean we're talking about Ancient Soul, for Christ's sake. You must have some idea what's locked up in that head. Read the Omega file. Then we'll see who's so quick to nitpick. Well, maybe nitpick is too trivial a phrase.

I'm seated in an obscenely large leather chair behind an acre of a desk made from Tanzanian African Blackwood, setting off a Tiffany Twelve-Light Lily Table Lamp, next to an expensive-looking blotter upon which lay a Montblanc Heritage Collection Rouge et Noir Special Edition Coral Fountain Pen. I'm in a partner's office of the firm Hungadunga, Hungadunga, Hungadunga & McCormick.

The door opens and in walks Ancient Soul. She sees me and, to the untrained eye, she does not react. I give her my best smile and say, "Here for the closing on your house?"

She sits opposite me and gives me the smile right back like a Venus Williams backhand.

She settles back further into the chair and speaks in an even voice. "It is a damn good plan but somehow I knew I would see you before I exited stage right."

I look at her. "It is a beautiful plan, meticulous, logical, and just about flawlessly executed. I find only one fault: it's with you. In the end you had to trust a few people off the ranch. You had very little choice but we both know amateurs never last, not like professionals."

She nods, then asks the question she has to ask. "My buyer?"

I have to be hard. "The victim of a tragic accident, trying to change a tire this morning on a near-deserted highway. Very poor light conditions. The elderly lady never saw him until it was too late. It happens every day. The poor woman is distraught."

Ancient Soul holds my gaze. "He was a civilian. Just wanted to buy a house on the north shore. The woman, is she Asian, walks with a limp?"

I nod.

"You bastard, you used Kong from your Beijing wet works."

I let that sit, but have to let her know. "Did you think we were going to just let you walk away? With all you know. Did you really believe I would let that happen?" As I finish the last sentence, I raise the HD Standard.

"Yes, yes I did." She stands and quietly walks out over the five-inch-high carpet.

I slowly lay the gun on the desk.

Chapter 33
Anita Would've Listened

Mad Frankie, alternate time:

The ceiling fan is off perpendicular, so the blades are rotating at an odd angle, causing the reflected light from the Isamu Noguchi 14A Floor Lamp to be cast in a flickering pattern on the rose Venetian plastered wall. I say this because I just listed half of the furniture in the room. Venetian plaster walls each a complementary color, dark-cinnamon concrete floors, an Osvaldo Borsani and Arnaldo Pomodoro Brass Enameled Italian Bed, circa 1960s, and a rare modernist table designed by Martin Visser and Joke van der Heyden, manufactured by 't Spectrum-Bergeyk. The table has an aluminum base and a blue cold-painted top with die-cut dot pattern. Placed in the center of the table is a 75-year-old Chinese juniper bonsai in a dark-blue enamel pot. There is a solid line of glass windows at the top of the west-facing wall. The ceiling is fitted with three 96-inch Curb Mount Circular Double Dome Skylights by Wasco.

I lie on a set of blue bamboo sheets with a blue-checked, Blue Ridge Home Fashions cotton down comforter, cast aside. In the night I make my way here, in the dark, I slip through the crowds, here. I wanted to call Dizzy, email Dizzy, text Dizzy, but I came to her. To this minimalist parody, to this. I have too much money to be practical. I do love it so. Oh, I forgot, on a corner shelf, sitting on acoustic foam, a BeoSound 2 wireless speaker playing my iPod playlist of Cambodian 1960s pop music. Chou Malai is singing my favorite, "Love Pillow." All before Phnom Penh became the city of ghosts, in case you've forgotten.

We've been chasing the dragon all night. My head is papier-mâchè. My lungs feel sore from the smoke. There is tin foil all over the floor. We still have half of what we purchased, so this is just a moment before the next barrage. I turn my head to look at her. Her eyes are open, looking up at the skylights. Short-chopped red hair, strong yet lithe body, she truly cares about me enough to let me do things to her which are illegal in many states. May this be love. How is it that I am here in this room, first third of the 21st century, with Anita Berber, when she died about 90 years ago?

Without looking, she stretches her arm and lays her hand over my heart. I have to ask, "Anita, what are we doing here? This is highly improbable. Don't you remember your Berlin apartment, the fall of 1932?"

She smiles. "Of course. You were in love with that guy in the Schiaparelli suit. He had a funny name, Daffy?"

I shake my head. "No, it was Dizzy."

She laughs. "I'll tell you how, but pay attention—this whole scene is an anachronism, a time-slip. Nigel, I'm not really here. None of this is. You are here. You, Mad Frankie, are here because the alternative is not survivable. You are holed up in an isolated house, you are chasing the dragon, alone. You have no one left, no one to talk to. Every attempt to make human contact is foiled. I'm not sure when or where this is, but I'm flattered you brought me back. I loved Berlin in the late '20s and early '30s."

When I don't respond, she adds, "You see, Mad Frankie, you are right. I died in '28 but you, your imagination, brought me back. That is the answer. All the details, all the sets are all rendered because, whatever reality, whatever world you currently occupy, is destroying you." She rolls over and puts her arms around me, laying her head on my chest. "I'm listening, describe my apartment again. In your dreams, take me there, I want to be at Gedendktafel 10707 Berlin-Wilmerdorf, Zahringerstrasse 13, again, to hold you and make the world go away."

I gently brush my hand through her hair. Why is she calling me Mad Frankie? Once more, dear God, once more, my eyes slowly close as I inhale Anita's citrus scent.

Nigel, Berlin, 1932:

I am standing at the entrance to Anita's parlor. It always draws me in, longs to hold me in an embrace like a gentle soporific. As if Le Corbusier has made an offhand remark, there is no sofa in the room. Your eyes first land on the chaise lounge. It has perfect dimensions, with stylized vines, leaf and fruit carved in a three-dimensional style which exemplifies the unique style that could only be Dufrêne. The fabric, a stylized floral motif, complements the bleached white wood. Occupying the perfect location, a Tomaso Buzzi floor lamp with a Murano glass, Alga glass, shade sitting on copper piping. The doctor seats himself in one of a pair of armchairs, in beech and fabric, by Jindrich Halabala. The chairs have a very dynamic appearance, due to the curved base that ends fluently in the armrests. The dark-brown-stained wood contrasts beautifully with the green and off-white fabric upholstery in a scribble pattern.

The doctor pulls out a package of cigarettes and reaches for the Karl Wieden (KW) lighter sitting on a side table, model H259 by Jindrich Halabala, in oak ebonized legs and oak varnished top with exquisite wood-grain details. The floor is covered by an area rug of white wool mixed with grey designed by the Finnish artist Greta Skogster. Pulling you in further and finishing the look and feel of the room, occupying the far wall, is a French Art Deco rosewood cheval mirror by Maurice Dufrêne.

I am about to join the doctor when Gilhooley grabs my arm and motions me to fall behind. He looks around and, for whatever reason, seems to be satisfied he can talk. He turns to face me, looking quite lovely under the entranceway light, a simple chrome pendant with central frosted glass disc by Josef Hurka. He asks, "What year do you think it is?"

Seems an odd question but it has been an odd evening. "Why, it is fall 1932," I say.

"Really," he says, "if that is the case, then once again we are on an aborted timeline."

I'm puzzled. "Why do you say that? Everything is as it should be, I see no anomalies."

He says, "I am going to let you in on a little secret. Do you remember the last iteration? Don't answer—I do, and for similar reasons I know this is an unrealized reality. There is an anomaly here."

"There is no fucking anomaly." I grind that out.

He lets go of my arm and shakes his head. "The past I know, or is it the present? Never mind, it contains the fact that Anita Berber died in November of 1928 from complications brought on by her alcohol and drug consumption. Yet, in this world, she is still very much alive in what you call the fall of 1932."

"Gilhooley, Dizzy, you know why? Why Anita is still alive. I'll tell you, it's because this whole set exists only in my imagination. I'm dreaming this, because somewhere I'm stuck in a hell, maybe the hell of loss, not here, no not here. Think about it. We're just two guys in a bar somewhere, thinking over our next move. I want to stay here, damn it, I'm not going back until I can no longer create any viable alternatives, until the world ends."

Gilhooley turns toward me, his mascara is beginning to run. He slides into my arms, my lips grazing the sapphire earring of his left ear.

I whisper into that ear, "Please leave me here."

He turns his head, a tear running down his cheek. "Let's both stay."

Anita emerges from her bedroom wearing a dressing gown in a sheer blue silk fabric. Its soft flowing lines accent her lithe body. Her feet are encased in red Moroccan slippers, matching the shock of short-cropped hair on her head. She is perfection. I feel it all the way to my toes. She moves next to me, sliding an arm around my waist, while her scent envelops me entirely. The laughter, the room, the warmth of Anita's body—the moment is perfect. It will not last, but then again what does?

Chapter 34
Zhou Yi

Mad Frankie, present time, in the woods:

I shake out two Gabapentin 300 mg into my hand and carry them into the kitchen, washing them down with a pull of milk. I close the refrigerator door, I look at my reflection in the stainless steel. Maybe this whole string has been played out. Maybe the words will not clear a path. Have I been fooling myself? As usual I need to occupy myself until the pills shut my mind up. If only the memories would fade, would end. The good ones, the bad ones, just an avalanche of despair. Dizzy, can you hear me? Dizzy, maybe you are in your study typing away or are you drawing? Can you make it stop? I close my eyes.

Nigel, somewhere in China, somewhen:

I lift myself off the bamboo matting that has been placed upon the rosewood bed frame. Her fragrance still lingers there. I quietly wander out into the rear garden. The early-morning sunlight reflects off the pines. I am facing east, the direction the rear garden is to be enjoyed, bathed in a most gentle light.

The center of the garden is occupied by her. She has been here since dawn. Walking the circle, she concentrates on its center. Her body is in constant motion, duplicating the movements of the cosmos. She is always becoming, always changing, beautiful, poetic, divine.

The whirling circles of BaGua Zhang. The BaGua, signifying its roots in the Zhou yi. She is the Lion 乾, the Monkey 兌, the Rooster 離, the Dragon 震, the Phoenix 巽, the Snake 坎, the Bear 艮, the Qilin 坤. She is standing, turning, striking, ever changing. Watching her I am as empty as I have ever been.

The sun striking my face is pleasant. The large square, while not overly crowded, contains many young women all dressed in red. They wear red coats, red trousers, red hats, red shoes, and each carries a red lantern in one hand and a red fan in the other. Their hair is not

167

worn in the traditional way, their feet are not bound. All together they sing. The Chinese is understood:

> *Wearing all red,*
> *Carrying a small red lantern,*
> *Whoosh, with a wave of the fan,*
> *Up they fly to heaven,*
> *Learn to be a Boxer, study the Red Lantern,*
> *Kill all the foreign devils and make the churches burn.*

Again and again they sing. I know them: they are all members of the Hóng dēng jì shǎn líng, 紅燈記閃靈, The Red Lantern Shining. They are all young woman convinced that they can leap up to heaven when they wave their red fans. I just know they will kill many yang guizi, 鬼子. They will all stand very still and their spirits will join the battle.

They all turn toward me. But even though they take no notice of me, I see Her. The woman from the restaurant, much younger but the same one. Her movements are masterful, holding a terrible beauty to them. With a wave of her fan, she locks gazes with me. The look in her eyes holds me as she raises her red lantern.

I have thrown the coins; the hexagram is Qian, 乾. I sit back and contemplate the meaning:

Vast is the primordial energy indicated by Qian. All things owe to it their beginning. It contains all the meaning belonging to Tian, heaven. The clouds move and the rain is distributed; the various things appear in their developed forms. There exists a connection between the end and the beginning, between the Alpha and Omega, and how the six lines are accomplished, each in its time. The Wu mount the carriage drawn by six dragons at the proper time, and fly through the sky. The method of Qian is to change and transform, so that everything obtains its correct nature as appointed by Heaven and thereafter the conditions of great harmony are preserved in union. The result is "what is advantageous, and correct and firm." The Wu appears aloft, high above all things, and the myriad states all enjoy repose.

She has appeared many times, over and over and over.

Giuseppe, Broadway, New York, 1906:

Something changes; I feel it in my belly. Time slows down, everyone appears to be underwater. Out of the deep shadows a figure emerges. All in black, including mid-back-length hair. It is a woman, a diminutive woman. She seems to glide and pivot to face the approaching thugs. Her arms and legs move as one as she comes to a halt, adopting a stance I recognize as a Chinese martial art fighting posture. Her left leg out, straight, foot inward, right leg bent and carrying the weight. Both arms up, left arm extended palm up, right arm back palm up, flowing into left leg pulled back, both arms down and crossing her chest, fists closed, shifting her legs, right leg forward, body into a crouch, arms extended, palms open, thumbs facing down, flowing back to her original posture. All with an incredible grace that holds a sense of power. It seems like a long time between movements, but she is controlling time and space: it may have been a second or forever.

The boyos stop their forward progress and at the same time both laugh.

One speaks. "Go home, little girl, we have business with these two."

As they begin to move past her, she is suddenly behind the gunman and grasping his gun arm, pulling it down and striking his back. He is propelled forward, releasing his gun as he hits the pavement. In one kick the gun is out of sight. All this happens just out of the peripheral vision of the knifeman. As he realizes what is happening, he turns and thrusts his knife at the empty air. She grasps his knife arm, pulling it down as she moves beside him. He falls to his knees but still has the knife in his hand. She whirls in a circle and delivers a devastating kick to the side of the assailant's head. He is out before he bounces off the pavement. She is everywhere and nowhere, passing like an empty cloud. Gone, without even waiting for a thank-you.

She has appeared many times, over and over and over.

Nigel, on the Great Wall, alternate time:

The hordes are swarming up the hillside through the center of the valley. Their shouts, drums, banging shields are deafening. We stand quietly on the Great Wall. I step back, draw my bow, and wait for the order. It comes and thousands of arrows let fly, with devastating effect. I step forward, she steps back, and the cycle is repeated and repeated and repeated, yet they still come.

The signal pots are lit. One pot, two pots, three pots, more than 10,000 of the Army of the North are trying to breach the wall. They will succeed, at great cost, but they will not hold the prize for very long. Our section of wall is under repair. This is where they will come. Our quivers are empty, they are scaling the wall below us.

The order comes to retreat to the guard block. A small detachment will hold the stairs until this can happen. I am chosen; she quickly joins me without any orders. Here we will fight and here we will die, together. They are over the wall, and behind us the guards are moving up the stairs to the guard block, our small detachment shooting arrows, throwing spears. We wait with our swords.

They are having trouble mounting the many small, narrow steps to reach us. I yell "Tiānzǐ!" she yells "Wansui!" I look at her one last time. I will meet her again and again, eternally. We turn and bring down the first line of attackers, together. Then we die, together.

Giuseppe, Chinatown, New York, 1906:

My three char siu bau buns and bowl of dan dan mian noodles are set noiselessly on the table before me by the same diminutive woman who has served me almost every day for the past three months. She never makes eye contact. I often observe her as she moves effortlessly around the small, overly crowded space. Her movements consist of ever widening and contracting circles. Each time I am sure a collision is imminent, she is not at the point of contact.

Nigel, Peking, late August, 1901:

I lie broken, bodies and parts of bodies litter the ground.

The rebellion has failed. There was no army of heaven, no sacred incantations, no intervention by spirits of the past. We met their guns with courage, their cannon with fearlessness, and we fell, by the thousands. I am bleeding badly, the end will come quickly. My throat is on fire, my lips cracked. Suddenly a wet cloth is pressed against my lips. I open my eyes. It is a young girl from the *Hóng dēng jì shàn líng*. She brings her lips close to my ear and says, "*Zài tiāntáng děng wǒ.*" I think, yes, I will wait in heaven for you. I am gone, a Magic Boxer, on his journey west.

I will meet her many times, over and over and over.

I roll the Qian and she appears as Kun. The two hexagrams, Qian and Kun, as trigrams or hexagrams, stand for Heaven and Earth, yin and yang. The trigram Heaven is made up of three yang lines and is pure yang, while the trigram Earth is made up of three yin lines and is pure yin. Because of this, the firmness of yang and the flexibility of yin, they are considered the substance of all things between.

Giuseppe, Chinatown, New York, time advance:

I sense someone is in the room, lift and turn my head. There is a woman in the shadows, just standing, motionless. I dare not speak lest voice will frighten her away. No, she steps into the room and into the light. I am not prepared for who she is. Slightly built but no matter, there is strength, spiritual strength, strength from other realms. I can feel it all because that is what she wants. Dressed in a simple Chinese robe, the colour of which offsets her pale skin, blond hair, and crystal-clear blue eyes. She approaches my bed, tentatively, but at the same time resolutely.

My eyes open, I am back in Hong Kong back sitting before the old man. He speaks…

Giuseppe, Chinatown, New York, time cycles back:

"When the world began, there was heaven and earth. You will seek your fortune elsewhere. You have done terrible things, been the tool of great injustice, drunk, gambled, smoked the poison, and given in to the pleasures of the flesh. You have mashed your boot on the innocent and guilty alike. While you have used women of my race as things for your satisfaction, there is one who will come out of the East. She will be of the Dao, and the look in her eyes will show you your true path."

Chapter 35
Waiting at the Imperial Bar

Nigel, Vienna, Austria, alternate time:

Every night for three weeks we come to the Imperial Bar, Krugerstrasse 5, sit in the "yellow saloon," have a few cocktails, smoke a few cigarettes, and wait. In the 1920s and '30s, this was the place to be. A quick cocktail before the opera, meeting friends, watching the merry-go-round of a dying Hapsburg era. The Imperial is a little rundown now, the tables are still covered in fine cloth but the cloth is just not as white, the cocktail glasses look a little dull, like they're tried, but after all, aren't we all. Yet it's still here. It survived Armageddon. Armando is still here, mixing up cocktails dating to the heyday of the Old Waldorf bar. He's still an asset, if you know what I mean.

I look over at Gilhooley. His left hand wrapped around his rocks glass of Old Bushmills. He's staring out into the bar's interior but Lord knows what those eyes are really seeing. Just the three of us now: me, the Major, and Gilhooley, old "L" Detachment buddies. Fighting a new war, not over the last one. I guess Plato was right, only the dead have seen the end of war.

I pick up my pack of Luckies, open it, pull out the first one, turn it upside down, and put it back in the pack and not smoking it until it becomes the last one of this pack. It is a symbol of *yangtou* from the local dialect in Shanghai. In Chinese the word means lucky thing or something that makes you lucky. We'd keep this pack of cigarette with *yangtou* in our pockets, not to bring us luck at cards or gambling in general but to make sure the bullet that went past your head, went past.

We've been here for about two months. Before that we were running operations out of Palestine, collecting intel on what Arab intentions are after the projected British Army withdrawal next year. We knew what those bastards were up to and reported that, knowing full well the UN was going to do fuck-all. Still, it pisses me off. I slam back my Martinez, even if it's made with that terrible local gin, and signal the waiter for a repeat. Doesn't take long before the waiter places my cocktail on the table with a flourish. I see the maraschino in the glass. Gilhooley has seen it also. So tonight it may happen. Not that I mind spending part of my nights in the Imperial. My hotel is comfortable and I am growing quite fond of the young BBC correspondent, Kaylee. She's managed to secure a room on my floor. She has a fiancé who's an Oxford don, but I turn his photo around when we play in her room; war, you know. Anyway, I know she's not buying I was in army requisitions during the war. One night she was running her hand gently over my shoulder wound, but all she said was, "It must have been dangerous ordering all that spam." It's her sense of humor I love so much. I even told her my requisitions unit's motto was "Who cares who wins." She laughed, but it really is an inside joke among our detachment.

Well, I've finished my second cocktail, smoked three more Luckies, lit a fourth, and nothing. Time to call it a night. I die out my Lucky in the crystal ashtray, stand buttoning the jacket of my Jermyn Street bespoke suit, and see her walk in scanning the crowd. She works for Shin Bet; she's smart and dangerous. She doesn't really trust us but has come around after I buried my Fairbairn-Sykes in the throat of that Arab holding a Luger on her.

Gilhooley and I have been waiting for her to meet us again. I see she's still looking over the room, but I know she spotted us before she was through the door. The Shin Bet agent, code name Ancient Soul.

Revelation

The cold, wet cemetery earth begs for sun but none is forthcoming. We all have our collars pulled up and hats pulled down. Quietly, somberly standing waiting for the padre to say what padres are obliged to say and he does not disappoint, in English, "He will wipe every tear from their eyes. There will be no more death or mourning or crying or pain, for the old order of things has passed away."

I cough to cover my pain because there are no more tears to wipe away. I've seen more death, crying, pain—well, what's the use. We won and I am left with one question: why am I so very empty? I stand here against the chill of a November without promise, and from the past, from an eon ago, I remember these words from T. S. Eliot's "The Hollow Men":

174

Those who have crossed
With direct eyes, to death's other kingdom
Remember us—if at all—not as lost
Violent souls, but only
As the hollow men
The stuffed men.

My mind wanders so I miss whatever other comforting words the padre has to say. Some of us stand in line to wait to be handed a small shovel filled with dirt to drop on the coffin. I do just that and am turning when the Major tilts his head toward a departing figure, one who does not stay to offer a modicum of dirt, walking away, and that hurts more than the wooden coffin. I take a step but the Major puts his hand on my shoulder and says in his soothing, controlled voice, "Now's not the time, lad."

Of course he is right. I have to let Dizzy walk away. How did we get here? A bombed-out city full of plots, crosses, double crosses, black market, Red aggression, murder. Yes, murder and that's why we are here but I've gotten ahead of myself. Would I change anything if I could? I'll lay out the facts, but be forewarned—I am a ruthless bastard. So I don't expect favorable opinions, but remember that's why you put me here.

It seems the war ended and a new one has begun, the stakes pretty much the same, world domination. Luckily, Gilhooley and I are focused on a lot smaller slice of the pie. Our slice consists mainly of activity at the Café am Ring. There you can get coffee, Imperial torte, and information. That's what the MGB agents are there to buy. We are there to sell disinformation.

The three of us have been working this section since VE Day. So I have been at this for more years than I care to remember. Does it matter? Well, no, because you see I lost my whole family on October 9, 1940, during the first week of bombing in Southwark, south of the Thames. I had been working in an engineering firm but like my father joined the Scots Guards, a family tradition, held by my great-grandfather, grandfather, my father, me. I'm named after my father's father, so Nigel is not my real name but why quibble. I was not in the Norway expedition, as I was still training. I was away when the bombs fell on my block. Dad had already passed but my mum was with my wife and son, all killed by those German bastards. The "Detachment" is all I have left.

We're sitting in the Café Imperial, which is not the Imperial Bar, located at Kärntner Ring 16, It is better known as Café am Ring. I am staring at my Viennese mélange, which is just a coffee and milk, while Gilhooley has a Pharisee, just a coffee with a shot of Old Bushmills. Everything is so fucking complicated. We are keeping as low a profile as possible and it is not too hard here. In true Viennese style, this place is huge. I am tucked behind my copy of the *Arbeiter-Zeitung*. The newspaper is back after a 1934 banning. We didn't miss much. Gilhooley has a copy of the *Tractatus* and is scribbling some note on the top right corner of page 23, the Cambridge cunt that he is.

Well, we are keeping an eye on the Shin Bet agent. She is having coffee with a gentleman we have interest in. She is looking quite coy while our POI is an overweight, pink-looking bit of pastry. God, I hope it doesn't come down to sex. She'd probably slit his throat fist. Anyway, Gilhooley—I can't remember if that is his real name—has another woman in line but he seems reluctant to use her. I met her last week. Seems perfect to me, broke, alone, and without proper papers. I shoot a quick glance at another table holding two MGB agents. Two stupid cunts sitting there in their cheap suits drinking water until they are forced to buy a coffee. I'd like to kill the two of them just on general principles.

Pretty much a stalemate, as I do not think the fat man is going to tip his hand to the Shin Bet agent. Her German is perfect but she has a Sudeten German accent; her parents had the chance to get out in '37, so they did. No, time to move in our local talent. Why is Gilhooley stalling me on this?

I look over at him marking another page and think, no, he can't be involved with Jana. He has been a little standoffish and really put it to me that our only shot was the Shin Bet agent. Here goes.

"Gilhooley, I think it is time to move in our other asset. The fat man likes blondes."

Gilhooley puts down his pencil and looks up, not at me but for an answer. His shoulders sag. "Yes. Yes, it is."

I have to get it all out. "You have gone to bed with her."

He has a sharp look which quickly resolves into a resigned state, our usual state. "Yes, yes, I have."

I decide to defuse what really is a breach of protocol and say, "No need to pass this along to the Major, he is not tolerant of this behavior." I look at him closely; we've been through so much. There is no need for words, I can read his thoughts and he mine. I do not know what the science behind this is, but I lay it down to bonding in moments of extreme stress.

An example is that Shin Bet agent agreed to work with us. She saw what I would do, what I am capable of doing. She watched the Arab fuck bleed out and then smiled at me; she knew he was going to kill her.

Last week I gave her a little present, a Fairbairn-Sykes dagger. She looked at me like I had given her a bottle of Chanel No. 5. So before she guts this fat bastard, I think we'd better move on to our next plan. This one involves whatever it takes, and I bet that fat bastard is into some serious shite.

We drop some marks on the table and leave. I will wait at my hotel for Gilhooley to call and we'll meet with the Major and decide on a plan of action with our new asset. Two days go by, no call, no word. I can't say I'm that disappointed, as my BBC friend, Kaylee, has gotten very inventive. I notice the Oxford don's picture is in a drawer. Tip-fuckin'-top.

I am lying in bed wondering why my shoulder is hurting, maybe it's the bite mark but I've had worse, when the phone rings. I pick it up; Gilhooley; it's all set, the Imperial Bar at 8:00 p.m., table 9. Our asset is to pick up the fat man and do whatever it takes to get into his good graces.

There is a problem, though, I can feel it through the line. I have to say something. "I'll be on this my china plate, no worries."

The phone is silent. Kaylee is slipping a dress over her head as she says, "More scoff to order?"

I smile and toss a pillow at her. At that moment, looking at her, her hair slightly wild, her cheeks a little pink, her hazel eyes bright with promise, I realize I've been playing a hollow man and she deserves so much better. Tip-fuckin'-top.

Later we are sitting comfortably at table 9, drinks and a good view of the bar and tables 3 and 7. Our asset, Jana, is at the bar and I must say looking beautiful in her new outfit and hairdo, fuckin' Betty Grable.

Gilhooley speaks without looking at me. "Two stiffs at table 7, I think they're on to her."

I suddenly get a very bad feeling, like I've seen this before and it doesn't end pretty. The two MGB thugs are sitting with a glass of the terrible local gin each, looking smug. I'd love to get them to a dark alley. I glance at table 3; oh yes, the fat man has noticed her. He calls her over to his table; some of the other girls look disappointed. She sits and he pours her a glass of champagne from his ice bucket. We are in but please, Jana, go slow.

Gilhooley speaks once more. "Nigel, this is a mistake, she's an amateur. The stakes are too high."

As soon as he says it, I know he's right. How could we be so stupid?

One of the MGB agents is smiling. We have an abort plan in place. I am to order a Slivovitz. Armando is to go to her and say she has a phone call. Out the door into a car and away.

Twenty minutes go by and the fat man is looking annoyed, as she has brushed away his hand from her thigh, once, twice, and then a third time. Damn—we rehearsed this for days. She knows what she has to get done. Now she's just a young girl, alone and afraid.

I had pushed this. I'd warned her that if she blew this, it would be off behind the curtain or a camp or a bullet. OK, still time to get her out; she is going to break.

I signal the waiter. He is at the table in a flash. "One Slivovitz, *bitte*."

He walks off, gets to the bar, and Armando nods, pours out a glass, and places it on a tray. He turns picks up the phone, lays it down, walks around the bar, approaches table 3, leans in. She waves him away, he leans in again, again she waves him away. He returns to the bar.

Fifteen minutes later she is leaving with the fat man. Both are followed out by our two MGB agents. We sit and wait.

The waiter comes over and drops a pack of Luckies on the table and four packs of matches. Four drove away in the fat man's car. I am staring at the matches. Gilhooley doesn't say a word; he gets up and walks away.

Sometimes There Is No End

I'm sitting staring in the mirror of the Imperial Bar, working on my forth Martinez. I guess I never told you how a Scots gent came about drinking American cocktails. It was late 1943 or early 1944, I was in China looking over the Kuomintang troop readiness. There I met a young American OSS agent. A seasoned veteran, I had just departed the Middle East after working with the special boat service and Anders Lassen. Got to know him a bit; now that was a soldier. Killed in '45, awarded the Victoria Cross—the only non-Commonwealth recipient of the British Victoria Cross in the Second World War. Still think about Anders every day. Taught me the meaning of courage.

The OSS agent and I both went down to French Indochina to help train the local Viet Minh to fight the Japanese. We met frequently with their leader, who called himself Bác. Always seemed to have a handle on things. Anyway, this guy was a big gin drinker, not that appealing to my taste but he had a case of quality English Old Tom style gin and began to mix us cocktails every night. So when Armando asked me what I would like, I thought I would play a little joke and asked for a Martinez. He mixed it up as quick as can be without batting an eye.

Somewhere along the way I lost my way. I should have been more in tune with the situation. I browbeat that young woman; she was more afraid of me that those Red bastards. That's why she waved off Armando and that is why she lost her life. They made her suffer. Sometimes when you least expect it, something you have done many times breaks you. Jana was that thing for Gilhooley. I let him down, pushed him and pushed him. He got close too close and I missed the real signs.

I remember a situation where our positions were reversed. It was happenstance. It was February 9, 1945, and we were operating inside the town of Kleve awaiting the 15th Division to take the town. They got hung up outside the town and the next thing we knew the place was overrun by the 47th Panzer Corps. We ducked into a bombed-out building and Gilhooley and I got separated from the group. We dove into a basement for cover.

Crouching down in the dark, I heard a low moan. I tapped Gilhooley on the arm and made hand signals that someone was in the basement. I pulled my dagger and crept over to the sound. That part of the house was partially collapsed, but the moonlight revealed the face of a woman. She had a terrible abdominal wound. She was dying. Gilhooley was next to me. He put his hand over her mouth and was about to finish her off with his knife but I grabbed his hand. He looked at me in disbelief. I shook my head. He tried to pull his hand away but I held fast. He read the signs and turned away. I pulled out a morphine syrette and injected her. Her breath was coming in gasps; I held her until she stopped breathing. Gilhooley never mentioned it to me, ever, but he knew. I did not return the favor. I got a cab back to the hotel.

No longer much fun at the hotel. Kaylee was reassigned to Palestine. She left without saying good-bye; war, you know. I brooded all night. I tossed and turned then woke up in a bad mood, a black mood. I know now what I have to do. I will be way off the reservation. I will be in Indian country, but then again I am from south of the river.

At 8:00 p.m. I am sitting at a table in the Imperial Bar with a local asset, a pretty young woman. She needed a job and I got her one at the embassy. She is quite the linguist, and her English is better than mine. She knows the drill: look pleased and talk to no one. I am watching them. I am not watching them. I have my Webley under my arm and my dagger behind my back. 8:00 turns to 10:00 and then 10:30. Celebrating, are we? They pay in their blood money, get up, and leave.

I wait, then follow them out. Light tail, light tail, a side alley. I close quickly, pulling my Fairbairn-Sykes. I break all the rules. I stick the one closest with a quick stab through the neck at the base of the brain. He is dead before he hits the pavement. I pivot quickly but the second is pulling his gun. I manage to kick it out of his hand but slip on blood on the pavement and go down, my dagger clinking away. I'm reaching for my gun when the second fuck is on me with a knife. I'm done for when a shot rings out and the fuck falls off me like a sack of taters. I look up; it is Gilhooley. He is shaking his head.

"Get up Nigel, stop mucking about."

He reaches out and pulls me up. I look at him and say, "We'd better Scapa." We run to a bar we know and duck in quietly. I order two whiskeys.

Gilhooley looks at me. "The Major is going to bust us for this."

I just plant a big kiss on his cheek.

Sitting Outside the Phkachhouk Café

Nigel, Safe House, unknown location, alternate time:

Looking over the meadow to the tree line, it is all dark greens and browns surrounded by a swirling mist. The only vibrant colors come from the 20-foot length of prayer flags stretched between two white pines. Green, yellow, blue, red, each with a pray offering every time the wind moves them, an offering to Her. How many times have I negotiated with the Divine, begged the Divine, pleaded with the Divine? Are our prayers heard? Who can answer that, who will have the audacity to answer in the affirmative? Is there a master plan? Is it that we lack the knowledge to understand this plan?

Maybe the wrong approach, the wrong questions, maybe the answers are right in front of us. Maybe there are no answers. It takes me back, as painful as that might be, to the last time I saw you. Right before the world revealed its true nature, right before killing became a national sport, right before I tried to save her, right before they killed her just because she had a beautiful voice.

The bastards pulled out and left the door wide open for those fanatics to come and destroy anything and anyone who questioned the sickening political paradigm that passed for a philosophy.

Nigel, Phnom Penh, Cambodia, alternate time:

So, there we are sitting out front of the Phkachhouk Café having our usual Vietnamese coffee and letting the sun beat down on our Hong Kong white suits, as the beautiful Khmer girls ride passed on their scooters. The Green Palace Hotel is right across the street so we did not have far to roll out of bed.

I will have two coffees before Choun shows up to shine some sunshine on my life. Her smile helps push away the memories of a lifetime of dealing in death. I know we have to move fast; the barbarians are at the gate. Gilhooley has paid off at least a dozen officials and I greased two suspected double agents, but not for our mission. No, our mission is strictly intel on troop movement and if it all goes south, get out. If the Major knew what we really have been up to, we would be counting sheep outside Auckland.

I look over at Gilhooley; damn, he looks tired. That knife wound running from his left ear to his jawline is healing nicely, which is good because that's often problematic in the tropics. I was a little slow to put one in that shit with my suppressed HD Standard and he almost got that knife into Gilhooley's neck. Gilhooley is putting it all on the line here, just to help me get her away from the coming deluge. After all we had to do, all the terrible things we did do for them, now we're doing something for each other.

I see her pull in on her bright-red Honda scooter. She pulls down the kickstand, parking the bike. She turns and sees me, and her face brightens as she puts her hands together bowing her head in the standard Khmer greeting, but she always uses Third Sampeah level in her greeting, I wish she wouldn't. I stand and return the greeting. She fluidly moves toward me, the sun reflecting off her bright-yellow sundress. She is perfection. She's small of stature but her heart is large, loving, and gentle. It lies outside this world.

Her English is quite good, far better than my Khmer. We watched her perform at the Kngaok Club last night. She sings in the most exquisite Khmer voice, pop tunes with a traditional turn to the music. I can listen to her sing for the rest of my life.

"Choun, we need to be ready to leave on a moment's notice. You must be ready to come with us. We will have a boat at the Trei dock, have your scooter filled with gas always. We will get word to you in plenty of time to meet us, travel light." She nods and smiles that smile. She is going to be a big hit in the UK.

I know what we need. I ask, "Hungry? Let's get some soup." I signal the waiter, one of our operatives, for two of the dried version of Phnom Penh noodles with soup broth on the side. Gilhooley does his best to avoid too much local cuisine.

The soup arrives and I feel good about our plan. Like all good plans, it is simple. We take our boat north to the Thai border hours away but off the roads. At the border, papers in hand, we have a local contact with a car to take us to Chiang Mai. Of course, in the back of my mind I know once the shooting starts plans are worth fuck-all. We have a backup plan but it is not very encouraging, as it involves some motorcycles, Sean Flynn, and Highway 1, back into Vietnam. He is a high-risk individual so some concern is always on my mind.

We finish our meal since it is getting very warm. It is time to fall back to the hotel and a modicum of air conditioning. I stand and drop some riel to cover the meal and a nice tip, then leave my small spoon in the coffee glass, a sign to our operative we are ready to move. Walking across the street to the hotel, I suddenly feel a lot less confident. Too many things to go wrong. After a while, lying on my bed with Choun beside me, sweat covering our bodies in spite of the air conditioning or maybe because of the air conditioning, I am running through as many worst-case scenarios as I can think of—and I am very good at worst-case scenarios. Choun stirs, placing a hand over my heart. Sometimes all you have left is trust in the Divine.

April 17, 1975

Nigel, Phnom Penh, Cambodia, alternate time:

Someone is shaking me awake, although I am awake.

"Stop shanking me, Gilhooley, I'm wide awake."

"Up, Nigel. It's happening—this morning they will be rolling into the city, God help us."

I sit up. "Got to get word to Choun immediately, get to the dock—shit, why did I let her go see her mother? I should have kept her here."

Gilhooley doesn't answer, no point, he's busy checking the guns on the table. I get up and walk over to the table. Not much of an arsenal but it's all we have. Two M3A1 variants, American made, we prefer it to the Sten, firing a .45-caliber ACP round. Useful since we both carry Colt .45 1911s.

Weapons check completed, we sling the M3A1s under our arms and holster the .45s at our sides, all beneath our suit jackets. In the lobby the clerk just nods and smiles. I want to tell him he won't be smiling in a few hours, but why? We slip out the door just as a jeep flies by, crowded with black-pajamaed little thugs. They are firing their SKSs into the air.

I look at Gilhooley. "Don't fucking tell me they folded without a fight!"

"Damn it, Nigel, you knew these people are just plain worn out, They're hoping for the best."

I shake my head. "It's going to a fuckin' blood bath."

"Nigel, you don't know for certain. Maybe they all want to end the fighting."

I grab Gilhooley's arm. He looks me in the eyes, then just nods. We've seen it all before, the little Maoist pricks. "Gilhooley, this will be no different, it's just the logical consequence of their sick system of values. Once they have power, they will define what morality is. It's always about the power of the gun."

Gilhooley pulls his arm away. He knows this is not going to end well.

I say, "Let's get to the dock, meet Choun, and get the hell out. Lon Nol is finished."

We run along the front of the hotel, across the street, and into the alley alongside the Phkachhouk Café. There is the Citroën DS 19, two tone, maroon with grey top, quietly purring with the waiter from the café behind the wheel.

We hop in, yell at the driver to step on it and not stop for any reason. Of course, as soon as we pull out, a jeep is right behind us.

Gilhooley says, "We'd better leg it."

I yell at the driver, "Lose them, I don't want to get into a gunfight already!"

As soon as I finish, the gunfire starts. The driver pulls a high-g right, the jeep attempts the same but veers off wildly and hits a pole. Hopeful our luck will hold...it does, and we arrive at the Trei dock, slow way down, and approach our boat. About 40 yards, and next to piles of tarps, I slip out. The Citroën glides another 10 feet and stops with its lights out.

Behind cover I raise my glasses and look the boat over. Our captain is standing on the dock looking apprehensive as he scans the street, the boat engines rumbling. I slowly and casually walk toward the boat, holding the .45 low at my side. As I get close, the captain recognizes me and starts nervously speaking to me in Khmer. I gesture with my left hand to be quiet, meanwhile the Citroën has pulled up alongside us. The driver gets out and I ask him to tell the captain we are to wait for one more person.

You can imagine how well this news is received. The captain very quietly but very forcefully tells our operative that it will be light soon and that means we will all be dead. Fuck, I know he's right but I hear a scooter. I would recognize that sound anywhere. It is a red scooter with a young woman on it, a young woman but not Choun.

It's Chantrea, Choun's cousin. She brakes and jumps off the bike. It hits the ground as she runs over to us. "They're already on edge of the city—they got Choun and her mother and put them into trucks. I jumped on her bike, they shot at me."

I sag. I know it is over, I know I fucked up, I know I'll never see her again. I look at Chantrea. "Please get on the boat, you have to come with us."

She shakes her head no. "I have to get to Choun, I have to get her out."

I grab her by both arms. "It means death if they catch you on that bike, do you understand? Get on the boat!" Knowing I'm right, she climbs aboard.

I wave over the diver. "Leave the car and get on the boat."

He looks at me and actually smiles, putting his hand gently on my shoulder. "I fought with American Special Forces in a Hatchet Force company, for two years. These people are evil, they will have to kill me if they want my home." He reaches behind his neck, unfastens a chain with an ivory Buddha attached, puts it around my neck, and kisses me. With that he walks to the car and drives away.

I look at Gilhooley. "How did these guys lose?" We both know why, we both know politicians are worth fuck-all.

We hear a jeep roaring down the road that runs alongside the dock. I motion Chantrea below and tell the captain to say he is going fishing, as Gilhooley and I scamper around to the other side of the wheelhouse. The captain does just that, but one of the four in the jeep wants to check out the boat, probably wants to steal it. There is a short conversation, and just to piss me off the fuck decides to take a walk around our side of the boat. His last walk. When he gets close and out of the shadows, I strike with my dagger—throat stab, rip, pitch him over the side. The only sound is the asshole hitting the water.

One of the three in the jeep stands up, only making for a better target as Gilhooley greases all three with his M31A. I yell to the captain to get going but no need, lines are off and we are already pulling away from the dock. The horizon is just beginning to lighten. I go below and find Chantrea sobbing, just the start of the tears.

In Khmer the name Chantrea, means moon full of light.
There will not be any light in Cambodia for too long a time.

Just a Moment

Nigel, Phnom Penh, Cambodia, alternate time:

The mirrored ball turns slowly, reflecting the twin spots that in turn light up Choun's sequined dress as if by the Divine. She has her right arm raised, holding the mike in her left hand, as she sings my favorite song, "Love Pillow."

In this moment of infinite moments, I realize how much I love her. I don't understand many of the words she sings, but the song speaks to me in another medium, not mindfulness, but mindlessness. My love for her cannot be explained not even by the poet. While it brings me such comfort, as with all things, it brings a sense of sadness. Why? Perhaps we really can glimpse the future, the swirling tides of time engulf us, carry us along on its current, and we are helpless.

I don't know how long, only the message of sweetness, the desire to hold her and never let go. Every time, each night, when she gets to the final refrain, no matter what, she turns to me with a smile, a smile like a sapphire bullet straight to my heart.

I down my martini and turn toward my table companions. Dizzy has an Old Bushmills in front of him and an arm around a beautiful young hooker. She is laughing at something he said, of course, Dizzy is not funny, she's no fool. While I'm waiting for Choun to join us, I really look at Dizzy, his hair slicked back, starting to grey, military regulation mustache, impeccable white suit, Hong Kong, azure tie with stickpin. He has a wide smile on his face, almost as if it can wipe away all we've seen and done. Fuck it, I haven't seen him this happy in a long time.

I get his attention and over the band I yell to him, "I love you, you cunt." Still smiling he raises his glass, turns, and kisses the young girl.

Burn List

Nigel, alternate time:

So here we are sitting in the restaurant on the rooftop of the Arcadia Suites, Plot 54A Kira Road, Kampala, Uganda, having our usual—me a cold martini, Gilhooley a Bushmills—enjoying a nice breeze coming from Lake Victoria, cooling out our, slightly wrinkled, Hong Kong white suits, watching the beautiful Asian girls circulate among the hotel guests. It is June 20 and we have reliable intel there is going to be an attack aimed at Israeli assets. No idea where but our source claims Idi is involved, so here we are at a hotel within spitting distance of the British High Commission, just two low-level bureaucrats, heavily armed but bureaucrats, nonetheless.

We are going to have dinner with the mistress of a local mining manager, British, who is passing intel to the Amin government. She is playing this passive Indo-European secretary he uses to blind-drop intel. Of course, if he knew who she might be—and I use "might" because neither Gilhooley or myself are really sure—he'd shit himself, the dumb cunt. All aboveboard, as Gilhooley has a front as a visa clerk and this guy has greased Gilhooley's wallet to help him fix her papers, so he can continue to enjoy her company back in the UK. The shit should know he is on our burn list. Gilhooley and I cut high card to see who gets to be removal man. High card gets the honor; I drew the King of Hearts.

I nod toward the entrance canopy and we both watch her scanning the crowd. I smile, knowing full well she spotted us a half step in through the canopy. She's wearing a Jean Varon brown floral cotton balloon-sleeve voile dress; it is quite hideous, but the genius bought it for her, so she wears it. I stand and wave her over. Her name is Rana Rahimi and her striking dark, sultry features fit her, purported Iranian background.

I walk around the table and pull out a chair for her. She greets us in Persian, wishing us well, etc. I order her a wine. Gilhooley and Rana engage in conversation about the prospects of her papers, while I look bored, scanning the crowd. There is the usual amateur tail on us, a young kid in a blue sharkskin suit, patent-leather shoes, white socks, green shirt, and sunglasses. I have grown quite fond of our young spy over the last couple of days. He has some potential but his talents lend themselves more to pop star rather than spook. He is not on our burn list.

I am half listening to the coded conversation when I hear Rana make note of an airliner coming in over the city. Damn—a hijacking, I better pay closer attention. A butterfly crosses the table and Rana says in French, "*Un beau papillon*," French airliner, but when, where, that's as much as she has. We silently eat our dinner. At one point I make eye contact with her; it is a special moment, one I haven't exchanged with her before. She has acknowledged me, and I acknowledged her, together, still fighting, still standing on that wall, even after all these years. Dinner over, she gets up, we stand, and she bids us good night in Persian and walks out of the restaurant, now with Mossad, Ancient Soul.

We pay, leave our tip, and begin to leave. I slap Gilhooley on his right shoulder. He says, "Have to hit the head, Nigel, meet you at the bar."

It is well known, among the foreign crowd, I have been making eyes at the bartender, which makes for a great cover. Since I'm British, they assume I'm ginger. The bartender's story goes like this: straight from Fidel's Cuba, ardent marxist, here to support his revolutionary brothers. In reality, Raul, his code name, is CIA. He helped the Bolivians track down that lowlife Che. Not sure who put a bullet in his head. Raul's job on station is to receive any intel we can give him. He knows we are not really spooks but is not sure what we are, though Gilhooley has special service written all over him.

Raul is talking with a young man, but when he sees me out of the corner of his eye, he turns and pulls a Plymouth Gin bottle off the shelves behind him and begins to mix a martini. I blow him a kiss, meaning I have intel, and he winks at me, meaning clear to relay. We engage in small talk, his friend joins us, and the three of us make small talk. His friend is a Spaniard, Miguel, an accomplished fresco artist. Nice kid, completely unaware of the world Raul and I live in, thank God.

Gilhooley sits at the other end of the bar, only because he can sometimes be a pain in the ass but probably he just wants everyone to think he's jealous. During our chat I pass along the intel Rana has given us and everyone has a few drinks and a few laughs. Miguel tells a funny story about Franco. I didn't think that possible but he pulls it off. I say good night and we head down to our rooms. Tomorrow at lunchtime Gilhooley has a meet with Rana at the Kisementi Gardens, off John Babiha Avenue and Kira Road. The intel seems to say this is going to happen soon; hopefully we can pin down where and when.

Just outside my door, I sense footsteps on the carpet. Without turning around, I get ready to pull my dagger until I hear a soft voice, "Nigel, can I have a word?"

I know who she is, a woman I've befriended, a woman who should have never been brought here, Jeannie, Jeannie Blears. I open my door and indicate with my chin for her to enter. Of course she has had too much to drink tonight—every night, really. She is married to a Brit who works out of the Commission. He is helping with farming quotas or some such nonsense. He's not a bad chap but is too absorbed in his work to notice his wife is fading away. The guy is a true believer, he actually believes you can be a force for good. OK, I sound like a jaded bastard but the help I provide comes out of the barrel of my gun or the point of my dagger. Maybe killing as many evil bastards as I can is helping.

I close the door after scanning the hallway, and as I turn, Jeannie moves into my arms. I hold her, and her scent of Nina Ricci's L'Air du Temps brings back powerful memories of sweet afternoons in this room, for a time blotting out the truths of this world.

"Nigel, I'm sorry, but I wanted to see you. I did what you suggested, had a long talk with Reg, he felt terrible and was very understanding, said he was caught up in his work, says he will request a transfer back to the UK."

"Good for him, Jeannie. That's the best course to take. I know you really love him. I hope I haven't behaved like a cad, taken advantage."

"On the contrary, you were there for me, gave me great advice. You and your friend are two of the most unique civil servants I have ever met."

"That's because we are old school, Jeannie, we come from a time when things were much clearer, the sides were well drawn." She is looking into my eyes as she reaches for the light switch.

The next day I am having a strong coffee on our rooftop, feeling pleased with myself, I may have helped save a marriage. I had a good sense that Reg would do the correct thing and he did. Good for you, Reg, she's worth it. She does love the gin, but who doesn't?

As I wave for another cup of coffee, I see the cultural attaché from the Commission, Margo Goodwhite. She is here to promote British theater and if possible start a small acting school. Of course, I know her as Portia, her code name. The irony is not lost on her that she is surrounded by so many dark complexions, but she had to explain that one to me. She is an embedded operative from SIS. She spots me and wanders over to the table. I stand and she greets me as usual: "'It droppeth as the gentle rain from heaven / Upon the place beneath.'"

It's from Shakespeare's *Merchant of Venice*, Act 4, Scene 1. So I have to recite in return, "'It is twice blessed.'"

None of this has anything to do with our assignment or any kind of protocol, she just enjoys her role. I pull out a chair for her, she sits, I sit, I look at her clear eyes and think she has so much vitality, I could use a dozen like her. But all I say is, "Coffee?"

"Please. Just left my second meeting today. The first was with the Minister of Culture, who thinks we should buy him a Rolls, the second with the Interior Minister, who wants a house for his mistress."

A young Asian woman I know sets down Margo's coffee and gives me a beautiful smile. I wish I could fix papers for her. I look back at Margo, who has sat back in her chair with a grin on her ageless face,

"What?" I ask.

"Nigel, that was no simple table service, unless there has been an upgrade I missed."

"No, I got her brother a job at the Commission. She thinks I'm a nice chap."

Margo laughs. "Very nice."

I straighten my tie and look at her, acknowledged.

She begins with a line from *Macbeth*, "'For the poor wren will fight…Her young ones in her nest, against the owl'" then follows with a line from *Julius Caesar*: "'but, for mine own part, it was Greek to me.'"

OK, these Shakespeare quotes tell me an airliner hijacking, Greece. We have what and where, now we have to wait for the when. We know in confirmed intel the hijacked airliner will end up in Uganda. I drain my coffee and wish Margo a good day. Can we just monitor every Air France flight? Can we track ingress and egress of known terrorist operatives? In a perfectly sane world everyone is in agreement, but there are high-ranking elements that believe the Israelis are the villains. The cunts, I was there when they dug up those fields in Belzec, Poland. I'll never forget it. I wish they'd seen it.

I will meet up with Gilhooley at 5:00 p.m. in our rooftop bar and coordinate our intel. Fist I have a meet at 12:00 p.m. in Kisementi Gardens with a Brit who owns a tailor shop, downtown Kampala. I often meet with him in the park as he is an avid ornithologist and is always showing me lots of photographs he has taken all around the town and beyond.

I arrive, after a pleasant walk, at Kisementi Gardens. After wandering around for a while, I spot my friend sitting on a bench, binoculars to his eyes, two cameras around his neck, notebook next to him.

I quietly sit down beside him. Without lowering the binoculars, he says, "Hello, Nigel, nice day for it."

Then he slowly lowers the binoculars and smiles at me. Under the notebook is a plain letter-size envelope, which he picks up, opens, and hands me a stack of pictures. Birds, birds, birds, airport building. I pass the building and look at the next batch of birds.

I put down the pictures. "What is so interesting about this building?"

He answers, "It's a disused airport building that has been getting a lot of attention the last couple of days. I stake my pension that is where whoever they take will be held. Probably for some sort of exchange. Will these assholes ever learn? Negotiation is not an option."

He places all the pictures back in the envelope and stands, shakes my hand, and walks away. David Goren, small of stature but with big balls.

June 26th, having a drink with Gilhooley. Gin and tonic, Gilhooley, well, fuck, you should know by now. We both feel it is going to happen in short order, the ground chatter has picked up exponentially. Gilhooley tells me he received a coded message today at the Commission that stated the hijacking will happen within the next few days. Those cunts at Cambridge and Oxford are so helpful.

I look across the bar and see Rana and Mr. Tosser enter. She is holding on to his arm and he is looking around as if to say, I have her and you don't. He sees Gilhooley and waves. Subtle; we should recruit this guy. Rana excuses herself and comes over to the table.

We both stand and I pull out a chair for her. She greets us in Persian, wishing us well, etc.

Seated, she looks at us. "I was hoping those papers would be ready tomorrow."

Gilhooley answers, "I can try, Rana. Where should we meet?"

"I think the airport, but I have friends ready to meet me there. Maybe they will be delayed but I don't think it can be avoided."

Gilhooley just nods. "We will do our best, ready to support all efforts."

She stands, nods to Gilhooley, and clasps my hand and speaks to me in Persian, "برو و شادی خودت را بیدار کن." She clasps my hand tighter. "It's an old Persian saying: 'Go and wake up your luck.'" She turns and walks back to the tosser's table. Damn, I love the group we have assembled.

The "when" happens on June 27. Air France Flight 139, an Airbus A300B4-203, is hijacked just after takeoff from Athens Airport by two Palestinians and two Germans. They divert the flight to Benghazi, Libya, hold the plane on the ground for seven hours, and refuel before taking it to Entebbe Airport in Uganda. All intel is in the hands of those who can and will do something about it. Gilhooley and I have to sit and wait.

The hijackers are joined at the airport by four other foreign elements along with members of the Ugandan army. Idi Amin visits daily, talking his usual BS to the hostages, trying to make them believe he's in their corner. The hijackers' demands: $5 million for the release of the airplane, the release of 53 Palestinian and pro-Palestinian militants, 40 of whom had been prisoners in Israel. Gilhooley and I both know there is no peaceful way to end this, so if the IDF do not act, it's not going to end well for the hostages.

The stalemate drags on until the night of July 3, when a group of Israeli commandos flies in from Israel and seize control of Entebbe Airport, freeing nearly all the hostages. Three hostages die during the operation and 10 are wounded; 7 hijackers, about 45 Ugandan soldiers, and 1 Israeli soldier are dead. The commandos leave Entebbe on July 4 with their cargo. Gilhooley and I think: a job well done.

We are handed a problem, though. Dora Bloch, a 74-year-old Israeli who holds British citizenship, is at the Mulago Hospital in Kampala. She has been left behind, and we get a request from control to snatch her from the hospital, steal a vehicle, and deliver her to a de Havilland

Canada DHC-2 Beaver sitting in Lake Victoria, then fly to Kenya. We both laugh, say good-bye to each other, and head for the hospital.

At the hospital we encounter chaos. I get a bad feeling as soon as we arrive. We go to the floor our intel told us Dora is on, but there has already been a gunfight. I see two dead Ugandan police officers, who I suspected were guarding Dora. I look at Gilhooley and he just shakes his head. I push into the room, and, as we expect, her bed is empty.

As we are leaving the room, a doctor grabs Gilhooley and says we have to wait for the army to arrive, as he just called them. I strike him under the chin, bring up my knee to his groin, and he goes down. He is about to get up but I point my Browning Hi-Power at him. He takes the hint. Smart doc. We quickly exfil the premises.

Outside I put my Browning to the head of a cab driver and inform him we need to borrow his vehicle. I tell him I will leave the keys. He jumps out and we jump in. I know Rana has already left with her IDF buddies, but there is one thing we need to do. We drive to a well-to-do area and pull up to a house. I get out and tell Gilhooley to leave it running. I ring the bell, a maid answers. I inquire if the gentlemen of the house is at home. Why yes, she says, he came home after the trouble at the airport, he is in his study. No bother, I know the way. I knock, enter, open the door.

"About time you got here," he says. "I need to get to the Commission office, I have all my important papers, you will take me there now."

"Need any help with you papers, sir?"

"No, I've got them all in this case. Let's go, it is open season on Brits now."

"You are right about that, sir."

He looks stupidly at my Browning as I put two in his chest, the cunt. I pick up his case, walk out as the maid starts screaming. I tell her to shut up and she does. I get in the cab and we head to the lake and our plane.

Sunset, we are comfortably ensconced in some plush leather chairs at the Mombassa Club, Kenya, me sipping my martini, made with Mombassa Club Gin, and Gilhooley having, fuck sake, a gin and tonic. We're both happy, all our group is safe, but we raise our glasses to the IDF and the one we couldn't get out. Here's to you, Dora Bloch.

Chapter 36
A .45-cal. Rimless

Giuseppe, Warren Street, New York, 1906:

Raymond Clark is sitting behind a Ming rosewood desk, spare, except for the Tiffany gilt bronze and glass Piano Counter-Balance Desk Lamp by Tiffany Studios decorated with a yellow iridized Tiffany Favrile damascene glass shade on top, an unusually extended piano counter-balance, with a gilt bronze and acid-etched base. Next to an open note-book is a Waterman #12 Mottled HR Slip Cap Eyedropper Fountain Pen with the flexible 14k gold nib. Immediately to his right on a red cloth lies a well-oiled Colt .45-caliber Rimless automatic pistol. In its 1906 catalogue, Colt boldly proclaims this: "The Most Powerful Small Arm Ever Invented."

"Yes, Finnegan, war in Europe is inevitable. There is too much of the old thinking, the old ways."

He tosses a handful of papers on the desk and says, "I read your report on Gilhooley, up to and including the problem with the Tong. He provided a valuable service. We still have to find his true meaning, for example, what are his long-term plans? Now, on another topic, I know you killed that man off 23rd Street. Tell me why."

I look at Clark, better come clean. "I got the information requested but he was an evil sod. He cursed my mother. I did it before I could even think. If you want me out, I'll leave."

Clark leans back in his chair, looking me in the eye. "He means nothing to me but I have to know can you or will you control your temper? I realize you are half Italian and I know that cursing out one's mother is not a pardonable sin."

I nod and let the chips fall. "You know my weakness, I still think I can be of service. Gilhooley is in my debt and now I am in his. Some-how we make a good team."

Clark looks as if he is thinking this over then speaks. "Yes, that is a valuable piece to this puzzle. One more question. I know you smoke opium, do you think that chasing the dragon will interfere with this job? Sometimes I think it may be an asset."

"No, Mr. Clark, it does allow me to enter circles closed to most men."

Clark laughs, "Yes, Finnegan, that it does. OK, you know what you have to do. Report back if you have further useful intel."

With that, I rapidly leave Mr. Clark, glad to be off the carpet. I nod to Marcus, and am in the Otis in a flash. Tired after a long night writing that report. Think I'll head back to the flat and have a nap and then go out later to McGinnity's.

I open the door to the flat; it is dark and damp. I move through the railroad style to my rear bedroom, throw off my coat, sit on the bed, pull off my boots, and stretch out on the bed. I'm so very tired. As I begin to drift, off images of that whirling, powerful Chinese woman fill my thoughts. Why did she intervene, risk her life? Just before world fades I realize I've known her, quite possibly, that I've loved her.

It is cold, and white, the air is thin, all around are the peaks of high, rugged mountains. I am on the edge of a steep cliff with rocky outcrops, ravines, and scrub pines surrounding me. I'm having trouble filling my lungs with air. I must be at an altitude over a mile. While thin, the air is sweet and pure.

Purely by accident I happen to turn my head and I see him, maybe 30 feet from me. Standing on the top of the snow, he's maybe four feet long and at least 70 pounds. His coat is grey with black spots on head and neck, with larger rosettes on the back, flanks, and bushy tail. The belly is whitish. The fur is thick and long. His body is stocky, short-legged, and slightly smaller than the other cats of his genus. His eyes are pale green. His muzzle is short and his forehead domed. It is a snow leopard, and if he thinks I am prey, I am a dead man. He is 30 feet away but that is an easy leap. Before I can take another breath, he can be on me.

Yet he just stands there, mewing, raising his muzzle. I see how very big and wide his paws are. The reason he can stand above the snow. He back legs are ready; in a moment he will be on me, I know it. Well, to end it all here in this pristine environ, the air, the pines, the snow, the sun reflecting off his wind-rippled fur, maybe it is my path.

I look again and the snow leopard is gone and replaced by her voice, from right in front me, to the centre of my skull. Sounds of all there is, was, will be. The primordial drone of all the uncountably infinite worlds. My body is weightless. It is too beautiful to bear, too painful to hear. We are not the author of our lives. It is the 32 paths of Kabbalah, the 72 names of G_D, the Alpha and Omega.

She appears angry, protective, loving. The sounds intensify, it is deafening; it is the music of eternity, the sounds of existence. It contains all things. I am her, she is me. She has shown me my spirit guide, the snow leopard. Follow his path, take his courage.

I love the Supreme because I came from Her. I devote myself to the Supreme because I wish to go back to Her. I surrender myself to the Supreme because she lives in me and I in Her.

Part Two

Chapter 37
Cinderella Ballroom

Nigel, New York City, 1927:

It is late night or early morning depending if you had been loaded most of the evening. So let's say it is late for an early morning. I realize I'm sitting on a gold davenport in a pair of boxers with a slight run of blood down my right arm. I lift my head and try to remember where exactly I am. Wherever I am it is damn expensive. My feet are buried in a plush oriental carpet, just under an acre, in fact the entire place is littered with Asian art, artifacts, and knickknacks. Whoever owns this place, they have money. There is a large carved table with Chinese characters cut into the top, covered with a slab of glass. On top of the table is a bowl that looks like it's from the Ming dynasty, filled with a white powder, two silver spoons, a Herend Lighter with a Queen Victoria Green Border, VBO Butterfly Flower, a length of cord that looks rubberized, and a serious-looking hypodermic needle lying on a black velvet cloth.

Suddenly the room is filled with music. I let it wash over me. It's a new recording by Frank Trumbauer and His Orchestra, called "I'm Coming Virginia," featuring a lyrical, brilliant solo by Bix Beiderbecke. Bix's phrasing is a thing of beauty. Every time I hear this piece, it feels like I'm hearing it for the first time. Bix, so understated, so haunting, like an invitation to a kiss.

Two hands gently slide down from my shoulders to my wrists, curly blond hair caresses my neck, and—that scent. That scent by Coco, her number 5. It's like an avalanche burying your senses. Yes, I know, I should be embarrassed…I begin to come back. The young lady from the Cinderella Ballroom on Broadway and 48th Street, the young lady from last night. I had gone to hear my friend David playing in a band and was sitting with his friend Sarah when a woman she knew stopped at the table. After that the details become frozen in a mist.

Her warm breath on my ear. "We are supposed to meet David and Sarah for lunch at the Puncheon Club. We have hours and I have an idea." She moves away from me around the davenport and sits beside me. I look at her; she is beautiful and trouble. Well, why blame her? I am trouble or am I in trouble, why split hairs.

I know David didn't look too thrilled when he finished playing his cornet and joined us. He knows her and he knows me. I wanted to tell him just keep playing beautiful music. We broke up early, promising to meet for lunch at the Puncheon Club. I came back to this estate of an apartment. Drugs, music, sex, drugs, music, more drugs. She sees the blood on my arm and wipes it gently with a white handkerchief with a red lace border. I am overwhelmed with a sadness I cannot explain. Now I remember she's an artist, her parents are wealthy, this is their place, she was so lost last night I saw it in her eyes, a pain you cannot fake. She asked me here, said she hated getting loaded alone. What could I say? All I do is get loaded alone and listen to the same music over and over.

I bury myself in Chanel and ask, "What is this idea you have?"

The Cinderella Ballroom, The Idea

Scratch, pop, scratch, pop, scratch, pop, the needle is jammed between the end of the record track and the label. A well-manicured hand lifts the phonograph arm and places it back at the beginning of the record. This same hand has done this maybe half a dozen times and shows no indication that this is in any way annoying.

I am sitting on the edge of a bed the size of Rhode Island. Silk everywhere, perfume and a sharp medicinal scent fill the air. The room is lit only by a pair Art Deco table lamps designed by Daum Nancy. They feature a mushroom form glass design in hues of aqua and navy with gold powder and gold leaf inclusions detailing a wrought-iron frame.

I am in a set of boxers. I cannot remember if I have been in these boxers or at some point I had other clothes or even if these are the same boxers. A rivulet of blood has partially run down my left arm and dried. A man in black tie is about to throw open the heavy, dark-gold drapes but I intervene. "Please, sir, I don't think I can stand more light."

The man spins around. "I beg your pardon, sir. I did not realize you were up. Might I add, sir, it is quite dark outside."

I feel pretty stupid. Do I even know what day it is? I just mumble, "Oh, sorry, I was not aware, go ahead."

He turns and opens the 10-foot drape then turns back to me. "Will you be needing anything, sir?"

I want him to get the last several days back, but why? "A whiskey, ah…" I realize I either do not remember his name or I never knew it.

He realizes this. "McDowall, sir, I have a very fine Speyside malt, a Gordon & MacPhail, if the gentleman would care to partake?"

I nod yes.

He asks, "A splash of water, sir?"

I nod yes again. He walks out with as much dignity as he can muster, considering what the hell is going on. I sit there with my head in my hands. Bix's solo always seems so fresh. It's something I can hold on to.

Finally I turn to look across the landscape. Now I remember the idea. The woman from the Cinderella Ballroom, Kaylee, and the upstairs friend, Lara, are sleeping in each other's arms. They both look so innocent, so comforted. The reality is they are both dope fiends. Isn't that the expression? I just wanted, in so many lives, so many circumstances, someone I could get loaded with and now I have two, such riches, such poverty of the soul.

I realize Kaylee's eyes are open, one perfect breast above the silk sheet, her face still slightly flushed, I am not sure if it is from the sex or drugs. Is someone keeping score? Well, Murderers' Row is. Somewhere off in the distance, considering the size of this place it is distant, a doorbell is ringing. It stops and a few moments later McDowall enters the bedroom. "Excuse me, there is a gentleman at the door with a package. I did not let him in."

Kaylee lifts both arms straight up, the sheet drops away, McDowall doesn't even blink. "It's OK, McDowall, pay the man and bring the package back here."

"Very well, ma'am." He leaves. Why does the guy do it? Money, I guess, but I think he does care about Kaylee.

Not long and McDowall returns. "Shall I place the package on the dressing table, ma'am?"

"Please do, that's all for now, McDowall."

"Excuse me, ma'am, but I was about to fetch the gentleman a drink." Kaylee just nods OK. McDowall goes off once more. Kaylee turns to me and opens her arms. It strikes me, I realize I love her. What I am to do now? I slide up the bed and lay my head on her firm stomach. As if she knows what I am thinking she says, running her hand through my hair, "Don't worry, love, we have enough to last a mighty long time."

"I know," I say. "I know, Kaylee."

Empress 1908

Kaylee is sleeping peacefully while I am one flight up in Lara's apartment. The apartment is a homage to the De Stijl movement. It has a minimal amount of everything. Sparse, muted primary colors with white and grey, all the layers independent of each other. We are sitting close on a low-slung davenport of her own design, in a restrained yellow. Kaylee is passionate in her art, her colors are bold, warm, inviting. Lara's design is introspective, clean, serene. No wonder they are so close. Together they close a loop, complete the square.

Lara is looking my way when she asks, "Would you like a taste of a special gin a just received?"

"Why yes, always ready to try a new gin."

She gets up, and seeing her in silhouette against the Poul Henningsen 4/3 Desk Lamp with base in brown brass and shades in copper, green, and gold paint, spreads a warm feeling over me. Like Bix's cornet solo in "Georgia On My Mind." She is quite beautiful. I guess, looking around and realizing the depth of her esthetic, my early assessment of her is quite wrong. She is a many-layered person.

She deftly pours out two glasses and brings them over, handing me one. An exquisite clear crystal glass with a gold band, probably by Moser; what is more impressive is the gin. It is the most striking shade of indigo blue. I bring it to my lips as she does the same. We take a sip at the same time. I nod, still enthralled by the color of the gin. I down the contents. She smiles, takes my glass, and refills it and brings it back. This time we both throw it back at once. She repeats the process but this time I hold up the glass to the light from the Poul Henningsen in order to fully take in the indigo.

As I am doing this, I turn and look at Lara—and for the first time I realize her eyes are a matching shade to the gin. She is looking deep into me, and for a moment there may be a hint of sexuality but it is more a recognition, a mingling of spirits.

She asks me, "Would you like to try something you may not know about?"

Well, strange question, but I feel quite comfortable. "Sure, Lara, I am game for whatever you have in mind."

She gets up and leaves the room. Not sure of the layout but she is gone a very short time. Returning, she has a sliver box in one hand and some foil and a lighter in the other. She hands them to me and brings over a Japanese black lacquered cocktail table with chrysanthemum design and I place the items on it.

She lays out the piece of foil about six inches square, opens the box, and, with a small wooden spoon, places a pile of white powder in the middle and spreads it into one continuous line. She hands me a rolled-up $100 bill, picks up the foil in one hand, the lighter in the other, and looks at me. "OK, when I hold the lighter under the foil, I will cook it briefly, it'll turn oily."

She does and it does. "Now the H will burn, you are to inhale the smoke with the bill, are you ready?"

I nod. This is got to be interesting since I don't smoke. I hope I will be able to handle it. She moves the foil toward me and fires up the Cartier stainless steel table lighter. Almost immediately smoke begins to rise as she moves the lighter across the foil. I chase the smoke. She says, "Hold it in." That I do as long as I can and then release it, and the smoke rises toward the white plastered ceiling. It's much different than a shot, subtle, like sliding slowly into a warm bath. She repeats the act and then I sink back into the silk pillows. Chasing the dragon is what Lara calls what we are doing. All I focus on is the indigo color of her eyes.

St. Quentin Canal

The cornet solo seems to blow the smoke away from in front of my eyes, clear the haze of the last couple of days. It is good but it's not Bix. That bar is set too high, so I settle back in my chair and look at my untouched martini. My hair is slicked back. I have on a set of evening wear in midnight blue, a deep, blackish blue, which even in this bright light appears muted, yet still appearing to be darker and richer than black.

The jacket sitting long on my hips, with moderately wide peaked lapels, cuffed at the wrists with satin trim. Single breasted, of course. Two flap pockets on the front, and a slit breast pocket containing a small white pocket square.

The trousers, a matching midnight blue, very high waisted, held up by a pair of white suspenders, with a satin stripe down each leg. The pants are cut narrow and cuffed. The shirt, starched white, crisp with a wingtip collar and French cuffs, buttoning up the front with mother-of-pearl buttons. Keeping with the popular style, the cuff links are initialed "K-L," in midnight-blue enamel.

The waistcoat is a stylish white brocade with a straight waist lined "tub" fashion, high-waisted cut with no points. The bow tie is a black silk. On the left jacket lapel, a boutonniere containing a mini yellow calla lily. The shoes are simple black patent-leather slip-on pumps with small stacked heels, the toes slightly pointed.

Hard for me to believe that about two weeks ago I was here with two friends who now have disowned me. In fact the little fuck called me a hophead. He's right, of course, but technically hophead refers to someone who smokes opium and is addicted. By now we are several levels up the synthesis chain; 80 years from now, who knows what pharmaceutical magic they will cook up.

Each night we appear at the Cinderella Ballroom, most of the time at the same table, talk, laugh, drink, they smoke, listen to jazz, go for a late-night bite. Lara favors the Nom Wah Tea Parlor at 13-15 Doyers Street, then back to the apartment. They are, of course, Kaylee and Lara. I enjoy their company immensely, I love them both, they love each other, who gives a fuck what anyone thinks.

I have had this brewing inside me for a long time, in fact since September 29, 1918. I was 18 and part of the US II Corps and we were thrown into the Battle of St. Quentin Canal, part of the 100 days offensive on the Western Front. It lasted to the armistice on November 11, and we suffered 13,182 casualties. I watched my best friend get vaporized by an artillery shell. I was in a coma for five days. There is no explanation that I can give or that I have heard to explain why nothing is what it should be after that day at the canal, at least what it can be. If I know one thing, it is I know what I do not know.

My eyes rest on my companions. Kaylee is wearing a Chanel evening dress with a straight design on top a fuller skirt on the bottom, with an open back, all in lipstick red. Lara is also wearing a Chanel of the same design but in a quiet, muted yellow. They are both laughing at a joke about Coco that I neither understand nor care about. These two are funny and I always thought women were not that funny. I must have learned something in that coma. I'm lost in that thought when Kaylee says, "Hey, there's McDowall at the bar."

I look and yes, it's him. I find nothing odd but I didn't peg him being a jazz fan. Why not say hello. "Ladies, I'm going to say hello, be right back."

I make my way through the crowd to the bar. I motion to the bartender, Armando, to get McDowall a refill. Armando nods. I slide in next to McDowall. He turns and looks at me and it takes a second but recognition washes over his face. I offer my hand, he takes it, and we shake as Armando places another Speyside single malt on the bar.

McDowall looks at it and then at me. "Thank you, sir."

I say, "No more 'sir'—I was an NCO."

McDowall turns toward me, his eyes casting a different reflection. "You served, sir? In the war?"

"Yes, I did, McDowall, and would you mind if I ask you your first name?"

"In Britain, sir, never, but things are different here. Johnston. I joined, sir, but never made it to the front. We were training and someone fired a short round, everybody yelled 'Duck!' and I yelled, 'What?'—and Bob's your uncle, I'm back in Manchester pulling pints."

I laugh then feel bad and apologize.

"No need to apologize, sir, I always play it that way and I realize what I missed. How about you?"

"Well, Johnston, I was at the Battle of St. Quentin Canal and got myself blown up, have been a little loopy ever since. Enjoy the single malt, Johnston, I never would have thought you liked jazz."

"I am immersing myself in all things American, sir."

I laugh and we shake hands. I have the feeling Mr. McDowall is looking at me a little differently now.

I get back to the table and Kaylee asks, "How is McDowall? Nice to see him enjoying his day off. He is a worrier. I am more trouble than I'm worth."

I lay my hand on her arm. "I don't think he sees it that way. How about a bite?"

Before anyone can speak, we all say, "Nom Wah Tea Parlor," and all laugh.

Cab it to Doyers, get out, and push our way into the Tea Parlor, it is that crowded. After a wait, standing at the door, we get a table. We order. My three char siu bau buns and bowl of dan dan mian noodles are set noiselessly on the table before me by the same diminutive woman almost every time we come here. She never makes eye contact. I often observe her as she moves effortlessly around the small, overly crowded space. Her movements consist of ever widening and contracting circles. Each time I am sure a collision is imminent, she is not at the point of contact.

Having had a fine snack upon exiting, Lara says she wants to stop in an herbal shop before we head back uptown. I follow them two doors down to a small Chinese herbal shop with a sign above depicting a beautiful crane at the edge of a pond. We go into the shop. It is dimly lit. Lara beckons me to follow her to the back of the shop, where a few candles are burning in the corner in front of a small reed mat. The mat is occupied by a very frail-looking old man. The old man's eyes open and he beckons me closer. I stop in front of his mat. He pushes both hands down. Sit.

I sit. He speaks. "Many years ago I learned your language at a young age as my father was involved with negotiations between English trading companies. I was called to help maintain some face during and at the end of the second opium war but after, because of the disastrous defeat of the Qing army, the death of the Emperor, and the burning of the summer palace, we had nothing with which to bargain. Now all that is left is rebellion. From the East it will come but it will not restore the Ming."

I look at him, perplexed. "So, you can tell me the future old man?"

He answers, "When the world began, there was heaven and earth. You will seek your fortune elsewhere. You have done terrible things, been the tool of great injustice, drunk, gambled, smoked the poison, and given in to the pleasures of the flesh. There is one who will come out of the East. She will be of the Dao, and the look in her eyes will show you your true path."

Later when we have exhausted ourselves and I am out in the parlor lying on the Adolf Loos Knieschwimmer Variant Rocking Chaise Lounge from Vienna, my eyes finally closing as I feared they might and I would see that shell explode as I have seen it explode almost every night. Not tonight; tonight as I go under, I see a courtyard filled with young Chinese woman all dressed in red and holding red lanterns.

On the Knieschwimmer

Consciousness returns as something wet and fluffy is striking each side of my face. I jolt awake and attempt to sit up but I am knocked back down by the force of the next blow. Why the hell is McDowall beating me with a wet towel?

Suddenly he stops. "Are you back, sir, are you aware of where you are?"

I realize I am laid out on the Adolf Loos Knieschwimmer Variant Rocking Chaise Lounge from Vienna. Sitting on the davenport, quietly crying, is Kaylee. She lifts her head and sees I am awake.

Her voice sounds frightened. "I thought I killed you with that last shot. It was a new batch, strong, I should have been more careful."

The top of my body is wet and my face is stinging. I look at McDowall and say, "Quite a beating you were administering."

He stands up straight with a look of relief on his face. "Yes, back home I helped tend war veterans who had acquired the habit. I had to invoke that procedure on more than one occasion, not always with success. I am very glad you are all right, sir, we lost enough of you fellows."

He turns to Kaylee. "If I may, I would like to fetch the gentleman some water."

She agrees. "Of course McDowall."

As he walks to the kitchen, I call out after to him, "Thank you, Johnston, I owe you one."

He tilts his head back toward me. "I am sure you are paid up, sir."

He's made of finer stuff, I'm thinking. I don't really feel my legs but that's not too rare ever since that shell burst at the canal. A hand brushes a lock of hair off my forehead. I look up at Kaylee. A tear drops off her cheek onto my cheek and runs down to my lips, kissing them. She melts into my arms, her hair brushing away the tear.

She whispers into my ear, "I'm so sorry. You know I'm no good."

I whisper back, allowing my lips to touch her lobe, "Why, you made a mistake. On July 1, 1916, during that single day at the Somme, the British took 57,470 casualties. You think one of those fucking generals said they were sorry? Forget it, Kaylee, I'm a big boy. I know I cannot control it anymore, but if somebody can make the images, make those sounds of the dying go away without the drugs, I still wouldn't care. I like getting loaded. I especially like getting loaded with you."

She slides a hand to my cheek and lovingly holds it. I continue, "Anyway, what would we miss?"

McDowall enters the room and announces, "Miss Lara, Miss Kaylee," and brings me a crystal tumbler filled with ice water and then retreats back out.

Lara comes over to the Loos, kneels down, puts her arms around us both, and says in her low register, "I missed you two dope fiends."

I am admiring the ceiling fresco, which I never noticed before, done in a Pozzo style of using the illusionistic technique called quadratura. I say to Lara, "Have you ever noticed the frescoed ceilings in this place?"

"Yes," she says, "yes, aren't they just too much." I am about to reply when I realize she is kissing Kaylee and it's not a kiss hello.

"Ladies, ladies, why don't you take it to the bedroom, it would be so much more comfortable and Kaylee would not be digging her elbow into my groin." They laugh their way to the bedroom. I'm left here alone. All things considered, at the canal they said I lay in a muddy shell hole for 10 hours. No, not bad, still feeling the effect of the drug, shoes off, tie loosened, lying on Adolf. No, all things in perspective, I'd rather be here than in that muddy hole.

Malory Arrives

I am not paying attention, as I am watching the young woman in the elevator with me. I am not staring, just interested because she is quite striking, well dressed in wearable knitwear that has a special double-layered stitch created by Armenian refugees for Elsa Schiaparelli. I let her enter first and her thank-you is in slightly accented English. When the doors open, I realize that I rode past Kaylee's floor and we are now on Lara's floor. Well, I might as well say hello and check to see if she has any ideas about tonight's activities.

Walking the carpeted hallway toward Lara's, I am five feet behind the young lady. Surprise, she stops at Lara's door and is ringing the bell. The door opens and Lara, who by the way refuses to employ any servants, steps out and embraces the young woman. They swing around and Lara spots me standing off to the side.

She smiles and says, "Look who's standing outside my door."

The young woman turns and says, "We rode up in the elevator together. I did not know he was coming to visit you." She breaks her embrace with Lara and steps toward me extending her hand. I take it, slightly surprised by the firmness of the handshake.

She says, "I am Malory. You must be Nigel." She carries a vibrancy that runs right through her handshake.

"Yes, yes I am."

Lara waves us into her apartment. "Please have a seat, anyone want a drink?"

I glance at my Rolex 1926 Oyster and it is 10:45 a.m. "Lara, it is not yet 11:00."

She laughs and puts her hand on my shoulder. "I was thinking of orange juice, love."

I feel pretty stupid and a little embarrassed. Am I trying to impress Malory? Malory shakes her head. Lara is looking at me with a slight smile, she has something in mind. She moves her hand toward Malory. "This is my cousin Malory, she has come over from France to stay with me to see if she likes New York. I am expecting you to show her all the sights and persuade her to stay. Malory, Nigel knows lots of interesting places and things to do."

Great, I'm thinking, turn your young cousin over to a shell-shocked dope fiend. "It would be my pleasure, Lara, I can think of a few things right off the top of my head." Give it right back.

Lara laughs. "I bet you do." She gets up, pulling her robe around her. "I going to make some coffee, you two get better acquainted."

I say to Malory, "I was going to make dinner plans with Lara and our friend Kaylee, would you join us?"

208

She replies, "If it is not too much. I would love to see the sights with real New Yorkers."

"OK, I thought we would have dinner at the Puncheon Club, it's on 49th street. Our friend Kaylee can open any doors. Let's see if Lara has any ideas."

Malory appears to be trying to word a delicate question. "No one can get a drink of alcohol, is that right?"

I laugh. "Technically, but we can get a drink anywhere. At the Cinderella Ballroom, they will serve certain guests drinks in coffee cups. That's how I get my martinis."

"Oh"—she lets out a little laugh—"it is that way everywhere, not so." She stands. "Excuse me," and leaves the room.

Lara returns from her coffee making. She looks around. "You didn't scare her off already, did you?"

I laugh. "No, not yet, I need more time."

Lara sits next to me and speaks in a low voice, "Her mother, my aunt, sent her here, truthfully, she is having a difficult time of it. Malory's father was killed at the Battle of Verdun in '16, her mother never got over it. Malory was old enough to know her father and she has suffered also."

I look into Lara's blue eyes. "It's all a terrible equation, who knows what far-reaching consequences have yet to be felt. The poor kid."

Lara is studying my face and suddenly she puts her arms around me in a loving embrace and whispers in my ear, "I have complete faith in you, I trust you with her."

Of course I go for the laugh. "Yes, but can she be trusted not to take advantage?"

Lara shakes her head. "Did you always have this sense of humor?"

"Honestly, only since I was blown up, everything seems funny to me. I know, funny how? It's just funny."

Lara gives me a quick squeeze and sits back. "She is here to study at The Art Students League at The American Fine Arts Society Building at 215 West 57th Street. She talks on and on about her interest in the Regionalist movement and some painter named Benton. I'm just happy she has a passion about something."

I nod. "Yes, the question before the house is, how are we to deal with her in light of our little proclivities?"

Lara leans further back, looking at me. "We must keep her out of that aspect of our lives."

I cross my legs, slightly pulling back the Brooks Brothers pants. "I guess we could find a young gentleman, I know a few who work downtown on Wall Street. They spend lots of cash but they're a wild bunch. I'm not sure…since the war everyone I know who made it back is not available, for one reason or another." All the time Lara is shaking her head.

I stop and ask, "What's wrong?"

She reaches over and takes my hand. "It's you, you're the one to help her settle in."

I pull my hand away. "Have you lost your mind? I thought you were kidding. Let's see, my qualities: loopy from an exploding shell, a dope fiend, a nihilist who cares about fuck-all, has no real interests, except the dope, and I get the shakes every now and then. Sounds like marriage material."

Lara takes my hand again. "No, can't you see you are loyal and honest and you will never make her cry?"

I pull my hand away again. "What are you, my agent? Honestly, Lara, I never got out of that mud hole, whoever I was before that moment is gone, replaced by some facsimile of a man. This kid deserves something better. Her father was slaughtered for nothing. She should be compensated and not with an addled veteran."

Lara takes my hand, again. "Listen, I'm not asking you to marry her, just show her a good time and a few laughs."

I hold on to her hand. "Oh, was I overreacting? Never mind, a few laughs, a good time, now you are asking for my Babe Ruth swing."

Lara smiles. "OK, it's settled. Tonight we begin."

Begin it we do, three nights running. We are having a marvelous time. Malory is a serious young lady but she is as warmhearted as she is serious. I wish I knew someone appropriate. I am not fond of the Art Students League crowd. Artists, then again the only artist I ever met, other than Malory, was a young man who got gassed at Belleau Wood in '18.

I arrive at Kaylee's apartment. Tonight I've decided on a different set of evening wear. A tuxedo jacket, fairly long, falling below my hips. Thin notched lapels, fairly wide. The jacket is cuffed at the wrists, with contrasting faille material. The jacket is single breasted with two buttonholes on either side of the jacket held together by a coat link. Matching pants that are very high waisted, coming above the natural waistline, and held up with suspenders. The trim on the side legs is a single narrow braid, in satin. The trousers have thin legs and cuffs turned up at the high ankle, a sharp crease down the center.

My shirt is buttoned up with shirt links made of black onyx. On the double cuffs (French cuffs) are a pair of initialed cuff links ("K-L").

Ivory waistcoat in the Prince of Wales style, backless vest attached around the back with just two straps. The bow tie fairly fat, black.

Black patent-leather slip-on pumps are my evening shoe of choice, with a small stacked heel and slightly pointed round toe.

McDowall opens the door to my ring, opens it wider and bids me enter. "How is the gentleman tonight?"

"Fine, Johnston, thanks for asking."

"There will be three ladies this evening, sir. Maybe a dram before leaving?"

"Yes, Johnston, that was very nice scotch you gave me, some of that with a splash of water."

McDowall smiles. "We'll make a Scotsman of you yet, sir." He walks over to the rosewood bar.

The three ladies appear out of Kaylee's bedroom, all dressed for an evening out. Each has on a dress of fine material, Kaylee and Lara in silk, Malory in chiffon. All three dresses are sleeveless with the fashionable drop waist, with layers of fabric, creating a fullness from the waist down and beaded. One dress in yellow, one in red, and one in turquoise. Each is wearing an understated, fairly long pearl necklace. All three have fur wraps.

McDowall hands me my scotch in a Waterford rocks glass, weighty. I throw it back.

"Thanks, Johnston. I'm fortified for the task at hand."

McDowall has a word. "Pardon, sir, but today is November 30, which makes it St. Andrew's Day. I believe the club will have something special. I recommend the haggis, the chef there does a marvelous haggis." Of course I vaguely remember what haggis is, but I feel confident in McDowall's food *compétence*.

We leave the apartment, cab it down to the Puncheon Club. Kaylee is greeted warmly and the four of us are shown to a table appropriate to her standing, fuck everyone else. Well, it's November 30, St. Andrew's Day, and the waiter informs us there is a special menu.

St. Andrew's Day

Mini haggis, tatties, and neeps to start, with a dram
(which turns out to be fucking iced tea),
Angus forerib with roasted seasonal root vegetables and
roast potatoes,
served with a red wine reduction,
Mackie's ice cream with raspberries to finish.

We all order the special menu, although Malory looks dubious after I explain what haggis is. Despite the misgivings, we all enjoy our meal. Of course, I spike everyone's tea with some Old Forester from my flask. Goddamn Prohibition, they don't want us to drink but there is certainly enough H to go around.

After dinner it is a short walk to the Cinderella Ballroom. There is a mediocre jazz band but it doesn't slow us down. They are doing a nice ragtime piece, though, so I ask Malory to dance. She declines, I persist, she relents. Once on the dance floor, I explain to her it is expected to do a fox-trot to this kind of beat. She is a little nervous but I take her in my arms and speak softly into her ear, slow, slow, quick, quick. Damn, she is doing a nice job right away. Her breath on my cheek, the scent of Chanel No. 5, her softness, her warmth, this is not supposed to happen.

Just then there is a loud crash—a waiter has dropped a very large tray of glasses.

Too late my body is reacting. I'm trying to stop it but I cannot. Sweat is already beading my forehead. Malory pulls away slightly, noticing how tense I have become.

She says, "I think I've had enough fox-trot. Let's sit awhile." We move off the dance floor. My hand is shaking. It was nothing, but that is how it happens. It could be anything, sudden movement or a loud noise. For the rest of the excursion, I am quiet. The ladies sense something is not quite right, so they call it an evening.

We get back to Kaylee's apartment and she says I should stay and sleep on the couch in Lara's apartment, Malory can have Lara's bedroom, and Lara will stay down here. It seems all a little convoluted but I surmise Kaylee thinks I want to sleep with Malory and Malory wants to sleep with me. Fuck it, I've slept on couches before. The two of us begin to head up to Lara's place. McDowall asks if I need anything. Yes, but nothing I will mention.

We get upstairs and I quickly wish pleasant dreams to Malory, just to relax the kid. She stands there for a moment and then turns to walk to the bedroom, saying, "I'll get a blanket and pillow for you."

"Thank you, Malory." She's back in no time and I say good night again. She hesitates. "Do you need anything?"

"Nothing, thank you." So formal. She retreats to the bedroom, lights out. I strip down and get under the covers, praying it won't happen tonight.

"Drew, Drew!" someone is yelling, someone in a panic. My body is being shaken. I come back to reality, I leave my dream, my eyes focus, it's Malory.

She is holding my shoulders. "You were yelling someone's name over and over, to get down, to take cover." My body feels cold and yet I am sweating.

Malory stands. "Let me get you some water."

I grab her arm; she looks a little frightened. "No, please stay for a moment. I'll be all right, it will pass."

She sits back down and asks, "Who is Drew?"

I avert my face. "My friend, he was killed at the St. Quentin Canal." I look at this talented young woman and say, "Go back to bed, Malory, it's just a dream I was having, it will pass, it always does." I really am thinking about a shot, because while it does pass it never goes away. She puts her hands back on my shoulders. "No, I will sit up with you for a while. Let me put some music on, that will help." She gets up and in a minute the room is filled with Ruth Etting's voice. "'After you've gone and left me crying / After you've gone, there's no denying /

You'll feel blue, you'll feel sad...'" God no, not that song, not that song,

I try again. "I'm fine, really, go back to bed."

This time she looks firmly at me. "It's the drug you want. I will stay here with you while you take it."

I sit up. "Have you lost your mind? I can't expose you to this. I promised Lara and it is not something you should see."

She looks at me sharply. "I have seen this and more. France lost a generation of men, including my father, some came home in body only. I will sit here with you, offering what meager support I can give to someone who is hurt so very bad."

I get up, get my works, and return. I prepare a shot, roll up my sleeve, apply the rubber hose, and inject the liquid relief. A few minutes pass and I am feeling fine until I look over at Malory and realize Lara was wrong. There are tears running down Malory's cheeks, I did make her cry.

Over a Tartine

Lara is pouring the French roast coffee from the 19th-century Naples/ Capo di Monte Boxed Coffee Service. Each cup is individually hand painted over raised and molded decoration, the handles all depict a piece of coral which is further decorated with gold enamel. The breakfast is some tartine, accompanied by Sara Jane Cooper's Oxford marmalade and butter. No conversation for a while, until Lara puts her second cup of coffee onto its saucer. "So, Malory, did you sleep well?"

"Yes, I did," she answers.

Lara says, "Oh, Nigel is still sleeping, anything I should know about?"

Malory sits back in her chair, putting down her tartine after so liberally spreading Sara all over it. "Yes, cousin, Nigel had a nightmare last night, I sat up with him for a while. The war, you know."

"Yes, I love the guy, he is so very damaged and yet he manages to be there whenever you need him. I don't think he will ever recover but he is coping the best he can. So much lost, so much he has lost. He was married, you know. He never talks much about her, married before he left for France. A sweet young girl from Sioux Falls, South Dakota.

She died of influenza while he was recuperating in hospital from his injuries. She was pregnant when she died. He's seen about as much death as anyone can have the courage to witness."

Malory is looking down into her coffee, lost, no doubt, in her own past and things that cannot be altered. She lifts her head. "Yes, when I was dancing with him, my head close to his, I recognized his scent as Acqua di Parma, a beautifully subtle men's cologne, his dancing smooth, the rhythm intoxicating, and in a moment it all changed. The loud crash and his whole body froze. I did not know what to say, so I pleaded fatigue. Tell me, cousin, he seems to have his own schedule, does he work?"

"Work? God no, I do not think he has ever held a job for any length of time. No, he cannot abide being in any kind of office. His father requested he work for a while at his uncle's shipyard but he left after beating another employee senseless. Seems the guy was disparaging the war and saying those who went to fight Europe's war were fools. Oddly it's the same sentiment Nigel has, but I guess he earned the right to voice it. Anyway, his family is very wealthy."

After a pause she elaborated, "Apparently the family on his mother's side are Croats, not sure where exactly but they were part of the dying Hapsburg Empire. Two of his uncles left for South Africa, and what became known as Rhodesia. Peter and Frank, cannot remember the last name, their stories are quite fascinating. One uncle, Peter, made a fortune connecting with the British South Africa Company and establishing mines of gold, copper, and diamonds. He died in a mine accident, leaving his vast fortune to his sister, Nigel's mother.

"The other uncle, Frank—Mad Frank, they call him—is, according to Nigel, a ruthless bastard. He was very experienced in some kind of counter-insurgent tactics, not sure what the hell it means but Frank created a small band of fighters—British, Croats, South African, local tribes—and was given the green light from top British military to conduct operations.

"Conduct them he did, systematically tracking down the highly mobile Boer guerrilla units and killing without question every Boer he could lay his hands on. His reward was shares in several gold mines. He also sent a large share of his money to his sister. That's how his family got their money, on his mother's side. Nigel keeps Frank's

Webley, well used, on his night table, brought it with him to France, shot a few Huns with it, I suppose.

"Nigel is quite a generous person. He frequently picks up our bill wherever we are, even though we are not exactly broke, and if he meets a veteran, their money is no good. We ran into a dinner of some veterans' group, must have been 20 of them, anyway, Nigel quietly paid for the whole meal, must have been $300."

Malory is taking it all in. "Lara, I do not think anything less of Nigel for all the shakes, the nightmares, the drugs. He's warm, funny, has been so kind to me and it was as intimate an evening, last night, as I have spent with a man in my life. It takes a special kind of courage to show how broken you really are."

As Malory finishes, music is heard coming from the sitting room. The sweet sounds of Bix's cornet, such a soulful tone.

Malory looks at Lara. "Nigel's awake, I think I'll go see how he is doing."

Lara nods OK but says, "Malory, you can love him but don't fall in love with him."

Scratch, scratch. I lift the arm off the record of "Davenport Blues."

"How are you feeling?"

I turn and see Malory standing in the sitting room holding a cup and saucer in her right hand. She's wearing a rose-colored dressing gown, trimmed in blue and embellished with embroidery. It has one trimmed pocket in the front, with a snap closing at the bust, and a self-belt with a floral accent.

"I brought you a cup of coffee, glad to see you up."

I happily take the cup, feel a little unsteady so I sit, putting the cup on the Japanese black lacquered cocktail table with chrysanthemum design. I am wearing some of last night's attire and feeling a little out of place. I should never have succumbed to the demons last night. How is Malory to perceive the situation now? The davenport cushions move as Malory sits down beside me. I can't really look at her; I would like to run out of the room but I just stare straight ahead. My head is empty, my body fatigued. This is all too much, what's going on here. You should leave these woman alone. Think, you have been a terrible influence on

Kaylee and Lara, now Malory has witnessed how far someone can fall. Get out, Nigel, get out and find whatever darkness is there.

An arm is placed around my shoulders. Malory is quietly holding me. She says in her soft voice, "I am going to sing you a song."

I have to look at her now. "I didn't know you sing."

She runs her hand through my hair, pushing it in place. "Oh yes, and I learned an American song." She stands.

Lara enters the room and sits beside me, putting her hand on my thigh. She says, "Today is going to be beautiful."

Malory begins to sing "My Blue Heaven" in a sweet, slightly accented, lyric voice, warming my heart with the popular piece, changing only a single stanza.

> *...Lara and me, and Nigel makes three*
> *...Just Lara and me, and Nigel makes three*
> *We're happy...*

Malory finishes and stands with her arms wide in invitation, as Lara's Arpège scent envelops me. Maybe it will be a beautiful day.

Chasing the Dragon

The record, still spinning, reaches an end as the needle bumps against the label, trying to continue to capture Ruth's voice. The room is bathed in a subtle lighting from two pairs of French Art Deco wall sconces by the French artist Degué, in clear and frosted glass shades with geometric and floral motif.

The only occupant of the apartment is lying on the davenport of pale yellow. He's in a dressing gown of Chinese embroidered satin silk, probably dating from the second half of the 19th century. It consists of a very fine polychrome embroidery of floss silk on a yellow ochre bronze satin background representing auspicious signs and Taoist symbols. His feet are bare, one arm is dangling off the davenport scraping the plush 12-by-10 carpet consisting of three arrangements of horizontal stripes in a composition, one at the upper left corner, one at the center, and one at the lower right corner, orange in color, each broken up by a brown streak of color running vertically at different points, all on an earthy background.

His hair is out of place, eyes closed, but he is not sleeping, while his breathing is regular, sweat is beading on his pale forehead. The occupant has no idea what time it is or even how long he has been in the apartment. His last memories consist of a long drawn-out discussion with the three ladies concerning a weekend excursion to East Hampton and a weekend of cocktails and boring conversation about politics—the owner holds some political office, and the stock market. Yes, if anyone mentions politics, they better make damn sure the davenport's occupant is not within reach of his Webley. He stirs, he lifts his arm…Nigel is stirring.

I sit up and regret it. I glance down at the Japanese black lacquered cocktail table with chrysanthemum design and see it littered with used tin foil, a Cartier stainless steel table lighter, and Lara's Chinese black lacquered box. I know the box is almost empty. Nice work, the only kind you're capable of, chasing the dragon for, how long?

The doorbell is ringing, it sounds like I'm inside the bell tower of St. Patrick's.

"OK!" I yell. Great, so mannerly. I manage to get to my feet and stumble to the apartment door and open it. In comes McDowall carrying a large tray. If he is shocked by my stumblebum appearance he does not show it. "Pardon, sir, I thought a spot of breakfast would be in order."

I stare at him for a few seconds and then realize that tray must be heavy. "Sorry, Johnston, please bring it in and put it down on the table in the sitting room."

I do my best to follow McDowall but realize I am still high from the drugs. It's all coming back now. The three ladies had me on the davenport and spent at least an hour trying to persuade me to accompany them to East Hampton. Let's see, I love being around them but I hate the island, I despise all politicians, and—the last straw—the bastards cannot mix a proper martini, as simple as that seems to me. Those assholes never even heard of orange bitters. The ladies all looked disappointed. Malory tried to appeal to my sense of camaraderie, that almost got me, but I knew the most danger they would face would be terrible cocktails and worse food. Reminds me of the old joke about terrible food and the portions are so small.

I manage to stomp on McDowall's right foot trying to seat myself back down. He doesn't flinch as I apologize, "So sorry, Johnston, I am a little under the weather this morning, late night."

McDowall says, "No harm, sir, it's not a real foot."

I look at him questioningly. "Sorry, sir, I told you about the training accident, it took away my right leg below the knee. I wear a prosthetic."

"Sorry to hear that, Johnston."

"Really a blessing, sir, lost most of my company at the Somme."

I don't say anything because there is nothing to say.

McDowall looks at the table. "Is the gentleman finished with the foil?" He conveys not an ounce of judgment.

"Thanks, Johnston, they are all used."

McDowall sweeps them all up and carries them to the kitchen. He returns, lifts the lid off the dish. It is a full English; not sure if the stomach can handle it,

"Looks beautiful, Johnston, but I'll start with coffee."

McDowall pours a cup. "Black, sir?"

"Yes, I really appreciate you going through all this trouble."

"It is not any trouble, sir, I'm more than happy and Miss Kaylee, Miss Lara, and Miss Malory all were adamant that I see if you require anything." McDowall hesitates. "Now, sir, in full light of the American democratic policy, I am going to take a chance of losing my service."

"Go ahead, Johnston, this will between us."

McDowall straightens up and begins. "Sir, it may not be my place, but I have grown very fond of you and I feel a need to offer my opinion. It is not in any way a condemnation of you, I would just hope the gentleman would go carefully. The world needs men like you to make sure people don't forget what a slaughterhouse that war was."

My eyes fill. "Johnston, I have nothing but respect for you and I am proud to know a man like you. We have seen more than our share. I will cherish what you have said to me. I am afraid that what we say, what we do, will have little effect because the world is a slaughterhouse. I wish it was different."

I pick up the lacquered box and open it, showing it to McDowall. "They will never be able to make enough of this stuff."

McDowall nods sadly. "I suspect you are right, sir. I just hope you go carefully in this world. It is a better place with you in it."

I am feeling a powerful sense of comradeship and decide on an empty gesture. I reach down and remove my Rolex 1926 Oyster. In 1926, Rolex created the first waterproof and dustproof wristwatch and gave it the name "Oyster." I hold it out to McDowall.

He takes it thinking I want him to put it away, but no. "It's yours, Johnston."

His head jumps up. "I could never accept such a gift, sir."

"I insist. It is a memento of our service."

"But I did not serve, sir."

"Oh, yes you did, every night you have to take off that leg. Look at the back case."

McDowall turns it over. It reads:

II Corps

McDowall closes his hand over the watch. "I will cherish it for the rest of my life, sir."

I smile at him. "You do me great honor accepting it, Johnston."

I can see he is moved. "Does the gentleman need anything else, sir?"

I think he better get out of here, no use both of us getting sentimental. "No, thank you again, please leave the tray, I might want something later."

"Good, sir. By the way, sir, it is, according to my watch"—he glances down at the Rolex—"15:35 hours."

I just laugh as he walks to the door.

I go into the kitchen and tear off a piece of foil and bring it into the sitting room. I pour an amount of H onto the foil, pick up the Cartier, pull the rolled-up bill out of my pocket, place it in my mouth, heat the foil gently, and then, lighter under, I chase the smoke the length of the foil. I sit back looking up at the ceiling and finally exhale, blowing the smoke to heaven. I am thinking to myself, yesterday was a beautiful day. Today is another day.

Darkness Covered the Sky
...it's your love.

All three woman are looking down at the figure lying on the davenport. Amazingly, he has a slight smile on his face. He is pale, unshaven, hair disheveled, the exquisite Chinese robe looking two sizes two big, feet bare, a small tremor in his right hand. None of the three have any idea what to do, should they wake him? Should they leave him be? What is happening in his dream state?

Malory turns to Lara, and Kaylee. "I am going to get a cool cloth and wipe his forehead." She leaves for the bathroom.

The tremor in his right hand increases by a small increment, his legs are starting to move, his lips are twitching. Behind his eyes...

Dark clouds cover the sky, stretching beyond sight in each direction, the landscape is a montage of upturned dirt, tangled wire, bodies, oh yes, lots of bodies. The advance has already stalled just past their own wire. The counter-barrage is intensifying with each passing second. Someone yells "Gas!" but it is just the smoke from exploding shells. Officers are shouting encouragement; how do you encourage men to run to their deaths? Explosions, dirt, shrapnel, body parts are all flying around him. Drew is off to his right. He sees the shells walking toward them, he screams for Drew to get down, to take cover, but the shell explodes and he is gone forever. The concussion knocks him into a shell hole, there he will lie for hours, unconscious, stepped on by retreating troops, covered in his friend's blood.

Nigel bolts upright, wide awake but standing on the Western Front. He's about to scream out Drew's name but suddenly a cool cloth is run over his forehead and he is in Lara's apartment, Malory standing beside him, in fact all three ladies are in front of him.

Of course Nigel smiles. "Back from the Island? Must have dozed off on the davenport."

Lara sits beside him. "God, were you right about the cocktails. They used a local distilled gin and mixed it awfully with a cheap vermouth, not a bitter in sight. We took great pleasure in batting about what would happen if Nigel was here. The consensus was a drink quietly but pointedly left untouched."

Kaylee laughs. "Nigel, time to rise, dress, and come down to my apartment. McDowall is cooking tonight, a pork loin and sundries."

I look uncertain. "Maybe I should go back to my apartment and leave you three to enjoy dinner."

Kaylee is already shaking her head. "No, we haven't seen you for two days and you have three Brooks Brothers suits, shirts, the works, in my apartment. Come down, bathe, shave, please, and mix us some drinkable cocktails."

I really don't want to be alone so I agree to Kaylee's idea.

Lara speaks up before I can gather myself and put on proper clothes in order to venture into the hall. "Nigel, please join me in my bedroom before you go downstairs." I nod OK.

Kaylee announces, "Malory come down with me and see what McDowall is whipping up." Both head out the door. I begin to rise when Lara pushes me back down onto the davenport.

She looks a little apprehensive. "Nigel, I have a favor to ask of you." I spread my arms in a just-name-it gesture. "There is a man I want you to talk to, a doctor, a psychologist. You know you cannot go on like this. We all talked it over on the trip back. We met this doctor at the East Hampton house. I heard his connection to our host is that he is treating his wife. Apparently she took a bunch of pills once and he is helping her."

I am listening but something strikes me as funny. "Well, considering the host, I would expect she would need treatment if she didn't take a handful of pills."

Lara looks at me a moment and then bursts out laughing. "Damn it, Nigel! Oh, I forgot, everything seems funny to you. Would you see this doctor, at least once, if not for yourself then for the three of us?"

"OK, Lara, I will. You always think you can control it but in the end it controls you. What's his name and where is his office?"

Lara pulls out a card from her suit jacket and hands it to me. It reads:

Dr. D. D. Gilhooley

110 E. 10th Street

Suite 100

I look at Lara. "D. D., what the hell is that?"

Lara starts to giggle but represses it. "His first name is Dizzy. Dr. Dizzy Daniel Gilhooley."

I flip the card onto the Japanese table. "OK, so you want me to go see Doctor Dizzy, what is this, some kind of burlesque skit? I suppose he has a blond assistant with large breasts?"

Lara laughs, putting her hand in front of her face. "Nigel, would you believe his receptionist is a blonde with big breasts?"

I continue, "So am I the punchline? How long did you speak with this quack?"

Lara places her hand on my thigh, a sure signal she is about to say something she feels is important. "You trust me, Nigel?"

"Of course, Lara. I will go see this guy. No shock treatments, please, no diets, no hydrotherapy, what does he indeed do?"

"He talks with you and he believes in some kind of hypnotism. He talked at length about somebody named Franz Mesmer and a *magnétisme* animal and a lot about William James."

"I have grave doubts but I will go see this doctor on your recommendation alone."

Lara smiles. "Thank you, Nigel. I hope he can be of some help."

It's Friday at 10:00 a.m. I find myself up almost at a work hour and am standing outside number 110. I walk into the lobby and introduce myself to the concierge, who announces me to the suite and directs me across the lobby to an office door, marked 100. I go into the minuscule waiting room. Behind the small desk is indeed a blonde with large breasts. I do not laugh but introduce myself as the doctor's 10:00 a.m. appointment.

"Please, have a seat, sir, the doctor will be with you momentarily." I take off my shearling collar chesterfield coat and my tonal ribbon fedora, handing both to the receptionist.

I sit on the quite uncomfortable chair, determined to see this through. Some sort of buzzer goes off and the receptionist says I can go in to see the doctor. I open and enter the doctor's office. It's not much bigger than the reception area. Desk against the wall, doctor in a small armchair positioned next to a two-cushion sofa. The desk is bare expect for a telephone and a bust of someone I do not recognize.

The doctor is sitting with his legs crossed in a grey double-breasted suit, white shirt, wing collar, solid red tie, cap-toe Oxfords in black. He is quite thin, greying hair slicked back, and a well-trimmed beard. I figure the beard is de rigueur for his profession. He points to the sofa, like I have another place to sit besides his lap. I sit.

He adjusts the pad sitting on his thigh. "If I may call you Nigel, please tell me what has brought you here."

"I am here at a friend's request."

"Why did you agree to her request?"

"Because she asked me to come here."

"Why do you think she asked you to come here?"

"She suspects I am a murderer."

The doctor sits up slightly and asks, "Are you indeed a murderer?"

"Yes, I have killed quite a few." I think the doctor is beginning to catch on.

"Nigel, I take it you were in the service. Possibly in the war, but your little fun with me has a ring of truth, does it not? It is about killing or being killed."

I nod once. "Nice, Doc. I owe it to my friends to play this straight so here it is, yes I was in the war, it has left me with frequent nightmares about death, about my friend's death. I can't be the first war veteran who has sat on this sofa."

"No, you are not, but we have quickly jumped ahead thanks to your honesty. Nigel, here is what I will try to accomplish. Listen, and if it does not sound like something you want to participate in, you can choose to walk out. Does that sound fair?"

"Yes, Doctor. I like to get down to it without much preamble."

"Nigel, I mainly deal with actions, events that have shaped our character. I will use talk, I will utilize hypnosis, I will utilize—no, I will stress—movement therapies. Strictly speaking, trauma involves bodily movement so too should a successful recovery from trauma. An insight from William James: 'All traumatic events, even ones that seem to leave no physical wound, are physiological because they are emotional.'

"Nigel, before any intervention by me, would you be willing to talk about your war experiences? How have they impacted your every-day life?"

So, I have nothing to hide even if this guy is not bound by some oath. What can they do, send me to the front?

It takes about one and a half hours to give him a pretty detailed overview of my life to this point. Not much, but that's all there is, folks. He doesn't say anything at first, making a few notes with his Waterman #58 Red Ripple Fountain Pen. Then he looks up at me. "Those events are horrific, Nigel, they no doubt have left deep psycho-logic impressions. You were also left with physical wounds. Tell me, were you thoroughly examined for any brain damage?"

"Yes, at a veterans hospital outside Philadelphia, it's when my wife died. I should have never agreed to go into that hospital. I could have been with her when she passed."

"Nigel, more trauma heaped unto your shoulders with a helping of guilt. The VA has programs for disability compensation; 9,000 veter-ans have undergone treatment for psychological disability in veterans hospitals. You should be compensated."

"Doc, I don't need the money and it would mean spending time in one of those shit holes. Pardon, but that is what they are. I self-medicate, Doctor."

"Thank you for sharing that. I was trying to think of the question."

"No, no, it's the way it is. There is no reason to hide it from you."

"Nigel, do you have many friends? People you can be with, talk to, do things with?"

"After the war? I have two close friends and now a third has joined our group, three women."

"Good, sex is a good release, motion and relief."

"Don't get ahead of yourself, Doc, two are lesbians and the third is a sweet kid from France, I am not having sex with any of them. You met them all at a house in East Hampton."

"Sorry, not the impression I got from the two woman. They openly said there was a three-way relationship. I am not shocked or judging, I was just wondering about the relationship. They seem to care deeply for you."

"I have no doubt they do, but I am not good for them, my nihilism is bound to rub off."

"Oh Nigel, what do you call nihilism?"

"Doc, what have all the religious and moral principles given us, take a run across no-man's-land toward a Maxim gun and then I'll ask, hold a dying young man in your arms when all he wants is his mother then I'll ask. It's all lies, and you know what? This is just the beginning of the 20th century."

"I do not have those answers but we are here to try and build a new destiny for you, Nigel. As James has said, 'Sow an action and you reap a habit; sow a habit and you reap a character; sow a character and you reap a destiny.'" He looks at his watch, a J. E. Caldwell in 18k yellow gold with Breguet numerals. "I afraid that's our time for today. Please call if you think we can work together."

I get up and hold out my hand. He takes it firmly and says, "I really would like to takes this journey together."

"Thanks, Doc, I will think about what we said here."

Looking for a cab on 10th Street, the air is cold, damp.

I look up, the skies dark, shouts—"Keep moving, keep moving, boys!"—incredible noise, confusion, hopeless, yet we keep running, falling, dying.

"Are you all right, sir?" The face comes into focus. I have pushed myself against a building wall, a young man's face, a face that never got past our wire, an 18-year-old face. I try, "I told you get through the wire, to keep moving. I tried, I'm so sorry, I tried…"

"Can I get anything for you, sir? I can stay here with you, it will pass, sir."

My mind begins to clear. It will pass? "Son, how do you know?"

"It's my dad, sir, he suffered a terrible head injury in the war. He talks like you did, sometimes. I think it's the war, sir. He threatens us sometimes, I think maybe we remind him of the Huns."

I am filled with a crushing sadness. "No, son, he's just never came back from that field. Go careful, please."

With that, I give the kid a handful of bills. He takes a look and is handing them back but I push them away. "Son, for your father's service, tell him someone from II Corps, St. Quentin Canal, he'll understand."

I am about to get in a cab when I hear someone call my name. I turn and see David waving from across the street. I close the cab door and wave the cab on. David crosses the street, I hold out my hand, he takes it and moves in for a hug. We embrace and move apart; he keeps my hand in his. "I hope you are well, I just want to say Sarah and I feel terrible about the way we left it last time we were together."

"You play a sweet cornet, David, and you are right, I am a dope fiend. You two deserve better company."

He grips my hand tighter. "Maybe, but you are our dope fiend and we should look out for one another, we all lost so much, I don't want to lose you, too."

"You might miss me at that." We both laugh. We decide to get together next week at the Cinderella Ballroom.

As he is walking away, he turns and shouts, "Please bring Kaylee."

I tip my fedora, get in a cab, and head uptown.

The night starts very well as we all dress, the three ladies looking divine, sensuous, sumptuous. I want all three but why be such a selfish bastard. We leave the apartment, cab it down to the Puncheon Club. Kaylee is greeted as obsequiously as possible as she has a pick of tables, reserved or not. She picks a reserved table with the name "White" on a small card on the tabletop. The maître d' pulls out a chair for each of the ladies without batting an eye. Kaylee picks up the card on the table, rips it up, and throws it over her shoulder, saying, "Fuck him, Mr. George White, Mr. Fancy Broadway producer." I vaguely remember he's done some big shows on Broadway but old money is old money.

Lara says, "Kaylee hates the guy, he promised a friend a part in a production after getting her to sleep with him. He reigned, of course, the weasel."

Well, not two minutes after we have ordered ginger ale for all, we hear a commotion at the front. In storms Mr. White with a very nervous maître d' following a yard behind.

OK, he's approaching the table. I stand and cut him off, slightly out of eye shot from our table. "Oh, so sorry, Mr. White, there is just a slight mix-up, I'd be happy to buy dinner for you and your friends."

This slows him down but no. "Fuck off, I want this table, tell those three chippies to move it."

I put my arm around his shoulder, smiling. He tries to shrug it off, to no avail. I whisper into his ear, "You see, Mr. White, it's this way. those three ladies are friends of mine and we are going to dine at that table, not only that but I am not buying you dinner now, you are going to leave, or—here's another choice. I will"—I reach behind and grab his collar—"rip your balls off and stuff them down your throat."

I shove him into the arms of the maître d'. He looks a little pale as he retreats with his party.

I sit back down. Malory says, "I was worried there was going to be a scene but you are such the diplomat, Nigel, he seemed satisfied."

"What can I say, Malory, I have a way with people." To myself, I'm glad he backed down. Who knows what I might have done. I do have the Webley tucked into a holster behind my back. I really should leave the thing at home. Could I have shot him? Yes, just as I did that Hun who bayonetted Elliot Gibbs.

What are you talking about, Nigel? This is a restaurant on 49th Street. The ginger ale arrives and all three woman look at me, a sign for me to take out the flask and add the Old Forester.

We spend a few pleasant hours at dinner. As we are leaving, the maître d' makes a point of shaking my hand. Naturally I palm a $100 and give it to him. He looks shocked but I just smile and as we exit he places his hand on my lower back, feels the Webley, and pulls his hand away. I look back and he nods. He is an Italian, from Rome, who likes a little muscle in his restaurant.

We hit a few clubs, enjoying some good jazz, and end up at the Cinderella Ballroom, where I spot a gentleman I know. He spots me and nods. I excuse myself and head for the men's room. It's fairly empty, so I head for stall three and go in. The gentleman is waiting. The exchange takes seconds, he leaves, I flush, and return to the ladies.

At a nice ragtime piece, I stand, and this time Malory offers no resistance. We move in a loving rhythm, a timeless moment, she holds me and I am as safe as I have felt in a long time. I pull her closer as a slow fox-trot starts, her body is pressed to me, I dip my head toward her neck and inhale the scent of Shalimar by Guerlain. Can this be real? After today it all seems to be coming back, can I make it stop? Maybe Dizzy can help? The song ends and we head back to our table. It is late so we decide to go.

At the coat check, Kaylee says, "Nigel, come back with us, we can all have a nice breakfast tomorrow at the Plaza. Malory is taking Lara's bed so stay up there."

Got to hand it to Kaylee, she is persistent. I give a little laugh and nod yes. Cab, we are back at Kaylee's and Lara's building, the beautiful Beaux Arts gem, the St. Urban, a 12-story apartment house at 89th Street, one of many French flat–style residences built all along Central Park West.

Lara and Kaylee get off on Kaylee's floor as Malory and I ride up one more flight. We silently traverse the hallway carpet then Malory opens Lara's door and we head in.

Malory turns. "I think I will change into a more comfortable outfit, you must have something up here?"

"Of course, my Chinese dressing gown." We both change and in no time are sitting on the davenport. When the doorbell rings, I answer, it's McDowall with a tray. I open the door wider.

"Good evening, sir, Miss Kaylee thought the two of you would like some port."

"Capital idea, Johnston, please pour." Of course the tray has the port in a Moser Pope decanter with two Moser liqueur glasses.

McDowall pours out two glasses. "Is there anything else I can get, sir?"

"No thanks, Johnston. Please bid Kaylee and Lara good night and thank Kaylee for the port."

"There is a nice Stilton under that glass domed dish, sir. I took the liberty."

"Excellent, Johnston, who can resist the king of cheeses."

McDowall laughs. "Have a pleasant night, sir."

After he departs, I look over to see Malory quietly sleeping, nestled into the corner of the davenport. The light is perfect from the two pairs of French Art Deco wall sconces. She looks so sweet...

No, Nigel, don't think about that. I let my head fall back on the softness of Lara's design. A moment of bliss, a moment and it is gone. Malory, someday, I know happiness will be at your door, please let it in.

Well, Nigel, time to get her to bed. I gently rub her arm and her eyes open. I should kiss her but why would I do that?

"Time for bed, angels sing thee to thy rest."

"That's beautiful, Nigel." Her legs unfold and she stands up. In her sheer gown, backlit, I can see what a lovely figure she has.

"Good night, Malory, we'll have a nice breakfast tomorrow, you will love the Plaza."

She stands there. "Good night Nigel, I hope you rest well. I had a marvelous time this evening." In a flash she is hugging me and there is a soft loving kiss on my cheek. She is off to the bedroom. I'm thinking Kaylee is going to be unhappy with the hapless Nigel. I close my eyes...

I am carrying him through the wire back to our trench, Wesley. I lay him down. There's no chance, the medic is shaking his head. Wesley is holding me with both hands, crying.

"I don't want to die here. Please help me, Nigel. I want to see my folks, take me home." His eyes are filled with terror, one last gasp and he is dead. I am holding him, the medics are trying to put him on a stretcher. I push them away. I put my arms around him, I tried to tell him, I tried, I'm so sorry, I'm so sorry...

I realize I am sobbing and I'm awake, I'm being held, someone is holding me, it's Malory, I push my head into her breasts.

"It's OK, Nigel, it's all over, I'm going to hold you as long as you want."

There is something in my darkness that sheds new light, it's your love.

The Palm Court

We have secured a table for four, just off the atrium in the Palm Court of the Plaza Hotel, at 1:30 in the afternoon, breakfast. Lara has taken Malory for a brief tour after we ordered. I am wearing my casual single-breasted flannel three-piece suit in medium grey Prince of Wales check, without Marquesa de Casa Maury hanging off my arm, with blue overcheck. Three-button roll-through lapel and jetted pockets with flaps. Cotton and cashmere shirt, silk tie, solid blue, with a geometric pattern pocket square. I am trying to avoid looking directly at Kaylee, who I know is staring at me, not in anger but expectation.

Lara came into the apartment this morning, about 10:45, and saw Malory and I curled up on the davenport in each other's arms. Lara could barely control herself with glee. It really is very touching that they both have taken an interest in gently prodding me into getting closer to Malory. I am sure that they are doing the same to her.

I can hold off Kaylee no longer, as she is now drumming her fingers and pointedly looking my way. "What?" I ask, silly but it is a starter.

She is nonplussed. "I want so much for you to find some happiness, I really like Malory, and I love you. Should I reserve the Plaza Ballroom?"

"Now that's funny, I cannot imagine it will be necessary. She is a very sweet kid—sorry, a very sweet woman. Honestly, Kaylee, I was in bad shape last night, it was a continuation of and I believe started with, my session with the doctor you three recommended I speak with."

"Nigel, listen, you don't have to marry anyone but why miss out on a chance to grab a little joy? I believe Malory is quite fond of you. It's not like you have some surprises to spring on her."

"No, no, I have shared too much. You'd think she would have run away at full speed by now but she's as persistent, in a subtler way, as you."

Kaylee is smiling at me; it's as if I am seeing her for the first time. She is projecting a transcendence I would have never thought possible. Steady, Nigel, you are close to sounding like one of the old reverend's sermons.

"Nigel, you're honest, your honor is loyalty, kind, and as men go, you are quite sweet, what the Huns think notwithstanding."

"Kaylee, I cannot get too close. Maybe, I have many doubts, this doctor will be able to help me cope. The real problem is I like getting loaded. That is something the doctor will have to make peace with."

"Nigel, I do not want to put any more pressure on you. Let's just enjoy ourselves and see where your relationship with Malory goes."

"That sounds like a plan. I do think she is sold on New York. If things are getting too tight at Lara's, I can rent a nice flat for her, without her knowing it is me, of course."

"She could just stay at your place, when are you ever there?"

We both get a good laugh out of that one and I add, "Yes, between Lara's and your apartment, I think I have most of my clothes."

Kaylee shakes her head. "Stop joking, Nigel, I've seen your clothes closet. The Prince of Wales should have such a collection and in as much style."

I laugh. "The doctor has got me interested in this psychologist William James, and he has said and I quote: 'a man's Self is the sum total of all that he can call his.' My wardrobe is part of that self."

"Very impressive, Nigel, I think you hit it off with that doctor."

"I might have, Kaylee, I might have."

Lara and Malory arrive with Lara's impeccable sense of timing, as our breakfast is being served.

I actually have an appetite and I am admiring the eggs Benedict in front of me. Malory has ordered the same and I can't resist, picking up my china coffee cup. "Thank you, Lemuel Benedict, and hangovers, or we never would be enjoying this meal." No one really gets it but who cares, you don't always have to play to the house.

We are almost finished eating our meal when Kaylee sets down her coffee, looking at me, and says, "Nigel, I think it is time that Malory hears the story how a man from Minnesota came about being named Nigel."

I'm about to say that it really is not that interesting but Malory claps her hands and says, "Please, I always thought it was a little strange, knowing you are not of English descent."

I place my coffee cup on its saucer. "OK, it does have point of interest."

Lara laughs. "Stop, it is a great story, an American story, worth telling."

I put my napkin next to my plate and begin, "It all started at the battle of Gettysburg in 1863. For those of us who are foreigners, Gettysburg was the pivotal battle of the American Civil War.

"My grandfather and my granduncle are both very young men in the II Corps, Second Division, 1st Brigade, 1st Minnesota and sitting atop Cemetery Ridge. It is the second day of battle, it is afternoon, and Major General Sickles' Third Corp units have been repulsed and were crossing the open space toward Cemetery Ridge being pursued by two Confederate brigades.

"Major General Winfield Scott Hancock, sensing he was about to lose this vital position, ordered the 1st Minnesota to charge into the gap to buy time for him to regroup his position. There were 262 men in the 1st Minnesota. They were about to be out numbered five to one. Colonel William Colvill repeated the order and all 262 men doubled-timed down the slope and broke the Confederate front line with bayonets. Nearly surrounded they held out for some time and when they retired, upon the approach of Confederate reserves, 215 had been killed or wounded, an 82% casualty rate.

"My granduncle, Thorvald Larsson, survived that day, and the next helped treat many of the wounded. He later went on to become a noted surgeon, although his career was marred by a drug dependence he acquired after being wounded in the war. He passed about five years ago, I have his green alligator instrument bag, I cherish it.

"My grandfather, Sigurd Larsson, got very sick the morning of the action and spent those two days delirious on a cot in the medical tent. Well, three days go by and my grandfather is worried about his brother. After hearing about what happened to the 1st Minnesota, he was sure he lost his brother. He's out for a walk along a road when a wagon rolls by and stops, out jumps my granduncle, Thorvald. You can imagine the greeting."

Malory cannot resist asking, "Where does Nigel come into this story?"

I nod. "OK, but it is the sad part of the story. Somehow there is this kid from the III Corps who stayed with the 1st Minnesota and charged down that hill with them. In the heat of the battle my grand-uncle's bayonet would not dislodge from a Confederate soldier, the enemy, and he was about to get shot when this kid jumped in from of him and took the bullet. He was killed.

"Turns out he was an English kid my granduncle got to know, he was from Manchester and came over to fight because his family were avid Abolitionists, hated slavery, his name was Nigel. My granduncle and my grandfather made a pact that for as long as the Larssons had sons, they would always name their firstborn son Nigel. Hence my father is Nigel, and I, being the only son with three sisters, Nigel also. Nigel Larsson, from Cold Spring, Minnesota, home of the company my father's side of the family helped to establish, the Cold Spring Brewing Company."

Malory is looking at me. "That is a beautiful story and I am very happy you told it to me. You are very worthy of your name, Nigel."

Domestic

I am sitting on Lara's pale-yellow davenport, still dressed in my three-piece suit in medium grey Prince of Wales check with blue overcheck, when the doorbell rings. I soon realize I am the only one in the apartment, so I will have to answer the door. It's not that I mind answering the door, but usually there is a person on the other side. Forget I mentioned it. I stand and walk to the door and open it.

A polished young couple is standing there with a pleasant expression on their faces.

"Hello," the young woman says. She has a lovely, inviting smile. "We are friends of Lara's. Ginny and Alistair, we have an appointment."

I swing open the door, bidding them enter. "Please have a seat." They both sit down together on the davenport. "May I offer you a beverage?"

The gentleman speaks. He is wearing a blue flannel suit, not of the highest quality but it fits his trim figure nicely. "I'll take a coffee, and what will you have, Ginny?"

I look at Ginny, who is dressed smartly in a tweed suit, white blouse, and a thin, understated string of pearls. "I'll have a coffee also, thanks."

Alistair crosses his leg and asks, "Excuse me, but what is your name?"

"Nigel."

"Nigel, do you know what time your mistress is due back?"

I get it; since I opened the door, they assume I am Lara's butler. OK, I don't see why I shouldn't play along. "I expect the lady of the house will be home momentarily, sir."

Alistair nods. "Thank you, Nigel, we'll take that coffee now."

"Of course, sir, coming right up."

I retreat to the kitchen. Prepare the pot, and place it on the stove. I fill in the time until the coffee is ready by putting together a tray with the 19th-century Naples/Capo di Monte Coffee Service with two cups, two dishes in a rare Coalport pattern showing a combination of one bright-orange flower among turquoise and pale-green leaves, pale-blue flowers, and deep-cobalt rocks, all with touches of gold. With a touch of whimsy, I place a Jaffa cake on each dish.

A few minutes and the coffee is ready. I transfer the French roast to the Naples/Capo di Monte, fill the Martele-style sterling silver sugar and creamer set made by Black, Starr & Frost. Tray loaded I pick it up and head for the sitting room.

They both slide forward as I place the tray on the Japanese table. I pour out two cups and explain, "There is cream and sugar for the coffee and a small cake." They both look pleased, maybe I can persuade Lara to keep me on.

Small-talk time. "Nigel, how long have you been in Lara's employ?"

Really, this has gone long enough. I don't want to be cruel so I might as well end this, even if I am enjoying my role. I look at them both and raise my left wrist but realize I gave my watch to McDowall and forgot to replace it. "How long have you been here?"

They look at each other and Ginny answers, "'Bout 45 minutes, why?"

"Then the answer is 45 minutes."

Alistair sets his cup down. "What do you mean, the answer is 45 minutes?"

"Why, the answer to the question, how long has Lara engaged you?"

He is not looking too happy. There are people who do not think everything is funny, maybe anything.

"Sorry, I am a friend of Lara's, I was just in her apartment when you rang."

Ginny covers her mouth and begins to laugh.

Alistair frowns. "Really, Nigel, you carried on with that joke a trifle too long, don't you think?"

I have to admit he's right. "You're probably right, but you have to approve of the service."

Ginny is nodding with a big smile. "Impeccable."

Alistair turns to her. "Ginny, please don't encourage this type of behavior."

"I do apologize, but no real harm done and you got an excellent cup of coffee."

Alistair is not going to let it go. "Playing people for fools is a bit much."

I am beginning to get annoyed. I've already apologized and he should be a good sport about my little joke. I'm hoping he drops it now, but he's going to say something else,

"Furthermore…"

Ginny puts her hand on his arm. "Alistair, really, shut up."

I am stunned, Alistair looks like he is about the swallow his Adam's apple. There is complete silence. Alistair's face is beginning to redden. I, for one, have never experienced such outrageous behavior in a woman. I cannot take my eyes off her. She just sits there sipping her coffee, puts down her cup, picks up and takes a bite of her Jaffa cake. I feel it is up to me to end this very tense moment. "Listen, it was very bad form on my part to take you both in like I did, my apologies, again."

Ginny puts down her cake. "Nigel it was nothing, and anyone with a sense of humor would have just laughed it off."

Great, here I am trying to smooth things over and she lands another right. Alistair looks like he's ready to go down. I am trying to think of what to say when I just start to laugh and Ginny starts to laugh. Alistair stands up.

"Alistair, sit down, it's all over."

My God, the guy is taking a beating, I give up. The doorbell rings, thank goodness, now Alistair's cutman can attend to him.

I open the door and to my surprise it's Lara. She smiles at me. "Thanks, Nigel, glad you're here, I forgot my keys, and it is such trouble getting the building staff to bring up a spare set."

"It's nothing, Lara. You have two guests who say they have an appointment."

Lara stops just inside the door. "Oh, I completely forgot, I had better make amends."

"Yes, I think you had better."

Lara is about to head for the sitting room when I take her arm. "I played a little joke on them, made believe I was your butler. I am pretty sure it is a very thick atmosphere in there."

Lara turns to face me. "Are they both mad at you?"

"No, Ginny took the whole thing in stride but Alistair is not pleased."

Lara takes my arm. "The appointment is with Ginny, I am to edit her book, I never met Alistair. I hope he doesn't muck things up."

"I would not worry about that, Lara, he seems to be quite pacified."

"Thanks, Nigel. I like this woman and I think her work is very sweet."

"Don't mention it. I just hope Alistair has not bled all over your davenport."

Lara is turning to head in to meet them when she spins around. "What, what happened!"

"Sorry, Lara, just a little joke. No one is bleeding."

Lara shakes her head and starts for the sitting room. I think it best I stay out of the way. I quietly slip out the door and gently close it. Halfway down the hallway, I see Malory exit the elevator. She sees me, and it is not the usual smile but a countenance I have not seen before. I have a moment of panic—you fool, you put this young woman through too much—and am feeling terrible when she reaches me. But she puts her arms around me and gives me a kiss I will be feeling till next Wednesday. When it finally ends, I am in a daze, as if a powerful shock has run through my body, charging all my cells with wonder. I really don't want to let her go but I must.

As the embrace breaks and I look into her dark eyes—what am I to do now?—Malory breaks the silence. "I have been thinking about you all morning. That story was so touching, a wonderful way to remember one who made the ultimate sacrifice. It makes so much sense from what I have come to understand about you."

"Malory, I really think I have been too much of a burden." She is about to say something but I place my hand over her mouth, gently. "No, it was not a statement meant to elicit a response. You are a talented artist, young, loving, and you have been a tremendous comfort to me. There are just too many negatives on my side of the ledger. I would dearly love to be your friend."

She places her hands, one on either side of my face. "It's a start, Nigel, it's a start."

Nigel at the Sherry

It is a cold and damp December morning, too close to Christmas for Nigel's liking. His earliest, fondest, childhood, seasonal memories have been obliterated, almost as if they are part of someone else's life. While he extracts as much comfort and happiness from mere moments and current friendships, he cannot escape those walking shells, the endless barrage.

He climbs out of the cab after overpaying, as usual. He is home, 781 Fifth Avenue, the newly opened Sherry-Netherland, or "The Sherry" as it has come to be known, and at 38 stories is the tallest apartment/hotel building in the world and one of the first to have a steel frame. He looks up at the skies, dark and unforgiving, and a shiver ruins through his body, a moment of panic until a small rift opens in the clouds and bold shafts of sunlight break through, illuminating the blue of the sky and the sidewalk before Nigel. He closes the cab door and turns toward his home.

The Romanesque Revival—think the Smithsonian Institution—building has an exterior base of travertine marble with lanterns and griffins dotting the facade, which includes a Gothic-inspired minaret. The intimate lobby's design is modeled after the Vatican Library with vaulted ceilings, ornate mirrors, high-relief carved limestone panels by Karl Bitter taken from the porte cochere of the demolished Cornelius Vanderbilt mansion, along with ornamental frieze roundels. The frescoes on the ceiling are based on Raphael's frescoes at the Vatican Palace and were re-created by artist Joseph Aruta. Its corridors all have vaulted ceilings and faux-marble columns hand detailed in gold leaf.

Nigel likes its proximity to the park so, when it became available, he purchased a 1,350-square-foot, two-bedroom suite overlooking Central Park with high ceilings, decorative fireplace, and marble bathrooms complete with silver-plated faucets. While some of the tenants hired designers to furnish their apartments, Nigel did no such thing.

238

The apartment is inviting, and sedate, mostly finished in the new Art Deco style. It is supposed to represent Modernism but Nigel is drawn to the possibility of replacing the old world and old-world ideas with the new. Probably, when he ponders it, he doesn't see a sofa changing man's basic drive: destruction.

He enters his apartment removing his fedora and chesterfield, placing both on a barber shop chrome hat-and-coat wall rack. Then he moves on to the sitting room, with its decorative fireplace and Art Deco sofa in high-gloss black from France, a striking design with straight lines and rounded side cabinets and backrest; a three-seat sofa covered with high-quality red leather, on the front side of which are six small drawers and two glass doors. Facing each other, there are two large armchairs, also from Paris, covered in black leather. Centering these three items is a René Prou black lacquer table, the circular top with molded edge above four tapering scroll legs, its Chinese influence clear in the subtle line of the legs. All these items are sitting on a Chinese rug with a solid red floral motif with a yellow/orange border. A spectacular piece, the rug measures 14′2″ × 16′8″.

The opposite wall has a black lacquer bar cabinet, with two drawers, in the French Art Deco style with a tulip-shape, patinated old salmon-mirror. Above the bar and on two of the adjacent walls there are Italian-design crystal Murano glass half-moon bronze-finish sconces. Lots of black lacquer, for Nigel the perfect expression for the rest of the 20th century. Across the sitting room, by the decorative fireplace, is a combination electronic radio-phonograph, the type that could use the radio's amplifier for reproducing records, eliminating the need for the horn, replacing it with a small paper-cone speaker. Fidelity is also much improved. This model has a sophisticated record changer, which allows a complete symphony to be played without having to stop and manually change records.

Adjacent to the sitting room is a semi-formal dining area, containing a dining suite in walnut, with a stunning walnut grain pattern throughout. The drop-in seats are upholstered in light-green fabric, blending in with the park's tree line. The table is supported by twin pedestals, each with a built-in door and cabinet. On the table, two Tiffany candlestick holders in lead crystal.

Nigel looks over his apartment and knows his maid, Adrijana, has been cleaning, the place looks tip-top. He hears someone in his bedroom and it must be her. She comes in twice a week as part of the building services. No one who has an apartment need hire their own service as it is part of the building amenities.

Adrijana is in her mid-forties, a strong woman with black short hair sprinkled with grey and deep-set dark eyes, of Serbian ancestry. Sometimes Nigel wonders what his Croat relatives would think. It's all part of his rejection of the past, of past prejudices and lingering hatreds. Nigel sees her and she sees him.

Nigel stops at the bar and fixes himself a Speyside malt and water then sits in his black leather armchair, loosens his bow tie. It has been a long evening into daybreak. The inseparable quartet out on the town, Nigel spending his relatives' money. Money they worked for, stole for, killed for. All in the hands of an addled veteran, going on 10 years since his last combat.

You are a complete waste. Well, here we go, fix wearing off, self-degradation coming on, each day, every day. Dr. Gilhooley calls it survivor guilt. He's right, the fuck, as we went through our wire I circled behind Drew and moved off to his left, if not he's hating himself instead of me hating myself. Gilhooley tells me there's no why in combat, it just is. Never thought that much about it, he could be right.

Adrijana comes into the living room and sees me. "Mr. Nigel, I did not hear you come in. I was just finishing straightening up your bedroom. Really, the place is so neat, you really do not need a maid."

I smile at her, stand and walk over to her, looking deeply into her dark eyes. I can only imagine what those eyes must have seen. Her family caught up in the anti-Serbian backlash, by Croats and Muslims, following the assassination of the Archduke, she lost everyone. In fact, the Kingdom of Serbia lost more than 1.2 million inhabitants during the war (both army and civilian losses), which represented over 29% of its overall population, a larger percentage than any other country. I take her in my arms, two broken people sharing a moment of relief, just a moment.

It's around midday and I am lying on my French queen-size bed comprising a headboard, footboard, and matching side rails in beautifully figured thuya burl wood by Maurice Dufrêne. The headboard is two tone and inlaid with mother-of-pearl rectangles. The elegantly curved sleigh-type footboard has swag-like drapery details in ebony and stylized floral detail in marquetry inlay. It is supported by six silver-tipped bun feet.

I climb out of bed, reluctantly, pulling my robe around me, and head for the sitting room, change my mind and go to the bathroom for a shower, something I am beginning to enjoy. Showered, dried, talcumed, new robe, I return to the sitting room.

Turn on the record player and place a record on the turntable. I return to my leather armchair and get lost in Ruth's voice.

My head falls back…I'm running, terrified, back at the front, the same path through the wire, see Wesley get hit, his rifle flies off to his right as he falls, see Wesley get hit, his rifle flies off to his right as he falls, see Wesley get hit, his rifle flies off to his right as he falls, and again and again. I jerk upward; I'm in my apartment, the light is fading. I drain my glass.

Ruth has not abandoned me.

I have grown lonely and I see no other way. Everything is worked out. I walk back into my bedroom, sit on my bed, and pick up the Webley from my nightstand. Pull back the hammer and hold it in my lap. I raise the gun, tighten my grip on the hard rubber handle, and think how easy it will be to pull the trigger. A voice in my head: *"I bet you miss, you dumb fuck, you could never hit anything."* It's Drew's voice. *"That's right, asshole, it's Drew, here to tell you to put that fucking gun down before someone gets hurt."*

I start to laugh, uncock the Webley, and place it on the bed, laughing, laughing because it's so damn funny.

Jazz Me Blues

My body is still shaking with laughter. It's not a laughter of mirth, it has a maniacal quality. My hand is resting on the Webley; I am aware that my doorbell is ringing. I don't want to answer but cannot be impolite.

I make my way to the door, open it, and there is Adrijana. "Please come in, Adrijana, did you forget something?"

She enters the apartment, never talking her eyes off me. "Mr. Nigel, I cannot accept this. I do not understand why, you have done too much

241

already." As she is speaking she is pulling an envelope out of her coat. I remember now: her Christmas bonus.

"Mr. Nigel, there is $1,000 in this envelope. How can I?"

I look at the envelope and recognize my terrible handwriting. "Adrijana, I want you to know it has nothing to do with the sex. You know we share a common bond, the bond of the real world, the way things really are. Money is worthless unless some good can come of it. Please take it and make your life a little better."

I look into her eyes and see the well of tears that has almost completely run dry. How many tears can one person shed? I take her hand and push it, with the envelope, back into her coat pocket. Her arms come up, around my shoulders, my arms cradle her in a loving embrace, together we open the world a little bit wider to the possibility that the Divine may enter.

We move apart slightly but the embrace is just as intense. "Mr. Nigel, how can I ever thank you, first putting my Melissa in that private school and now this."

"Adrijana, your daughter is going to make something of herself. I really believe she is going to be a doctor, regardless of the current fools who think women can't be anything but school teachers."

She puts one hand on either side of my face. "*Neka te bog zaštiti, uvijek.* May God protect you, always."

I place a gentle kiss on her forehead. "Go now, Adrijana, go find some happiness with your daughter, take her to a nice dinner."

She is about to become emotional, so she turns and leaves the apartment.

"Well, Drew, It's not much, but maybe today I did some good."

Drew answers, *"Sure, and I guess you forgot the big house on Lake Minnetonka you bought for my parents?"*

"Drew, they needed a new start, new vistas. I saw the house and loved it, no way I'm going to live there, so why not someone I care about? Nothing can make it right but maybe I can help make it bearable."

"You're really something, Nigel, did I tell you I love you? Also, put that Webley away before you shoot yourself in the foot. Sorry about the crack about not hitting anything. We all remember your quick draw and shooting that Hun that popped up, 50 yards into no-man's-land."

I go into my bedroom, pick up the Webley, and place it into the cloth bag and put it away. I head back to the sitting room and my favorite chair, get back up and fix myself another drink. McDowall has got me hooked on this Speyside malt. Hooked; I laugh, laugh because it's funny.

Drew has more to say. *"Now that we are talking, I'm going to ask you a question. What are you thinking about, you want to be friends with Malory? Brother, I may be wrong but I think she's soft on you."*

"Drew, you know why, I can't get involved with her. I know what you're thinking, what about Adrijana? We're not really involved in that way, she loves me on another level as I love her. Too much baggage being carried around by us to be romantically linked. That doesn't mean I can't help her a little bit."

"You've done some good in that direction, generous to a fault."

"Drew, it's easy to be generous with other people's money. They made it, I spend it. Honestly, sometimes I think I'm not really here, in the world I mean, somehow I left myself at that canal. That this is all a dream. Although, I have to admit to you, brother, if I was going to conjure a scene, I would be hard pressed to top being loaded and in bed with Kaylee and Lara." I start to laugh, remembering something. "Do you remember those two brunettes in Paris on our first leave? Damn, we were fresh-faced kids from Minnesota, and after the first night they thought it would be fun to switch."

"I remember, we were going to meet up again on our next leave but those fucking Huns had other ideas."

Drew begins to fade in my head. I try to will him back but he's gone for now. I know he'll be back, I just can't let the little fuck down. You are going to have to take it, Nigel, no more gunplay. They are certainly enough ways to die. I think back after Drew was killed how many night patrols I volunteered for into no-man's-land. Maybe I want to join you, buddy.

I know I have enough people who care for me and want me to stop taking such risks, Kaylee and Lara steering me toward Malory, Malory so loving. David, poor David, I treated him so harshly, yet he still took the time to tell me how much he is worried. In some ways I really am a callous bastard, I just wish I could let them all know that the dice have to be thrown, the cards turned over, I have left it to a supremely dark fate.

There is a ghost of a chance, go left or right, and we make it or we don't.

I go over to the Victrola and put on a stack of records. The first drops and starts playing. Ruth again. Soon as her voice hits, I know what I want. No, not tonight, yes, just a little, no harm, not good you have to get ready for dinner guests. What get ready? All you did was order, so just chase it halfway around the block. There's a long, long trail. Remember that one? It takes me back to our first leave again. Damn, you were a handsome kid, Drew. Someone is squeezing my heart.

I get up and go into my bedroom, unlock my desk, withdraw what I want, and head back to the sitting room. I lay the pack on the table, pull my armchair closer, open the bag, and spoon some powder onto a piece of foil, spread it out, take out a small glass tube I had made, put it into my mouth, pick up the foil, fire up the lighter—and the doorbell rings. Damn! I place a magazine over the stuff and walk over to the door. Opening the door, there's Malory holding a beautiful bouquet of gardenias. I'm quite flustered. I can't keep her standing in the hallway so invite her in.

She sees I am still in my dressing gown. "I'm sorry to be so early, Nigel, Kaylee was insistent I bring over the flowers in case you wanted to use them in an arrangement."

I smile. "I bet she was. Let me take those."

I place the bouquet on the bar, then take her coat and hat, placing them on the hat/coat rack. I turn back and my breath is taken away. Malory is stunning in a velvet evening dress, knee length, with a wide rounded collar, sleeveless, with longline extended armholes that are so sensuous, finishing with a mink hem, gorgeous velvet burnout fabric in golden pile with a sheer indigo base.

"Malory, you look spectacular." I take her in my arms and we execute a few dance spins, wonderful. I release her. "Please come in. Are Kaylee and Lara on their way?"

"They said they would be here in about 45 minutes." Malory sits on the sofa, I pull back the armchair, very cognizant of the drugs on the table under the magazine. I will have to excuse myself in order to dress for dinner.

"Need to freshen up, Malory?"

"No, I'm fine, did I interrupt something?" She has picked up on my discomfort.

"No, I just need to get ready for dinner."

"Nigel, were you about to use those drugs under the magazine?"

Hopeless. "I apologize, Malory, I will put them away. I hope I did not make you uncomfortable. I am so sorry to be subjecting you to this. It's bad enough we engage in this behavior. To get you involved, well, I could never forgive myself. I could just see myself trying to explain to your mother. 'Oh, I'm so sorry Mrs. Leblanc, I exposed your daughter to heroin and it had a terrible effect on her life.'"

Malory tries to mitigate the situation. "I see the three of you using the drug and you all have lives and are living quite well, as a matter of fact. I was at an Art Student League gathering in an apartment in Greenwich Village, there was cocaine available."

I freeze in the process of picking up the magazine, and slowly turn to her. "What? Who gave you cocaine?"

"No one. I didn't want any but I was a little nervous."

I sit down in my chair. "Malory, I am going to tell you something and I want you to listen. That drug can lead to some very bad choices. It's a powerful stimulant and can be used to help men seduce woman. You have to be very careful, do you understand what I'm saying?"

"Yes, I came close, I have to admit."

"Please tell me that you'll steer clear of this drug."

"OK, I will make it known I'm not interested."

"Thank you. I know you can handle this. Please do not accept any drugs from anyone. There are some truly evil people on the street and they mean to do you harm."

I walk over to the bar and pick up the large bunch of gardenias and bring them into the kitchen, trim the stems slightly, fill the blown-glass and wrought-iron vase—by Daum Nancy and Louis Majorelle, decorated with clear rippled glass with added multi-colored fractured glass all blown out into a decorated wrought-iron frame—with water, and place the lovely scented gardenias into it. I carry the vase to the dining area and place it in the middle of the table Adrijana so beautifully set for me today. Then I glance at my notes on the menu:

Old Tom Gin Martini
with Beluga caviar on toast points

Antoine's original recipe Oysters Rockefeller
W/2 Bottles Dom Pérignon 1921

Spiced Crown Pork Roast with Glazed Root Vegetables
W/2 bottles 1926 White Burgundy.

Delmonico's Baked Alaska

I go back into the sitting room. "Malory, I have to dress for dinner, can I get you anything?"

"No, I'm fine, is there anything I can do?"

"If you want to play some music, feel free to make a selection."

I quickly pick up the drugs and carry them into the bedroom. I lay it all out on my Georgian-period Campaign triple-slope writing desk, or "Captain's Box" for it is commonly used by ship officers for storage of valuables, documents, and writing supplies. This particular one was my uncle's, Peter Studenich, who at one time was a ship's captain. The box is mounted by lacquered brass guarding the corners, which lends strength to the joinery. The top lifts to reveal a leather document storage folder secured in place with two tiny steel tabs that flip out of the way to reveal the folder and the stringing. The upper slope lifts with a fabric tab to give access to a document storage area and also a spring-loaded hidden compartment. I depress a hidden button and the wooden slat beneath the inkwells pops open to expose two drawers, where I store my drugs. I am about to empty the foil back into the bag and put the stuff into the drawers but I hesitate. "*I know what you are thinking.*"

Damn, Drew is beginning to show up at the most inopportune times.

"How's that, Drew? I don't even know what I'm thinking."

"*You hesitate because Malory is here and you don't want to get loaded in front of her, ergo, you have feelings for her beyond friendship.*"

"Drew, we're not back at university—'ergo,' really, Mr. Sherlock Holmes. I do have feelings for her but why does your deduction preclude friendship?"

Before he can answer, I place the glass tube in my mouth, dump some H on the foil, and ignite it, inhaling the smoke. I hold it in as long as possible and blow it out.

Drew speaks in a quiet voice, *"I'm sorry, brother, I pushed a little too hard. Let's go slow, Nigel."*

I throw down the glass tube. "No, Drew, I was just acting like a child. I'm confused about my own motivations. Well, let's dress for dinner, what do you think, the Brooks Brothers tux?"

Drew chuckles, "Oh, be careful Nigel, you are devastating in that tux."

I sit down on my bed, putting my hands on either side of my head, resting my elbows on my knees. I realize I am duplicating exactly what Malory and Adrijana did with their hands. Drew continues, *"Let's not beat on Nigel now, there's going to be three very attractive women out there and you never let down dinner guests, no matter what photographs are being displayed behind your eyes. Go out there and enjoy their company."*

Dressed, hair combed, dosed with Acqua di Parma, I head out to the sitting room. Kaylee and Lara have arrived and are sitting together on my sofa. Kaylee sees me. "Oh, doesn't our man look handsome tonight."

They both stand and again I am so impressed. Kaylee is wearing a dress from Goupy of Paris, one of the most elite couture houses operating. The dress is very special, all hand stitched, in a vibrant tangerine silk-chiffon and metallic-gold lace. The perfection of the tangerine color is beyond compare, while the gossamer delicacy of the metallic-gold spiderweb lace inserts make it magical, with a scoop neck and sleeveless bodice so flattering to Kaylee's figure.

Lara is stunning in a sheer evening dress, primarily made of black chiffon, featuring two embroidered panels in the front and one in the back. All panels display blooming roses made of interwoven gold metallic thread. The dress has gathered fabric on both sides at hip level, as well as some panels on the lower half of the long sleeves. The sleeves, front of the dress, and back of the dress are decorated with gold cord trim.

Of course I am thinking, how is it I deserve to be in their company? "Ladies, you are perfection. This is exactly what the designers had in mind when they first sketched out their ideas. Please have a seat, while I mix up a batch of illegal cocktails."

The doorbell rings. I cut away from the bar and open the door. It's Johnston. If I am surprised I don't show it. "Johnston, please come in, let me take your hat and coat."

"Not to bother, sir, I can manage. Miss Kaylee asked if I could come to your apartment to help serve tonight. I presume she has informed you of these plans?"

"Of course not, Johnston, but we'll just acquiesce to her wishes."

"My apologies, sir, had I known."

"Forget it, Johnston, I have learned that more often than not Kaylee's ideas are spot-on. I was about to mix some cocktails, would you care for one?"

"Most generous sir, but no. Anything I can attend to?"

"If you would ring the kitchen to check on our dinner, that would be great. Thank you."

I open the bar and take out the bar glass, bar spoon, jigger. I go into the kitchen and fill the ice bucket, grab a lemon, and return to the bar. I can readily mix individual martinis, which I do, one, two, three:

2 jiggers Old Tom Gin
1 jigger French vermouth
Dash orange bitters
Twist lemon
Stirred

I hand out the three cocktails to the ladies, make one for myself, and ask the ladies to join me at the table, where I like an eclectic collection of dinnerware. McDowall has already plated the beluga and toast points on my sterling silver appetizer plates, Tiffany & Co., each plate with a circular well, short foot, tapering shoulder, and scrolled and molded rim with applied scallop shells. I raise my glass. "Ladies, we have been through thick and thin, harum-scarum, and all manner of death-defying adventures. Allow me to include: a beautiful young woman with child, all my lost boys from II Corps, to all of them, to us, and fuck everyone else."

I drain my glass, as do the ladies. I look over at Johnston and raise my glass to him. He nods with a smile.

Plates removed, next course Oysters Rockefeller, on a set of Limoges oyster plates, painted and gilt trimmed for six oysters with central sauce wells painted in rose, violet, blue-green, and yellow. McDowall pops the first bottle of champagne, a 1921 vintage Dom Pérignon, and pours for each into the Murano MVM Cappellin amber champagne glasses with wide and shallow octagonal bowl with applied teardrops to a wrythen knopped stem and spreading circular foot with gilded edging.

"Johnston, please bring another glass, fill it." He places it beside me and fills it. I pick it up and hand it to him; he's reluctant but he takes it. "For the purposes of a toast," I say, raising my glass again. "To those doing their best to hold back the tide, you wonderful bastards." I drain my glass again.

Lara is laughing. "Nigel, what's with all the toasting?"

"No idea, just thinking about us and some lost, but no need to get maudlin, let's enjoy these oysters."

McDowall opens the second champagne, asks the ladies, only Kaylee nods, he fills her glass, fills my glass, no need to ask, and then places the bottle in the French marbled brown Bakelite stepped champagne bucket. The oysters are fabulous and are devoured quickly. The women make a few oyster jokes in my direction, which I ignore, in good fun. We also finish off the second bottle of champagne.

Next course: Spiced Crown Pork Roast with Glazed Root Vegetables, which McDowall has plated in the kitchen on my grandmother's Limoges plates accented with a 24k acid-etched gilt band and gilt medallion, which she ordered from the Philadelphia retailer John Wanamaker. After serving each plate, McDowall fills each tall stemmed green wine glasses by Belgium glass maker Val Saint Lambert, in an Osram pattern, with the vintage 1926, impressive vintage, white burgundy.

The roast is done to perfection and complemented beautifully by the glazed root vegetables. Everyone agrees the roast is superb. Pork is not a big favorite here but in the Midwest it is king.

Final course is Delmonico's Baked Alaska. I do not ordinarily have dessert, but for a dinner party, it is an impressive ending.

McDowall brings in the coffee service by Black, Starr & Frost jewelers, the creamer, sugar, and coffee pot in sterling silver, all on a silver tray. He pours the French roast coffee for each of us into the Copeland & Garrett tobacco-leaf-pattern cup and saucer in blue, red, peach, pink, and green with gilt highlighting. He then serves each of us a slice of Baked Alaska on the tobacco leaf/cabbage leaf plates.

I feel the meal was successful and as I am thinking that, the three ladies burst into applause. "Ladies, please, I just put the menu together."

The doorbell rings again. I know who it is, since I asked McDowall to call down. McDowall answers the door and brings the building chief and his staff into the dining area. The women are looking excited at my little idea. I stand, "Ladies, let me introduce Master Chef Henri Jacques Cartier and his staff, those who are truly responsible for tonight's magnificent repast." They are greeted with a vigorous round of applause. The chief and staff bow and turn to leave, though first the chief steps up to me and clasps my hand, whispering into my ear, "The staff and I want to say how *très généreux de votre part*, how very generous your gift was."

"Nothing, Henri. Food is more important than money."

He laughs and kisses my cheek. Malory has a few words in French with the chief. He looks impressed with my choice of dinner guests, can't say I disagree.

"Ladies, if you please, let's head for the sitting room and some music. Johnston, please, leave everything in the kitchen. I asked my maid to come in tomorrow to clean up. Thank you."

Before we leave the table, we all fill our wine glasses, finishing off the second bottle of white burgundy. Malory heads over to the Victrola, makes some selections, and puts the stack onto the player. Music starts at a newly engineered fidelity, which we enjoy immensely. We had all seen Yvonne Printemps in *Mozart* on Broadway and Malory loved Yvonne. Of course, Kaylee got us backstage and Yvonne was very gracious to her fellow countryman but declined the invitation to a quiet dinner with the three ladies, nothing other than she had another engagement. Malory picked Yvonne singing, "C'est la saison d'amour"; nice choice. McDowall, finished in the kitchen, says, "I have done as you requested, sir. Is there anything else I can do for you?"

"You have been terrific, Johnston. No need to go back uptown, I booked you a room on the second floor with breakfast. The key is at the front desk, room in your name."

"Most generous of you, sir. Miss Kaylee, is there anything at your apartment I should do this evening? I can always return."

Kaylee smiles at McDowall warmly. "Not at all, I'll see you back at the apartment tomorrow."

I show Johnston to the door with a word. "I hear there is a singer in the lounge who is very fond of Scotsmen, have a drink on me, Larsson tab."

"Thank you, sir, most kind, I might just do that."

"Her name is Ann, cannot miss her—bright-red hair, met her at Saratoga Springs last season." I open the door, shaking Johnston's hand. "To us, Johnston."

"Thank you, indeed sir, to us, good night."

I gently close the door, hoping Johnston takes my advice.

Back in the sitting room, Lara and Malory are dancing to "All of Me," Ruth Etting singing. Kaylee gets my attention. I look at her and she is nodding in their direction and mouthing, "Cut in." I walk over and tap Lara on the shoulder, she turns and bows, holding Malory's hand out. I take it and spin her into my arms. We move as one, looking over at the two ladies, wide smiles. I can see they think this is it, book the honeymoon in Paris now.

The song ends and I bring Malory over to an armchair and she sits. Everyone is quite tipsy but I make another round of drinks anyway. Malory manages to down hers a little too fast. She is all smiles, a smile to lighten any room. Lara is resting against Kaylee and both have love in their eyes.

I speak, quietly, trying not to break the mood. "Ladies, please stay tonight, I can use the company and everyone looks so comfortable."

Kaylee says, "Thank you, Nigel, the consummate host."

I laugh, knowing what Kaylee is thinking.

"If you and Lara don't mind sharing my bedroom, Malory can have the guest bedroom."

Lara agrees. "That will work for us. I am quite fatigued, can we turn in?"

I look over at Malory. "Malory, I can call a cab if you would like to go back to Lara's apartment."

"What, and miss all the fun? I'll stay."

"Great. Ladies, let me get some extra pillows in my closet and I know I have some nightgowns to fit. A real slumber party."

I head for my bedroom, get the extra bedding and two exquisite nightgowns. I cannot remember why I bought them, but here there are. I lay them on the bed. Then I stop at my desk, open it, and remove the drug package and slip it into my inside pocket. Back in the sitting room, Lara and Kaylee are in a sweet embrace. I look over at Malory, who is watching them.

"My bedroom is ready when you care to retire, nightgowns on the bed."

They both stand, a little swaying, but they simultaneously embrace me warmly, lovingly, planting kisses on each cheek. I really love the both of them and feel sad. Why, I wish I could say. Drew chimes in. *"I've a feeling, brother, that it is the realization how much you can lose, so fast."*

I think, yes, you're so right, Drew, savor this moment. They break the embrace but not before Kaylee whispers in my ear, "I want a full report in the morning."

They turn and walk into my bedroom. As if someone has sent up a signal flare, Malory stands and walks in my direction. God she is radiating warmth, enough to last a mighty long time. I do notice she has quite a list to one side, weaving my way. The fates, not to be outdone, a record drops: "My Blue Heaven." On cue Malory begins to sing, such a sweet voice.

Malory finishes and slides into my arms. Drew says, *"Nigel, it's time to go home, time to go home."*

Love, Devotion, Surrender

For a west-facing bedroom, it is amazingly bathed in a sweet, gentle light at mid-morning. Malory's eyes open to the new day, bittersweet that it is, but still holding a promise of love. Thinking about it, she realizes that is how we have gotten to this point. Her mother's love for her and her father, her cousin's love for her, her love for Nigel, Nigel's love for Drew, Kaylee's love for Lara. On and on, this is what is important to Malory. She believes this is where we find redemption, salvation, peace. She loves Nigel, she is devoted to helping him, she has surrendered herself to walking this path.

She rolls over onto her back, wearing a set of Nigel's silk pajamas from Brooks Brothers. There is a certain level of excitement, feeling Nigel's silk against her bare body. She hugs herself and even though the night did not end as she had hoped, as in most things in life, it ended, unexpectedly, beautifully.

The mood was perfect, as was most of the evening's atmosphere, simply because of the incredible attention to detail that is Nigel. Just the table setting was astounding. How does he even know these things exist? How can he decide what will work with what? She had thought for a while that Nigel is a depressed person, but she called her uncle in Paris, who is a psychiatrist, and he explained that Nigel's symptoms are a result of traumatic events he witnessed in the war. He has treated many such cases and the prognosis is not inherently positive, especially when the patients self-medicate.

Malory has other ideas. She firmly, and admits possibly naively, believes that love, kindness, and everyday support will help him, maybe not cure him because how can those events ever be dispelled? She thinks the key may be in that attention to detail, but also that same detail invades his nightmares. It is a fine line. Her new idea is seeing if Nigel has any interest in art, get him to do some drawing, painting, who knows. Help that creative energy—he has it—thrive.

Malory throws back the covers and stands. Immediately the pajama bottoms fall down. She lets them sit there for a moment, looking at the bed, and that same excitement passes through her. She pulls up the bottoms, tying them a little more tightly, properly rolled, then heads for the sitting room. Empty. Hmm, where is Nigel? Maybe in with Karlee and Lara. She feels no jealousy, just interest. She sees the coffee table has some spent foil on it and, though not positive, is pretty sure Nigel took some drugs last night.

The dining room table is set for breakfast. She can smell coffee and pastry. Answering her question, a striking-looking woman emerges from the kitchen. The woman sees her and gives a slight bow of her head. "Good morning, miss, I am Adrijana, Mr. Nigel's housekeeper. Coffee is ready if you would like a cup."

"Hello, my name is Malory and I would love a cup."

"Coming right up, Miss Malory, please have a seat."

If Adrijana thinks anything of a young woman appearing in Nigel's pajamas, she does not show it. Those kinds of things never hold much importance to Adrijana.

Malory takes a seat at the table and as she is waiting for Adrijana to return, the door opens and in walks Nigel. Malory is in disbelief, even feeling a little light-headed, yet here comes Nigel across the sitting room in a morning suit of an Oxford grey coat/waistcoat, cashmere striped trousers, starched white double-cuff shirt, blue enamel links, with a blue striped tie.

"Good morning, Malory, just popped down to the lobby for a word with the concierge and guess what I saw? No, I can't wait. Johnston, leaving the building but not before he had a rather passionate embrace with a very well formed redheaded young woman. Damn, I knew they would hit it off."

Nigel pulls out a chair and sits. Malory is touched by his enthusiasm for Johnston and this young woman.

Nigel is not done. "I'm going to send them to California on their honeymoon."

Malory is a little surprised but then again it is Nigel. "Are they thinking of marriage? I didn't know McDowall had a woman friend."

Nigel laughs. "No, no, they just met last night. The thought of the two of them in California and in love just seems so pleasing to me, I don't know why. I may be compensating."

He reaches across the table and takes Malory's hand. "You are a blessing in my life, Malory, I just don't know how to thank you. You may be the most patient and understanding person I have ever met."

Drew: *"True, Nigel, and I have to tell you not many men could have resisted sleeping with her last night. You have an impeccable sense of when the right moment is occurring."*

Nigel sits back and decides to voice his idea. "Malory, would you ever consider getting a place of you own?"

"Sure, I have thought about it. Lara has been so kind and has said repeatedly that I am welcome as long as I care to stay, but I hope I am not too much for her. Her apartment is big but not that big. I have been looking but I have not found anything. There is a young man at the league who wants me to move in with him. No, no," she laughs, "he is a communist and is big on the importance of art supporting the international movement. He really is an unbelievable bore and incredibly pedantic. Anyway, he is mad at me because he insisted on sitting by me in a drawing class and was going on and on about what a great man Stalin is, until I threatened to stab him in the eye with my green Castell 9000 pencil. He hasn't said a word to me since but a friend told me he calls me a counter-revolutionary, the ass. Sorry, Nigel, that was quite a long-winded answer to a simple question."

Nigel just smiles at her. "The reason I ask is because there is a very smart one-bedroom one floor down. I'm afraid it looks east but still very nice views."

Malory laughs. "Nigel, how can I ever hope to afford anything in this building? Buying into this place, it must be very expensive."

"That it is, Malory but here is my plan. I already own the apartment, you rent it from me."

Malory is excited but realistic. "Nigel, I could never pay you what the rent would be on an apartment in this building."

Nigel holds up his hand. "Yes, I understand, but the rent is very affordable and very possible for you to manage."

"Nigel, my allowance is tiny. Lara has been incredibly gracious to me, spending far too much money on me. I could not ask her to foot another bill."

"No, she would not have to pay anything, your rent would consist of giving me art lessons."

At first Malory thinks she heard wrong, so she just sits there. Nigel looks a little worried that his idea has fallen flat. "It is no burden on me and it would be nice…"

Malory holds up her hand. "Nigel, you have an impeccable sense of when the right moment is occurring."

Quand Les Papillons

Sitting on my leather armchair, I have every reason to be pleased. Today I handed the keys to my one-bedroom to Malory. The flat is completely furnished, and I was a little concerned it would not be to her liking, but then I remembered it is Malory and it is her first apartment, so the excitement level is quite high. Kaylee and Lara helped her move in, not that she had that much to bring over from Lara's. I had the building send up a case of Dom Pérignon 1921; she seemed to love it so, what's not to love? I've already set her up with Adrijana, who is to come in three times a week. Adrijana has taken a liking to Malory and I know she will do right by her.

As a celebration the three ladies are going out for dinner and expect to meet me later at the Cinderella Ballroom. Their plans are dinner at 9:00 p.m., the Puncheon Club, and give me a call to rendezvous at the Ballroom. I raise my left wrist to check the time and realize I gave my watch to McDowall and have not replaced it. I look over at the bar and my rose-pink glass and chrome clock by the French clockmakers JAZ, easy to read because it is quite large for a normal JAZ, tells me it is 8:00 p.m.

I am on dangerous ground and I know it, I'm out in no-man's-land. Alone, time to kill, music that takes me back, back to France, back to Drew, back just before the world revealed its true nature. Stacking all my favorite Yvonne Printemps'—"C'est la saison d'amour," "Quand les papillons," "Au clair de la lune"—I've played through the stack at least five times. Each time I sink lower into the chair, I grip the armrests a little tighter. Tears, oh, the tears have been flowing, my chest is tight, and that feeling of unspeakable loss is beginning to mount.

Stop—focus on better days, focus on college, focus on Drew and me playing hockey, focus on the first time I got Drew drunk, our first double date with the Lindgren sisters. Drew was so mad because I ended up with Sonia, and we all knew what Sonia liked. We had a great laugh on the way home because it turned out to be the short straw, as Pop Lindgren caught me with my hand in Sonia's dress. She does have a wonderful set of breasts, good thing he had trouble finding that Fox double barrel. The old man did like us and never told my dad, for which I am eternally grateful. Come to think of it better, he did not tell Mom, who has a little Mad Frank Studenich in her.

OK, little laugh over, now, record drops, Yvonne, if you never heard her sing I suggest you acquaint yourself with her work, marvelous voice. Everything I remember about Drew is colored with an unbelievable sadness. I cannot separate his loss on that fucking battlefield and all the things we did before that moment. I get up and go into my bedroom, go to my desk and open it, raise the binder, and pull out the photograph, more memories and just as painful.

Slightly out of focus, it is a couple, man in an Army uniform, woman in a long spring dress, cinched at the waist, looking white in the photograph, I remember it was a light lavender with a dark lavender cinch with matching hat. Her face has already begun to fade in my memory. We met summer 1917, I was with my parents at our lake house. She was with her parents at their lake house. I remember the golf course, country club where on Friday nights there would be a social. My cousin Nordea introduced me to a rather tall Norwegian girl from Wayzata, originally from Sioux Falls named Signe Valfours. From the very first moment I was enthralled by the sparkle in her green eyes.

It was never a question, from the first moment we met, although I was not very aggressive, I wanted her. We dreamed of the two of us living in New York. She wanted to play in the New York Philharmonic; I believe she would have, she was an accomplished violist and had a deep love of all things classical.

Both families approved of our match. Her family, while not rich, were solid middle class. My mother loved music and was happily looking forward to telling all her friends she had a daughter-in-law playing in the Philharmonic. My father was fine with her pursuing a musical career, classical, and really believed it was up to me to provide.

Her father was a bit of a dreamer, who went from scheme to scheme, some successful, some not, but he always provided. He was a kind person and supported his daughter. Her mother, well, I hate the bitch. She loved the marriage, of course, the money-grubbing lowlife. The rest of the Valfours clan is not much better. I often think that Signe must have been left on a Norwegian doorstep. She certainly looked more like a Laplander. Her father died in '18, one month before his daughter. After Signe passed I never spoke to those people again, they didn't deserve a daughter/sister like her. Mrs. Valfours, if you are still alive somewhere, fuck you.

Married in the spring of 1918, we spent part of the summer on a lake in Minnesota. It was fun, so much fun. We had this cat who came with the house, or owned the house, not sure, but he sure loved Signe. We swam, I cooked, we stayed in bed late, not wanting to let go of each other. I actually was thinking of finding employment in New York. I have a friend on Wall Street, he was enthused about my coming to his firm. I was sure I could lose lots of money for lots of people.

We moved to New York and stayed at the Waldorf Astoria. I had joined the Army, felt I had to do my part. Drew was going to join me in New York and we would be transported to France as part of the II Corps. At that time everyone felt that since America had entered the war, it would be over, over there, quickly and it was—but at a cost we never could have fathomed.

The shell sitting here is what came back, sans Drew, sans most of his psyche. I am lost, part of a new generation of men who are invisible, go about their daily lives, concealing an insight into the coming horror. Nothing was settled on those mud fields; men died, more men died, and our leaders, in their memories, just created more brewing hatred. The real apocalypse is coming, as we are continually perfecting ways to slaughter ourselves.

Drew: *"Nigel, Nigel, time to get up and get ready for the girls. We both know it's a shit hole but so much less so with Malory in it with us."*

"Drew, what, tell me what was it worth."

"OK, fuck-all, but here we are, listen to Malory's dream, there is light, there is love."

"Can it make a difference? I have been seeing a psychologist, only three visits, not sure that he can put back these pieces."

"Let him try, Nigel, think of all the people in your corner, all the people who care."

"I am bitter, Drew. I was thinking about Signe and our child, they never had a chance, the canal, how so many died, so many crippled, was it a son she carried?"

In one of the great ironies of life, it was the Norwegian vessel *Bergensfjord* which steamed into New York City's harbor on August 11, 1918, its crew and 10 passengers infected with a new and particularly aggressive form of influenza, the start of the epidemic. The fools in charge, as usual, had no clue what they were in for. It was worse than the Somme: it slaughtered men, women, and children. It was a precursor to what is waiting for us, it is a symbol for our times.

258

"Nigel, these are things we cannot control. Duck, brother, get down, find happiness where you can, sometimes the soul shines with light."

"Drew, sometimes there is only darkness. I cannot escape it, you know what I need."

"Love, Nigel, it may be right in front of you."

"No, Drew, I cannot let her make that mistake. I will probably die in this expensive apartment; for now I crave the one thing I cannot corrupt. Sorry, Drew, I love you, brother, but I have to ease this pain."

"We'll take it slow, Nigel. Medicate yourself but mitigate the risk, it is not time for you to leave."

I get up off the chair and enter my bedroom, open the hidden compartment in my desk, and take out my friend, but not my true friend, it doesn't love me like you do. I go back to my sitting room and begin to chase something I will never catch. It laughs the harder I try but it is so sweet. The smoke rises and rises. How much time has gone by?

I lift my head and Kaylee is sitting opposite me. "Nigel you didn't answer your phone. The girls are in Malory's apartment, I persuaded them to let me come up and see what happened. I know full well, what's happening but I didn't let on to them. Are you all right? I hate to see you alone and getting loaded."

"Then let's get loaded together. It's what I really want—you and me, Kaylee, and heroin make three."

She laughs as she picks up the lighter and sets the dragon loose. Kaylee is the one as Yvonne sings.

Death of the Virgin

I am tying my wonderfully woven Macclesfield tie with a weave in the shape of silver and purple chevrons, looking down at Kaylee fast asleep on my bed. One finely shaped leg outside the deep-blue silk sheets, her left arm extending outward, her right arm curled, hand resting on her stomach, her head turned to the left, her hair splayed out on the pillow, the light, the silk, her skin, I find myself wishing Caravaggio was here to capture the beauty of her pose, but he did: it is hanging in the Louvre. Caravaggio is one of the things that seem to make it worthwhile.

We chased the dragon last night and I am grateful to Kaylee, even though she joined me in my habit, she also joined me in my pain, she also created an atmosphere of peace, of caring. I get very angry with myself…how long has it been, Nigel? How many have told you to move on, let it go, bring yourself into the present and leave the past in the past and not carry it forward into the future? I wish I could explain that I believe, if I leave them in the past, then they're gone; if I carry them with me, then they're still here. It's my path, it's my obligation, to keep them alive, if only in my mind.

I pull on my dark-grey Brooks Brothers suit jacket, bend down and place a gentle kiss on Kaylee's forehead. Can you support someone on an unconscious level? In her way, Kaylee is so very hurt, I have never been able to get to the origins of her pain. Maybe it has been carried through from another time, place, some other life. Lara is at a loss also. She has met Kaylee's parents, and if anything they are overly indulgent with her, with her lifestyle, not aware of her drug use, and have welcomed Lara at many a family dinner. Very broad-minded if you ask me, but the wealthy have a way of making their own social rules.

Today we are all going down to Kaylee's studio in Greenwich Village to take a look at some of her artwork. Malory has expressed an interest, as she has only seen the two pieces hanging in Kaylee's parents' apartment. Kaylee has been trying to persuade Malory to leave the Art Students League and attend her art school, the New York School of Fine and Applied Art. It's all very convoluted, but I recall that Kaylee's father was good friends with William Merritt Chase who was the founder or co-founder of the school. Like I said, I don't follow much of the constant competing discussions, but I like the bold style of Kaylee's portrait work.

The bell is ringing. I leave Kaylee, reluctantly, and open the door to Malory. Feeling a little like a cad, I say, "Please come in, Malory. May I take your coat?"

She removes her blue crackle, deep-pile velvet coat with a satin de chine lining. She is wearing a simple patterned suit in a dark blue, fitting her trim, athletic figure beautifully. On the lapel is a gift I gave her, a Victorian sword-style jabot brooch in silver-topped 14k yellow gold, set with rose-cut diamonds and lapis. She sees me looking at the brooch and touches it gently with her left hand. "It's so beautiful, Nigel, I just had to wear it. Is it too much?"

"It was made for you, and if you had it on at a Yankees game it would still be appropriate."

She laughs. "Baseball, is that right?"

"Yes, I have tickets for opening day and you will be my guest, where I will introduce you to Murderers' Row."

"Sounds sinister, do they scare people?"

"I think only the opposing pitchers, Malory, only the opposing pitchers."

"Bowlers, right?"

"Yes. Have a seat, can I offer you a coffee or tea?"

"Nothing, thank you, I guess you and Kaylee got involved, Lara and I thought that would happen, she went home after about an hour. May I play some music?"

I don't think she is hinting at anything so I merely say, "Yes, we got involved, and, anyway, chose some music."

I go back into the bedroom. Kaylee is up and in the shower. I persuaded her and Lara that it's the only way to go.

I return to the living room and see Malory looking out my windows at the park. I walk over to her, I don't know why but I put my hands on her shoulders, nervous. I'm about to pull away but she moves back into my arms. She's wearing Chanel, and she presses her backside into my groin. The sun has just dipped low enough to place the trees in shadow but washing us in soft, bright winter light, her scent, Yvonne singing "Quand les papillons," my head drops down, my lips just make contact with her neck, she sighs ever so sweetly.

Drew: *"Kiss her, you moron, take her in your arms and kiss her."* I slide my hands down her arms and gently place them on her hips, pulling her back into me.

Kaylee comes out of my bedroom. "I have to admit, Nigel, your shower is fantastic, it's—" She stops as she realizes what she has stumbled onto. She tries to turn and retreat back into the bedroom but now the doorbell rings, and just a moment, just a brief moment, is gone.

"I'll get it," Kaylee declares, but the embrace is already broken. Lara enters, Malory and I are standing a foot apart, backs to the windows.

On My Victrola

I am sitting on my favorite chair, cleaning my Webley, when the doorbell rings. I put the gun down on the cleaning cloth and go to the door and open it. It takes me a second but I recognize the young woman as the one I met in Lara's apartment, the one I played that joke on about being Lara's butler, Ginny the writer.

"Ginny, please come in, what brings you here?"

"I hope I am not being too forward but I have something I would like to discuss with you."

"Fine, fine, please come in." I take her fur coat and hat, directing her to an armchair in the sitting room.

"Can I offer you something to drink, tea, coffee, wine, cocktail?"

Ginny laughs. "Quite a list, a coffee would be lovely."

"Please relax, I will be right back."

She looks at my Webley then turns her attention toward the windows. "Would you mind if I took a look at your view?"

"Of course not, please do." I pick up the Webley and cloth and carry them with me into the kitchen, thinking, what could she possibly want to ask, let me prepare some coffee. Adrijana is already on top of it, plus putting together two small plates of her *torta praska*, a Serbian apricot torte made with layered yeast dough that requires no rising, apricot filling, and a nut-dusted meringue top. A nice treat for us, compliments of my double in another gender.

"Thank you so much, Adrijana, this is very nice but unnecessary. You have other apartments to attend to."

She turns and gives me a light slap which turns into a gentle caress and a smile. When Adrijana smiles, her face, her whole persona, is transformed. It is just an indication how very beautiful this woman is and how, despite life having taken so much from her, she is still standing. On my Victrola, Bix's cornet solo transitions into the chorus, of "I'm Coming Virginia"; it always grabs my heart. To hell with it. I bend down slightly and place a kiss on Adrijana's lips, a light, tender, kiss. It bring that smile as she waves me toward the sitting room.

"Go, see that your guest is comfortable, I'll bring a tray in as soon as the coffee is ready."

I return to the sitting room/dining area and see Ginny looking out the windows at the winter park below. For a moment I remember the scene yesterday with Malory and my stomach tightens. Thank goodness, Ginny turns and starts to walk away from the windows. I ask, "Coffee will be ready in short order, now, what can I do for you?"

"I don't know if you know, but I am a writer and our mutual friend Lara has consented to edit the book I just finished. I have a small reading group, consisting of four women, they read all my work and have read my latest and all have given me comments and helpful suggestions. I think it would be very helpful to have someone read through the work from a male perspective, so here I am, asking you if you would have any interest."

I'm not sure but I want to start off positively. "I am, please tell me about the story."

She looks happy with my response. "Great, OK, here is a brief synopsis of the plot but first a little background. I write books for girls, approximately ages 9-13, and this is my third book. The first two were well received."

I sit back slightly, wondering what have I gotten myself into? —children's books, girls, well, I'm in it now, thinking of titles: *The Welford Sisters and The Ghosts of Belleau Wood, The Creature From St. Quentin Canal*…I'm hoping I still have a smile on my face.

Drew: *"Nigel, this might be good for you. You accepted, so get on with it."*

Ginny continues, "A brief outline of this one, called *Treasure of the Everglades*, takes place in Florida. Two girls, Marley and Kate, ages 11 and 12, find a map in an abandoned house on the street where they live, and the map appears to indicate a treasure that was buried by Spaniards in the Everglades. Is it a fake, has the treasure been found, isn't it dangerous to travel in the Everglades? That's the gist of the story, with the two girls trying to keep everyone in the dark but hoping they can find the treasure and help Marley's mother, who needs an operation. The only male characters are Kate's father—Marley's father left them—and an old Seminole, who may have a copy of the map and seems quite scary to the girls. What do you think? I was thinking the story is quite dark."

Dark? I envy this woman, her life, but what do I really know about her? Maybe she writes to extinguish terrible things or thoughts surrounding her. I do have a question but I have to be delicate. "What does Alistair think of your stories?"

She laughs. "Alistair thinks I should write books teaching young girls how to be good mothers and wives, not fill their heads with fiction. What do you think?"

Drew: *"Go carefully, Nigel, sidestep this one if you can."*

I continue, "Alistair seems to be a very serious man, and people like that are more inclined to see things in black and white. I'm a little more confused about things than I used to be."

She is about to say something but Adrijana is bringing in the tray. She sets it down on the table between us and moves cups, plates, milk, sugar, and silverware off the tray, pours coffee, and sets the pot down. She looks at me, nods, and asks, "Is there anything else I can get for you, sir?"

Damn, she thinks this is some sort of liaison, single women just don't drop by men's apartments in the afternoon, not where Adrijana comes from. For some reason I want to explain it to her. "Let me come into the kitchen and review the list of things to get done."

She has a questioning look on her face at first. "Certainly, sir, I will wait in the kitchen." She leaves the sitting room.

"Ginny, please excuse me, I will be right back."

"Certainly, Nigel, you will have to tell me what this tasty-looking cake is."

I head for the kitchen. Adrijana is putting things away. I approach her. "Adrijana, this woman came over to discuss her book with me and please stop calling me sir."

She gives a little laugh and raises her eyes to look at me directly. "Mr. Nigel, it would not be proper or fair to you if I was to judge anything you do. We have to take what happiness comes to us. I will always offer any support I can in return for your kindness to me and my daughter."

I put my hands on her arms. *"To nije ništa,* it's nothing." She looks startled for a second and then her eyes fill with tears. I pull her into my arms.

From behind me I hear, "Oh, I'm sorry, I just spilled some milk."

Adrijana breaks the embrace. "I will see to it." She grabs a cloth and goes into the sitting room. Ginny gives me a little smirk and goes back to her coffee. For a moment I am furious but I realize what she thinks must be going on. This situation is quite common, wealthy men getting involved with their female staff. I feel bad for Adrijana; me, I could care less what anyone thinks about my behavior. Should I straighten it out or ignore it?

Drew: *"Honestly, Nigel, I did not care for that look in her eyes, but there is nothing you can say that will change what she already has decided, is going on."* I know he is right but it is a point of honor.

I sit in my armchair and stare at Ginny, who is avoiding my eyes. Adrijana appears with her coat and hat on. "I must leave now, sir, I will be back tomorrow morning."

I stand. "I will show you out, Adrijana." She just nods. When we get to the door, I open it and lean in and whisper in her ear, "Adrijana, you mean more to me than whatever that woman thinks. I will see you in the morning, love to your daughter."

She smiles at me; I can't imagine what she must be thinking, I just want to let her know that what happened means nothing to me.

I sit myself down in my chair, still feeling a little angry, but I think I will let Ginny say something, which she does. "Nigel, I realize these types of things go on all the time, I am not shocked."

"Ginny, if you mean by 'these types of things' like men's lungs destroyed by gas so they slowly suffocate, or shooting a young German solider with my pistol, so close his last breath is blown in my face, or having a vengeful mob drag out your family and slaughter them in front of you, if that is what you mean, then you're right."

Ginny looks taken aback. I have one last thing to say. *"Patnji nema kraja.* Serbian. It means there is no end to suffering. Now *that's* dark."

Bix is playing his solo.

Gotovo je, gotovo je

My breathing is slowing, slowing, Adrijana throws an arm over my chest, a sigh of contentment, a moment of respite, an interlude of relief, my eyes are closing but I feel the panic rising. Stop, stop, no—not here, not now, with Adrijana in my arms. Too late, you belong here, in the darkness, in the mud, in terror.

Holding the hand of an arm draped across my chest, my lungs are going to burst, my legs are screaming, I cannot carry him any further but I must carry him further, 60 yards, 50 yards, I'm surrounded by complete carnage. Wesley has stopped groaning when I hit every rut, my breath is coming in jagged rasps, my eyes are burning, I feel like I might vomit, no time, Wesley needs help and it's you and only you. Through the wire, over the top, shouting for a medic, shouting for help, Wesley needs help. I lay him down, his blood has soaked through my tunic, the medic takes one look, shakes his head, moves on to others crying out for help, it's too late. I drop to my knees, Wesley grabs me, he doesn't want to die, not here, not in this shit hole, but you see, he does die, in that shit hole, and no matter how many times I will myself to run faster, to react quicker, to get him help sooner, he always dies, dies wanting to go home.

The scene fades as it always does, on my knees, with that blood-soaked tunic, tears tracking through the dirt on my face, unable to accept he's gone. Warm breath on my ear, words, words, foreign words, spoken so softly, so gently, "*Gotovo je, gotovo je.*"

As my eyes open, a tear runs down my cheek. I'm in my bedroom, a hand is caressing my face. I turn my head and look into the warm, dark, eyes of someone who does not need an explanation, who, on too many nights, had no one to hold her and say, "*Gotovo je, gotovo je*, it's over, it's over," yet she lovingly does just that for me. I pull her closer. "What would I do without you, Adrijana, who has seen what we have seen?"

"This is all that's left, Mr. Nigel, just a few moments of *Nežnost*, tenderness. You are the *svetlost u mom životu*, my light, so often I thought that God had abandoned us, how could this happen? But now, I think that there is hope, that God is with us."

I brush a strand of hair off her forehead. "Your faith is much stronger than mine, to go through what you have gone through and still believe God cares. I cannot take that leap, I'm still down in the mud, still surrounded by death."

266

"Yes, Mr. Nigel, I turn to my faith and you turn to narcotics, we have to find the light, it will save us in the end. No one can lead you to God; God will show you the path, God will deliver you. It has been a long time since I have been held like this, Mr. Nigel, it means so much to me. Have faith, believe in the Holy Spirit."

"I admire your courage, Adrijana, there is no denying that I have been blessed in many ways. I must try to remember that there are beautiful moments that happen around us if we just look for them."

She gently bites my neck, then kisses it.

"Adrijana, I'm spending money I never made, I do no work, I chase the dragon, I pretty much lead a life of a dilettante."

"What is this dilettante?"

"Someone who has a passing or casual interest in things unlike a serious person's interest."

Adrijana laughs; I love to hear her laugh. "Mr. Nigel, you have already given more than one life's worth, you do so much good, you try to make people happy, is there a greater job than that? You are harder on yourself than anyone I ever met. You can't save everyone, sometimes you cannot save anyone. Forgive yourself, love."

She puts her arms around me, holding me, my holy spirit, with *Nežnost.*

Out of Time Interlude
Nigel – Adrijana

Devotion

On the hand-carved Louis XV-style Parisienne Bed by La Maison London, finished in a white lacquer patina, is a naked, muscular, small-breasted, brunette with short-cropped hair and tattoos covering both arms and her right thigh. Those on her arms depict scenes from the crucifixion of Christ, and on her thigh a Madonna with a single tear running down her right cheek. The woman is lying on her back on top of crumpled grey sheets, her darkly mascaraed eyes closed, her breathing shallow. Next to her, on one of a pair of 19th-century Italian gilt wood consoles with marble tops, is a stainless steel Cartier table lighter, several pieces of foil, a seven-inch plastic straw, and six dime bags containing a greyish-white powder, a narcotic.

There were 10 bags when they entered the bedroom. The other person on the bed is a tattooed man, not young, all his tattoos are on his right arm and the right side of his torso. They all have some sort of devotional meaning and are fairly cryptic, including many in traditional Chinese characters. His right hand is holding a six-inch Chinese melon knife, which has a very slender, sharp blade, folding into a bone handle. At the moment the blade is open. He transfers it to his left hand and quickly slashes his right arm three times. The five-inch cuts begin to bleed immediately.

As he makes each cut, he is heard to say, "This is for you. This is for you. This is for you."

He cannot really explain why he is cutting himself; he figures in the absence of a new tattoo, he needs to feel the pain and blood as a symbol of his devotion.

The woman stirs, opens her eyes, and sees what the man is up to. "Nigel, please stop that, what the fuck, you're not doing enough to harm yourself? Put the knife down and come over to me." This is all said in a surprisingly tender way.

The man turns at the mention of his name. "Adrijana, I'm sorry, I didn't want you to see this."

He slides across the sheets. The woman takes his right arm and, looking down at the blood rising off the cuts, says, "Nigel, Nigel, you did all you could, all anyone could have done, please stop this. I'll get loaded with you but this self-mutilation must stop."

She kisses his mouth, almost as if afraid to bruise his lips, then she breaks the kiss and smiles at him, raises his right arm, and gently licks the blood from the cuts.

Surrender

Sitting on the hand-carved Louis XV-style Parisienne Bed by La Maison London, finished in a white lacquer patina, is a naked, muscular, small-breasted, brunette with short-cropped hair and tattoos covering both arms and her right thigh. Those on her arms depict scenes from the

268

crucifixion of Christ, and on her thigh a Madonna with a single tear running down her right cheek.

She has just poured half a bag of white powder onto a piece of foil, and now brings it up, slides the lighter under, and ignites the substance, inhaling the smoke through a plastic straw, holding, exhaling.

She pours the rest of the bag's contents onto the foil, then, bringing a beautifully proportioned, muscular leg up and under, she turns her upper body, which shows off the firmness of her core. She offers the narcotic, like a tribute to a God, who seemingly has abandoned the figures in this room.

I turn to her, leaning in so she can transition the powder to smoke and I can inhale the result. I do, holding the smoke, then lean back onto the antique hand-knotted Chinese pillow depicting a peacock on a tan background. Exhaling, God's gift or a demon's work, who can say? The cuts on my arm have stopped bleeding, and already I would like to add more slashes, but I do not vocalize these thoughts.

Adrijana rolls over to me, placing her leg over both of mine, moving her mouth just close enough to my neck so I can feel her deliciously warm breath. It sends a shiver up my spine, my stomach tightens. She gently bites my neck, then kisses her bite. A new song fills the room as Timi Yuro sings to me. Yes, Timi, I hear you. I turn my head and bury my face in Adrijana's thick brunette hair, inhaling her scent like it's another hit of narcotic. By now, it's a familiar Jo Malone scent of honeysuckle and Davana. In India Davana blossoms are offered in daily rituals to Lord Shiva; here, it is an offering of release. Adrijana slides onto me, raising her upper body and pinning me to the bed. She is incredibly strong. She looks down at me, her eyes flashing, sticks her tongue out. How the fuck can you resist this? Of course I surrender.

My breathing is slowing, slowing, Adrijana throws an arm over my chest, a sigh of contentment, a moment of respite, an interlude of relief. Like she can read my mind, she fixes another foil and we finish another bag, loaded, no panic. We lie back down in perfect unison, me looking deep into her warm, dark eyes, and she placing a hand on my cheek, in a light caress.

All I want to do is stay in this room and chase the dragon, and let Adrijana have her way. I pull up her head and place my lips on hers, our tongues make a ghost-like contact, our eyes open together, and we recognize what this all means, what we have been doing, what we will be doing. My head is swimming from the drug and I don't give a fuck. I love getting loaded and I love her for being here with me. As if she can read my mind, she kisses me passionately, sits up, opens the melon knife, and runs the blade across her right arm. I see the blood begin to seep out of the wound. I don't know what to say. Yvonne is singing "*Quand les papillons*." I pull Adrijana to me and embrace her like I never want her to hurt herself for me ever again and to acknowledge what she has just done.

Love
"Said, I'll protect you."

Sitting on the hand-carved Louis XV-style Parisienne Bed by La Maison London, finished in a white lacquer patina, is a naked, muscular, shaved-headed man with tattoos covering his right arm and the right side of his torso. Each separate tattoo holds a devotional meaning. On both sides of his wrist are sayings in traditional Chinese characters, one reads, "The way of the Shaman," and on the opposite side the characters read, "Is the way of danger." There is a goldfish in red and orange, a Chinese symbolic representation of Motherhood; there are names of the dead with various incantations; there is a Magic Boxer spell that holds great power. On his torso is the Tibetan knot of life, which proclaims the interconnection of all things; and a pair of wings with the Chinese character signifying the courage of a warrior. He has just poured half a bag of white powder onto a piece of foil, and now brings it up, slides the lighter under, and ignites the substance, inhaling the smoke through a plastic straw, holding, exhaling.

I turn and look down at the naked, muscular, small-breasted, brunette with short-cropped hair and tattoos covering both arms and her right thigh. Those on her arms depict scenes from the crucifixion of Christ, and on her thigh a Madonna with a single tear running down her right cheek. We have been in this room for, well, who really knows. All I do know is that with each passing moment my feelings for this woman have intensified.

Watching Adrijana sleep holds a kind of comfort. Yes, to my eyes she is quite beautiful, but that's just her facial features, and the way she has worked her body. The beauty of Adrijana lies in her strength, courage, devotion, and loyalty. She fearlessly walks the path of protection, she will do whatever it takes to stand between me and my demons, she will entice them, seemingly join them, trick them, scare them, all this to protect me, all at great peril to her, evidenced by the blood drying on her right arm, a sign of her devotion.

Her hazel eyes open and notice I am looking at her with, what I hope, is a look of love and appreciation. She smiles at me. "Time for more?"

I nod. We are down to one bag, either this interlude comes to an end or I get more. I look at the cut on her arm once more and guilt overcomes me. Why should she put herself in such a position? We have not known each other for very long, although it is clear we have much in common. The sex is somewhat violent—I have the bruises and bite marks to prove that—but it really is like two martial artists engaging, maybe different styles, ba gua, wing chun, for instance, but still the battle is equal, it is for keeps, no quarter given or taken, our qi flows through us and between us, when it is over we are both stronger.

So, the question is, if I love Adrijana, why I am exposing her to these dangers? Am I such a selfish cunt? Doesn't she need protection? What the fuck, Nigel, are you going to let her harm herself? At the very least this is risky behavior, mixing two narcotics, chasing them across all time and space. I need to let her free, save her, even if I spiral down into the abyss. Yes, get her out of here, she is a talented artist, she has a loving family, why should she risk it all? Nigel, you have reached the end of the line, the last stop, the terminal. She needs to transfer the fuck out of here.

We split the last bag, the last dime, the last high, the last...

"Adrijana—"

Before I can say more, she rolls me over onto my stomach, sliding on top of my back, then takes my ear lobe in her teeth, releases, replaces it with her tongue, teeth, tongue.

"Adrijana, I need to tell you something."

She withdraws her tongue. "Go ahead Nigel, but choose your words carefully." She pushes her groin into my backside to emphasis her point. It's her sense of humor that I love so much.

"Adrijana, I think you should call it a day, here, time to get back to your studio, you need to finish that large canvas, your agent has been calling every day."

She moves off of my back, lying on her side. I face her, running my hand down her arm and placing it on one of her firm buttocks.

"I like it here with you. I would rather stay. I'm not sure how I want to finish that canvas, it has been rolling around in my head, I can't quite make out the last scene."

"Adrijana, this is the last scene."

She laughs, kissing my nose. "Stop being a writer for a moment, too much drama, anyway, you need someone to help you navigate, by yourself you'll get lost, we'll do this together. Aren't you having a good time? The canvas will be on the easel tomorrow, so for now, get back on your stomach." As I roll over I'm thinking she has a point.

Ubij me sada, molim te

I am lying on my back on a Post-Modern enameled steel bed with a curved steel headboard and integrated flooring steel nightstands. I reach out for the foil on the nightstand closest to me, but before I can reach it another hand picks it up. The hand is attached to a naked, muscular, small-breasted, brunette with short-cropped hair and tattoos covering both arms and her right thigh. Those on her arms depict scenes from the crucifixion of Christ, and on her thigh a Madonna with a single tear running down her right cheek.

I blink. "Adrijana, what are you still doing here, didn't I scare you away?"

She slaps my face, then kisses it. "You're not getting rid of me that easy, you cunt." She straddles my body, pours some of the blue powder, from the foil she picked up, onto her tongue, then proceeds to push her tongue into my mouth. The bitterness of the crushed pills is strong and unpleasant but soon that will fade. The bitterness is replaced by a metallic taste of my blood, as she has bitten my lower lip.

272

She puts both her hands around my neck, looking down at me. "Can I strangle the life out of you?" Her eyes are flashing passion and desire.

"Please, do it Adrijana, my last sight would be of your perfect breasts, the feel of your groin pressed into my genitals, *Ubij me sada, molim te*, kill me now, please." She rolls off me, handling the foil and lighter to ignite the blue powder. I inhale it all and let my head fall back onto the pillows.

"Adrijana, how long can we stay in this room?"

"As long as the words last, after that, who knows."

I pull her closer and notice the bruise under her right eye, did I do that?

She is fingering my latest tattoo, just below my right elbow on my forearm, 天馬行空, Heavenly Horse Moves Through the Air. "I love looking at the Chinese characters on your body. I put the bruise above your Under The Banner of Heaven tattoo, it seems fitting."

I take stock of our bodies. We have beaten each other in terrifying ways, and I'm thinking we are just resting for the next round of violence.

She looks at me. "Nigel, isn't this perfect. We found each other at the right moment, the moment of complete disregard. We both realize that it means fuck-all and we have the bruises to prove it." She produces the Chinese melon knife, opens it, and runs the blade down my chest, for 10 inches, the slash turning red, dotted by blood. With her finger she takes up the blood and transfers it to a line between her breasts.

I pull her into me and whisper into her ear, "If you really loved me, it would all end here and all the pain would stop, all the pictures of those terrible things would all go away."

She shakes her head and looks deep into my eyes, hers dark pools drawing me into her world, or is it the other way around? Something has happened—the very atmosphere in the room has changed. I look once more into her eyes, her tear-filled eyes.

"Adrijana, we can never hurt each other more than what life has dealt out."

She lays her head on my chest with a small sob. I hold her tight to me. "*Gotovo je, gotovo je, ljubavi moja.*" It's over, it's over, my love.

Tea for Two

I open the door to my house. Inside music is playing from Resonant Drift Radio, the lights are low, there is a lingering scent of lavender from the three incense sticks set before the statue of Guan Gong, Guan the Holy Great Deity. I hear sounds coming from the bathroom. I push the door open and find Adrijana soaking in my Tea-for-Two Kohler tub, a citrus scent rising from the steaming water. Her wet hair is slicked back, accenting the beauty of her Slavic features, the nipples of her breasts just above the water.

I strip down and climb into the tub with her, slowly lowering myself into the hot water, the citrus bath salts stinging the cuts on my body. Once I'm submerged, Adrijana slides over to me, folding her legs and planting her muscular thighs over mine. We place our hands on each other's shoulders and look into each other's eyes. I love her and I'm about to say it but she speaks first.

"I love you, Nigel, can we ever break free from this reality? It's as if some despondent writer is typing away his pain onto us."

"Adrijana, we've hurt each other but we've saved each other. You are my strength, no matter what you do to me, I will always feel safe with you. There is no one who understands why we do what we do. Men blame you for taking me down and women blame me as an abuser. Who will understand what we really mean to each other?"

She moves in closer, gently holding me, lovingly holding me, her hand behind my head, her other hand running up and down my arm.

Maybe we, soon, will die in this house, maybe we will live together in love, for many years, but we eventually will die. Maybe she will run; can you blame her? Maybe I will run, plenty to blame there. How many more outcomes, how many more ways that always end the same way. The beauty of life, it's why it's so precious.

"I got more, let's dry off and go back to our room." I step out of the tub first, drying myself, Adrijana is looking at me. "Nigel, your body, look what we have done."

"Stand up, Adrijana." She does and I look at her body, cut and bruised just like mine. Before she can get cold, I help her from the tub and hand her a fresh towel. I take the towel from her and begin to dry her body. She is solid, she is powerful—God, she is so strong, in many ways, she has catered to all my stupidity. Her body bears the scars of the many battles she has fought in the many realms.

I hope it is clear by now, she is a shaman, she is my protector, each bruise, each cut, every ounce of drug she takes, because she has sworn to protect me, to do battle for me. The same for each cut she gives me, every bruise, each bite, every bit of smoke from the narcotic, you understand, right? She does it to keep me alive, so I feel life, pain is life, life is pain, so I am fully in this world, this realm.

We sit back down on the bed and I pour half a bag onto a piece of foil, light it, and let Adrijana inhale the smoke. I pour the other half and do the same for myself. Loaded, we lie down on the soft bamboo sheets, in a light-blue shade; we embrace, I pull her close, and bite her shoulder, the next round has begun. Who would do that for you?

Adrijana, *Moja ljubav*, my love.

Dreamland

I slowly become aware…it is morning, dawn, the sun is shining in my eyes, so I turn over onto my left side, wince from the sore ribs on that side of my body, the bed is empty on this side. Lately it has been filled with a remarkable woman, can I say I love her? She said it to me, how long have we known each other, months, maybe, weeks, definitely. Some old man told me she isn't good for the human spirit, but in fact she is everything the human spirit needs to survive, to fend off the darkest of the dark.

I am hung over from the drugs, the battle, the loving. It was an even match, both falling asleep in the twisted sheets. I wonder where she goes in dreamland, what battles does she fight, is she just as fierce in those realms as this one?

I get off the bed and pass through the hallway into the great room. She is on my golden Nepalese rug, naked, with her back to me, oblique to the glass wall. She has a 20-pound weight in each hand doing curls, the muscles in her arms taut, her shoulders flexing. She completes a set and slowly places the weights on a mat, then turns, sees me, and opens her arms.

I slowly become aware...it is morning, dawn, the sun is shining, reflecting off the curls of wire in front of our trench. Explosions off in the distance, off in front of the Hun trenches, hopefully obliterating their wire, or at least making avenues. Right, Nigel, just like Broadway. I wish I could laugh. I look down and to my left where corporal Wesley Hobbs is standing, just off the stairs, looking up at me. I pull the Webley with my right hand while raising my left hand to look at my watch—two minutes, one minute 30 seconds, one minute—then I lower my left hand, grab my whistle, and place it in my mouth. Look at my watch—30 seconds, 20—I climb up the stairs and crouch on top of our trench. Their barrage has started, not as intense but just as deadly.

I slowly become aware...it is morning, dawn, the sun is shining. I am standing in a dense coniferous forest, sounds of the forest all around me. I make my way in a direction I can only follow, follow the path. I reach a small clearing, where a woman stands in the center. She is wearing a ritualistic costume. The costume is filled with metal pendants, each representing different ideas and having its own qualities. In the Yakut language she is an ojun, a shaman. The air around her vibrates, the vibrations of a female ojun. Hostile spirits are scared away by her presence. Her drum beats, beats, beats and in her song can be heard sounds imitating the howling of the wolf, and the voices of other animals, her guardian spirits. The sounds are from in front of me, next to me, behind me, they are everywhere.

I slowly become aware...it is morning, dawn. I step through a door into the courtyard, facing east. The sun striking my face is pleasant. The large square, while not overly crowded, contains many young women all dressed in red. They wear red coats, red trousers, red hats, red shoes, and each carries a red lantern in one hand and a red fan in the other. Their hair is not worn in the traditional way, their feet are not bound. All together they sing.

I slowly become aware...it is morning, dawn, the sun is shining, I turn to my left to see a woman lying there, wearing a dressing gown in a sheer blue silk fabric. Its soft flowing lines accent her lithe body. Her feet are bare, her short-cropped hair is bright red. I know her, it is

Anita, Anita Berber, and she is perfection. I feel it all the way to my toes. I move next to her, sliding a hand up her taut stomach and cupping her small breast, her scent envelops me entirely. Her bedroom, the warmth of Anita's body—the moment is perfect. It will not last, but then again what does?

I slowly become aware…it is morning, dawn, I look up at an awe-inspiring sight, a sight no humans should ever see. The Sun, bloated and red, fills much of the heavens, its luminosity reflected in the narrow dust belt circling the horizon. Long ago the Moon reached the Roche limit and began to fall toward the Earth, breaking up and forming our own Saturn ring. The object of so much literature and thousands of years of the moon festival, long gone. Where has Chang'e gone now? There is a small disturbance behind me, as someone has kicked a few loose rocks on the way toward me. I turn to see Gilhooley. He nods and walks up to stand beside me.

I slowly become aware…it is morning, dawn, I lift myself off the bamboo matting that has been placed upon the rosewood bed frame. Her fragrance still lingers there. I quietly wander out into the rear garden. The early-morning sunlight reflects off the pines. I am facing east, the direction the rear garden is to be enjoyed, bathed in a most gentle light.

The center of the garden is occupied by her. She has been here since dawn. Walking the circle, she concentrates on its center. Her body is in constant motion, duplicating the movements of the cosmos. She is always becoming, always changing, beautiful, poetic, divine.

The whirling circles of BaGua Zhang. The BaGua, signifying its roots in the Zhou yi. She is the Lion 乾, the Monkey 兌, the Rooster 離, the Dragon 震, the Phoenix 巽, the Snake 坎, the Bear 艮, the Qilin 坤. She is standing, turning, striking, ever changing. Watching her I am as empty as I have ever been.

I slowly become aware…it is morning, dawn, I realize I'm sitting on a gold davenport in a pair of boxers with a slight run of blood down my right arm. I lift my head and try to remember where exactly I am. Wherever I am it is damn expensive. My feet are buried in a plush

277

oriental carpet, just under an acre, in fact the entire place is littered with Asian art, artifacts, and knickknacks. Whoever owns this place they have money. There is a large carved table with Chinese characters cut into the top, covered with a slab of glass. On top of the table is a bowl that looks like it's from the Ming dynasty, filled with a white powder, two silver spoons, a Herend Lighter with a Queen Victoria Green Border, VBO Butterfly Flower, a length of cord that looks rubberized, and a serious-looking hypodermic needle lying on a black velvet cloth.

Suddenly the room is filled with music. I let it wash over me. It's a new recording by Frank Trumbauer and His Orchestra, called "I'm Coming Virginia," featuring a lyrical, brilliant solo by Bix Beiderbecke. Bix's phrasing is a thing of beauty. Every time I hear this piece, it feels like I'm hearing it for the first time. Bix, so understated, so haunting, like an invitation to a kiss.

Two hands gently slide down from my shoulders to my wrists, curly blond hair caresses my neck, and—that scent. That scent by Coco, her number 5. It's like an avalanche burying your senses. Yes, I know, I should be embarrassed...I begin to come back. The young lady from the Cinderella Ballroom on Broadway and 48th Street, the young lady from last night. I had gone to hear my friend David playing in a band and was sitting with his friend Sarah when a woman she knew stopped at the table. After that the details become frozen in a mist.

I slowly become aware...it is morning, dawn, Adrijana is helping me to my feet. After a night in my armchair, I am stiff as a, you know. Next thing I know, I'm stripped down and put to bed.

I slowly become aware...it is morning, dawn, I get off the bed and pass through the hallway into the great room. She is on my golden Nepalese rug, naked, with her back to me, oblique to the glass wall. She has a 20-pound weight in each hand doing curls, the muscles in her arms taut, her shoulders flexing. She completes a set and slowly places the weights on a mat, then turns, sees me, and opens her arms. *Moja ljubav*, my love.

Return to the Cinderella Ballroom

Common Knowledge

Nigel, Sherry-Netherland, New York, 1927:

I've laid the Webley down on the cleaning cloth, after I made sure it's not loaded. I check my cleaning supplies: Hoppe's No.9 solvent, Remington Oil, my English bore brush, some dry cleaning patches, old toothbrush.

I press the latch lever and open the pistol. I pick up my George V shilling, a keepsake from my uncle, and use it to remove the cam lever lock screw completely, then rotate the cam lever upward. The cylinder retaining cam rotates clockwise to release the cylinder flange. I slide out the cylinder assembly. This is all you need to do for a routine cleaning. I dip my bore brush in the cleaning solvent and feed the bore brush through the barrel of the gun, making sure the brush goes all the way through, exiting at the other end. Then comes back through the barrel in the opposite direction.

I take a cleaning patch and dip it in cleaning solvent then feed it all the way through the barrel. I always use one solvent-covered patch followed by two dry cleaning patches. Next, using my old toothbrush, I clean around the muzzle of the gun; then, using a little cleaning solvent, I clean the rear cylinder opening using the toothbrush again and some cleaning solvent. I brush the cylinders, both outside and on the ends. I clean the sometimes problematic extractor rod with the brush and solvent, cleaning the front side then pushing it out and cleaning the star and the rest of the rod normally housed between the cylinders. Back to the bore brush and the cleaning solvent, I clean each cylinder. I repeat the barrel process for each cylinder. Replace the cylinder assembly, rotate the cam lever, and replace and tighten the cam lever lock screw.

Using a clean cloth, and a small amount of gun oil, I begin covering the gun, with the exception of the rubber hand grips, and inside the barrel and inside the cylinders. I wipe off any excess oil with a different rag, polishing up the gun.

Cleaned and polished, I'm sitting in a dugout.

Corporal Lancaster: "Have you been hit, Sargent Larsson? there is blood on the right side of your face." I holster the Webley and with a cloth I wipe the right side of my face. Yes, it is blood but it's not mine, it's the young German soldier's I shot in their trench. I saw the light go out of his eyes.

"Sargent? Are you all right?"

"Yes, Corporal, it's a Hun's blood."

"Yes, I saw you shoot that kid, he look so scared." There is a little laughter, not because it is funny but because we are all just as scared.

A whistle, a whistle—over the top, boys, through the wire, the barrage is lifting—no, it's not a whistle, it's a bell.

It's the doorbell, someone is ringing my bell.

I get up and open the door, it's Lara.

"Lara, good to see you." She just nods. "Please come in."

I take her coat and hat and put them on my rack, recognizing she is unhappy about something. We enter the sitting room and sit opposite, on my armchairs.

"Can I offer you something to drink?"

"Nothing at the moment," she says. Lara is wearing a rather severe, hand-tailored suit, dark grey. On her right lapel is a brooch with a European-cut diamond at the center, surrounded by European-cut and rose-cut diamonds, all set in 14k yellow gold with a platinum top, a spectacular, if understated, piece. Under her suit is a strict white blouse; she means business.

As she is removing her black leather gloves, she begins, "So there I was having lunch at the Plaza, a few friends, I didn't think you knew anyone except Ginny. I was telling a story about you and your dinner party at the Sherry. Anyway, Kitty Van Heusen said she met you at the Cinderella Ballroom a few months ago and that you are quite funny and charming."

"Oh yes, Lara, that is me to a T."

"Wait, Nigel, it gets so much better. I finish my story and Ginny proceeds to tell her own story about you. Can you guess what it might be?"

I know immediately what the story might be, and Lara's overall demeanor makes it obvious.

"I can imagine. Is it anything to do with her visit to my apartment to discuss reading her book?"

Lara puts her gloves in her lap. "Well, that is the day, but the gist of the story revolves around you interrupting her visit to go into the kitchen and have sex with your maid."

I thought it was going to be bad but had no idea it would be this bad. Why would this woman embarrass Lara, the person who is going to edit her book?

"Lara, why would she do this to you?"

"Honestly, I think she was just trying to be funny. She did attempt to make you out as some sort of Bohemian, but the whole thing landed flat. Unfortunately, the consensus was, since the story is now common knowledge, you should fire your maid."

I laugh but I realize that really is the consensus. Lara has more. "Oh, did I mention Malory was at the lunch?"

"No, damn, poor Malory. And fire Adrijana? Is this what you think?"

"Of course not, but Malory's face turned red and Kitty made a remark about that. Nigel, you don't know these people, how they are, what passes for propriety in their circle."

I am about to say what I think about their circle but it is not just about me, now, it involves Lara and, terribly, Malory. "Lara, common knowledge—that's a real comic phrase, common knowledge, almost nothing has hurt us more than that phrase, because that sort of knowledge is almost always worthless. You know that I will never fire Adrijana. Anyway, I can buy and sell the Van Heusen clan, all their money is tied up on the stock market with a little property thrown in."

I am beginning to get angry. Lara sees this and attempts to settle things down. "Nigel, please, I did not come here to ask you to fire Adrijana."

"Lara, if you want to know, I am sleeping with her. I will go down into the lobby and shout it at the top of my voice, I will invite everyone to lunch and proclaim it written on a layer cake." I am begging to lose control, I can hear the shells in coming, I have no place to run. The barrage is starting, I'm in no-man's-land, there is no place to run, Maxim guns in front, shells exploding on top and behind us, I am yelling to everyone to get down, to take cover.

I realize Lara is standing next to me, looking down at me, holding her hand on my forehead. "Nigel, I am so sorry, I did not mean to upset you so, these people are not worth it, let's have a drink and a few laughs."

At that moment the doorbell rings. "I'll get it, Nigel, I'll send them away."

I am sitting in my armchair, I am in my sitting room, there is no barrage, no mud, no blood, no wire, no Maxim guns, just a tired man, a man who cannot stop the memories.

I hear voices, there is a discussion going on. "Lara, whoever it is, bring them in here."

Quiet, then I look up and Lara has brought my guest into the sitting room. It's Ginny. I am at a loss. What would possess her to come here now, after what happened at the Plaza?

She looks apprehensive, and as she starts to speak her voice has a slight trill to it. "Nigel, I know Lara has told you about what happened at the Plaza. I wanted to come here to see you and offer my profound apology for the story I, so callously, told everyone at the table. I just want you to know there is no excuse for my behavior, but please say something, yell, tell me what a silly fool I am, anything."

Honestly, I am furious with her but I can never stay that way toward anyone who has the courage to admit their mistake and offer no excuses.

"Ginny, please sit. You have caused some consternation on the home front, something that has to be addressed. I am happy you came here to tell me, I admire that in a person. So what can we do about what happened?"

Ginny sits on my sofa and Lara retakes her armchair. I start, "Let me say this, I will never fire Adrijana. So we have three of us and Malory who supposedly are affected by this story being told at a luncheon. As far as I am concerned, this bit of gossip has no effect on my life, but since it can have some effect on those I care about, then it must be dealt with. Any ideas, ladies, since this is your social circle?"

Ginny speaks up, "I thought we could get everyone together at another lunch and I could say I made it all up trying to be funny."

Lara says, "If you did that, Ginny, you would become persona non grata in this circle."

"Lara, I really am not in the circle, I was only there because you invited me. Can you see me having tea at the Van Heusen house on Madison Avenue? It would be perfect in the sense that it would only reinforce their stereotype of the middle-class girl trying to move up in high society."

Lara is smiling, "Damn, Ginny, you are a writer. It is too brilliant for words but you realize where that does leave you?"

Ginny nods. "Yes, Lara, but it is a fitting punishment and in a way a just reward, because I may have redeemed myself to the people in this room."

I didn't think she had it in her but I am impressed. Still one more item: "Honorable suggestion Ginny, and quite brave, but one other problem. What happened with Malory?"

Lara says, "That's actually took care of itself. Kitty thought it was sweet that Malory would blush at the mention of you fucking your maid."

"Lara, her name is Adrijana and she means more to me than that. It is amazing how much more complex things really are than what people make them out to be."

Lara is looking down at my Webley. "Nigel, why is it almost every time I come to your apartment your gun is out on the table?"

"I was just cleaning it, Lara. Let me put it away, if it makes you nervous."

"Nigel, I am not afraid of the gun, but what it has been used for, that is unnerving."

I put the cleaning supplies back in their case and pick up the Webley. I love the heft of it, the solid feel of my hand around the slightly worn rubber grips.

I look at Lara. "Yes, yes it has, but it will never see what I have seen, for that it must be grateful."

Semi-darkness
A little white light.

The apartment is dimly lit, because, what's to see? I am in my favorite armchair admiring the newly installed Fog & Mørup pendant light in black patinated brass suspension with a milky-white opaline glass with a concave bottom part and convex sides matching the glass holder. The lamp is hung from the glass holder with a textile cable, so that it is 38 inches above my René Prou black lacquer table, highlighting my gun-metal-black, war-finished .455-caliber Webley top-break revolver.

Next to the gun, a Cartier stainless steel table lighter, several pieces of tin foil, a rolled-up $10 bill, and two bags of H. A portion of one bag is spread on a piece of tin foil. Malory left about 30 minutes ago, after we had words. They were not pleasant words. I thought the problems caused by Ginny's story had been repaired. I was wrong.

Originally she came here to offer support, thinking the bit of gossip might have caused me some unrest. At first she was solicitous, talking about what a terrible thing it was to say over a lunch, that it was callous and cruel. The very idea that I could be sleeping with the help, taking advantage of a working woman, just was not possible for me to be doing.

There I was, painted into a corner. I decided to explain the situation to her. I mucked it up, of course. It came out like a creep making excuses for sleeping with his maid. I should have just kept my mouth shut. The worst part was the look in her eyes, that look of total betrayal. She didn't say much, I think because she was so thunderstruck. She wasn't mad, she wasn't sad, she was just stunned. I may have killed her love, just as surely as I shot that young German.

I feel a sense of terrible loss, so get up and walk over to the windows in my dining room, lights twinkling from adjacent buildings, the park dark. I look down at the window ledge and there, sitting on the ledge, alone, is a sparrow. It looks up at me and flies off into the semi-darkness.

Just wait—the repercussions will be like an earthquake. Kaylee and Lara are going to be furious. What was I thinking? It was completely unnecessary, why to clear my conscience, to make myself feel better. The truth, that holy, lofty ideal, what is it? In this situation, was a lie preferable? Would it just have been for my benefit to keep Malory in the dark? Why, because I want to sleep with her? Why, because I was being selfish? Malory, it is almost like you exist only in a dream, only in my imagination.

A friend is coming over. I raise my left wrist to check the time and remember I gave my watch to McDowell and have not replaced it. I glance over at my desk clock: 7:35. He should be here any time now. I pick up the lighter and chase the dragon. Better put all this away. He will not approve of what is going on here. I have just finished putting everything in it place when the doorbell rings.

Right on time. I open the door and David walks in, extending his hand. We shake, embrace, and I take his hat and overcoat. "David, please go into the sitting room."

He does as I hang his overcoat and place his hat on my rack, following him into the sitting room.

"Please have a seat, can I fix you a cocktail?"

"No, thanks, Nigel, I just wanted to stop by and say hello. I'm having dinner with Sarah at 8:30. Well, how have you been, Nigel? We both miss you and were wondering if we could have dinner Saturday night? I'm thinking The Palm Too, for a nice steak and beverages, about 9:30, what do you think?"

"Well, David, it is awfully nice of you two to be thinking of me, I would like to have a nice dinner with you. I'll meet you at 9:30."

"Great, Nigel, I'll make the reservations, all you need do is show up."

I laugh, I sense David is trying to reconnect and I appreciate the effort. He's a nice talented kid, who is going out of way to re-establish a friendship I've been callous about.

He is looking my way. "How are you, Nigel?"

Should I be perfectly honest? I hate to burden him with my troubles. "I have managed to keep my head above water, things are looking better." Half a lie.

"Nigel, you ever thought about going back to university and finishing your degree? You were studying to be an engineer, right?"

"Yes, civil engineering, but I don't think I have the patience anymore, it seems a lifetime ago. Could you see me among all those fresh-faced kids? I'm afraid that ship has sailed."

"How about a job? You are qualified to do so many things. You were a sergeant in the Army."

"David, yes the Army taught me many things, like killing Huns. I was very good at it. If you have a question about how best to set up a mortar, I'm your man."

"You lead men, that must translate into some business need."

"David, thanks, I really appreciate your concern but I'll find something to occupy my time."

"I hope so, Nigel, I really hope so. Well, I best be going. We'll firm up plans for Saturday later in the week."

"Great, I will enjoy seeing Sarah again. Let me show you out."

We get to the door. David puts on his coat and hat, turns, and looks at me before he embraces me. "Go careful, Nigel, please go careful."

I ease the door closed. I say to the closed door, "Everyone, should go careful in a place like this."

I go back to my bedroom and return to the sitting room, placing the Webley, drugs, and paraphernalia on my René Prou lacquered table under the Fog & Mørup pendant light. I sit and stare at the Webley, I stare at the Webley, I stare at the Webley...

He runs out of the dugout, I shoot him in the chest, his momentum carries him into my arms, his clear blue eyes filled with fear, his last breath caresses my face, he slides down my body into the mud.

I pour half the contents of a bag onto the foil, light the Cartier, and chase the dragon across the foil, lean back into my leather armchair. I turn to the right, a little white light, my blue heaven, the released smoke is illuminated by the pendant light, a little white light, once more, once more, once more.

I jerk awake, the light is filtering into the dugout. No, I'm in my sitting room, the apartment door opening has woken me before he can run out of that dugout again. I look up and there's Adrijana, her beautiful face looking at me lovingly. She glides over to me, bends down, before a kiss, her breath caresses my face.

The Match

Adrijana is helping me to my feet after a night in my armchair. I am as stiff as a...you know. Next thing I know, I'm stripped down and put to bed.

"Mr. Nigel, I have a few things to clean then I will go down to Miss Malory's apartment, since you are paying I think it will still be all right to clean there."

"Adrijana, did she say she would be home this morning?"

"She said she would be at school today until this evening. I can get it all done, well, before she comes home." She bends down and lightly caresses my face. "Mr. McDowall told me what has happened. If you want to end my service I would understand, I have brought shame on your house."

I am startled by her statement. "No, Adrijana, you have brought love to my house. I will try to make others understand what this means, but in reality it is none of their business. I cannot stop their fantasies, let them think what they want. There is one person I would like to talk with but my first try was a complete failure."

Adrijana looks sad. "Miss Malory, I heard she is very upset. Mr. Nigel, I came between the two of you and for that I am sorry. If I leave that would help to bring the two of you back together. It is a good match, the two of you."

"Adrijana, you are beginning to sound like my mother. If she had her way, I'd be married to Liz Hansen, and have two kids, big desk at the brewery, mucking up whatever one does behind a big desk. Mother is a good woman, though she knows the war changed everything, she just hopes I can find some peace and a semblance of a life, you both have my best interests at heart."

Adrijana smiles. "I want to clean up something quickly, I'll be right back."

She leaves my bedroom. I put my head back down and I'm beginning to think of how I can make amends to Malory when Adrijana returns. She places the lighter on my nightstand, lifts the Webley, breaks the revolver, and looks at the cylinders.

"The gun is loaded, Mr. Nigel."

"Of course, Adrijana, what good is an unloaded gun? Lay it on the nightstand, I'll put it away later."

She does just that. "Mr. Nigel, accidents happen all the time with loaded guns and people who are drunk or on drugs. I know you have a great deal of experience handling firearms but I wish you would go careful."

I look up at her, a lock of dark hair has fallen onto her cheek, her dark eyes, her sensuous mouth, I want to kiss her, I want to let myself drown in those eyes. I want to go inside her and never come out.

"You're right, Adrijana, a loaded Webley is not something to have around when one is loaded. Can I ask a favor of you?"

"Of course, Mr. Nigel, anything I can do."

"Please hold me, please get in bed with me, and make the world go away."

Later, after Adrijana leaves and the world has returned, I am sitting on my favorite armchair watching the sinking, cold, February sun wash the wall opposite my windows. I have made a mess of things, unintentionally, of course, which is what is happening more and more. Malory deserves better but I will not be the one to give it to her. I'm just too far gone, into the night, into the darkness, I cannot presume she can follow me, come with me, there, live with me, there. The doorbell rings; answer it I must but I do so reluctantly. I am surprised to see Johnston McDowall.

"Pardon me, sir, but I was attending Miss Malory and if it is convenient, might I have a word?"

I open the door wider. "Certainly, please come in and join me in my sitting room."

I am about to turn around when I receive a blow to the side of my head and go down onto the floor. I am stunned for a second, then I realize Johnston has hit me. I look up at him, astounded to find him reaching down and helping me to my feet, saying, "Please be careful sir, you all right?"

He leads me into the sitting room, his arm around me, and eases me into a chair. "Drink, sir, a nip of scotch perhaps?"

"Well, Johnston, from that greeting I suppose you heard what happened between Malory and me."

"I am dreadfully sorry, sir, I cannot imagine what came over me, only she reminds me so much of a younger sister."

"Forget it, Johnston, I deserved that and more." I'm rubbing my jaw. "Do any amateur boxing? That's quite a right."

"Again, I beg the gentleman's pardon, not very sporting of me, my anger got the best of me."

"I understand, no harm done, please have a seat so we can talk this through."

The doorbell rings again. "Excuse me, Johnston, let me get that."

I walk over to the door and open it to a stinging slap to my face. It's Lara and she is winding up for another when I step back, holding up my hands. "If you are here to finish the bracing, Johnston has already delivered the message, please come in and join us, since this is Hit Nigel Night."

I look both ways in the hall, expecting to see Kaylee with a shiv. No, not yet. I close the door. Lara is already sitting on my favorite armchair, so I sit on the sofa.

Lara cannot control herself. "Nigel, how could you! That girl is devastated. Oh, nice of you to drop by, Malory, by the way I'm fucking my maid."

"Lara, not quite how it unfolded. Listen, I need to make some things clear. I think the world of Malory, she is a talented, exceptional woman. I also think you need to know more about Adrijana."

Just as I am about to begin the door opens and in walks Adrijana. She stops when she sees I have company,

"So sorry, Mr. Nigel, I just have to finish one or two things in the kitchen."

Lara stands. "No, no, please come in, Nigel was just about to explain his relationship with you."

Adrijana flushes. I see how uncomfortable she is and I yell, "Stop!"—startling everyone.

I'm standing, suddenly there are three air bursts in succession, taking out many of our forward line. I know I have to keep everyone moving, to get to their wire, to the damaged parts I can see a few dozen yards ahead. The noise, the smoke, I've already lost so many, we'll never hold their trench, even if we take it. Any sane man would run the other way but no, I'm yelling, yelling for the men to go forward to the wire, to death.

I realize I'm in my sitting room, Lara and Johnston are staring at me, Adrijana has her arm around my waist, helping me onto the sofa. It's as if all the air has left the room, but Adrijana speaks softly to me, "I will be right back with glass of water. You're here, in your home, with friends." She leaves to get that water.

I hear Lara's voice. "Nigel, I'm so sorry, things have gotten out of hand, please accept my apologies."

I give her a weak smile, more embarrassed than anything because I don't really know what I must have said, I never do.

There is a hand on my shoulder, it's Johnston. "Sir, I have behaved in a most appalling manner. After all the kindness you have shown me, not to give you the benefit of the doubt, well, it's unforgivable."

I place my hand on top of his. "Not to worry, brother, a guy needs a good sock on the jaw every now and then."

Adrijana returns with that glass of water. I take a drink and thank her. She bends down and whispers in my ear, "I should leave you, I have made things too difficult for you, Mr. Nigel. *Moja ljubav*."

"Please sit, Adrijana, I need to set some things straight."

Reluctantly, she sits next to me on the sofa. I turn and look at her. "Adrijana, if you don't mind, friends, Adrijana lost everything in the old country. Endured terrible tragedy, has come to America to start a new life with her young daughter. I am supporting her as best I can because she is deserving of our support and I love her. Adrijana, I want you to know that I have nothing but respect, admiration, and love for you, you and Melissa mean the world to me. I was a fool to let this relationship blossom and still think it is fine you are my maid, in fact apologies all around, my friends. I have been selfish and inattentive to others' needs. I know now that I will never be able to stop these memories from playing endlessly in front of my eyes. It cheapens their sacrifice, using it like a crutch. I will try to explain myself to Malory, she is just beginning to spread her wings and there are great things in store for her."

Lara speaks. "Nigel, what is so wrong with the status quo? Malory will be told how you really feel about Adrijana, she can decide how she wants to proceed. You've suffered, Adrijana has suffered, why should we impose rigid rules? McDowall?"

"All I have to say is, God Bless America. Again, sir, my deepest apologies. Life has been quite good for me since I arrived on these shores. I would be remiss if I failed to support others trying to find their way in a new country. Miss Adrijana, if there is anything I can do, do not hesitate to ask. I must leave to return to Miss Kaylee's apartment and fix her supper. Good night, I'll show myself out, thank you." With that Johnston departs.

Lara stands. "I should go too, Nigel, we can work all this out, everyone overreacted. I am sure Malory will understand, I know she is already regretting having words with you. Let's make this all work. It's a new day, the old rules are dead, we can make our own."

I stand. "Let me show you out, Lara." I escort her to the door, but before I can open it, Lara embraces me. "Nigel, in all this I forgot how much I care for you. The best way I know how is to learn more about Adrijana. If you love her she must be special."

I pull her closer into me. "Lara, I should have been more forthright but I hope things can be put right."

"They can and I will try to make it so, good night, love."

I close the door feeling better now that things are completely in the open. I will speak with Malory, I'm not sure what to say but I have the feeling it will work out. I walk back into the sitting room. Adrijana is on the sofa, her head bowed, she is crying. "Adrijana, things will work out, what is the matter, can I help?"

"Mr. Nigel, it is something no else knows, it is a secret I have been carrying since I left the Kingdom. Only a handful of people still alive know this. After tonight, I feel it is time I told it to you. I know you will hold it to your heart and tell no one else."

"Adrijana, I will never betray your trust, so if there is something you feel I must know please tell it to me, your secret is safe with me."

"It is so hard, Mr. Nigel, if Melissa ever found out, I don't know what she would do. After what you have sacrificed, I owe it to you to tell this to you."

I pick up her hand, she is trembling, I pull her close to me. "Unburden yourself, *moja ljubav*."

She moves her head to face me, tears running down her cheeks. "They came to our village from adjoining villages. I knew some of them—Croats, Moslem. They killed all the men and boys, they dragged me into my house after the murders. They raped me all night. I don't remember much, how many, only when the sun came up they fled. I was in disbelief when I realized I was pregnant. I knew none would ask any questions; if I killed the child, it would be no sin, they told me."

"Adrijana, it is too terrible a decision to have had to make. You cannot be faulted for doing this."

"Wait, Mr. Nigel, God gave me life from hatred. I had the baby, she is a beautiful young girl named Melissa."

All I can do is pull her closer, hold her like I never held anyone, *moja ljubav.*

The Webley

I am sitting on my favorite armchair, the only light in the sitting room is my Fog & Mørup pendant light, its illumination reflecting back off the René Prou black lacquer table. In the middle of the table is my Webley, loaded as I am about to be. I am mulling over the session I had this afternoon with Dr. Dizzy Gilhooley. He tries, he really does, but in the end he cannot stop the young Hun from running out of that dugout, Wesley dying in the mud, and most of all my beloved friend, mate, being incinerated. How much talk would it take to erase all those things and more? No, Dizzy, there is nothing you can really do to help. I like the guy, he is smart, warm, and very sincere, but in the end, ineffectual. Not his fault. Someday, maybe they'll invent some pill you can take, but what pill can control your dreams?

This is one of the few times I've thought about ending it, checking out, punching my ticket, shit, blowing my brains out. My answer is usually the same: haven't we seen enough death? Young men, woman, children fighting with all they have to live and you want to kill yourself? Wesley wanted so much to see that house in Wayzata, see his parents, sisters, friends back home and you are going to shoot yourself? I feel ashamed, I feel angry, I am mad at myself, mad at Dizzy, why, because he thinks he is helping me. Maybe he believes he is? I am trying to hold out, trying not to do the only thing that helps and at the same time hurts me so very much. It's in my desk, it's calling, it's beautiful, it's dangerous, it may very well kill me but I can't stand the film any longer. I want to leave the theater, I don't care to see the last act. Why, because I know how it ends. I've talked about all of this, described my dreams, given vent to my anger, my rage, yet I am still sitting here with a loaded Webley.

I get up go to my bedroom and retrieve that which I crave so much, hoping to make the world go away, hoping for that little white light. I pour half of the light brown powder from the bag onto my foil, ignite the Cartier, and inhale as much as I can, please hear my cry, straight to hell or paradise.

After the bag is empty, the foil blackened, I settle back into the comfort of my armchair, the Webley feeling lonely. Now the real pain wants its due. The thing that has driven me to this chair and a loaded pistol: Adrijana is gone. She left me a note, trying to explain how my life will be so much better with a bright young woman like Malory rather than someone who has seen the horrors that one person can inflict on another. I know I will do everything I can to convince her she's wrong but she is so willful, yet another sacrifice. My God, Adrijana, *moja ljubav*, please listen, I'll do whatever it takes, I need you so much, I'm lost without you. I know what she is thinking, that together we multiply the horror. That we've seen too much for one person and together it might overwhelm us, bury us. I don't know, maybe she feels ashamed now that she has told me her secret. Fuck, I know nothing, you know why, I'm no fucking good, who am I fooling?

Yes, once again the joke is on me, you see, I played the joke on myself. I alienated Malory and in the process drove Adrijana away. Malory thinks I should be with Adrijana and Adrijana thinks I should be with Malory. I start to laugh because it's so fucking funny. It's not? Where is your sense of humor? I parlayed two beautiful women into a bag of heroin. Funny, right? You had better start laughing, my friend, because I am within reach of my gun.

I am loaded. Remember what Adrijana said about being loaded around a loaded gun? I pick up the Webley. God, I love the feel of it in my hand, the slightly worn hard rubber grips. The sound it makes when I cock the hammer.

Suddenly a voice through all the drug fog. Drew: *"Nigel, you are such an asshole. How did you manage to lose both women? You'd think by default one would stick around. I am going to say something, I want you to know it is out of love, you are thinking about your young wife and dead child. It was not your fault. You don't have to beat yourself up, deny your chance at some happiness. It's just life, Nigel, you cannot control the dice. Grab one, Nigel, hold her with all your* strength. *Forgive yourself. Please put down the weapon. I've seen what it can do.*"

"Drew, she trusted me. If she had stayed in South Dakota, she would have been safe. No, I persuaded her to come here, to New York, where we conceived, she got sick, and I lost both, only to reinforce my darkest fears, after that slaughterhouse called a victory, nothing will work out. So I am left with guns and drugs."

I'm thinking I'd best put an end to this film but then realize it will never end, because who knows what is beyond the sky. I put the Webley down, pour out a bag of narcotics onto my foil, ignite it, inhaling all the smoke, then lean back, holding my comfort until it can work its magic. I release the smoke, having stolen all of its power. My eyes begin to close, a welcome relief. Suddenly the apartment is filled with the howling of a wolf. I struggle to reach my Webley but I drift further into dreamland.

I am standing in a dense coniferous forest, sounds of the forest all around me. I make my way in a direction I can only follow, follow the path. I reach a small clearing, where a woman stands in the center. She is wearing a ritualistic costume. The costume is filled with metal pendants, each representing different ideas and having its own quali-ties. In the Yakut language she is an ojun, a shaman. The air around her vibrates, the vibrations of a female ojun. Hostile spirits are scared away by her presence. Her drum beats, beats, beats and in her song can be heard sounds imitating the howling of the wolf, and the voices of other animals, her guardian spirits. The sounds are from in front of me, next to me, behind me, they are everywhere.

I do not know how much time has elapsed, am I still in dreamland? As I slowly open my eyes the *ojun* is gone, replaced by the smiling loving face of Adrijana, my love, how could I let you go? I say it out loud, "Adrijana, I can't let you go." She cups my face with both of her hands. "A dream, Mr. Nigel, I am here, I will always be here."

The Other Side of the Door

I am standing in the hallway of my building wearing my Brooks Brothers navy-blue suit, white rolled-cuff shirt, dark patterned red tie, my II Corps cuff links. My palms sweaty, my pulse racing. I know she is in there, in her apartment, she is unaware I am standing on the other side of her door. I try to raise my right arm to ring her bell but so far, no luck.

Someone has grabbed the straps of my field gear and is pulling me up and over the trench wall. It is Sergeant Wilkins, he is yelling at me, he is yelling at everyone. I am pulled off the wall and fall on my knees, pulled to my feet and pushed forward. Forward, why would I want to go forward? My eyes take in the scope of the battlefield. Smoke, explosions, yelling, thunderous concussions, it stretches as far as I can see, bleak, overcast, mud, stagnant water, bodies, blood, death.

My feet have a mind of their own—they are running, running, dodging geysers of dirt, bodies and eternity. The line, a dozen or so yards ahead of me, is cut down like wheat before a scythe, we are in range of the Maxim guns, veteran gunners, I am well within their sights. An explosion picks me up, turns my body head over heels and I land on my feet, running, running. I try to lift my arms to aim my Browning Auto-5 self-loading, semi-automatic shotgun, but the explosion has entangled it in my gear and I almost shoot myself, pulling the trigger before the weapon is pointed in the right direction.

I try to raise my right arm to ring her bell, no luck.

My feet have a mind of their own—they are running, running, dodging patients, nurses, doctors, through the corridors of Bellevue, get to the ward, the epidemic ward. I burst through the double doors startling a young nurse, whom I grab. "Mrs. Larsson, which bed, which bed is she in?"

She averts her eyes. I have attracted the attention of a doctor, who approaches me. "Mr. Larsson, please come this way." He takes me to the end of a row of beds, to an empty bed.

"I am so sorry, Mr. Larsson, she passed away last night, peacefully." The bile rises in my throat. I say in a lifeless voice, "No one dies peacefully." I walk out, I crawl out, I run out.

I am standing in the hallway of my building wearing my Brooks Brothers navy-blue suit, white rolled-cuff shirt, dark patterned red tie, my II Corps cuff links. My palms sweaty, my pulse racing. I know she

295

is in there, in her apartment, she is unaware I am standing on the other side of her door. I try to raise my right arm to ring her bell but so far, no luck.

I am not paying attention, as I am watching the young woman in the elevator with me. I am not staring, just interested because she is quite striking, well dressed in wearable knitwear that has a special double-layered stitch created by Armenian refugees for Elsa Schiaparelli. I let her enter first and her thank-you is in slightly accented English. When the doors open, I realize that I rode past Kaylee's floor and we are now on Lara's floor. Well, I might as well say hello and check to see if she has any ideas about tonight's activities.

I get up, get my works, and return. I prepare a shot, roll up my sleeve, apply the rubber hose, and inject the liquid relief. A few minutes pass and I am feeling fine until I look over at Malory and realize Lara was wrong. There are tears running down Malory's cheeks, I did make her cry.

Opening the door, there's Malory holding a beautiful bouquet of gardenias. I'm quite flustered. I can't keep her standing in the hallway so invite her in.

She sees I am still in my dressing gown. "I'm sorry to be so early, Nigel, Kaylee was insistent I bring over the flowers in case you wanted to use them in an arrangement."

The bell is ringing. I leave Kaylee, reluctantly, and open the door to Malory. Feeling a little like a cad, I say, "Please come in, Malory. May I take your coat?"

She removes her blue crackle, deep-pile velvet coat with a satin de chine lining. She is wearing a simple patterned suit in a dark blue, fitting her trim, athletic figure beautifully. On the lapel is a gift I gave her, a Victorian sword-style jabot brooch in silver-topped 14k yellow gold, set with rose-cut diamonds and lapis. She sees me looking at the brooch and touches it gently with her left hand. "It's so beautiful, Nigel, I just had to wear it. Is it too much?"

I return to the living room and see Malory looking out my windows at the park. I walk over to her, I don't know why but I put my hands on her shoulders, nervous. I'm about to pull away but she moves back into my arms. She's wearing Chanel, and she presses her backside into my groin. The sun has just dipped low enough to place the trees in shadow but washing us in soft, bright winter light, her scent, Yvonne singing "Quand les papillons," my head drops down, my lips just make contact with her neck, she sighs ever so sweetly.

I am standing in the hallway of my building wearing my Brooks Brothers navy-blue suit, white rolled-cuff shirt, dark patterned red tie, my II Corps cuff links. My palms sweaty, my pulse racing. I know she is in there, in her apartment, she is unaware I am standing on the other side of her door. I try to raise my right arm to ring her bell, it lifts, I point my finger, I place it on the bell button, I push and hear the bell sound. Moments pass…over the top boys, over the top.

The door opens. Malory in her dressing gown, hair a little out of place, draping along one cheek and slightly covering her left eye, she brushes it back behind her ear. I have rehearsed this speech for hours but it is gone as soon as I see her. The only sound is Bix's cornet, soulful, a touch of sadness. Her left hand by her side, her right hand, which is clutching her gown closed, drops to her side also, the gown opens, partially revealing her breasts.

Her arms rise and open. I step into them and she whispers in my ear, "Take your happiness where you may."

Part Three

Chapter 38
In Her Arms

The door opens. Malory in her dressing gown, hair a little out of place, draping along one cheek and slightly covering her left eye, she brushes it back behind her ear. I have rehearsed this speech for hours but it is gone as soon as I see her. The only sound is Bix's cornet, soulful, a touch of sadness. Her left hand by her side, her right hand, which is clutching her gown closed, drops to her side also, the gown opens, partially revealing her breasts.

Her arms rise and open. I step into them and she whispers in my ear, "Take your happiness where you may." It all fades, all the beauty, all the horror.

Mad Frankie, alternate time, Siberia:

She takes a long pull of her drink and her gaze drifts out the window for a moment. She takes in the expanse of white landscape and deep-blue sky. She turns back to me and begins, "How many times have we crossed paths, do you remember? Do you remember when? Do you have any details after I met you and Gilhooley at that rundown farm-house?"

Now it is my turn. "I remember you arriving at the farm; after that, I'm not sure. Also, have you seen today's date?"

"Yes, yes, the boys back at the lab have done all the math. They're scared shitless. Something is controlling local time. At least they think it is a local phenomenon. Who knows, the disturbance may have far, very far, reaching effects, maybe outside our galaxy and beyond."

The waiter silently puts my ice-cold martini in front of me. I nod and he backs away.

I look at Ancient Soul. "Is this the plan to lure me to desolation? Are you going to finally kill me? Let me tell you something, there will always be a world where I survive with a family, grandchildren. My wife will grow old with me and close our eyes to this world. Is that so improbable?" I throw back my drink, stand, and look out over the lake.

The shaman is standing in the middle of the lake. In the mist she raises a knife in her right hand and brings it down, piercing her breast.

I am kneeling in a small hut, sage fills the air along with pine bark. I am stripped to the waist, devotional tattoos covering the right side of my body. Ancient Soul approaches me, puts a gun to my head, and pulls the trigger. I am so very grateful.

I look at Ancient Soul. "Is this the plan to lure me to desolation? Are you going to finally kill me? Let me tell you something, there will always be a world where I survive with a family, grandchildren. My wife will grow old with me and close our eyes to this world. Is that so improbable?" I throw back my drink, stand, and look out over the lake.

The shaman is standing in the middle of the lake. In the mist she raises a knife in her right hand and brings it down, piercing her breast.

I am kneeling in a small hut, sage fills the air along with pine bark. I am stripped to the waist, devotional tattoos covering the right side of my body. There is an old man on a straw mat. He speaks in English: "When the world began, there was heaven and earth. You will seek your fortune elsewhere. You have done terrible things, been the tool of great injustice, drunk, gambled, smoked the poison, and given in to the pleasures of the flesh. You have mashed your boot on the innocent and guilty alike. While you have used women of my race as things for your satisfaction, there is one who will come out of the East. She will be of the Dao, and the look in her eyes will show you your true path."

I look at Ancient Soul. "Is this the plan to lure me to desolation? Are you going to finally kill me? Let me tell you something, there will always be a world where I survive with a family, grandchildren. My wife will grow old with me and close our eyes to this world. Is that so improbable?" I throw back my drink, stand, and look out over the lake.

The shaman is standing in the middle of the lake. In the mist she raises a knife in her right hand and brings it down, piercing her breast.

I am kneeling in a small hut, sage fills the air along with pine bark. I am stripped to the waist, devotional tattoos covering the right side of my body. Ancient Soul approaches, kneeling next to me. We wait for the Sakha ojun in costume. I am scared. I look at Ancient Soul, into her eyes; she returns my look, placing a hand on my shoulder. "I'm here now, I will face the demons with you."

The ojun, the Sakha shaman, enters with Vasily, who is dressed in local garb. She commences to beat the drum softly and to sing in a plaintive voice. Then the beating of the drum grows stronger and stronger; and in her song you can hear sounds imitating the howling of the wolf, the groaning of the reindeer, and the voices of other animals, her guardian spirits. The sounds seem to come sometimes from the corner nearest to where I am kneeling, then from the opposite end, then again from the middle of the house, and then to proceed from the ceiling. Her drum also seems to sound, now over my head, now at my feet, now behind, now in front of me. I can see nothing. Yet it goes on and on.

My eyes open, I am lying on a wooden pallet, the room is dimly lit by several low-burning candles. The dream is still with me, the dream of another, I was another, I had a woman I loved and who loved me. I am overcome with a sadness as strong as I have ever known, it was not real, this time, this place. No, no, it was real, I was on the other side of a door, one more door and now I am through this one, in this world. The pallet creaks as someone lies down next to me and puts their arms around me. I recognize her scent, her warm breath on my ear as she speaks.

"We were so very worried, we all thought that last shot sent you on your way to another, better world." I bring my arms up and return the embrace. It's Jeannie and I feel so safe in her arms.

No Riffraff

Giuseppe, Lower East Side, New York, 1907:

I have been walking around in a daze for two days. Clark has terminated my employment due to circumstances that make sense: the dragon has gotten hold of me and I am a liability. Clark's right, of course. I think I may have given Jeannie my last $20. Maybe McGinnity has a few ideas. I slowly make my way over to Broadway.

While walking along Broadway, I pass Kid Twist. He nods; that might be a possibility, but I am not a Hebrew so might be a problem, can't see myself converting at this point, foreskin or not. I arrive at McGinnity's Tavern. He has been trying to attract a better class of clients, dropping Saloon and replacing it with Tavern. I let out a small laugh when I see the sign in the window: "No Riffraff." That should keep the lowlifes out. Of course, I push open the doors and get my usual nod hello from McGinnity. Fancy that, I guess I'm not riffraff, how that is, I cannot explain.

Walking toward the bar, I notice McGinnity has created a section for dining, tables, tablecloths, waitress service, and a nice menu. I get to the bar and Armando has already put a nice martini in front of me.

"Armando, he's really fancied up the place."

"Finnegan, please take a look at the menu. He has hired a real chief, no Irish or English cooking. Believe it or not, Italian cooking."

I am glancing at the menu when I feel a hand on my shoulder. "Giuseppe, *amico mio come stai?*"

"Tony, *Sto bene, tu?*"

"Eccellente, ora sono nel settore della ristorazione."

"A restaurant, *dove?*"

"Questo, amico mio."

Now it all makes sense. McGinnity has a new partner, the Mano Nera, all this explains the "No Riffraff" sign. Those boys want to sit and have a nice quiet dinner.

"Tony, you've done well, *fatto bene.*"

"Si, the chief he's mio cugino di Napoli."

What a shock, the chef is Tony's cousin. I look at Armando, who says, "The food's very good, the kid can cook."

I nod. "OK, how about a plate of ravioli?"

Tony smiles. *"La mamma sarebbe felice, La mamma sarebbe felice, dagli un braciole d'agnello."* Mama would be happy, lamb braciole, my favourite. Tony puts his hand on my shoulder. *"Vieni, amico mio, il miglior tavolo, I tuoi soldi non vanno bene."*

Good thing because I am broke. Tony ushers me to a fine table, signals, and a bottle of wine is placed on the table. "Waitress will come to your table, *divertiti amico mio*, enjoy my friend, *mangia, quindi parliamo.*"

Well, he wants to talk and I need the work. What kind, we'll see. I'm thinking about pouring myself another glass of wine when a hand picks up the bottle and fills my glass. I look up, there is a strong-looking woman with black short hair sprinkled with grey in her mid-forties, I would say. She has deep-set dark eyes.

"Hello, my name's Finnegan."

"Please to meet you, Mr. Finnegan, I am Adrijana. Tony asked me to wait on you tonight, anything you need, just ask."

I am staring, I know, I cannot help it, I feel my heart stir, a smile on my face, I feel a satisfying sense of comfort and trust. Why, I cannot explain. Thought I would ask, "*Sei Italiano?*" I guess, I'm hoping.

"*No, sono Serbo.* Most of the kitchen help are Serbs. Tony hired me because I speak Italian and can direct the Serb staff."

I am sitting like a fool with a smile on my face. She looks at me and gives me a slight smile in return. "I will check on your food." She turns and walks to the kitchen.

I catch Tony's eye and wave him over. "Tony, she seems very lovely, Adrijana, pleasant, she should make a nice addition."

"*Si*, hard worker, speaks *bellissimo italiano*, can run the entire staff. Here alone, husband killed in a *faida*, very complicated. She will make her way, though, *forte, capire?*"

I nod. "Yes, I believe she will, *attraente*, yes, *forte*." I motion Tony closer and whisper, "What about McGinnity's other business, his *opium e donne*, his women?"

Tony looks at me, not too happy. "*Tutto venduto ai Cinesi.*"

Damn, the Chinese, the Tong. "Tong?" I ask.

Tony wavers his hand. "*Buon uomo*, Wu."

I feel some relief, Wu is running the women. I am worried about Jeannie and her history with the Tong. I'll have to ask Wu. I didn't think the boys would want dope fiends staggering through their restaurant to get to the red door, which I see is now white.

Tony stands up straight. "Giuseppe, I will change *il nome del ristorante sarà La Luna di Marie, il nome di mia nonna, La Luna.*"

Well, the final straw, Tony's changing the name of the place to Marie's Moon, after his grandmother. I guess McGinnity is being forced out. I feel bad. Tony sees that I am not as happy as I should be.

"Giuseppe, *il tuo amico McGinnity è stato curato*, paid well."

I smile at Tony; he did take care of McGinnity, though what Tony thinks is taken care of, I best not ask.

A piano starts up. I turn and see an elderly gentleman playing. Hogan has left town, his show on Broadway having ended, too bad, he was good for the place. Walking from the shadows to, in front of the piano, she appears as if from a dream, wearing a stylish dress in a French grey Henrietta crepe de chine. Her hair is not in the current style but short in a dark-blond colour, her figure is very trim, she stands poised ready for her cue.

Tony taps me on my shoulder and I turn around, he's all smiles. *"Lei viene dalla Francia, bellissima tale classe, il suo nome è Malory."*

I am captivated, I cannot take my eyes off her. She takes a single step forward and, making a slight turn, she looks directly at me and begins to sing, in a wonderfully, lyric voice:

Beautiful dreamer, wake unto me,
Starlight and dewdrops are awaiting thee;
Sounds of the rude world, heard in the day,
Lull'd by the moonlight have all passed away!
Beautiful dreamer, queen of my song,
List' while I woo thee with soft…

I am overcome with a sense of loss I almost cannot bear. A tear is running down my cheek. Malory, lead me to the moonlight.

Adorando la Madonna

A young, well-dressed man greets Malory after her song and they depart to a far table. I am sure I have met her but judging by the young toff, it is doubtful. The demons give and the demons take away.

A plate of beautiful cheese ravioli is put down in front of me, followed by another plate with a *braciole d'agnello*.

I look up into the dark eyes of Adrijana. "This looks delicious, Adrijana. I'm quite hungry."

"Yes, I had the ravioli for dinner, they're very delicate and tender. Is there anything else you need?"

"I think I'm good for the moment, thank you, Adrijana."

"You're welcome, Mr. Finnegan."

"Adrijana, please call me Giuseppe, seems more fitting in this place."

She gives a short laugh. "Giuseppe, it is," as she refills my glass. "Let me tell you about dessert, we have a fired pastry dough shell in the shape of a cylinder which we fill with a special cream."

I laugh of course. "Adrijana, I was born in Manchester but *mia madre è di Venezia, so cos'è un cannolo*, I know what a cannoli is."

She lays her hand on my shoulder, lightly laughing. As soon as she touches me, I do not hear a word she says. It is as if a current is running through my body. Again that feeling of safety, a loving gentle, spell. "Then I will bring you one with *un caffè espresso*. Tony sent for a new espresso machine from Naples."

She returns to the kitchen. I miss her touch already. She is right, the ravioli is tender, the gravy sumptuous, and the lamb braciole is, well, *solo mia nonna è migliore*. I look over to the bar and Tony nods with a gesture toward the white door. He moves from the bar and through the door. Adrijana arrives with the espresso and pastry and puts them in from of me.

"Adrijana, I have to speak with Tony," this as I am throwing back the coffee. "I would love to have this later."

"No problem, Giuseppe, I'll have a fresh one when you want it."

"Sorry to put you out, Tony is ready, and…"

"It's nothing, *moja ljubav*." I look at her as if I know what she is saying. She places a hand on my face lightly. "When you are ready."

I nod and head for the white door. I open it and see Tony had some work done, as there is a small foyer containing a shrine setup with a dozen fresh flowers, candles that can be lit asking for wishes to be granted by the representation in a three-foot statue *per La Madonna*. I light a small white candle *per mia madre e Jeannie*, I place a dollar bill at her feet, and *fai il segno della Croce, PATER, FILIUS, SPIRITUS, SANCTUS*. I know what Tony requires, I just hope I can do what he wants.

I walk through the passageway approaching three tough-looking, well-dressed gentlemen. I raise my left hand displaying three fingers, the left hand of God, the *Scutum Fidei*, and they nod, slightly. I knock on a dark, hand-carved oak door bearing a depiction of La Madonna.

"*Accedere.*"

I open the heavy door. Tony is behind a desk of the Louis Philippe period with classic shapely legs, subtle and classy. He sits on a Venetian Chinoiserie decorated red-lacquer and parcel-gilt gondola chair. The curved sides cantered with a pillow seat and padded back and sides, decorated with parcel-gilt scrolls with floral, leaves, birds, and tree decorations and an allegorical painting of two Chinese male figures. He is holding a Moroccan dagger with a wooden handle inlaid with mother-and-pearl and brass. He gestures toward a straight-backed wooden chair in front of his desk. "*Siediti, amico mio*, sit."

I sit.

Tony begins. "English, Giuseppe, I do not want any *malinteso*, misunderstanding. We have become close, we have shared difficult things, done difficult things. My friend, I want to help you but first *chiacchiere, La verità*, ah, plain talk, the truth. In this thing of mine there is no room for someone who takes the drug, they are not reliable. You take this poison, you degrade yourself. *Amico mio*, you are brave, loyal, and honest. I would like you with me but my associates vote no, they say *mettilo lui nel Fiume*, put him in the river. I, *il affare*, bargain, I can give you a job, you must *dimostra a te stesso*, prove yourself."

I am waiting for the other shoe to drop. This will be difficult, knowing full well it is not a request, I have gone too deep, I'm in it to my neck. I sit and wait. Silence, silence, Tony is looking at me and he does not look pleased.

"There is a man, he has sold us his business. He took *i nostri soldi*, our money, but it is heard he bad-mouths us, talks about *La nostra cosa*, our thing, he was told, *gli fu detto di stare zitto*, to shut up but no, he comes in our place with *La mancanza di rispetto*, no respect. He *deve essere messo a tacere*, must be silenced."

Tony opens a small drawer and removes a gun and an envelope, places the gun atop the envelope, and slides both across the table. A stolen H&R .32-caliber revolver and an envelope which I know contains $200.

Tony sits and waits, he waits, I pick up the gun.

"Bene, sì, amico mio, fai questo per restituire il favore, you repay a debt of the *dell'ebraico*, the Jew. The man's *il nome è McGinnity*."

My brain refuses to acknowledge what my ears have just heard. What shit I have made of this life, first Jeannie, now McGinnity.

"Can I talk with him, Tony, persuade him to shut up?"

"Troppo tardi, quei bastardi siciliani hanno sentito, sarebbe un segno di debolezza. Sorry, too late, those Sicilians have heard, they will think us weak."

I pick up the gun, pact made, promises to keep. It's McGinnity or me, there are no other options—but McGinnity, for fuck sake! He took me under his wing, looked out for me, this place was like a second home. No, no, I cannot do this, how am I to get out of this?

Make no mistake, McGinnity is a dead man, he crossed the Mano Nera, he insulted them in their own place of business, this after he took their money, fuck, like he had a choice. If not I then another. Tony smiles at me. *"È fatta, accendi una candela per chiedere protezione alla madonna.* Light a candle, ask *La Madonna* for her protection."

I stand. *"Grazie Tony, è finito."*

He answers, *"Buono, amico mio, arrivederci."*

I walk out of Tony's office on legs I cannot feel, passing the three gentlemen. They all give me the three fingers of their left hand, they know, it is a sign of respect, I am the blackest of hands, I am an *assassino*.

I stop in front of the beautiful statue of *La Madonna*. A loving smile on her face, arms out, as to embrace, to embrace all the suffering in this world. How can she protect me, if I am about to bring about more suffering? I light a candle and kneel on the pad reciting a prayer *mia madre* taught me:

Ave Maria, piena di grazia,
il Signore è con te
Beati voi tra le donne,
e benedetto è il frutto del tuo grembo, Gesù.
Santa Maria, Madre di Dio,
prega per noi peccatori, ora,
e nell'ora della nostra morte. Amen.

Hail Mary, full of grace,
The Lord is with you.
Blessed are you among women,
And blessed is the fruit of your womb, Jesus.
Holy Mary, Mother of God,
pray for us sinners, now,
And at the hour of our death. Amen.

The envelope in my pants, the gun in my jacket, I push through the white door. There is a ruckus by the dining area—it is McGinnity, he is loud, he is yelling at Adrijana, "Keep your hands off me, you dago bitch." He shoves her against the bar. I rush over and grab him, drag him toward the door and out onto the street, there are people there, there are several Mano Nera, standing outside the place. He is yelling all the way, how he was cheated, how they stole the place he built. It is hard to hear. A cab arrives and two men get out and shove McGinnity into the back, nodding for me to get in also. I climb in. McGinnity is quiet, I suspect he's been sapped.

We drive for a little while, we arrive off Christopher, the river, some gaslights, few people. There is a hand gripping my heart. What to do, what to do, the blood is pounding in my ears. The cab stops, the two gentlemen get out, pulling McGinnity out after them. He is un-steady on his feet, stumbling toward the water. I get out and he turns, "Finnegan, Finnegan, you can't do this, not like this!" He is holding up his hands.

"McGinnity, why couldn't you just shut the fuck up!" I yell. We are slowly walking toward the water. McGinnity turns and sees he is at the river's edge, then turns back to me. "Finnegan, please, I'll leave town, disappear…"

He doesn't finish. I shoot him twice in the chest, he goes over the side, there is a splash, the gun follows. The two Mano Nera men give me the left-handed sign and nod. I wave them into the cab with, "*Camminerò*," I'll walk.

They get into the cab and drive off. I start walking, heading I know not where, but I can hear *mia madre, Ave Maria, piena di grazia, il Signore è con te.*

308

Somehow I arrive back at La Luna di Marie. I push open the doors and am ushered straight back to Tony. I enter his office where he is behind his desk eating dinner. He looks up.

I say, "*È fatto, Tony, ha finito.*"

"*Bene, amico mio, mangia?*" I shake my head. Tony calls out, "Roberto" and door opens slightly. Roberto pokes his head in the room. "*Mostra a Giuseppe un letto, vedi che prende del cibo*, a bed and some food for Giuseppe."

"*Si*, Tony."

I follow Roberto to the back and a room with a single bed, chair, small table, lamp. I loosen my tie, take off my jacket, and lie down. My mind is completely blank, some time passes, how much, I am not sure, the door opens, a woman carries in a tray, which she sets down on the table. The lighting is dim but I recognize Adrijana. She sits down on the edge of the bed. A single tear runs out of my right eye. Adrijana bends down and puts her arms around me, quieting the sobs.

I Woke Up Feeling Dead

I woke up feeling dead, one moment I am sweating, the next chills, headache, joints aching, I am still in that backroom, Tony's room. During the night someone must have covered me in blankets. I dare not move because it will only set off a new wave of discomfort, so I just lie there, the white-painted ceiling getting my full attention. What have you done, Finnegan?

What have you done?

I killed a man, I killed a man on orders. Not policing, or war, but to shut someone up, to silence them forever. A stranger, interfering with business? A molester? No, a friend, someone who looked out for me, someone who let me indulge, only because he thought a man should make his own decisions about such things, without coercing. I shot him down while he's pleading for his life, without mercy, without regard.

The door opens, admitting Adrijana, carrying a bottle and a small glass. She runs a damp cloth across my forehead, it feels good. I look up, into those dark, deep, pools and see only love. Her smile lifts my leaden spirit, her touch is magic. I am not worth it. I have to go.

"Adrijana, I have to get up and go."

"Giuseppe, stay, let me take care of you."

"You've already done too much, I'll be back later."

I stand up, Adrijana looks hopeless, she knows where it is I am going, she gives my face one last, gentle caress, turns, and walks out of the room.

I am out of the room, out into the restaurant, out the front door and in no time at Wu's Bath Emporium. Money exchanged, pallet chosen, table moved over as I lie down on the wooden pallet in the gloom of Wu's Bath Emporium's opium den, with everything a hophead would want, meaning a nice ball of dope. I notice how beautiful the young Chinese woman is as she twirls the ball of dope over the opium lamp. Maybe it's because she has the thing I want. The thing that so fleetingly quenches the fire.

All set, she hands me the plain pipe. Her eyes are averted as I notice she is missing the ring finger of the hand offering me the pipe. I take it from her, bringing the stem to my mouth with more anticipation than with any lover. I take a long pull, allowing my head to fall back among the cheap pillows. As I exhale time slows and the cosmos opens to its terribly beautiful, infinite possibilities, but it is one I am falling toward.

I jerk awake, not so quickly realize where I am. I look down to see someone sitting on the pallet, a young girl, very young, naked to her waist, thick blond hair partially covering her small breasts. She notices I am awake and leans in toward me, her hair falling on my chest as she whispers into my ear, "Fella, if you buy me a ball of dope, I'll suck your cock." She licks the side of my face. I say nothing, staring at her.

"Quiet fella. OK, I'll suck you off and then you can buy me the dope."

I reach into my pocket and pull some bills out and push them into her hand. Her smile shows some missing teeth as she turns and begins to pull down my pants.

I grab her arm. "It's on the house."

She sits up, stands, and walks from the dimness of my pallet into the darkness.

I am shaken and all I can say to her back is, "*Che Dio ti protegga*, may God protect you." Out of the darkness into dimness walks Wu, shaking his head as he looks down at me. "Enough, get up, I take you to herb shop, you stay until cure, my orders, or you, *Nǐ huì xiāoshī de*, disappear. Very close, called Heavenly Crane, old man and young woman, white, she wu, 巫, *Shàngdì bǎohù nǐ*, may the heavens protect you."

I know what he is saying: cure or I will be in the river.

The wu 巫

All I know is that Wu and a young Chinese woman are helping arrange my clothes and pulling me upright. Wu looks very nervous, when was the last time I saw Wu this frightened, Jeannie and that Tong member. Why the rush? Slowly dropping, floating down into in my consciousness, like a weighted body in the river, is the reason. I'm already a dead man. They must have decided I am too much of a liability. Why not just shoot me down and dump me in the river after McGinnity? They were Tony's men, he still had hopes, he was trying to protect me.

He was outvoted. Once I left Tony's place, I was marked for death. They have finished pulling me together, I am upright and looking stupid. Wu is trying to be patient but he knows, the time to go, go, go, so Giuseppe went.

Wu tries not to look too conspicuous as he leads me down the street in a sort of half carry, half pushing style. Even in Chinatown, a Chinese man doesn't put his hands on a white man, so I am aware of the risk Wu is taking and know that disappearing a body might present an easier problem, so he is putting himself out.

Somehow we arrive at the Heavenly Crane herb shop. I stumble down two stairs and through the door, startling two customers. They look scared to see a white man being manhandled into the back room but avert their eyes and say nothing.

Once in the back, which is a fairly large room with a vaulted ceiling, Wu is joined by a very old man. Both help me onto a small bed then Wu quickly departs. The old man is looking down at me. "Many years ago, I learned your language. I'm a yi, a physician who practices Chinese medicine. I must prepare you, there's a wu here."

I'm confused. "He just left." Then I realize, not this again, he is talking about a shaman, I thought this gentleman was the shaman.

I ask, "I thought you are the wu?"

The old man smiles, bent over, then momentarily straightens himself. The filtered light catches him at a different angle, making him look young, strong, confident. Can a wu do these things? He bends back down and is the old man once more.

"No, no, wu special being, earth tiger, my name Ching Ling Foo, I'm yi, together we are wuyi. If the signs are auspicious she will appear. Your friend Wu told me your birthday, December 27, 1881, you are metal snake, it is May 15, month of the snake, it is 5:00 p.m. so the wu will not appear now, she will wait until morning between 9:00 and 11:00 a.m., time of the snake. If she appears at all, only the wu can see what you are and what you might become, as the master has said, the true wu do not simply read the omens."

Time is passing, but I do not know how. I am being administered to by Ching. Every so often I know he gives me smaller and smaller doses of opium but he has mixed a concoction of Chinese herbs. As he is preparing his mixture, created for my qi, he recites the ingredients: ginseng, yanhusuo, Cocculine, found in the root of the climbing plant *Sinomenium acutum* and Stephania root. What proportions I have no idea. After a while my yen begins to recede but I am a shell. I feel weak, listless, lifeless.

I sense someone is in the room, I lift and turn my head, there is a woman, in the shadows, just standing, motionless, I dare not speak, as if my voice will frighten her away. No, she steps into the room and into the light. I am not prepared for who she is. Slightly built but no matter, there is strength, spiritual strength, strength from other realms. I can feel it all because that is what she wants. Dressed in a simple Chinese robe, the colour of which offsets her pale skin, blond hair, and crystal-clear blue eyes. She approaches my bed, tentatively but at the same time resolutely. She holds both hands out, palms up, and speaks.

"*Tiān kěyǐ bǎohù nǐ*, I am Anja Wangemann, I help Mr. Ching, restocking and organizing his herbs."

My head falls back onto the pillows and I smile at her. "Thank you for the blessing, nice to meet you. Have you lived in China?"

"I was born in Guangzhou and lived with my parents until I left to come to America. sadly they were both killed in the Boxer rebellion. I wish I could have saved them but Anja could not convince them of the danger."

"Anja, sometimes you cannot save people, people you love. I know, because of that, I am the master of self-hate."

"Yes, I have come to grips that Anja can only do so much, what she can do is surrender to Taiyi, the great oneness, who holds the ladle of the big dipper providing the movement of life to the world."

She looks away and is silent for a few seconds, looks sad for a few seconds, looks resigned for a few seconds, and then she looks back at me, the light illuminating the outline of her body as she smiles at me. I feel as safe as I have ever felt. She takes one step back, as if she is departing, but has one last thing to say: "Trust me and you will let go of what you are and become what you will be." Then she is gone, vanished, was it a dream?

I slowly close my eyes, painfully aware of my broken body.

Someone is staring at me. I recognize Ching and Wu, they do not look happy. Ching says, "You not among the living, you in spirit world, only the wu can reach you now."

"Ridiculous, I'm awake in your back room."

Neither acknowledges anything I just said. To prove my point, I sit up and then, with a fair amount of difficulty, stand, yet both men are still looking down at the bed. I turn, scared of what I will see, because I know what I'll see. Yes, it's me, lying on the bed, Giuseppe, pale, gaunt, empty, dead. I woke up dead. I move over to a corner and sit down on the floor, feeling almost nothing, maybe just relief.

People come in and out of the room, their movements leaving a visual trail that begins to curve in on itself, again and again, and then it begins to fade, grow dimmer and dimmer, as I realize I am departing, leaving, on my journey, my journey west. Someone or something is shaking me awake. I smell incense, a beautiful aroma of lemongrass, that picks my consciousness up, in a gentle and loving way, but it is not the shaking or the incense, I sense her presence. It is morning, the time of the snake. I open my eyes, she is just standing, her back to me, in the centre of the room, the centre of my energy, the centre of everything. The journey's end?

I see clearly: three Chinese women enter the room, two with drums, the other with a flute. They begin to play. Three more Chinese women enter, dressed in simple white gowns under robes of pale green, trimmed in turquoise. They are priestesses and they begin to dance to the music of drums and flute, dance to the music of drums and flute, dance to the music of drums and flute, they reach a trance-like state, they are receiving *shen* (spirits) into their bodies, they begin speaking in tongues. In the power of the *shen* gathering around the whirling dancers, object suddenly begin to rise into the air. The dancers slash themselves with knives but do not bleed. All this creating an energy vortex, all swirling around the central figure, she lifts her arms, the tiger on the back of her red robe, trimmed in gold and yellow, begins to move, almost as if it is going to leap from her back—and then she turns.

It is Anja, pale, blonde, blue eyes—or is it? I am terrified—but she looks directly at me and all fear departs. She moves toward me and the vortex shifts with her, she is the source, she is the vortex, she is controlling the energy, she is controlling time, it is timelessness, it is the alpha and the omega, occupying the same space, the same moment.

She reaches the bed, raises her arms, and throws back her head. There is a flash so bright I think I must have been blinded but no, I can see. Her head drops down and she places her left hand on my chest over my heart, her right arm extended upward, and speaks: "What you were is no more, what you have become is, this is the way of change."

A Monday Afternoon

I scan the place, not a bad size crowd, still the lingerers over lunch, enjoying their espresso, Tony's crew at their usual table, fairly nondescript in expensive dark suits. A lively bar crowd, Armando working that cocktail shaker, McGinnity holding court, Gilhooley looking my way and nodding. Adrijana, catches my eye and gives me that warm, slight smile that I love so much. I straighten my Brooks Brothers jacket, pick up a check, and head for a lone, distinguished, gentleman finishing his coffee.

I place the check on the table. "I hope the meal was to your satisfaction, Dr. Larsson."

He nods, which is about as much as you are going to get out of him, probably lost in one of his cases. I return back to my gilded wood centre table inspired by decorative and architectural motifs of the Trecento, the Italian pre-Renaissance of the 14th century. Tony has taste. I review tonight's menu then look up. Jeannie catches my eye, check. I pick up her check and approach her table and slide the check face down on the tabletop. Jeannie is striking in a beautiful day dress of grey satin and muslin in printed circular patterns. High collar and modesty in cotton lace with a collar trim in a polychrome floral print, satin waistband and piping, Art Nouveau style. Jeannie's lunch guest, Alice Paul, is wearing a similar style dress in a light-blue satin.

"Planning some new strategies, ladies?"

They both laugh. Jeannie says, "Yes, and we expect your full support, Mr. Finnegan."

My turn to laugh. "Without question, Miss Culbard, without question. Whenever you are ready, no hurry with the check."

I am returning to my workstation when I notice a woman sitting alone at a far table. Funny, I don't remember seating her; well, maybe Adrijana did. There is a pot of tea and a cup in front of her. I met her once in that herb shop, the Heavenly Crane. She guided me, picking out a few herbs to help with my headaches. As I am walking, I'm thinking about the encounter. She was helpful, knowledgeable, friendly but she has an otherworldly quality to her. There is talk that many Chinese fear her, that she does some sort of divination that is intense, evidently too intense for some. Anyway, Wu has regaled me with a few stories about her as I soak in a tub at his Bath Emporium.

One story circulating is a tale that she can travel in the spirit realm and even bring people back. I think it's all a bit much but I lived in China so I do believe she holds great power. Who knows, maybe someday I will need her services. I glance back at her table, and suddenly it strikes me how much she has given. I can feel what her powers have cost her. Damn, Finnegan, go say hello, she looks so lonely.

When I arrive at her table, without looking up from her cup she says, "Why, hello, Mr. Finnegan, you look well." She turns toward me, her clear eyes look at me, I feel she sees all I am, she smiles at me as if she is quite pleased with what see sees.

I feel the need to say something, to make conversation. "Anja Wangemann, is that right?"

"Yes, you visited the herb shop. I'm grateful you came to me."

I'm a little confused; she's grateful? "No, Anja, may I address you by your first name?"

"Yes, Giuseppe." A small smile.

"I'm grateful to you, Anja, whatever you concocted for me cleared away my headaches."

She takes my hand. "Giuseppe, it was the Divine that stabilized your virtue through ritual practice, I was only the medium."

As she holds my hand, in my mind's eye I see someone on a pallet, lifeless, colourless, that person is me. I am frightened but I don't want to pull my hand away. Her hand, she is pulling me, leading me, she brings me gently toward her and whispers in my ear, "Can you hear her singing?"

Reality stops, this life is transformed, this is the way of change.

Nigel, The Sherry, alternate time:

I am feeling spare. Monday afternoon, last night I chased the dragon until I nodded off. Adrijana, having let herself in to clean, found me unconscious on my black leather chair, made some strong coffee, and rang Malory downstairs to come up and sit with me while she worked. Malory is standing about 10 feet away, toward my dining room, sunlight outlining her body. In an effort to cheer me up, she is singing, in a wonderfully, lyric voice:

> *Beautiful dreamer, wake unto me,*
> *Starlight and dewdrops are waiting for thee;*
> *Sounds of the rude world, heard in the day,*
> *Lull'd by the moonlight have all passed away!*
> *Beautiful dreamer, queen of my song,*
> *List while I woo thee with soft...*

Malory finishes and stands with her arms wide in invitation, as I am enveloped by the Arpège scent from a woman sitting next to me. Maybe it will be a beautiful day. Anyway, I'm feeling better and I'm interested in the woman next to me, Malory's new acquaintance from the Art Students League, a young German woman, Anja Wangemann.

The Magi

I am sitting quietly, watching Malory and Lara in animated conversation. Lara seems perturbed about something. I am thinking the woman next to me might be feeling a little uncomfortable. I turn to say something to her, in an effort to make her feel more relaxed, but from across the room Lara says, "Nigel, may I have a word?"

"Of course." I get up. "Excuse me, Miss Wangemann." She nods.

I walk over to Lara and Malory. Lara says, "In private, for a moment."

Malory is looking unsettled. I think I know what is going on, but best wait until people explain themselves. I follow Lara into the bedroom, and she opens up soon as soon as she thinks we're out of earshot. "Nigel, she didn't mean anything, it just happened, she was so young you see, now she feels terrible, I just—"

I hold up my hand. "Wait a minute, what's the matter?"

"It's Anja, she's German."

"Lara, I appreciate your concern and I find it quite touching. How can I hold her responsible, a little girl at the time?"

"I understand, Nigel. It must've been terrible."

"Worse than that, Lara, worse than that."

I leave her and walk into the sitting room. Malory and Anja are in conversation. They both stand, and Malory walks over to me.

"Nigel, thank you for a nice morning, I think it best if Anja and I go down to my place." Malory is looking a sheepish. I glance over at Anja, who is looking down at my Chinese carpet.

"Please stay. I will order a light lunch to be brought up, it would make me very happy if you and your friend would be my guests." I take Malory's hand and lean into her, realizing they are both wearing Arpège, a subtle scent that suits them both.

I whisper in her ear, "The horror is mine Malory, and no one here is to blame."

She turns her head, her lips brushing my cheek ever so lightly, her breath warm and inviting. "Thank you, Nigel, I would never do anything to hurt you."

Short time later we are all seated comfortably around my dining table having a light lunch of:

Poached Dover Sole in a Lemon Caper Sauce
Glazed Julienne Carrots
Pommes Frites with a touch of Rosemary

Lara is regaling us with a story about her trip to Florence with Kaylee. Of course they stayed in luxury and saw all the sights there are to see—Cathedral of Santa Maria del Fiore, Ponte Vecchio, Galleria degli Uffizi, Palazzo Vecchio, Galleria dell'Accademia—I lost the thread after all that but it did sound like a fantastic trip. They asked me to join them but traveling has never been my strong suit.

While over coffee and a slice of Adrijana's *Lenja pita sa višnjama*, or in her translation, Lazy Cherry Pie, either way it's delicious, I look over at Anja and notice she is wear a striking pendant, cross in yellow gold, at its center a small red rose. I hesitate to ask about it in front of everyone, so I say nothing.

I excuse myself, and walk into the kitchen to thank Adrijana for setting a beautiful table and adding a nice Serbian treat. She is quietly stacking dishes as I move up behind her. She senses me and gently pushes into me. Lowering my head, my lips graze her ear, I whisper, "*Mnogo te volim.*" I love you very much.

She replies in her fatalist fashion, "*Dobro što sam ti učinio.*" What good have I done you? It's hard for me to talk with her when she is like this, words are not useful. I put my arms around her and rest my head against hers. Just a moment, the world goes away, just a moment, it is just us, just a moment, *moja ljubav.*

"I will send a car to pick up you and your daughter and bring you back here, would the two of you have dinner with me?"

She brings her hands up over her head, placing them on either side of my face. "Yes, Melissa always enjoys your company. You spoil her so, what will she become?"

"Adrijana, she will become a very successful woman at whatever she decides she wants to be. Now, I must get back to my guests."

I reluctantly break our embrace and return to the sitting room, where everyone seems quite comfortable. I sit in my armchair next to Anja. Lara and Malory are talking further about her trip, so I decide I will ask Anja about her pendant.

"Miss Wangemann, that is a very interesting pendant you are wearing."

"Please call me Anja. Yes, it was my father's, he passed when I was 13, he intended that my brother have the pendant and follow in his footsteps after he was gone, but my brother was killed in the war. My brother, Wilhelm, was a talented artist, what a waste. I love him very much." She pauses for a moment, then goes on. "I was fascinated by the pendant, and the society my father belonged to. I decided to do some research. That led me to a whole system of beliefs and through them I have become a member of the Rosy Cross, the Rosenkreuz."

I lean back in my chair. I am a little taken aback not because it is true—I know almost nothing about the Rosy Cross—but because it reminds me that each side suffered, how we all lost someone we loved.

"If I may ask, Anja, how is it that you ended up at the Art Students League?"

"My brother and I shared artistic talent and many family members have similar talents. My father was an accomplished stained glass maker, my mother was a gifted organ recitalist, she played every Sunday at our local church, in Leverkusen, a city north of Köln. She died six months after hearing her only son was killed, one month before the war ended, it broke her heart. After that, I thought I would try and find a new life in America."

"Anja, I was in the war, and would be hard pressed to point out anything good that came of it. Costs so high and no gain. I would like to say it was the war to end all wars but Plato was right, only the dead have seen the end of war. I fear the violence is just beginning."

Anja nods and says, "That is why it's so important to forgo the old ways and look for answers in new realms, different ways of thinking, fresh visions for a new faith."

I smile and say, "Hence, the Rosy Cross."

"Yes, many beliefs come from the Magi. The Magi are said to have been from the land of Shir, at the shore of the Great Ocean. In other texts, Shir is associated with silk production, leading many to identify Shir as China and the Magi as Chinese. Yes, from the land of Shir, where the believers offered up the Magi, this knowledge has come. Brought back from the Middle East by Christian Rosenkreuz, not from Sufi or Zoroastrian masters but from those we call the Magi,

319

referring to prayers they would silently offer to heaven, from the land by the great sea, China."

I say, "So the society's name is derived from his name. When did he live and are they the same Magi present at the birth of Christ? I read somewhere that Christian Rosenkreuz is an allegorical figure. That texts said to be from him are considered apocrypha."

I quickly realize I may have insulted her and start to apologize, but Anja starts to speak. "The legend is: Christian Rosenkreuz was born in the 13th century, and had a rebirth in the 14th century. I believe that his first appearance was Lazarus/St. John. Lazarus the disciple Christ had raised from the dead and who would remain active until the Lord's return. The phrase 'C.R.C.'s deceased father's brother's son' is considered a deeply enigmatic one. Many believe, as do I, it refers to the rebirth process. Believers of the Rose-Croix are mentioned in Dante's *The Divine Comedy*."

I say, "Anja, that is a very concise explanation. I respect your belief system, especially when it is delivered with such confidence and passion. Sometimes I wish I still had that zest for life, that *raison de la passion*, but I never really got out of those trenches."

Drew says, *"You brought up a subject that must be very painful for her. Shut up, Nigel. Don't make her feel uncomfortable, apologize. Let her keep what she is holding on to."*

I realize Drew is right, but the words just came up before I knew what I was saying. "I'm sorry, Anja, for bringing up the war. I meant that it is impossible for me to believe anything will ever be better, that the world is in great jeopardy."

She replies, "No need to apologize, I have no idea what it must have been like, but your pain, my brother's death, I want it to have meaning. That there is still a chance, maybe a ghost of a chance, but one nevertheless. If you open your heart, magical things can happen. Like the believers have said: 'the World shall awake out of her heavy and drowsy sleep, and with an open heart, bare-head, and bare-foot, shall merrily and joyfully meet the new arising Sun.'"

Adrijana enters and addresses me. "Pardon, is there anything else you need?"

When I look at her, my stomach tightens. Why have I sucked her into my pitiful life? I've helped her financially, but I have placed so many additional burdens on her.

"I think we are fine. Thank you for all your help."

Adrijana says, "Then I'll finish in the kitchen."

Anja continues, "To answer your question about the Magi, yes, there are cities in China on the same relative latitude as Bethlehem. It is believed that the star visible in Bethlehem was seen by the Magi. This star fulfilled a prophecy that a great deliverer would be born. They came from the east to bear witness to the birth and bring offerings."

I am amazed by this young woman and her depth of knowledge.

"Anja, I never heard about a connection between the Magi and the Chinese. It is quite plausible, since it is common knowledge that the Chinese have many esoteric belief systems."

Anja replies, with a bit of excitement, "Yes, tomorrow I am going to visit a Chinese yi, an herbal physician, at his shop in Chinatown. Would you like to join me? The shop is called the Heavenly Crane."

"I know the place. Lara took me there. She wanted me to buy some herbs. I did and I brewed a tea with them, it tasted awful."

Anja laughs. "I won't make you buy any herbs. I want to speak with the owner, his name is Ching Ling Foo, about the Magi. Will you come with me, around 11:00 tomorrow?"

"It's a date. Just come upstairs from Mallory's place and we'll go to Chinatown together."

Next morning after several cups of coffee to clear my head, Anja and I head downtown to the Heavenly Crane. We enter the shop, it has a pleasant, earthy smell, and Anja greets the proprietor, Mr. Ching Ling Foo, then introduces me. He remembers me and says, "Happy to see you again, Mr. Larsson. If I can be of assistance, please ask."

"Thank you, Mr. Ching."

He returns to conversation with Anja. I enter a section of the shop devoted to statues, incense, and Chinese relics. I am looking in a glass case containing pendants when Anja enters this section of the shop.

"Have you seen these pendants?" I ask. I get no reply. I'm about to repeat the question when I notice she is staring at something in another glass case. I join her, wondering what has attracted her attention. It is a crudely carved figure made of a translucent crystal. I say, "It's beautiful."

She doesn't reply. Without my noticing his arrival, Ching Ling Foo is standing on the other side of the case.

He says, "I see you are drawn to this statue. It is a sacred totem from Neolithic China, depicting a figure thought to represent a wu, or shaman. I believe that the wu attached the statue, by that small groove at the top, to her garments, most likely worn during rituals."

He reaches into the case and withdraws the item. "Please examine it, if you would like."

He offers it to Anja and she takes the statue. She takes a step back and pulls the totem to her breast. The atmosphere in the room changes. The light level rises. Street sounds are dampened. The moment freezes. I feel a vortex of immense energy.

Ching Ling Foo says, "The totem has summoned the wu, she is here."

He drops to his knees. Anja is speaking in a language I don't understand. I'm trying to say something but I can only look at her, Anja pale, blonde, blue eyes, or is it? I feel the same terror as when a bombardment commenced, but she looks directly at me and all fear departs. She moves toward me and the vortex shifts with her, she is the source, she is the vortex, she is controlling the energy, she is controlling time, it is timelessness, it is the alpha and the omega, occupying the same space, the same moment.

She turns toward me, raises her arms, and throws back her head. There is a flash so bright I think I must have been blinded but no, I can see. Her head drops down and she places her left hand on my chest over my heart, her right arm, holding the crystal, extends upward, and she speaks. I understand what she says: "What you were is no more, what you have become is, this is the way of change."

A Monday Afternoon

I am in my favorite armchair helping Melissa with her math homework. Adrijana is in the kitchen, she wanted to prepare dinner tonight. Lucky for us she is preparing Sarma:

One large head of cabbage
One pound mixed minced meat (2/3 pork, 1/3 beef)

322

A couple of dried pork ribs, smoked sausage
Rice, six cups
Two onions, three cloves of garlic
Chicken and herb salt, pepper, bay leaf, sweet and spicy
paprika powder
Oil

The doorbell rings. "Melissa, excuse me." I answer the door.

Drew is standing there with Malory, smiling as usual. Drew says, "Nigel, we're anticipating a spectacular dinner. We did mention we were bringing a guest?"

I laugh, he hands me a bottle. "Of course you did." Of course he didn't but no matter.

Drew says, "She's a new friend of Malory's, her name is Anja Wangemann." After the introduction, they both step aside, the heavens part, and there is a pale, blonde, blue-eyed, woman. She is wearing a striking pendant of a carved figure made of a translucent crystal.

Mad Frankie

Mad Frankie, present time, in the woods:

I shake out two Gabapentin 300 mg into my hand and carry them into the kitchen, washing them down with a pull of milk. I close the refrigerator door, I look at my reflection in the stainless steel. Maybe this whole string has been played out. Maybe the words will not clear a path. Have I been fooling myself? As usual I need to occupy myself until the pills shut my mind up. If only the memories would fade, would end. The good ones, the bad ones, just an avalanche of despair. Dizzy, can you hear me? Dizzy, maybe you are in your study typing away or are you drawing? Can you make it stop? I close my eyes.

I turn off the highway onto the rutted quarter-mile driveway that leads to a rundown old farmhouse. The yard surrounding the house is packed clay and hard as concrete, yet still filled with potholes. I park the jeep, get out, and look at the house. it needs more than a paint job, it is on a terminal track.

I climb the warped three stairs to the front porch covered by a leaking overhang, a few uncomfortable-looking chairs placed haphazardly around, the porch railing looking like a crackhead's dental work, barely supporting a few empty flower boxes. No reason to knock because no one would answer the door, although just barging in could lead to an exchange of gunfire. Not today, thank God.

The man sits in a double leather recliner, in a faded mauve color, his shoe box next to him, filled with the obligatory paper bags. He turns and nods at me, knowing I always have cash and offer no hassle. I walk around the L-shaped couch layout, each one occupied with a loaded person. Next to Mr. Supplier is his friend in a dirty Rolling Stones T-shirt, for fuck sake. I hand my money over and get my 10-pack. "Mind if I get off here?" I say.

"No, be my guest, plenty of room."

I turn and a guy I do not know gets up and leaves the room, so I sit down, pour some of the greyish powder on a slip of foil, light it, and inhale the sweet smoke. I sink further into the grimy couch and close my eyes. The couch moves and I open my eyes, to Mr. Supplier's sister, a young blonde, she might be 17 but looks older, she is waif thin, her nipples poking out of her Joy Division tee, I love her for that.

Kneeling on the couch, she places a hand on my thigh. She knows I cannot resist her. I pick up her hand, lick it, and pour the rest of the bag out on the back of her hand. She gives a short laugh before inhaling the powder, licking off the residue. She curls up next to me on the couch. Her left hand rubbing my stomach, has a tattoo of a rosy cross. I run my hand through her hair, thinking I really hit a high note.

"And descant on mine own deformity"

~From *Richard III*, Shakespeare

The rain is beating against my windshield, the road barely illuminated by my headlights, darkness, heading into the heart of it. What am I doing? I have no answer. Ever been at the beginning of an act, knowing full well that it's not the right move? My dear Gloucester, you weren't such a cunt. I admire a guy who can call himself out. Who knows, maybe you fucked up. Here I am, dear Gloucester, calling it as

I see it, I'm about to fuck up. How could I possibly have anything re-sembling true feelings for this person, that would justify coming out in the night of the deluge, the night where all the signs said travel not?

Turning onto the rutted, road of sorrows, leading to the house of little joy. I will cop, as an excuse, but I come for her, Sami, not to res-cue her but to abandon me. For a few bags she will fuck me, for a few bags she will lay her head on my chest and let me hold her. Admitting to you, dear Gloucester, I cannot prove a lover and realizing I am a villain.

My headlights play off the house and its peeling paint of faded love. I get out of the Jeep, walking slowly, all the rain and clouds that lour'd upon the house, ignored, while the last quantum of hope, buried deep in the bosom of that ocean, my hopelessness. I mount the three stairs, fearing my tread, and quietly open the door.

Candlelight hides as much as it can, while Slim Whitman sings about the end of the world. The man in the double leather recliner, in a faded mauve color, acknowledges my entrance, almost like he's glad I came. I walk around the awkward couch setup and hand him the bills. He smiles. "Been a slow night, the rain keeps traffic down."

He hands me my packet, held together with a tiny rubber band. "Get off if you want."

I feel my stomach tighten, not from this shit but because I have to ask. I try for causal, sitting down on the sofa. "Sami around?"

The man laughs. "She's up in her room. I know she'd love to see you, carrying, up the stairs first door on your left."

I get off the sofa and as I corner the couches, heading for the stairs, he lets me know something that should stop me but it doesn't. "You know she'll be 18 in July."

I turn to him. "That makes me feel so much better."

He laughs and turns toward the soundless TV.

The soiled, rug-covered stairs echo not my steps as I reach the top, pause, only to highlight the plot I have laid, arriving not so nimbly at the lady's chamber. I knock, a sweet sound, "Yes."

I enter, she's lying on her twin bed, holding a phone, dressed in sweat pants and her Joy Division tee shirt. She gives me a coy smile. "Why, it's Mad Frankie and on night like this."

I throw the packet on her bed. Seeing it, her eyes light up and she opens her arms. Dive, thoughts, down to my soul; here Mad Frankie comes.

Picture me there, in your dreams

Consciousness returns by olfactory stimuli. A divine citrus scent, mixed with a delicate hint of white tea and jasmine, gently prods me awake, while lightly coming to rest on my face. Awake, I am lying on a sea of silks. Silks dyed in shades of red and yellow. A feather-light comforter covers me to my waist, red, bordered in yellow, decorated with a large five-clawed yellow dragon with red eyes. The immense bed sits on a round dais within a perfectly square room. The ceiling is set with blue ceramic tiles. A set of large windows to my right are open, allowing a gentle breeze carrying a light whiff of working braziers.

Two men approach the bed, dressed in servant attire. At a certain distance, they drop to their knees and bow their heads to the floor. They address me, "Wàn Suì Yé, 萬歲爺/万岁爷, many dishes have been prepared, tasted, and are ready for consumption."

I open my eyes as the dream fades. There is no immense bed sitting on a round dais within a perfectly square room. There is no citrus scent, divine or otherwise. Just a little sweat and Chanel No. 5. Remember? Yes, I brought her a bottle of the spray cologne. I am naked, my tattooed right arm lying on top of a comforter depicting Hello Kitty. Another person has pushed me up against a wall on my side of a twin bed, her Chanel scent lingering on the pillow. What have you done, Mad Frankie, what have you done?

She stirs, turns over, lays an arm across my chest, snuggles her head into my shoulder, and throws a leg over mine. She is also naked, I can feel her groin pressed into my thigh. I put my arms around her and lightly kiss the top of her blond head. Better we had sex than do what we did. We spent hours chasing the dragon. Though, the ever present possibility of sex hung in the air like the storm clouds outside.

I feel a slight bite on my shoulder and a muffled laugh; she's awake.

"Sami, be careful, you don't want to start something we can't finish."

326

She raises her head. I look into her green eyes and in an instant I am overwhelmed with remorse. What have you done, Mad Frankie, what have you done? I bring her head up and lightly kiss her on the lips. She lets out a little moan and pulls herself up so she is on top of me. I want to break off the kiss but I can't, I want to kiss her, lick my way down her body, put myself inside her, but it's Sami, and Sami has already been abused by countless others. I am already on that list. Do I need to compound my sins?

"I can't make love to you, Sami."

She licks my nipple, saying, "Then let's just fuck."

I put on my best adult face. "Sami!"

"Oh, all right." She sits up, casting aside Hello Kitty, and straddles my middle. From out of nowhere she produces a bag. "Let's get loaded." She picks up a piece of foil and dumps the brownish powder out of the bag. She lays the foil on my stomach. "Don't move, Mad Frankie. I got you covered. We need some music." She picks up her phone and begins to scroll.

I ask, "Is it connected to the speaker?" I'd brought her a Bluetooth B&O speaker.

She just nods and says. "Here's one I found the other day. Do you know The Clash?"

I smile. "Saw them live at Bond's in New York."

She lowers her phone. "That's unbelievable, they're, like, from the '80s."

"I'm old, Sami."

She lays her hand over my heart. "See if you can tell me the name of this one." She starts the music. As the song starts, I wait for the rhythmic beat of the tom-toms. I recognize it, of course: The Clash's "Straight to Hell." Sami makes a small funnel of the foil, holds it for me, and fires up the Bic. The smoke rises up the funnel and licks at me, the dragon's tongue. I inhale deeply, letting my head fall back onto her pillow. Holding my breath forever as I stare at Sami's beautiful breasts, Joe Strummer sings.

As the last chords sound with Joe's diminishing vocals, my arms around this damaged young woman, I stir. Echoes of that night at Bond's still resonate. It is a cherished moment with my then new friend, Tommy. Here's to you, you Scottish basa, from your bawheid at the black gate.

Sami, I wish I could have been more than an enabler, but maybe I added a quantum of happiness to your life.

"Sami, I have to go. I will text you."

She sits up, her eyes sparkling with altered consciousness. Fuck it, maybe as a species it is a primal drive to lose oneself, to peek through the door into another, perhaps better, realm.

Dressed, I put one knee on the bed and give Sami a light kiss. She lies down, wrapping herself in Hello Kitty, content to stay in her room. Can you blame her? What's out there? I remember a phrase a Chinese shaman once told me: *Life is a dream walking, death is a going home.* I gently close her bedroom door, leaving a piece of my heart.

No one downstairs as I exit the gloom of the house into the gloom of the day. It's still raining as I walk across the yard to my Jeep. It starts, ready to carry me wherever I want, with no judgment. I slowly drive down the rutted road to the main highway. I turn right, heading south, heading home, my mind throwing me daggers of regret. I try to will them away but now the demons are too strong. They sense weakness, they know when you've had enough, when to strike.

I am driving too fast for someone who is not paying attention. Around a bend and I lose control, leave the road as the Jeep struggles to compensate for the careless driver. Somehow, without hitting the numerous pines, I end up in a clearing about 30 yards from the road. I curse myself but I am grateful for avoiding what might have been. How did I do that, or did I? I step out of the Jeep, looking around, it seems impossible I did not hit a tree, that I came to rest in this clearing. The engine stops, the only sounds are rain hitting leaves, and the pines whispering to me.

The whispering grows louder, rising in volume until I can distinguish voices. Female voices, chanting a phrase over and over. I cannot move. I try but I am incapable of movement. Then, steeping into the clearing, I see her.

Suddenly, the whole world is transformed and:

Cold, cold, cold forest, the conifer branches bent low by the weight of the pure white snow. I know I'm in Sami's bed, so this is a dream; is this a vision? Is this the past? Is this the future?

A low frequency begins on the forest floor, I can feel it through my Adidas. Getting stronger, penetrating my shins, thighs, hips. Spirit-awakening vibrations.

Suddenly I hear her voice from behind me, right to the center of my skull. Sounds of all there is, was, will be. The primordial drone of all the uncountably infinite worlds. My body is several feet above the pine-needled floor.

It is too beautiful to bear, too painful to hear. Are we the author of our lives? It is the 32 paths of Kabbalah, the 72 names of G_D, the Alpha and Omega.

She appears angry, protective, loving. The sounds intensify, becoming deafening; it is the music of eternity, the sounds of existence. It contains all things. I am her, she is me. The Divine in us all and yet I turn to the darkness.

She sends me a young woman. A beautiful, surprisingly tender, young woman, left alone, not nurtured, yet she embraces me, holds me, and for a moment I see the path illuminated. Then the dragon takes it away and I am lost. Yet my dream woman beckons, lovingly, she envelops me as I lay my head on her breast. Then it is gone. I am cast on the shores of a magnificent fjord. I hear a voice behind me: "Why, it's Mad Frankie and on a beautiful day like this."

Turning I see it's a woman I've written about, who transformed a desperate young man named Giuseppe's existence circa 1907. Who intervened to restore the life of a WWI PTSD sufferer in 1927. Now she stands before me. I thought her storyline ended with Nigel in jazz-age New York.

"Hello, Anja," I say.

She smiles at me. "Don't I get a hug?" I step forward and embrace her as she runs her hands gently up my back. The scent of peonies and:

A blond-haired woman enters. She's wearing on her feet, slippers with peony pattern embroidery. Above them she is wearing a long white silk pleated skirt under a silk peach waistcoat with porcelain buttons. Her arms are filled with peonies, red peonies. She bows slightly, turns, and begins placing the flowers in a Ming dynasty, Xuande mark and period (1426–35), imperial blue-and-white vase, which sits upon a deeply lacquered, green Ming-style stand.

The moment is perfect. The flowers, her robe, the sun striking her hair as she pauses, five flowers in the vase, one she is holding in her left hand—the perfect tableau, a Caravaggio vision. Only a breath, a second, revealing a minuscule island of beauty surrounded by darkness and coming doom.

"Pick one, Mad Frankie," Anja whispers in my ear, and:

I lie down on the wooden pallet in the gloom of Wu's Bath Emporium's opium den. Everything a hophead would want, meaning a nice ball of dope. I've never noticed how beautiful the young Chinese woman is as she twirls the ball of dope over the opium lamp. Maybe it's because she has the thing I want. The thing that so fleetingly quenches the fire.

All set, she hands me the plain pipe. Her eyes are averted as I notice she is missing the ring finger of the hand offering me the pipe. I take it from her, bringing the stem to my mouth with more anticipation than with any lover. I take a long pull, allowing my head to fall back among the cheap pillows. As I exhale time slows and the cosmos opens to its terribly beautiful, infinite possibilities, but it is one I am falling toward. I dream of a ship that sails away, far, far away.

Anja is holding me, like she's not willing to let me go.

"Pick one, Mad Frankie," she whispers in my ear, and:

I slide over to the rosewood bar, tucked into an alcove. I mix myself an Old Tom style martini; and as I add the twist, I decline a gilt mirror piled high with cocaine. Anita emerges from her bedroom wearing a dressing gown in a sheer blue silk fabric. Its soft flowing lines accent her lithe body. Her feet are encased in red Moroccan slippers, matching the shock of short-cropped hair on her head. She is perfection. I feel it all the way to my toes. She moves next to me, sliding an arm around my waist, while her scent envelops me entirely. The laughter, the room, the warmth of Anita's body—the moment is perfect. It will not last, but then again what does?

"Picture yourself there and if I dream it you will be there. Pick one, Mad Frankie," Anja whispers in my ear, and:

"Another world, another life, I know there is a sphere just beyond my senses. Somehow I am tied to another time. I cannot grasp it, I want to hold on but I cannot."

Ching Ling Foo lays a hand on my arm and speaks in an exquisite voice of the Divine. "It is time for the truth of the Dao. The world belongs to those who let go."

"Picture yourself there and I will dream you there. Pick one, Mad Frankie," Anja whispers in my ear, and:

Dizzy chuckles. He reaches between us and turns on the tabletop Catalin radio by Addison Industries. It takes a moment to warm up and then we hear the voice of Hank Snow.

Suddenly I notice a dust cloud rising, moving toward us. A car, running fast, the driver unconcerned about the advance warning. As it gets closer, I recognize the car and by connection, the driver. It is a 1955 Mercury Montclair two-door hardtop in black and grey with a 429 engine and a C6 auto trans. The driver pulls hard right while stomping on the brake, causing the car to perform a beautiful drift as it slides to a stop 50 feet from the porch. Coating us in fine grit. The driver opens the door, moving clear, and then slams it shut and casually leans against the front panel.

The predictors never said a damn thing about this but they didn't need to. I knew she'd show up. The situation demanded it. I smile at her while she is looking us over in her crisp field tan and not a bead of sweat.

She says, "Did you really think I would leave you two assholes to rot in this iteration?"

Dizzy says, "You rode off into the sunset, content to dwell in a non-replicating closed loop. Said good-bye, adios."

I am trying to hide my emotions but I say, "We need you on this one, we need the old magic."

She smiles at us. A slight wind begins to pick up, carrying a promise of rain. Adios is not so long.

Anja is holding me, like she's not willing to let me go.

"Picture yourself there and I will dream you there. Pick one, Mad Frankie," Anja whispers in my ear, and:

The sun breaks through the clouds, illuminating the white heads of each tulip like stars in an alternate universe. In the middle of the field stands a young man, a beautiful young man. The tears in my eyes catch the light like diamonds rolling down my cheeks. Somewhere, somewhen I know this young man. He gently places his hand over his heart. It all fades away.

Beautiful dreamer, wake unto me,
Starlight and dewdrops are waiting for thee;
Sounds of the rude world, heard in the day,
Lull'd by the moonlight have all passed away!

Anja is holding me, like she's not willing to let me go.

"It can be a closed loop, one to last an eon or a moment. Time has no meaning," Anja whispers in my ear. I pull her closer.

"I dreamed I was in your arms. Join me, we'll awaken in Tangier, sip a mint tea, and enjoy a bit of kif at the Café Hafa. We'll sit at the same table as Burroughs and Bowles. At night, under the stars, there will be music next to the Phoenician Tombs."

"Pick one, Mad Frankie," Anja whispers in my ear, and:

We are both kneeling on a bed of soft bamboo sheets in a pale green, the tears are running down my cheeks, my eyes beginning to bulge, sweat dotting my forehead. My tattooed right arm hanging limp at my side. My left arm is holding the rope. I can smell her Jo Malone Velvet Rose & Oud Cologne, feel her warm breath on my right ear, the sharp points of the nipples topping her breasts, slippery from the heat, pressed into my back. I am a gasper.

She tightens the rope around my neck with another twist. This strangulation game played by my partner is purely erotic. Nothing else matters to her but bringing me to the edge of death then orgasm. Who am I to argue with her premise. She, being a very smart mathematician of Syrian decent, coal-black, short-cropped hair with green eyes.

I am almost there, that point between this life and death, the moment when I enter a lucid, semi-hallucinogenic state, becoming hypoxic. Tighter, my love, almost, I'm thinking. Suddenly it's here, the moment I can see the door open, the moment I can step through and make this world go away.

"Mad Frankie, it would be best if you picked one in which you aren't being murdered," Anja says, without the slightest hint of sarcasm, and:

I lift myself off the bamboo matting that has been placed upon the rosewood bed frame. Her fragrance still lingers there. I quietly wander out into the rear garden. The early-morning sunlight reflects off the pines. I am facing east, the direction the rear garden is to be enjoyed, bathed in a most gentle light.

The center of the garden is occupied by her. She has been here since dawn. Walking the circle, she concentrates on its center. Her body is in constant motion, duplicating the movements of the cosmos. She is always becoming, always changing, beautiful, poetic, divine.

The whirling circles of BaGua Zhang. The BaGua, signifying its roots in the Zhou yi. She is the Lion 乾, the Monkey 兒, the Rooster 離, the Dragon 震, the Phoenix 巽, the Snake 坎, the Bear 艮, the Qilin 坤. She is standing, turning, striking, ever changing. Watching her I am as empty as I have ever been.

"You are getting close." She hugs me a little tighter. "Pick one, Mad Frankie," Anja whispers in my ear, and:

I see her pull in on her bright-red Honda scooter. She pulls down the kickstand, parking the bike. She turns and sees me, and her face brightens as she puts her hands together bowing her head in the standard Khmer greeting, but she always uses Third Sampeah level in her greeting, I wish she wouldn't. I stand and return the greeting. She fluidly moves toward me, the sun reflecting off her bright-yellow sundress. She is perfection. She's small of stature but her heart is large, loving, and gentle. It lies outside this world.

Her English is quite good, far better than my Khmer. We watched her perform at the Kngaok Club last night. She sings in the most exquisite Khmer voice, pop tunes with a traditional turn to the music. I can listen to her sing for the rest of my life.

"Pick one, Mad Frankie," Anja whispers in my ear, and:

The order comes to retreat to the guard block. A small detachment will hold the stairs until this can happen. I am chosen; she quickly joins me without any orders. They are over the wall, and behind us the guards are moving up the stairs to the guard block, our small detachment shooting arrows, throwing spears. We wait with our swords.

They are having trouble mounting the many small, narrow steps to reach us. I yell "Tiānzǐ!" she yells "Wansuì!" I look at her one last time. I will meet her again and again, eternally. We turn and bring down the first line of attackers, together. Then we die, together.

"Pick one, Mad Frankie," Anja whispers in my ear, and:

An arm is placed around my shoulders. Malory is quietly holding me. She says in her soft voice, "I am going to sing you a song."

I have to look at her now. "I didn't know you sing."

She runs her hand through my hair, pushing it in place. "Oh yes, and I learned an American song." She stands.

Lara enters the room and sits beside me, putting her hand on my thigh. She says, "Today is going to be beautiful."

Malory begins to sing "My Blue Heaven" in a sweet, slightly accented, lyric voice, warming my heart with the popular piece, changing only a single stanza.

...Lara and me, and Nigel makes three
...Just Lara and me, and Nigel makes three
We're happy...

Malory finishes and stands with her arms wide in invitation, as Lara's Arpège scent envelops me. Maybe it will be a beautiful day.

"Pick one, Mad Frankie," Anja whispers in my ear, and:

My breathing is slowing, slowing, Adrijana throws an arm over my chest, a sigh of contentment, a moment of respite, an interlude of relief. Like she can read my mind, she fixes another foil and we finish another bag, loaded, no panic. We lie back down in perfect unison, me looking deep into her warm, dark eyes, and she placing a hand on my cheek, in a light caress.

All I want to do is stay in this room and chase the dragon, and let Adrijana have her way. I pull up her head and place my lips on hers, our tongues make a ghost-like contact, our eyes open together, and we recognize what this all means, what we have been doing, what we will be doing. My head is swimming from the drug and I don't give a fuck. I love getting loaded and I love her for being here with me. As if she can read my mind, she kisses me passionately, sits up, opens the melon knife, and runs the blade across her right arm. I see the blood begin to seep out of the wound. I don't know what to say. Yvonne is singing "Quand les papillons." I pull Adrijana to me and embrace her like I never want her to hurt herself for me ever again and to acknowledge what she has just done.

"Pick one, Mad Frankie," Anja whispers in my ear.

"I can't. So much love, devotion, surrender, how can I lose all those moments for one?"

"That's it, Mad Frankie, there's not one to pick. The eternal recurrence of each moment, the endless cycle of creation and destruction, the alpha and the omega again and again. It will wash over us, beside this fjord, here I'm not Anja and I'm Anja, the wu has shared your Dao through every iteration and will again, holding you, eternally."

I lean back slightly from her embrace and the look in her eyes explains it all, that this is:

The Way of Change.

道

I'll Wait

Weeds grow around cold evaporator, my heart.
Will I ever see such brilliance again.
If...if only I had gone into the house, away.
What would the path be, without her,
Without the look in her eyes
I saw, a portal, a doorway, away from the chaos.
The briefest of moments, she revealed herself.
Does she know, can she admit to herself,
In this here and now?
Anja, how many times have I reached out my hand,
Only to be left holding emptiness?
How many lifetimes until I see the look in your eyes
Once again?
Now, chaos and degradation, cycle and re-cycle,
Bent is the path of eternity, so, infinity, is meaningless
As I sit and wait for that moment again,
When all things converge around us,
And I hold it all in my heart.

Made in the USA
Middletown, DE
03 September 2022